Books by Janelle Clawson

Trilogy: FOR ALL TIME

Part 1 – ABOVE THE CLOUDS
Part 2 – BENEATH THE MOON
Part 3 – THROUGH THE MIST

RIDE THE WIND

CODES OF HONOR

By

Janelle Clawson

U.S.A.

Codes of Honor

ISBN: 13: 978-0692435540

ISBN: 10: 0692435549

For information visit
Fablespinnerbooks.blogspot.com

Printed by CreateSpace in the U.S.A

Acknowledgements

CODES OF HONOR *was edited and proofread by: Cherri Williams, Anne Banks, and Lark Woodbury. Thank you so much for your time and input. Each of you added to the quality of this book.*

Special thanks *to Director Cindy Hines, of the Frontier Historical Society Museum in Glenwood Springs, for digging out the newspapers, the telephone directory, the maps, the photographs, and the information on the people and events I needed to add realism and depth to life in Glenwood Springs in the year 1908.*

Codes of Honor

Prologue

Cliff Springs Ranch, Colorado—June 1947

Sunset was painting the sky when Jack Garrison slipped through the barn door and inhaled the mingled scent of horses and hay. He paused for a moment to savor the barns familiar sounds and smells. His pleasure was suddenly interrupted by a discordant sound—sobbing.

Jack's brows drew together. *This isn't a day for crying.*

Today was the first time since World War II ended that all his children, their spouses, and his grandchildren had been together. It was a day of celebration. Neither his son, nor his sons-in-law, which included Ryder, Kytan Bendarson, Clint Gilbert, and Sky Brannigan, had died in the war. All of them, with the exception of Kytan, had suffered wounds but nothing life threatening or permanently debilitating. The family had celebrated the day with a feast and a family photograph.

Quietly following the muffled sobs, Jack rounded a tall stack of hay bales. Behind them he found his eldest granddaughter sitting on a fallen bale. Her face was pressed against her knees. Her long black hair tumbled around her legs as her shoulders shook.

"What's this?" Jack asked, sitting down on the hay bale beside her.

Her head jerked up. "Oh, Grandpa, I'm sorry."

"For what?"

"Everyone is so happy today, and . . . I didn't want to spoil it."

He gazed into her large tear filled eyes. "Why aren't you happy today? Did someone spoil the day for you?" Jack wrapped her in his arms. "Why don't you tell me what's troubling you, and let me help."

Tears overflowed. "There's nothing you or anyone can do."

"Maybe not, but I'd like to try. Tell me what's troubling you, and let me decide if anything can be done."

Jack drew her close against his chest as she again began to sob.

"Oh, Grandpa, I'm the . . . ugliest one. My cousins are all beautiful. That's what everyone said all day. Harley has beautiful blond hair and silver-blue eyes. Baby Jayling has golden-red hair and her eyes are the color of a tropical sea. Kateea is petite . . . as gorgeous as Auntie Taya is, and she has Uncle Kytan's dimples too. Everyone said my cousins will grow up to be great beauties. No one said that about me." She sniffed. "Just look at me! I'm taller than all the girls in my school class are—the boys too. I have ugly black hair and everyone says my eyes are like a wild animal's."

"Who dared to insult my great grandniece?" asked Zedekiah Long-Sight from the door of the barn.

He and his niece, Kedra Garrison, rounded the stack of hay bales and sat down.

"I'd like to know that too," Kedra said.

"Our granddaughter is thinking her beauty is the least among her cousins," Jack explained to his wife, while their granddaughter hid her face against his chest. "I was about to tell her how exceptionally beautiful I think she is and why."

The girl's head came up. "Do you mean that, Grandpa?"

Jack smiled down into her magnificent gold eyes. "Oh yes, my little darlin'— Tell me who do you look like?"

She wiped her eyes with the back of her hand and looked at her grandmother, Kedra. "I look like Grandma, everyone says so."

"That's right, and that's why you are the most beautiful one to me."

The girl looked at her grandfather skeptically.

Kedra smiled at her husband. "Maybe you ought to tell her how we met, and why you think so highly of my particular kind of beauty."

"You can't tell her that story without telling her about her heritage too," Zed said.

"I know I'm part Nahtow Indian, Uncle Zed," the girl said.

Zed took her hand. "But you don't know how special you are among your cousins, nor have you been told of the responsibility that belongs only to you."

As Jack wiped her damp cheeks with a big handkerchief, she looked up at her great Uncle Zed, expectantly.

Zed consulted Kedra. "May I teach her from the book of Nahtow?"

"Yes," Kedra said and turned to her husband. "If you're going to convince our granddaughter of her beauty, she needs to understand her Nahtow heritage and why you found the beauty of a savage, not to mention, ruthless criminal, so irresistible."

"Grandma, you aren't a criminal!" the girl exclaimed.

"Oh, but she is," Jack confided to his granddaughter. "She stole my heart thirty-nine years ago and has kept it ever since."

"Oh, Grandpa!"

Jack chuckled. "Zed, tell this child how the Nahtow became a tribe. Then, I'll tell her how I fell in love with the most savage, irresistible criminal, and you can insert vital Nahtow history as we go."

1

The Book of Nahtow, Cumorah—AD 385

I am Nahtow. My mother was a pure descendant of Nephi. My father was a pure descendant of Laman, whose ancestors became the people of Ammon and laid aside their weapons of rebellion to become a righteous people in the land of their brothers, the Nephites.

I will tell you of the night I received my calling, for it lives in my mind and is never far from my thoughts. It is the reason I live in the frozen country of the far North.

For four years the people called Nephites gathered together all their strength to make one last stand against their enemies—the Lamanites. The night before that great battle there was silence in the camp, but it was not the silence of sleep. It was that of mourning. Every man, woman, and child in the camp knew what the outcome of the battle would be—as did I.

I held my wife, Elan, close. Both of us were dressed for battle, our swords by our sides. All we felt for each other had been shared. Elan's gentle breathing made me hope she had found refuge from the coming battle in a few hours of repose.

Footsteps outside the tent moved my hand to the hilt of my sword.

Elan's eyes flew open. They searched mine as she too gripped the hilt of her sword.

I gazed into her hypnotic gold eyes. Even in the dim light of a small oil lamp they intoxicated me, just as they had the first time I saw them, only two months ago. But it was more than her eyes that drew me to her.

In her I saw all the greatness of Lehi's children, for she is the pure descendant of a stripling warrior—a Lamanite by birth and a Nephite by faith. She is fearless against evil, courageous in battle, and the most beautiful woman I have ever seen. I love her with all my heart, and rejoice that not even death can take her from me.

The flap of our tent lifted. Moroni ducked beneath it as we rolled out of the warmth of our blankets and came to our feet.

"My father has had a dream." Moroni gripped my shoulder. "He wishes to see you and Elan, for he must tell you what the Lord has ordained."

My arm tightened around Elan. "We will come," I said.

We followed Moroni out of the tent and into the darkness. Not a single ember from a cooking fire lit the camp. Only the smells, which lingered on the air, spoke of the hastily prepared meals that had been cooked before darkness fell and all the fires were extinguished. No one wished to be exposed by firelight to the arrows of our enemies, who we knew lurked beyond the borders of our camp.

Using only the light of the stars, we wove through the tents into the heart of the camp. We stopped in front of a large, multi-roomed tent where Mormon, Moroni's father, and my uncle, had just finished a council of war with his captains.

It had been a terrible disappointment to me when I wasn't named as one of the captains. I had worked long and hard to earn that rank. But my disappointment was soon turned into joy when I was given the honor of being in charge of my Uncle Mormon's personal guard. Protecting my uncle in the many skirmishes we've engaged in with the Lamanites, over the past few years, has been a source of great satisfaction.

We stepped aside as the captains of our army emerged from the tent. Shem, one of the captains, stopped in front of me. He was a large and mighty man, but no one in the camp was my equal in height or breadth.

Shem smiled at me, reaching for Elan's hand. He looked up into her face, for she too was taller than he was. "I have not had the opportunity to congratulate you two. It lifts my heart to know that even in this dark hour there are still things to smile about." He squeezed Elan's hand and clasped my arm in the hand to elbow grip of a brother and friend, then quickly walked away.

Moroni lifted the tent flap. Elan entered. I followed, and Moroni closed the flap of the tent behind himself.

Mormon, the Nephites' great champion, sat at a large table covered with maps, his head bent over one as he marked it and wrote notes along its upper left edge.

Elan and I stood silently beside Moroni in the bright light of the oil lamps that chased all shadows from the room, but could not be seen through the densely woven fabric of the tent.

Mormon finally laid aside his pen, rolled up the map, and looked up. The old warrior's face was lined with the burdens of the many years he'd seen; years of war, destruction, and the sorrow of seeing his people turn from all that was good to embrace all that was unholy. And yet, I also saw his unwavering love for this people, even though they had rejected the great light they had been given.

As Mormon's eyes met mine, a feeling of peace settled over me.

He stood and came around the table. "Nahtow, you are the son of my sister and have been my son since your noble father was taken from us. You have preserved my life many times at great risk to your own, as did your ancestors–the stripling warriors–when they fought for and protected the Nephites. You carry the scars of many battles, still fearless of those who inflicted them."

I took my uncle's out stretched arm. "I count it a great privilege to serve you."

"Thank you, but now there is one who needs your service, and that of your wife, more than I do." Mormon smiled at Elan and gestured to a couch of soft lamb's wool, flanked by a pair of chairs, in the corner of the room. "There is little time, but come and sit with me while I tell you what the Almighty has shown me."

The hope in Mormon's voice lifted my spirit. I knew Elan felt it too. Her hand, which held onto mine, communicated her wonder and anticipation of what we were about to be told.

I kept my hand closed around Elan's as we sat down. Mormon and Moroni drew their chairs close.

Mormon leaned forward. "Although you both have been blessed with great physical stature and strength, you will not fight in tomorrow's battle."

"But, Uncle—" I exchanged a startled look with Elan, who finished my thought, as she often did.

"Who will protect you from our enemies?" she asked.

Mormon waved away her concern. "It matters not. My work is finished, but yours is just beginning." He laid his hand over our clasped ones. "I have seen the great work you and your children will do."

"What work?" I asked.

"You both have been endowed with a great gift. You each have the capacity to remember all you see and hear. This gift will bless many generations of our father Lehi's children."

I wondered at his words, but knew that our capacities to remember had already blessed our own lives. A memory contest was how Elan and I met. Both my comrades and her friends had boasted of our astounding memories. Our friends contended with one another as to whose memory was the best. A challenge was issued from Elan's friends to mine. Both of us were badgered into taking part in the contest, against our wills.

The memory of that contest has become one of my prized possessions. Again, I let my mind watch Elan walk into the small clearing where our contest was held. She bore herself with regal grace. Tall and straight, she held her head high, towering over her friends. She looked up into my eyes and offered her hand in a gesture of sportsmanship.

"I am Elan," she said in a voice that sang through my soul and filled my heart.

I stared down at her, hypnotized by her magnificent gold eyes, unable to do or say anything. An elbow to my ribs made me raise my hand and take hers. I closed my fingers around hers, still unable to find my voice.

"And you are?" she asked in an amused tone.

"I am–I am . . . ah . . . Nahtow," I stammered, keeping her hand enclosed in mine.

The smile in her voice grew. "I am happy to know you can at least remember who you are."

Everyone, including my friends, laughed.

She tried to withdraw her hand, but my fingers refused to release it, until another elbow dug into my ribs.

"Shall we begin?" she asked as she stepped back.

"In a moment," Jenus said, pulling me aside. "What's the matter with you?" he hissed. "Have you lost your wits because Elan is a beautiful woman? Or are you trying to lull her into the false assumption that you can be easily beaten?"

"No. I just didn't expect to be competing against such a spectacular woman."

"Well you are. And from what I've heard, her memory is exceptionally good. You are going to need to concentrate if you want to win. So I will help you by reminding you that most the men in this camp have laid wagers on you. Don't disappoint us, or make us look weak in the eyes of our women. Too many of them have already become our equals in contests of arms. We can't afford to lose in a contest of minds."

Although I am known as a ferocious warrior, I am not by nature a competitive man. I am confident of my skills and abilities and have never felt the need to prove them to anyone, which was why I had resisted this contest. However, because I had agreed, I was determined to do my best.

"Let's get this over with," I said to Jenus.

"You will stand back to back," Jenus said, "and describe each other. The one that provides the most details will win this round." Jenus bowed to Elan. "Ladies first."

I squirmed with discomfort as Elan described me. Her voice was business like as she spoke of my long black hair, which was held away from my face by thick braids pulled back from my temples and secured behind my head by an etched clasp of heavy silver, ornamented with two white feathers. She described my light, gold-flecked, brown eyes, mentioned the small scar under my left ear and the long one that runs down the inside of my left arm, before she described my clothes and their worn condition.

My face grew warm. She didn't miss a single detail. Her description was largely flavored with, what I took to be, her opinion of what she saw. I concluded that she wasn't impressed.

When it was my turn, I struggled not to make my description of her sound like a man who was totally besot, but that is exactly what I was. I was sweating by the time I finished my description of her knee length black hair, ornamented with a string of tiger-eye stone beads that matched her enormous gold eyes, which were fringed with heavy black lashes under sculpted eyebrows. My voice nearly cracked as I described her clothes, her figure, and the way she carried herself.

When the round was over the judges declared it to be a tie.

In round two we were each taken to a separate location, a stone's throw apart, and allowed to turn in one continuously moving circle. Then we were blindfolded and asked to describe the three hundred and sixty degree panorama we had just seen in as much detail as we could remember.

Again the round was declared a tie.

The last contest was one of objects. It started with twenty-five different things, which we were allowed to look at for ten seconds, then describe in the order they were laid out. Round after round ended in a tie as the objects were shuffled, removed, and traded for others. The number of objects grew until there were fifty. The time we were given to study the items decreased. When the items reached seventy-five and we could both still name each one in order, the judges declared the contest a tie, amidst the groans of those who had bet on the outcome.

Many urged us to continue the contest. Elan and I declined. By then, we both knew there would be no winner.

"Your memory is perfect," I said, extending my hand to congratulate her.

She accepted my hand with the grace that characterized her. "As is yours."

"May I walk with you to your tent?" I asked, and then hesitantly added, "I would like to get to know you, if you will permit me."

"I would like that," she said, her gold eyes softening.

After that first meeting, we spent every moment we could together. It surprised me that she was as interested in me as I was in her.

Three weeks later, Mormon united us in marriage.

Elan's question to Mormon brought me back to the present. "How will our memories bless generations of Lehi's children?"

"It has been shown to me that you two must not take part in the coming battle. You and your posterity are to be the record keepers for the children of Lehi until the Lord gives this land to the Gentiles and restores the gospel. You must see, remember, and record the names of those who have dwindled in unbelief, for the day will come when these lost children of Lehi will be reclaimed, and all those who have not known the truth will come to that knowledge. Then, their work will need to be done. This can only happen if their names are recorded and preserved."

"How are we to escape the battle, when we are encompassed about on all sides by the Lamanites?" I asked.

"There are those who have escaped into the southern countries," Moroni said.

"But you will not go south," Mormon said hastily. "Those who have gone south will be hunted until they are found and slain."

"Then where are we to go?" Elan asked.

Mormon turned to Moroni. "Go see if everything is ready."

Moroni left the tent as Mormon went to the table. He brought back the map he had been working on when we entered and handed it to Elan. "Memorize it, while I explain your mission to Nahtow more fully."

Elan nodded and unrolled the map. I watched her eyes absorb every detail of the map as I listened to Mormon's instructions.

"You will travel far to the north, into a land of ice and cold. It will be a forbidding land, but for you it will be a safe haven, a place your enemies will not want to go."

I glanced at Elan. Her eyes met mine.

"You must follow the path I have outlined if you are to reach your destination safely." Mormon held out his hand. Elan put the map back into it. "I will burn this map, so no one will know where you have gone and follow you."

"How is it . . . you know about this frozen sanctuary and the path we must take to reach it?" I asked.

"I have seen it in a dream. You and your posterity must stay there for three generation–until the Nephite and Lamanite people are forgotten. You must teach your children the importance of their mission, even though they too will dwindle in unbelief as to thing pertaining to the truth."

Those prophetic words pained my soul.

Mormon must have seen my grief for he smiled and said, "Your children will possess the gift you and Elan have been given and their desire will be to know and remember all they see and hear. They will come forth from your sanctuary in the north and go among their brothers in this land. They will establish themselves as the keepers of histories, genealogies, and agreements, acting as arbitrators and interpreters between the many tribes that will inhabit the land. They will be accepted and respected for the long memories they have. They will be the means of teaching those who have a desire to learn what each of you knows of science, math, writing, art, and astronomy–though few of the people they live among will care for those things."

Again Mormon went to the table. This time he retrieved a set of blank metal plates. "Teach your children to keep the history and genealogy of the Nahtow people and always remind them of their mission as historians for the remnants of Lehi's children. Teach them to record the things that are of most worth on these plates, which won't deteriorate over time, as a safe guard for all they hear and see. This is wisdom, because the minds of men, even strong ones, can fail, and a chosen people can be destroyed. But these plates, along with all those your people keep, must be safe guarded. This is wisdom, for in a time far distant, when the Gentiles possess the land, one, like unto Elan, will be shown what to do with your records."

Moroni reentered the tent, coming in through the back. "Everything is ready and the way has been cleared."

"Then it is time," Mormon said solemnly. "But before you go, I will pronounce the blessing of the Lord upon your heads."

Elan and I knelt at Mormon's feet, our hands clasped together, as the prophet of the Lord laid a hand on each of our heads. Great and marvelous were the blessings, admonitions, and counsel the Lord gave to us.

We rose from our knees filled with peace and purpose. Mormon and Moroni embraced us. We donned the long dark cloaks Moroni handed us and followed him out through the back of the tent.

"Your supplies are waiting in the stand of trees by the stream just inside the northeast section of the camp," Moroni said.

He embraced us one last time.

I took Elan's hand, and found strength. Together we turned our backs on the fate of our people, and escaped.

2

Kansas City, Missouri—Monday, June 8, 1908

Jack Garrison took the elevator up to the top floor of the Savoy Hotel and stepped off in front of the penthouse suite where Theodore Roosevelt was currently staying. President Roosevelt was making a swing through the country's heartland, campaigning for William Howard Taft, his handpicked successor.

The secret service agent stationed outside the door of the suite asked to see Jack's identification. Jack showed him his badge and the agent knocked on the door. They waited silently until the door was opened by the President Roosevelt's private secretary.

The small man's eyes widened as they moved up Jack's body until they found his face.

"Jack!" President Roosevelt boomed from inside the large, stylish living room as the door swung open. "Come in."

Roosevelt waved Jack in with one hand and shooed the wide-eyed secretary out with the other.

Jack removed the Stetson he wore, which pushed his already impressive height of six feet nine inches to over seven feet, and ducked under the doorframe.

The president came toward him with a smile that lifted the corners of his bushy mustache, his penetrating blue eyes twinkling. "It's been too long, Jack," he said, holding out his hand.

The corners of Jack's mouth slowly lifted. He gave Mr. Roosevelt one of his rare smiles and shook hands with the man he still thought of as Colonel.

"It's good of you to see me on such short notice, Mr. President."

"Not at all—if you hadn't called me, I'd have called you." Roosevelt led Jack over to a comfortable set of brocaded chairs and motioned for him to sit down. "I've been hearing great things about you and your recent achievements."

"So you've already heard about the capture of Ace Donavan and his thugs?"

"And the gunfight that led to it. That was a bully piece of investigative law work. The citizens of this country are grateful to have that thug and his gang off the streets and safely behind bars. Their crime spree of robbery and murder through the nation's heartland almost forced me to call out the army." Roosevelt chuckled. "That is until I sent one of my Rough Riders after them."

The memories of those days drifted over each man's face.

Jack had won Colonel Roosevelt's respect when he was the first man to follow Roosevelt up San Juan Hill. He'd immediately leaped forward with Roosevelt's initial shout and charge, doggedly trudging up the grassy slope of the hill through a hail of enemy gunfire. Miraculously, Jack hadn't been hit, but when he reached the top, a retreating Spanish rifleman took aim at Roosevelt. A glint of sunlight bouncing off the rifleman's gun barrel was all the warning Jack had. He yanked Colonel Roosevelt out of his saddle just as the sniper fired. The bullet creased Jack's shoulder and saved the future president's life.

Roosevelt never forgot it.

Slouching back in the tall wing-backed chair, Jack ran a hand through his short-cropped red hair. The fiery color of his hair had been the bane of his life during his growing up years. It had started more fights than he could remember, and had taught him the bruising art of self-defense. In recent years, the fiery red tone had begun to soften, but not by much. Even now, he kept his hair short to minimize its offensiveness. And, in an era where facial hair was popular, he was clean-shaven, because his beard was even brighter than his hair.

"I'm just grateful no one on our side was killed in that skirmish with Donavan's gang. It was fortunate that my source was good, and my deputies and I were able to surround Donavan's gang in that isolated barn. It would have turned out badly, if we'd been forced into a gunfight in the middle of a crowded St. Louis street."

Mr. Roosevelt's eyes glowed through his oval spectacles. "I wish I could have been part of that fight, or at least have seen it." He gave Jack's somber face a knowing look. "But you didn't come here seeking my praise for your work. So tell me what's on your mind."

Jack said slowly, "I've been a U.S. Marshal for five years now."

"And one of the best this country has ever had."

"Thank you, sir. Being a marshal has been everything I hoped it would be, exciting, dangerous, and rewarding, but—"

The famous Roosevelt scowl creased the president's brows and tugged at this mustache.

"But what?"

"But . . . I came to tell you that tomorrow morning I intend to submit my resignation to the Department of Justice. I thought I should tell you before I did, as it was your influence that landed me the job."

"Why do you want to resign now, especially when your career is going so well?"

"Because being a marshal, at least for me, has always been a means to an end. I've been paid well, and I've finally put away enough money to buy a ranch. You know ranching is what I've always wanted to do. It's time I settled down and lived like normal folks do."

"As opposed to running all over the country hunting down dangerous criminals?"

"Yes."

"I can appreciate that." Roosevelt lifted the lid of a cigar box that stood on a small table next to his chair and took out a long Cuban cigar. He rolled it between his fingers and ran it under his nose, inhaling its aroma. His eyes met Jack's. He put the cigar back in the box and shut it.

"Thank you, sir. It's kind of you not to smoke for my sake."

"Not at all—I really should give the habit up." Roosevelt rested his elbows on the arms of his chair, leaned back, and pressed the tips of his fingers together. "Is there a girl waiting somewhere?"

"No."

"That surprises me. You're quite a romantic figure. I would think droves of females would be chasing after you and that at least one of them would have taken your fancy."

Jack snorted. "I seem to scare most women, not charm them. They don't chase me in droves—they run away from me in droves. And the ones that do hound me aren't the kinds that interest me. Besides, when I became a marshal, I decided it wasn't the sort of job that lent itself to the pursuit of domestic bliss."

"I see your point, but as a rancher, what kind of woman would interest you?"

"One that doesn't spend her days looking at fashion catalogs, doing up her hair, dreaming of silk dresses, diamonds, and seeing Paris in the spring."

Roosevelt laughed. "You're a wise man, Jack. A rancher needs a woman who can ride a horse, shoot a gun, herd and brand cattle, mend clothes, cook, and work as hard as he does."

"Exactly! That kind of woman isn't going to be easy to find, but then, I'm not in any particular hurry to find her."

"But you are anxious to buy a ranch. Have you found one?"

"I've heard about a few places, but I haven't bought anything yet."

"I'm glad to hear you say that. I had a feeling when you asked for this meeting that you intended to tender your resignation." Roosevelt leaned forward, his forearms resting on the arms of the chair. "Up until an hour ago, I would have wished you well and accepted your resignation."

Jack slowly straightened in his chair. "What happened an hour ago to make you change your mind?"

"I was informed by the Department of Justice that Marshals Will Forbes and Harry Walsh, were found shot to death in an express car."

"No!" Disbelief twisted Jack's normally stoic face.

William Forbes had been his mentor and friend, not only during his training as a U.S. Marshal, but also as a Rough Rider, where they had first met. Will had seen through Jack's size and scruffy beard covered face to the sixteen-year-old boy who was posing as a man to get into the Rough Riders. Initially impressed with Jack's ability to handle tough training situations and do the work of a man, Will also found Jack had the grit to endure hardship, as well as the teasing and buffeting of the other men because of his flaming hair and towering height. All that had convinced Will to keep quiet about Jack's age and help him fit into the troop. In many respects, Will had been a father to Jack, and Jack loved him for it.

Jack searched the president's grim face, trying to accept the death of Will Forbes. Grief, then anger, grew.

"Where and how did it happen?" he demanded.

"Does that mean you won't be handing me your resignation?"

"It does," Jack said tightly. "Until I find the person or persons that killed Will, and Harry, I'm not going to turn in my badge."

"Then the case is yours. I want the people who did this as badly as you do. I've known Will since we were boys. There isn't a man I respected more than I respected William Forbes."

"That's exactly how I feel." Jack leaned forward, gripping the arms of his chair. "Tell me everything you know."

"It's pitifully little." Roosevelt sighed and removed his spectacles. "Will and Harry were escorting the notorious smuggler, Haru Ito, across the country, by train, to face federal smuggling and black marketing charges in Washington."

"I had heard he'd finally been apprehended in San Francisco, but not who was in charge of transporting him back to Washington." Jack frowned. "Did Ito escape?"

"No, that's the confusing part. Ito appears to have been deliberately killed too."

"If Ito was the target, maybe Will and Harry were just the fallout. There must be a lot of people who wanted to keep Ito from revealing his list of buyers here in this country. You know the black market for ancient foreign artifacts is growing."

"Yes, but according to Tate Hadlock, the sheriff of Glenwood Springs, Colorado—"

"Is that where it happened?"

"Yes. Just about a mile after the train left Glenwood Springs for Denver, shots were heard coming from the express car. The train stopped immediately. Once the conductor knew what had happened, he brought the train back to Glenwood Springs. Sheriff Hadlock examined the scene and contacted the Department of Justice. As soon as I was informed, I called him."

"Why does he think Will, Harry, and Ito were murdered?"

"He says the express car they were in was carrying a, *supposedly,* secret shipment of rare emeralds. Their owner, Señor Luis Montoya Ortiz, contacted his embassy before he arrived in San Francisco, requesting they ask the State Department for protection for himself, and the emeralds, on his trip across the country to New York, where he had buyers waiting. The State Department contacted the Justice Department and arranged for Will and Harry to guard the emeralds, since they were headed across the country anyway."

"I'll bet Ortiz was delighted to have a couple of U.S. Marshals guard his emeralds."

"I'm sure he was. From what Sheriff Hadlock told me, those emeralds are worth more than most diamonds. The only place in the world they can be found is in a small region of Columbia. Apparently, their color and quality are exceptional."

"I assume the emeralds were stolen?"

"Yes."

"Did Sheriff Hadlock find any kind of evidence or leads as to who killed Will and Harry and stole the emeralds?"

"Our connection was bad, so our conversation was short. You can talk to him about it as soon as you get there." Roosevelt stood. "My personal express train is ready and waiting to take you to Denver. The Denver & Rio Grande Railroad Company has agreed to hold their regularly scheduled train to Glenwood Springs until you arrive in Denver."

"How long will it take your express train to get me to Denver," Jack asked his green eyes darkening to the shade of the emeralds that had been stolen. The hardness in his voice matched the steel in Roosevelt's blue eyes.

"You'll be there tomorrow and in Glenwood Springs by Wednesday." Roosevelt offered Jack his hand. "I want you to keep me informed, and if you need anything, let me know. I want the murderers who killed Marshal Walsh and my dear friend Will Forbes found and hung."

Jack clasped President Roosevelt's hand. "You have my word of honor. I'll bring their killers to justice—no matter how long it takes."

3

Glenwood Spring—Wednesday, June 10, 1908

It was mid-afternoon by the time the train reached Glenwood Springs. By then, Jack was thoroughly tired of being cooped up. Yet, when the train stopped in front of the red sandstone depot, he stayed in his seat. He waited until the departing passengers had left the train and the platform. Then he got off the train on the Colorado River side of the tracks, keeping the train between himself and the depot.

As soon as his boots hit the ground a peculiar thought popped into his mind—*home.*

"Now where did that come from?" he muttered.

Certainly the ride through Glenwood Canyon had been spectacular and escaping Kansas City was a relief. It was far too civilized for Jack with its crowded streets, overdressed men and women trying to impress each other, and the growing number of automobiles that honked and belched gas fumes. Denver hadn't been any better, but here the encroaching fingers of civilization hadn't intruded as much, at least not in terms of people and automobiles. But Jack knew it was just a matter of time. It was one of the reasons he hadn't given the state of Colorado any consideration in his long-term plans. Montana was the place he'd been thinking about for the past few months. Civilization was a bit farther behind up there.

Nahtow—AD 385–400: Long did Elan and I travel north. The land through which we traveled was pristine and desirable. It abounded in game, and provided for our needs. We avoided the haunts of men, though they were few.

After many days, we turned east and traveled to the shores of the great waters. The map in Elan's mind led us unerringly to a land bridge that ran out into the eastern sea. It was with faith and prayer that we took the land bridge and came after many days to the land Elan and I named Sanctuary.

We have made our home in a valley on an inlet from the sea. A river of pure water flows from the glacier above our valley. The land is fertile, though the growing season is short, yet we have found edible plants and grains which we grow for food. There is grass for the native cattle of the land, which have large antlers and run in herds. We have found the fox and the wolf here, also the great white bear. The sea too has given us of her abundance and we lack nothing for food, clothing, shelter, heat, and light.

Pushing the word *home,* which continued to linger, out of his mind, Jack rounded the engine and slipped between the railroad cars in the rail yard. Making his way toward the back of the yard, he read the number on each car until he spotted the one he was looking for, set off by itself.

The horse, tied up to the car, told Jack Sheriff Hadlock was inside. He stopped and stared at the boxcar that had been converted into an express car. This was the place Will died. No doubt his blood was still there. *I have to go in there and be a marshal. I can't let my feelings interfere with this investigation or blind me to what happened.*

He strode to the end of the car and climbed the stairs to the small platform in front of the door. It was open. He ducked and stepped in.

A man got up from a small table at the other end of the car. He was thirtyish, tall, and broad shouldered. A wide-brimmed, slouch hat covered his eyes. His face sported an impressive black handlebar mustache, which obscured his upper teeth when he smiled.

Jack walked toward the smiling man.

"Marshal Garrison?" the man asked, holding out his hand.

Jack dropped his gear, gripped the man's hand, and looked into his cobalt blue eyes, immediately liking his open, confident manner. "It's Jack, and you must be Sheriff Hadlock. Thanks for meeting me here."

"I'm Tate, and I'm happy to oblige, but curious as to why you wanted to meet me here, instead of in my office."

"Tell me, Tate, how long have you been the sheriff here?"

"About two years."

"Then you may not know about the train robbery that happened six years ago on this line, thirty miles east of here, near Eagle."

Tate looked blank.

"That's what I thought. As soon as I heard about what happened here, I had the Department of Justice put together all the information they had on that unsolved train robbery." Jack pulled a sheet of paper out of his shirt pocket and handed it to Tate. "This information caught up with me in Denver."

Tate took the paper and gestured at the small table he'd been sitting at. "Why don't we get comfortable while I look this over?"

They sat at the table while Tate read all the known facts in the Eagle robbery.

Tate looked up when he finished. "You think there's a connection between this robbery and the one six years ago in Eagle."

Jack stretched his long legs out in front of him. "Can you see any similarities between them?"

Tate looked back at the paper and studied it. "Now that you mention it, both robberies happened at this same time of year. The bandit got on and off the train unseen. The train was carrying a U.S. Marshal and his deputy, who were guarding both a wanted criminal and a sizeable payroll deposit. In both cases, shots were heard, which stopped the train. "

"Anything else?"

"The bandit wore a flour sack hood during the robbery, which reminds me—" Tate pointed to a flour sack, lying on the table. "I found that on the floor near the safe."

Jack picked up the sack inscribed with the words and logo of the Glenwood Springs Flour Mill. He slid his fingers into two holes, obviously cut out for eyes. "This fits the description the marshal gave of the hood worn by the bandit in the other robbery."

"If the bandit in the Eagle robbery was also wearing a hood like this one, then how did he get on and off the train unseen?"

"That's the unknown in both these crimes. I'm convinced the hood was the reason no one got killed in the Eagle robbery. In that case, the bandit locked the marshal and his deputy in the cell with the criminal they were guarding, walked out of their range of vision and somehow escaped the car and the train unseen by anyone." Jack turned the crude hood over in his hand. "It makes me wonder why this hood was left behind. Did it get pulled off by Will or Harry? Was that what made the bandit kill everyone—to keep from being identified?"

"That would make sense."

"It also gives us a possible motive for the murders. And now that you know the facts in the Eagle robbery," Jack said, reverting to their original subject. "What can you conclude about the two robberies?"

Tate set the paper down and looked at Jack thoughtfully. "Well, I'd say they were both done by the same person, and whoever did them lives somewhere along the rail line between Glenwood and Eagle."

"That's why we aren't sitting in your office. I don't want anyone to know who I am—including your deputies. I can work this case better if the folks around here don't know I'm a U.S. Marshal."

"But everyone knows that two of the men that were killed were U.S. Marshals. They'll be expecting a U.S. Marshal to show up to investigate their murders."

"One will. Marshal Luke Laramore, out of Denver, will be here tomorrow. You're going to help him conduct a very visible investigation, which will put everyone's eyes on him. What his investigation—in conjunction with yours—turns up will be the starting point for my investigation. Next week, Luke will hold a press conference to announce he's escorting Will's and Harry's remains as far as Denver. He'll give the public any information we decide might help with the investigation and publicly leave you in charge of continuing to look into anything you find."

"You want to lull the bandit into a false sense of security by making it appear there aren't any leads, while you poke around."

"Exactly—I hope you and Luke can come up with a solid lead. I want to start tracking whoever killed Will and Harry and heisted Señor Ortiz's emeralds before the trail gets any colder."

"I can hardly wait for Marshal Laramore to arrive. I'll be happy to let him take charge of the investigation—and Señor Ortiz. Since the day of the robbery, he's been in my office complaining that nothing is being done to recover his property." Tate paused. "I suppose you know he got in touch with his embassy."

"And lodged a number of complaints— When the train stopped in Denver, I contacted his embassy and asked for their help. I convinced them there would be a better chance of recovering the emeralds if Señor Ortiz wasn't dogging us. Thankfully, they convinced him."

Tate smiled. "So that's why he hasn't been in my office today."

"Luke will take Señor Ortiz to Denver when he's done here. Ortiz's ambassador talked him into waiting in a swanky hotel, courtesy of the State Department, while we investigate."

"Good!"

"Now I want to examine this car." Jack stood up. "Which end of the car was facing the engine?"

Tate pointed at the other end.

"Then the jail cell was on the river side of the tracks."

"That's right."

Jack began his investigation by pushing open the wooden door to a toilet stall, which was situated in the back corner. It was the old-fashioned kind that emptied directly onto the tracks. Jack lifted the raised seat off the hole in the floor and studied its diameter. *It's narrow, but not too narrow.* "Was the toilet in place when you examined the car?"

"Yes."

He set the toilet seat back over the hole.

The jail cell, where Ito had been locked up, sat next to the toilet stall. It contained a short bunk and a bucket. The cell was enclosed by wooden walls on three sides, with flat iron bars facing out. There was a two-foot gap on the other side of the cell wall before the mail bins and cubbies started. They were followed by a shelved compartment, meant to hold smaller bags, and several tall package lockers, which ran down the side of the car to the front.

Jack opened the lockers and examined them.

"A thin man might be able to fit into one of those lockers," Tate suggested.

"Or a woman," Jack replied, visually measuring the height and width of the lockers. "Either one could also have used the toilet as an exit route when the train stopped."

"I hadn't thought about that."

"But that doesn't tell us how the bandit got into the car unseen. With the train moving, I don't think anyone could have come up through the toilet. I also know Will Forbes. With a safe full of rare emeralds, and a prisoner to guard, he wouldn't have left this car unguarded for an instant."

Tate's handlebar mustache drooped into a frown.

Jack shut the empty lockers and stepped across the narrow aisle to another set of tall lockers and opened them. "The key to this crime is in how the bandit got into this car, and out of it, unseen."

Again, the lockers were empty with no sign that a person had used them as a hiding place. Shutting the lockers, Jack walked along an empty section of wall, where a sliding door rested when it was open. The windows on the door ran along the top and were meant to allow light into the car. Most people wouldn't have been tall enough to see out of them. Jack glanced out and kept moving.

He stopped as he reached the safe at the end of a bunk style bed, set against the wall. The small table, where he and Tate had been sitting, sat in the aisle between the bed and the toilet stall. He stared at the rust colored stain on the gray wool blanket covering the bed, before he asked, "Find anything under the bed?"

"I found a gun."

"What kind? . . . And had it been fired?"

"It's a Colt Navy, .36 calibers six shot revolver. All its rounds were still in their chambers. I believe it belonged to Marshal Forbes."

"Why?"

"Because the letters WF are tooled into the gun's handle, and when Marshal Forbes's body was removed, I noticed his shoulder holster was empty."

"Where is the gun?"

Tate pulled it from a saddlebag on the table and handed it to Jack.

The gun was as familiar to Jack as his own weapons were. He handed it back to Tate, his jaw a hard line. "The gun is Will's. Give it to Marshal Laramore tomorrow, along with the flour sack hood."

Jack sat back down and pushed his hat to the back of his head. "Did anyone move the bodies before you looked at the scene?"

"No, Frank Sullivan, the conductor, and the engineer, Joe Knapp, just checked the bodies for signs of life. After they confirmed that everyone was dead, Frank closed and locked the car."

"All right, tell me where each man was in the car and what wounds he'd sustained."

Tate walked over to the cell. "Ito was huddled in the corner of his bunk. There was a single gunshot wound to the side of his head . . . as though he had been trying to cower away with nowhere to go."

"He may have been the last one to die and knew it was coming."

"That fits, since he wasn't a threat to the robbers—being unarmed and locked up."

"Where was Harry Walsh?"

"He was over there, on his back with his head toward the front of the car." Tate pointed at a bloodstain on the floor a few feet from the safe, in front of the large sliding door. "He took a single shot to the front of his head, and"—Tate frowned—"His gun was in his holster."

"What did you make of that?"

"I thought it was odd. It seems to me, if the robber was holding him at gunpoint and forcing him to open the safe, which is what I think happened, then why didn't he take Marshal Walsh's gun?"

"Good question?" Jack examined the large bloodstain. It told him Harry had been shot at close range, and there would be an exit wound in the back of his head. "Did you find the bullet that killed Harry?"

Tate pointed out the embedded slug to the right of the door at the front of the car.

"Extract it, after Marshal Laramore sees it. He'll enter it into evidence." Jack turned away. "Where was Marshal Forbes?"

"He was on the floor in front of the mail bins—also on his back. His left temple had been grazed by a bullet and there was one in his chest."

"Did you find the bullet that grazed Marshal Forbes's head?"

"Yup." Tate pointed out the imbedded slug in the wall along the side of the bed.

"Extract that one too. They'll tell us what caliber the weapon was." Jack frowned. "It's not much, but little things can add up. Now, what did you initially see and feel when you first entered the car."

Jack knew Tate's initial reaction and feelings when he first entered the express car were important. He believed in gut reactions. They had helped him solve many of his cases.

"I came in through the back door, the one that had access to the dining car. The first thing I saw was an overturned chair between the table and the bunk. There was a blood trail from the middle of the bed to the safe, and it looked to me, by the blood splatters and smears, that there was a brief struggle before Marshal Forbes was shot in the chest and landed on the floor next to the mail bins."

Jack's chest tightened as he traced the blood drops from the dark discoloration on the bed to the safe and examined the smeared blood spots on the floor around the safe. He noted that there weren't any in between the safe and the stain on the floor where Will had fallen.

Some of what had happen he could picture in his mind. *But how did the bandit get into and out of the express car unseen?* Figuring that out was going to take time. He put it aside for the moment and asked, "Where did the train stop after the robbery?"

"On the other side of the Jackson tunnel."

"Can we get through the tunnel before another train is due?"

"Yup—the next train isn't due until 8p.m.," Tate said, following Jack as he grabbed his gear and headed for the door of the boxcar.

"I'll get my horse and meet you at the tunnel in . . . thirty minutes."

Tate locked the express car and mounted his black horse. "I'll be waiting when you get there."

Jack waited until Tate disappeared around the end of a boxcar before he pulled off his hat and crawled under the express car.

If the bandit entered the car through the toilet then there had to be a place he could brace himself while the train was in motion, and it had to have easy access to the toilet hole. *Unless the guy was an acrobat and a contortionist, I don't see how it could be done,* he concluded. *Unless . . . he came up through the toilet before the train started. Except crawling under the car without being seen by someone at the station or making a sound that would have alerted Will . . .* Jack shook his head.

Baffled, he walked back through the rail yard and alongside the train until he came to the stock car. The door to the car was open. He swung himself up inside.

The car's attendant, a rosy-cheeked man in his fifties, came forward. "May I see your claim ticket, please?"

Jack produced the ticket and the attendant checked it.

"I was beginning to think that no one was going to come for this big fella," he said opening the door of a split rail stall.

A huge chestnut stallion stomped his feet, and snorted.

"I know, Soldier"—Jack caught the stallion's head and patted his velvet nose—"I hate trains too, but it's over now, so let's get moving. We have an appointment to keep."

He saddled the stallion that stood seventeen hands and was a crossbreed between a draft horse and a quarter horse. After he cinched the saddle tight, he strapped his satchel and saddlebags to the saddle, walked Soldier out of the stall and down the ramp of the stock car. He swung onto the stallion's back and let him lope along the tracks beside the bank of the Colorado River, heading east—out of town.

The wind in Jack's face swept the lingering stench of coal smoke out of his nose and lungs. The sounds of Soldier's hooves pounding along the side of the train tracks and the roar of the Colorado River were a welcome duet in Jack's ears. He reined Soldier in as they neared the Jackson train tunnel, which they'd come through just before arriving in Glenwood Springs.

On the riverbank side of the tunnel, a clump of trees had grown into the rocks. Tate's horse was tied to one. Above the trees, the sheriff was standing on a narrow ridge of rock, overlooking the river. As Jack pulled Soldier up, Tate scrambled down from his perch and mounted his horse. From his saddlebag, Tate produced two flashlights. He handed one to Jack. Switching them on, they entered the tunnel.

"What was the express car's position in the train?" Jack asked.

"It was the fifth car from the engine and sat in between the stock car and the dining car."

"Did the passengers hear the shots?'

"They did . . . they did . . . they did." Tate's answer echoed through the tunnel.

"Where was the train when the passengers heard them?"

"The people in the rear observation car said they heard gunshots ricocheting off the walls of the tunnel, just as they entered it. The other passengers said they heard—what they assumed was a rockslide—while the passenger cars were inside the tunnel."

A faint light from the other end of the tunnel came into view. Jack urged Soldier to pick up the pace. He hated enclosed spaces. His size made automobiles, carriages, train coaches, and even many houses feel cramped. They just weren't built for a man of his size. He was always happiest when the horizon was his only enclosure, and the sky his only roof. That was one of the reasons he wanted to live in the country on a ranch, where he wouldn't feel closed in and could build a house to suit his size, one with towering windows that let the sky and horizon in.

When they emerged from the tunnel, Jack wheeled Soldier around and looked at it, examining the face of the rock around the tunnel entrance, then higher up the mountain it ran through.

"I know what you're thinking," Tate said, "and I've been up over the top. There aren't any footprints, rope marks, areas where rocks have recently slid or vegetation that has been flattened."

"Then the bandit *was* on the train when it left Glenwood Springs."

"And according to the conductor, no one—crew or passengers—were permitted to get off the train, until I allowed them to disembark after the train got back to town."

"Did you get their names? . . . And search everyone's bags?"

"Yup. I had two dozen deputies with me. We divided the people up into groups, let each group get their bags, and then took them directly to the courthouse to be searched and questioned. We took care of the folks from Denver, and beyond first, so the train could get underway again, but didn't find anything. We took down everyone's names and addresses—including the train crew's—in case you want to question them further. The train left Glenwood early the next morning. We held up the local folks who were on the train, asking them to wait until they'd been interviewed before they resumed their travel plans. After we searched them, we let them go home. I've spent yesterday and today interviewing them. I'm not done yet, but so far none of them have been any help. They all say the same thing."

"They thought it was a rockslide."

"A few recognized the sounds as gunshots."

"Who raised the alarm?"

"Drew Ellis, the head dining car steward. Ellis was standing at the front of the dining car when he heard the shots. According to him, they were still well inside the tunnel. He immediately stepped onto the platform of the express car and knocked on the door. When he didn't get an answer, he tried the door, but it was locked from the inside. He pounded and shouted, but got no response. He pulled the emergency brake inside the dining car just before the engine came out of the tunnel. When the train stopped, the conductor used his key to unlock the car."

"Is the conductor the only train official who had a key?"

"Yup, and he told me both marshals had keys too."

"And no one saw anyone get off the train when it stopped?"

"Not so far."

"How far was the train from the tunnel when it stopped?"

Tate pointed down the tracks that were heavily wooded on each side for about fifty yards. "It stopped just before it got out of the trees."

Jack walked Soldier over to the steep downhill slope where the trees ran right into the river and dismounted. Tate joined him. They walked along the edge of the trees, looking for footprints or any kind of ground disturbance that ran down the slope.

"There." Jack pointed at a narrow dirt slide that ended beside a tree at the water's edge. A rope, tied around the tree's trunk, trailed off into the water.

"That rope has probably been there for a long time," Tate said.

"Let's find out."

Jack held onto Soldier's reins, using the weight of the horse's powerful body as an anchor, while he slid down the bank and pulled the rope out of the river. He held it up for Tate to see.

The color of the rope clearly indicated it was new. The part that had been submerged in the river hadn't yet taken on the discoloration of long contact with the river's flowing silt and plant life, and it had obviously been cut.

"This could be the escape route, and our bandit's first mistake."

"Mistake?"

"I wondered why there were shots fired in the Eagle robbery, especially since the marshal didn't put up any resistance." Jack ran a finger along the cut edge of the rope. "This makes me believe the shots fired in the Eagle robbery were specifically meant to stop the train, allowing the bandit to get off at a predetermined point, where he most likely had some kind of getaway transportation."

"If that's true . . . then—"

"This robbery was deliberately planned to happen inside the tunnel. Shots were supposed to be fired after the robbery was complete . . . simply to get the train to stop. But things didn't go according to plan. People got killed. When the bandit reached the boat, instead of untying it, he cut the rope—an indication he was scared and wanted to leave the scene as quickly as possible. Now if we can just find someone on the train who saw a boat on the river during the time the train was stopped . . ." Jack mused.

"I'll ask, but it's unlikely. The passengers were all gawking out the windows on the other side of the train, waiting for the conductor and the engineer to unlock the express car door and tell them what had happened. Besides, if the bandit held the boat in close to the riverbank, the trees would have covered it as it went around the bend in the river. After that, I'm afraid the distance would have been too great for anyone who might have seen it to make out any useful details."

"Ask, just the same," Jack said, pulling himself hand over hand, up Soldier's reins, to the tracks.

When he was again on the tracks, he and Tate walked their horses back toward the tunnel on opposite sides of the track, looking for anything that might give them another clue.

Neither found anything.

They mounted up and again switched on their flashlights.

As they started back through the tunnel, Jack asked, "Is there a private boardinghouse in town? . . . A quiet respectable one—I mean. I need to keep a low profile."

Tate grinned. "I suspect, for you, that's pretty hard to do."

"It can be a challenge."

"I'd say the best place for you would be the boardinghouse on the southwest corner of 9th and Palmer. Just get off the train tracks where 7th Street starts. Palmer is the third street on your left. The boardinghouse belongs to Maggie Allen. She'll take good care of you.

"Thanks. Now, lastly, I need to see Will's body. I understand you have him and Harry on ice."

"They're at the undertakers. J.C. Schwartz runs both a furniture store and a funeral home. If you want to be unobserved, come around nine o'clock tonight. The furniture store will be closed. Walk around to the back. That's where the mortuary is—I'll meet you there."

"I'll be there at nine-thirty."

After Tate gave Jack directions to the Schwartz furniture store and mortuary, Jack said, "I saw a trail leading off into the mountains just as I left town. Where does it go?"

"It leads to a mountainous plateau. There's a spread up there called the High Peak Ranch. The saddle track you saw leads to it."

Tate pulled up his horse at the start of the saddle track just before they came into town.

"The owner of the High Peak Ranch, Eli Moore, has a contract to cut lumber up on the plateau in the White River National Forest. His ranch butts up against the forest. Come to think of it—Moore's property runs down to where the train stopped after the robbery. Just beyond where the train stopped, the Moores own a logging chute. It runs off the plateau to the Colorado River. The train stops there whenever Mr. Moore has a load of lumber to be picked up."

Jack's green eyes narrowed. "Interesting." He leaned over his saddle horn. "One more thing . . . If anyone should ask about me while I'm here, the story I'll be spreading around is that I was the foreman of the Canyon Rim Ranch outside San Antonio Texas. I came up here to look around and see if I liked Colorado enough to possibly buy my own ranch. If anyone checks that story out, it will hold up. The owner of the Canyon Rim Ranch, George Decker, is an old army friend of mine. He knows the story and will vouch for me." Jack shook hands with Tate. "Now I'll let you go into town first. I wouldn't want to seem too friendly with the sheriff on my first day in town."

4

Maggie Allen's boardinghouse was a big Victorian place. The three-story house, fronted by two cantilevered gables, featured a large semicircular oriel window. It overhung the roof of a wraparound porch, supported by spindle columns and enclosed by a white balustrade. The front door was bright red, indicating the house was a place travelers would find room and board.

Jack tied Soldier to a hitching post in front of the house, opened the gate in a low picket fence and walked through it, closing it behind him. Ducking under the overhanging roof, he stepped up onto the porch and straightened up.

A sturdy woman with gray-streaked brown hair was sitting in a rocking chair, fanning her heat-flushed face. She rocked back as Jack approached her.

"I'm Maggie Allen, the owner of this place. If you're lookin' for a bed, I've got one available, but it won't fit you."

"I've learned to adapt," Jack said, removing his Stetson.

Maggie stared at his hair and laughed. "I'll bet living with that hair has made you into one tough hombre."

"It's taught me a thing or two."

"What's your name, Red?"

"Jack Garrison."

"Irish, I should have known. Take a seat, Jack"—Maggie waved at the cane back chair next to her rocker—"and I'll tell you the rules of my boardinghouse. If you're agreeable, we'll do business."

Jack sat and stretched out his long legs. "Name your terms."

"There's no fightin', drinkin', swearin', or gamblin' allowed. If you smoke, you do it on the porch. There will be no flirting with the maids, or the kitchen help I employ. No lady friends are allowed up stairs, and I lock the doors promptly at midnight.

"What do you charge?"

"Twenty-five cents a night for a shared room and fifty for a private one. Both include breakfast and dinner. Private room renters use the house bathroom. Everyone else uses the privy and bathhouse outside the kitchen. There's also a stable out back for your horse. My son, Ned, will look after him. The room is paid for up front. Laundry service is pay for as you need it. If you're planning on stayin' a week—in a private room—then I'll do your laundry at no extra charge."

Jack dug into his pocket and pulled out a five-dollar half eagle. "I'll take the deal for a week in a private room."

Maggie put the gold coin into the pocket of her apron and stood. "Go put your horse in the stable. When you have him settled, I'll show you to your room and give you your change. Just come in through the backdoor. I'll be in the kitchen."

The stalls in the stable were small, but clean. Ned Allen favored his mother, and his waistline advertised her cooking. He met Jack at the door with a carrot for Soldier. He told Jack the stable, like the house, was always locked at midnight. Satisfied with the stable, Jack left Soldier in Ned's care.

Going through the backdoor and into the kitchen, Jack inhaled the enticing aroma of dinner. His stomach immediately reminded him that he hadn't eaten in several hours.

"What time is dinner served," he asked.

Maggie put the lid back on the pot she'd been stirring. "We eat promptly at six-thirty," she said, wiping her hands on her apron. "Follow me, and I'll show you to your room."

She led the way up the back stairs to the second floor, stopping at the first door on the left. The room was small, but held a full sized bed, a chest of drawers, a washstand with a mirror, and a straight-backed chair. A small closet was tucked into one corner of the room, across from an open window.

The room was clean and the bed looked as comfortable as Jack could expect, for one that was obviously too short for him. He dropped his satchel on the chair, and Maggie handed him his change.

"The key is in the door, and I always recommend you lock your door. Remember, dinner is at six-thirty, and I like to have all my guests in the parlor five minutes before we sit down. The parlor is just down the front stairs and to your left," Maggie said, going out the door.

"Thank you," Jack called after her.

He checked the clock on the dresser. There was about twenty minutes before dinner. He sat down on the bed and pulled a small pad of paper and a pencil from the pocket of his jacket. The ride to the boardinghouse had given him a chance to think. There were several more questions he needed answers to.

He finished writing his questions down about ten minutes before he needed to be in the parlor. Pocketing his notebook, he took a brush from his satchel, removed his jacket, exposing his shoulder holster, and brushed the dust from his pants and jacket.

Maggie Allen hadn't mentioned any rules about weapons. He usually carried three: A Browning, self-loading semi-automatic in either a shoulder holster or his jacket pocket. A Remington derringer, which he carried up the right sleeve of his shirt, and a knife, concealed inside the leg of his boot. He shrugged off his shoulder holster, removed the derringer from his right sleeve, and rolled up both his sleeves. After washing in the basin on the washstand, he replaced his weapons. Few people ever knew he carried weapons and he preferred it that way.

He hadn't seen or heard anyone else in the boardinghouse since his arrival, but as he put his jacket back on he heard doors opening and closing in the hall. Curious about his fellow tenants, he locked his room and went down the stairs to the parlor.

From the high arched doorway of the parlor, Jack studied Maggie's other guests.

"I'm glad you came down a little early," Maggie said, taking Jack's arm and drawing him into the room. "Gentleman, I'd like you to meet Jack Garrison. Jack, I'd like you to meet, Professor Norman Falkner, Mr. Morris Young, Hank Callister and Trent Wade."

Morris Young, an elderly man, stood and offered Jack his hand. "Glad to have you in the house," he said brightly. "I'm one of Maggie's permanent residents. When I retired, I decided I wanted to be close to the hot springs. They do my bones a world of good."

Jack detected a slight tremor in Mr. Young's fingers as they shook hands. "Nice to meet you Mr. Young."

"Just call me Mory, everyone does."

Jack nodded and held out his hand to Norman Falkner. The man looked terrified to put his hand into Jack's enormous one.

A little cough from Maggie made him raise his hand.

"Nice to meet you, Professor Falkner."

"And you," the professor said, quickly snatching his hand back.

"The professor is also one of my permanent tenants," Maggie said.

"I, too, came here for the healing power of the springs. Bathing in the hot springs and drinking the water has kept me from falling into an intolerable invalid state of existence."

Jack turned to the cowhands and shook hands with them. "Where do you two work?"

"We work for Eli Moore, the owner of the High Peak Ranch. We work the cattle end of his operation," Trent, a big rawboned kid, sporting a barely visible brown fuzz on his upper lip, said.

Jack thought he didn't look old enough to be out of high school.

"It's up on the plateau, just a couple of miles east of town," Hank, a more seasoned cowpoke with thinning black hair and a heavy mustache said. "We had a few of days off comin' to us and decided to spend them here," he added.

"It's fortunate you arrived in the middle of the week," Mory said.

"That's right," Professor Falkner agreed. "If you had arrived on Friday, Maggie would have been all booked up."

"This place fills up on the weekends with coal miners. They come here for a good meal and a hot bath," Mory explained.

"Yes, and then they spend all their money on cheap entertainment or gamble it all away," the professor muttered sourly.

Jack turned to the cowpokes, a hint of a smile in his green eyes. "Is that what you two are here to do?"

Before they could answer, Maggie said, "Let's go in to dinner. We can continue this conversation there."

Dinner included baked potatoes, hot rolls, honey glazed carrots and roast beef. The beef had been marinated and slow cooked. It seemed to melt in Jack's mouth.

"I can see why your house would be a popular place to stay," Jack said. "Everything is delicious."

Maggie smiled and dipped her head, accepting Jack's compliment.

Filling his plate for a second time, Jack asked Hank, "Do you think Mr. Moore would mind if I rode out and took a look at his spread? I'm in the market for a ranch. That's why I'm in Colorado."

"Mr. Moore isn't interested in selling the High Peak Ranch," Trent mumbled, his mouth full. "At least he hasn't ever said he was looking to sell the place."

"I'm not going to try to buy his ranch. I just want to see his operation. The area around Glenwood Springs interests me. Seeing some of the ranches and how they operate will help me decide if Glenwood Springs is the right place for me."

Hank said, "I'm sure Mr. Moore would be happy to show you his spread. He's mighty proud of it."

"If you'll give me directions on how to get there, maybe tomorrow I'll go out and take a look at it."

After finishing off two slices of strawberry pie, Jack excused himself from spending the evening in the parlor with Maggie's colorful guests and went to check on Soldier.

Finding Soldier was well taken care of by Ned; Jack patted the big horse's neck and fed him a lump of sugar. Soldier looked so content that Jack decided not to ride him over to his meeting at the mortuary. He'd already located the mortuary and thought the walk would do him good after being cooped up in a train for nearly twelve hours.

As darkness fell over Glenwood, Jack began his trek along the quiet streets. He listened to the sounds of crickets, and the occasional bark of a dog. Even the rolling of the river could be heard in the distance. Again that unexpected word came into his mind—*home.*

He acknowledged that he liked the feel of Glenwood Springs, but reminded himself that this resort town was already sporting all the niceties of civilization. In fact, it was one of the first cities in the

United State to have electrical lights. It also had a telephone system. Jack ascribed that to the two stays Teddy Roosevelt had made in Glenwood Springs, not to mention the international popularity of the hot springs.

No. Montana is the place for me. Still, I guess it wouldn't hurt to just look around at the possibilities. After all, looking for a ranch is part of my cover story. So . . . I'll go see the High Peak Ranch tomorrow morning.

Nearing the furniture store, Jack reviewed everything he'd learned so far. The impression taking hold in his gut left a bad taste in his mouth. *There had to be an inside man.* It wasn't a possibility he wanted to consider. *But I have to,* he told himself as he rounded the corner and spotted the building that housed both a furniture store in the front and a mortuary in the back.

It wasn't unusual for an undertaker to have another business and house them together. Making a living as an undertaker in a small community like Glenwood Springs wasn't lucrative.

Jack walked around to the back of the building. Like the bodies it housed, the mortuary was silent and lifeless. No welcoming lights burned in its windows.

A little shiver skated over Jack's skin. He stopped and gathered his courage, stilling the emotions building inside him. It was going to be hard to look at Will, to come face to face with the reality—and finality—that Will was dead. However, it was something he had to do, not only had Will been a dear friend, and he needed to say a final farewell, but because he was the marshal in charge of finding out who had killed such a fine man.

The nagging in the back of his mind, which insisted seeing Will would tell him something or give him a lead—a place to start—intensified. Nurturing that hope, he knocked on the mortuary door. Tate opened it, making him shade his eyes against the sudden light.

"Glad you're here," the sheriff said. "I don't like this place even in the daytime. Being alone in it at night is like walking through the Linwood Cemetery—something the tourists like to do."

"I'm none too fond of these places either, so I'll keep it short."

Tate led him down the hall to a closed door and stopped. He inserted a key and turned it in the lock.

Before he could open the door, Jack said, "I'd like to go in alone. Will was a good friend of mine. I'd like to spend a few minutes with him by myself—pay my final respects."

"Sure. He's in the first locker to your right. Marshal Walsh, and then Ito are next to him," Tate said, stepping back from the door.

Jack turned on the light and closed the door behind him. The icy room held six lockers. A printed card, inserted into a small metal frame on the door of each locker, held the name of the person inside.

Passing the locker with Will's name on it, Jack took hold of the frigid handle of the locker with the name Harry Walsh on it, opened it, and pulled out the slab. He uncovered Harry's face and looked down at the young man with the black hair.

"Handsome Harry," Jack whispered.

That had been his nickname. "He's as pretty as a woman," Luke Laramore had once said. He always wore a ready smile, liked the ladies a bit too much, and wore the most fashionable clothes. Those weren't exactly the qualities that characterized most U.S. Marshals. Jack wondered if that was why it took him five years to become a marshal.

He'd been promoted from deputy to marshal six months ago. *And that's what got him killed,* Jack thought sadly.

An ugly hole above Harry's right eyebrow had been plugged with a piece of cloth. *At least he died instantly, without feeling a thing.*

Jack rolled Harry's head to the side and examined the bullet's exit wound. As he suspected, the wound was substantial. Harry had been shot at point blank range.

By Jack's order, nothing had been removed from the victims' bodies, nor had any preparations been made for their burials. Jack felt he needed to see Harry and Will exactly as they were when they died—if he was to sense or feel anything about what had happened.

The first thing Jack examined was the gun in Harry's shoulder holster. Questions about the fully loaded, holstered gun rose in Jack's mind as he searched Harry's pockets, turning up the usual things. There was a wallet with twenty dollars, some loose change, his badge, a clean handkerchief, a comb, and a key ring, which included a key to the express car. After looking at each item, Jack replaced it, until he found a small notebook. The train schedule from Grand Junction to Denver, dated June 8th, had been written in the notebook, along with the initials D.E. He tore out the page and continued his search.

In the inside breast pocket of Harry's coat, he found a white spirit feather ornamented with a string of five tiger-eye stone beads.

The beads' differing bands of gold caught the light and shifted as Jack rolled them between his fingers, making them seem fluid—almost alive. *Just like the eyes of a tiger.*

The spirt feather, often given as a token of friendship, was an unusual item. Not the sort of thing he would have imagined finding in Harry's pocket. Jack put the spirit feather into his own coat pocket with the intention of learning more about the feather, wondering who had given it to Harry and if it was important to the case. He pushed Harry back into the locker and shut it.

For several moments, he just stared at the locker with Will's name on it. He closed his eyes, inhaling and exhaling slowly, before pulling Will out. It took a few more moments before he could make himself uncover Will's face. When he did, it was with quiet reverence.

He gazed down on the man who'd been his most influential father figure. Dried blood ran along a groove from his left temple back into his iron gray hair and down the left side of his face. *The bullet probably dazed him for a couple of minutes.* Jack's eyes blurred. A tear ran down his face and dripped onto Will's collar before he could stop it.

The faint smell of decomposition made Jack swallow and step back. He blew out a breath, took in a shaky one, and held it. Quickly, he pulled down the sheet covering Will and examined the bullet wound in his chest. There was blood and powder burns around the hole in Will's vest. The bullet had hit him directly in the heart.

He, too, died instantly.

Grief's powerful embrace encircled Jack in sorrow. He hadn't even been able to say goodbye—express his gratitude, his love. The need for comfort made him reach for Will's hand.

It was balled into a fist.

Gently opening Will's fingers, he discovered a pendant in the palm of Will's hand. The breath he was holding whooshed out of him. Even at a glance, he knew the pendant was unusual—unique. He took it from Will's hand and carefully examined it.

The stone pendant was a translucent emerald green. *Jade,* he decided, but its clear vibrant color was one he'd never run across. It was triangular in shape, with gold scalloped edges. He examined the gold inlaid symbols on the stone, thinking he'd never seen anything like them. *No, that's not true.*

A few years ago he'd gone to an ancient Egyptian exhibit. The symbols on the pendant reminded him of the hieroglyphics he'd seen at the exhibit. He rolled it over and found a tiny spot of dried blood. *Will's blood—*

A tingling sensation ran through his hand as he closed his fingers around the exquisite treasure. There was only one way this pendant could have ended up in Will's hand. *This must belong to Will's murderer.* Now he had a place to start his search for the bandit that had taken Will's life.

"Thank you, Will. I knew you wouldn't let me down."

Sliding the pendant into his breast pocket, Jack quickly searched Will for anything else of importance to the case, but found nothing. He paused and looked down on his mentor. Grief distorted his face. He didn't try to restrain the tears as he bent down and kissed Will's forehead. "Until we meet again," he whispered, pulling the sheet back over Will's face.

Tate was pacing the hall when Jack came out. "Did you find anything helpful?" he asked as they walked toward the outside door.

"Yes, and we'll talk about it tomorrow when Marshal Laramore gets here. He'll want to see the bodies too. Once he does, tell him to authorize Mr. Schwartz to prepare the bodies as their families have requested. I know they're anxious to lay them to rest."

"I can't imagine how hard it must be for them to have to wait on our investigation before their loved ones are returned to them."

Jack stopped Tate before he opened the door. "Hold off on doing more interviews with the local train passengers until Marshal Laramore gets here. I want him to be in on those interviews."

"Okay."

"Also"—Jack pulled the list of questions he'd made from his pocket—"after you brief Marshal Laramore and question the passengers, you can both start looking for the answers to these questions." He handed the list to Tate.

"What are you going to be doing," asked Tate, pocketing the list.

"I'm going to be establishing my cover story with the locals—letting myself be seen around town, asking all the questions someone interested in becoming a citizen of Glenwood Springs would ask."

"Sounds like more fun than questioning passengers."

"Just part of the job— I want to meet with you and Luke tomorrow night . . . go over what you've learned and decide on our next move. Is there an out of the way place we can do that?" The corner of Jack's mouth lifted. "I don't want to be seen with you two."

A wry grin lifted Tate's mustache. "We could meet at my house, after dark. I live alone, just a few blocks from your boardinghouse."

He gave Jack the address, and they went out the mortuary door.

"I'll be there at nine-thirty," Jack said and walked into the darkness.

5

Thursday, June 11, 1908

Jack ate a delicious breakfast of fresh strawberry crepes. When he couldn't eat another bite, he thanked Mrs. Allen for a memorable meal and went out to saddle Soldier, wondering about the trail that led to the High Peak Ranch. Its easy access to both the train tunnel and the river made it a good getaway prospect—if he was wrong about the boat. *The bandit could have gone back through the tunnel unseen, after the train stopped, and then up the track and onto the plateau. He could have had a horse waiting and gone back into town using the southern route off the plateau that Hank told me about this morning.*

Drawing in a deep breath of the cool mountain air, Jack walked Soldier north, up Palmer Street to 7th Street, and turned east. He found the saddle track and started up—his thoughts turning to Will, still struggling with his death, still mourning his loss.

The job of transporting Haru Ito across the country was supposed to have been Will's last one as a U.S. Marshal. *And it was,* Jack reflected bitterly. Will had been about to retire. He and his wife, Emily, were planning to move back to Texas and settle down near their grown children. *At least Emily can still do that.* It was a comfort to think of Emily surrounded by her children and grandchildren.

Jack held on to that thought as Soldier rounded a blind curve in the trail and stopped.

The trail dead-ended into a cross track, running roughly northwest to southeast. To the northwest, the trial climbed. To the southeast, it descended.

Soldier looked over his shoulder at Jack and stomped his feet.

Leaning on the saddle horn, Jack pushed his hat to the back of his head. "I don't recall Hank mentioning there was a T in the road or which direction to take when I came to it."

Soldier snorted.

"It doesn't matter," he told the stallion, patting his neck. "We haven't got anything else to do this morning. So which way will it be?"

Soldier jerked his head to the north.

"Okay, up it is."

He was about to urge Soldier onward, when the stallion turned his head, his ear pricking forward. An instant later Jack heard the thunder of hooves. He turned in his saddle just as a bay colored mustang with a black mane and tail galloped around the blind corner.

Jack yanked on Soldier's reins, pulling him out of the middle of the trail as the mustang flew around them, taking the descending trail.

The rider was bent over the mustang's neck. A hat hid his face. All Jack saw before the mustang rounded another bend was the buckskin jacket and pants the rider was wearing, along with a long black braid, decorated with a silver clasp, a string of some kind of gold beads, and two white feathers, which flew out behind the rider.

Nahtow—AD 405: In this year the land bridge disappeared, but not before a small group of people came across the bridge and into the land. They, like us, were seeking sanctuary from the wars they say are raging upon the land of our ancestors. They tell us the children of Lehi have broken into large tribes and small bands. They fight for land and dominance.

Those who have come, say they were led here, as were we. Their leader, Jonoc was shown the way in a dream. They desire to join with Elan and me and be our people. They have made me chief over them. We are now known as the Nahtow. We have combined my two white feathers and silver clasp with the string of gold stones Elan wears to form a totem for our people.

Elan and I will do all we can to teach them the ways of this harsh land and of the mission given to the Nahtow. I know they have been sent to us that our children may have the opportunity to marry and that our people will increase. The whisperings in my soul tell me that all who join with our children will inherit the memory Elan and I possess. This is needful that the Nahtow may be equal to the mission we have been given.

Jack's eyes narrowed, thinking about the white spirit feather tucked away in his satchel. "An Indian wearing white feathers," he mused, keeping Soldier from charging after the mustang.

The big stallion stomped and snorted.

If the Indian hadn't been such a skilled rider, they would have collided. But the Indian had ridden as though he was part of the mustang. Jack had to admire his skill, even if he deplored his manners. *No one should bolt around a blind corner like that.* And instead of stopping to apologize for the near miss, the Indian hadn't uttered a word as he flew around Soldier and pounded down the trail.

Jack rubbed Soldier's neck and the stallion quit stomping. "Well, since we couldn't ask the Indian where he was headed or which way leads to the High Peak Ranch, what do you say we follow the trail the Indian took and see where it leads?"

Soldier's head bounced as though he understood every word. Jack gave him his head, and Soldier took the descending trail.

Kedra Moore was late. Her errand into town shouldn't have taken her more than thirty minutes to complete. All she was supposed to have done was to pick up the mail and return the books she'd borrowed from Sarah Powell, her schoolteacher friend. She hadn't meant to spend so much time looking through Sarah's extensive library, but she couldn't resist looking through the new science books Sarah had just received for the coming school year. If she could have, Kedra would have borrowed all of them. As it was, her saddlebags bulged with the maximum number of books they could carry. Which ones to take and which ones to leave until she next raided Sarah's library had been an agonizing decision, one that took considerably longer than she'd realized.

She urged Flyer to cover the ground faster. *Effie is sure to blister my ears with her tongue, and I deserve it. I did promise to be back before it was time to prepare lunch. If only I wasn't so . . . book greedy.*

Nahtow—AD 410: Elan has given me many strong sons and beautiful daughters. I named my eldest son Ammon, after my father. All of my children have Elan's gold eyes. This pleases me, for I never tire of her eyes. They also all possess the gift of perfect memory.

We began to teach them of our mission to the lost children of Lehi when they were very young. Their minds were eager for knowledge and we have taught them all we know of faith and God. We have taught them the history of our people, as far back as the coming of our father Lehi into the land of our inheritance. We have also instructed them in science, mathematics, astronomy, medicine, and to read and write in our language, and still their minds are hungry for knowledge.

Reading books was an addiction Kedra couldn't seem to satisfy. She blamed it on the fact that her father had only allowed her to go to school through high school, which she'd finished two years ahead of most students her age. High school hadn't satisfied her hunger for knowledge. It was something she'd never understood, but her longing to learn was insatiable. Not only that, but the more she learned the more she wanted to know. The strange part about it was that she could remember everything she read, saw, or heard.

Somewhere over the years, that ability had made her want to know how much information she could put into her mind before she couldn't learn or remember anything more. To date, she hadn't found that point.

Her mind flashed back to the man on the big horse, and the collision she'd just barely managed to avoid. She'd been too busy trying to keep Flyer from ramming into the big stallion to even give the man a glance. *Not only am I book-greedy and incapable of keeping a promise, but I'm rude too. I should have at least stopped and apologized. Yes—and been even later.* She groaned as her shortcomings multiplied.

The ranch finally came into view. The house, which was more like a lodge, sat on the edge of a large meadow. A row of half a dozen small log cabins sat beside the house. A barn stood at the rear.

Kedra raced around to the back of the house and jumped off Flyer's back, almost before he came to a stop.

Buck Gilbert, the ranch's ramrod, caught Flyer's reins and said, "Effie has been searching for you." He grinned. "I'd say a thunder storm was in a better mood."

"Oh, no— Buck, do you mind taking care of Flyer for me?" Kedra asked the blond, bearded cowboy, pulling off the saddlebags that held the mail and her books.

Buck eyed the bulging bags. "I'll take care of Flyer. You best high-tail-it in and hide those books before Effie finds you—if you don't want a tongue lashing the whole ranch will be privileged to hear."

"Thanks," Kedra threw the word over her shoulder and ran through the back door of the two story, split log house.

She stopped, just after she entered, and pulled off her boots. On stocking feet, she crept down the hall to the right, and then padded softly up the back stairs and into her bedroom. She closed the door with a sigh. *Safe!* Taking a relieved breath, she quickly took the mail out of the saddlebags, pulled off her buckskin jacket, put her boots back on, and hurried down the stairs to her father's office.

He was working on the accounting books when she stepped into the office. "Here's the mail, Papa," she said, setting several envelopes on the desk. "I don't think the letter you were expecting is there."

"Thank you, dear," he replied, without looking up.

"You're welcome," Kedra said and left the office. Steeling herself, she marched into the kitchen.

"You're late!" Effie Blue pushed a damp strand of faded blond hair off her forehead, her blue eyes snapping with annoyance. "You promised me you'd be back to start the rolls for lunch." She looked up at the big clock on the wall. "Well it's too late now. The men will just have to settle for biscuits, so you best get started—if there's nothin' more pressing on your social agenda today."

"I'm sorry, Effie, really I am," Kedra said, slipping a big apron over her head and tying it behind her back.

"Being sorry don't feed the men." Effie shook a metal spatula at her. "You know I need your help on wash day to get the cooking done."

Kedra brought out a large bin of flour from the pantry. "I know, and you have every right to be angry with me."

"I certainly do, but my ire can wait," the Moore's cook and housekeeper, grumbled. "Right now I need to go hang up the clothes before they dry into a wrinkled heap. That is, if you think you can get the biscuits started and keep the meat from scorching while I'm gone."

"Of course I can."

Effie glowered at her and went out the door grumbling.

"Whew," Kedra blew out a relieved breath. "That wasn't as bad as I thought it would be," she confided to the big mixing bowl she took out of the cupboard.

She quickly gathered the rest of the ingredients from the pantry and the butter from the icebox and began to measure out the flour, tripling the recipe. From the corner of her eye she saw the masked, ring-tailed thief slip into the kitchen and knew Effie hadn't latched the screen door when she went out.

"Oh no you don't, Swindler. You know you aren't allowed in the kitchen. If Effie finds you in here she'll make a hat out of you."

Swindler hissed and scampered into the large pantry. Kedra ran after him, grabbing the broom as she entered the pantry. The raccoon was already climbing the shelves, knocking things off as he went.

"Come down now, or else I'll—" Kedra poked him with the broom.

He batted at the broom and hissed.

"Don't make me do it," she pleaded, but she could tell Swindler was in one of his moods.

As if to affirm her assessment, he batted a can off the shelf. She dodged it just in time to keep from being hit in the head. Swindler scrambled along the shelf, knocking things over as he went. Reaching for a hold on the shelf above him, he knocked over a box, and Kedra was showered with macaroni.

"That does it," she growled and swatted the raccoon with the broom, just as he tried to pull himself up to the next shelf.

Swindler fell off the shelf, landed like a cat, and shot out of the pantry. He ran across the floor and scrambled up to the counter top.

For a moment Kedra thought he was going to escape out the window, over the sink. Instead he leaped across the sink and headed for the open flour bin.

Kedra dropped the broom and sprang across the room. She managed to grab the flour bin just as Swindler reached it. His clawed hands curled over the rim. She gave the bin a hard tug. Swindler released his grip. She fell backwards, the flour dousing her.

The thief saw his chance, seized the bowl of butter, and jumped off the counter top.

Kedra rolled over, grabbed a pot from the under the large butcher-block table in the center of the kitchen and threw it at the raccoon as he ran for the door. The pot missed its mark and she threw another one just as a man's legs appeared in the doorway.

Swindler scooted out the door between the man's legs.

The man jumped aside to keep from being hit by the pot that followed the thief out of the kitchen. Ducking his head, he came through the door and looked down at Kedra, his face impassive.

"That's . . . um . . . an interesting pet."

"Swindler."

"Is that his name or his occupation?"

"Both."

Kedra stared up at the man. She'd never looked into such green eyes, and found herself unable to break away from them.

He tugged politely on the brim of his hat. "I beg your pardon for interrupting you, Miss. I was told Mr. Moore's office was just inside the back door, but I didn't see it."

His voice was rich and deep and Kedra almost sighed, until she suddenly realized she was still lying on the floor covered in flour. She jumped to her feet and turned away, her cheeks flaring with heat beneath the white flour that covered her face.

"Excuse me," she said as she took the dishcloth out of the sink and tried to wipe the flour from her face. Her efforts only made matters worse. The wet dishrag turned the flour into a sticky paste.

"Ah . . . would you allow me?" the man asked, reaching over her shoulder and taking the rag from her hands.

"I'm so embarrassed. I wish I could just sink through the floor," she moaned, dropping her head.

She heard him rinse out the rag. Then he put a finger under her chin and lifted it. Butterflies fluttered in her stomach as he carefully wiped the flour from her face.

"You'll have to wash your hair, but at least your face is now the right shade," he said without a hint of laughter or mockery.

Kedra searched his eyes, but found no trace of ridicule there.

"Thank you," she said; then gasped, "The meat!"

The smell of sizzling meat filled the kitchen. She slid across the flour dusted floor to the huge frying stove, grabbed a spatula, and started turning the meat over as fast as she could. The man was beside her in an instant, turning over the long strips of beef too.

She glanced up at him as they worked. He was the biggest man she'd ever seen. He towered over her and that was very unusual. At six feet, she was as tall as, or taller than, most men. She found the necessity of looking up to see his face . . . pleasing

When they were finished, the man stepped back, took off his hat, and wiped his brow with his shirtsleeve.

Kedra gawked at his fiery red hair, decided it suited him, and realized she liked what she saw. He was not only very tall, but also powerfully built, with strong even features, a square jaw, and a very attractive crease down the middle of his chin.

She fought a sudden urge to reach up and run her finger down his chin. Tightening her grip on the spatula, she stepped back.

As though he sensed her scrutiny, he put the hat back on his head, hiding his face in the shadow of its wide brim.

"I think we managed to salvage lunch," he said.

"And we did it without even being introduced."

"We may not have been introduced, but we have met. At least we *almost* met."

He lifted the silver clasp on the end of her long braid and dusted the flour from the tiger-eye beads and white feathers.

She groaned.

"You're quite a horsewoman. That was a remarkable piece of riding you did out there on the trail. Most people would have collided with me, if they'd come around that bend at the rate you were going."

"I am *so* sorry. It's just that I was late and—"

"You don't owe me an explanation, but I do think after all we've been through together, you might at least tell me your name." He held out his hand. "I'm Jack Garrison—and you are?"

"Kedra Moore."

A warm tingling sensation ran up her arm as his big fingers encased her hand. She tried to smile, but her embarrassment was too great. If there was a more humiliating way to meet a man she felt so strongly attracted to, she couldn't think of it. Not only had she almost run him off the trail, but his patient , willing, and timely help had made her feel like a rude, incompetent idiot, although, she had to admit that wasn't how he'd treated her.

From finding her on the floor covered in flour, to washing her face, and then helping her save lunch, he'd treated her as if she was just an awkward kid. Worst of all, nothing in his expression or manners suggested he saw her as anything else and that hurt.

She pulled her hand out of his and turned away as her face grew warm. "I'll take you to my father's office," she said, starting for the door, suddenly anxious to be rid of him.

She would never be able to look at Jack Garrison again without feeling awkward, and embarrassed. It wasn't vanity that prompted the way she felt. She simply hated being seen as an incompetent child. After all she was twenty-one, almost twenty-two.

I hope I never see Jack Garrison again. Then I can just forget this horrible encounter. But that was impossible. Her mind never let her forget anything. Sooner or later, it would force her to relive this humiliating episode—and her undeniably strong attraction to this big redheaded cowboy.

Nahtow—AD 440: Elan and I have lived to see the beginning of the fourth generation of our family. The gold eyes abound, and we have seen that the strongest gift of memory is always found in those who possess Elan's gold eyes. Those children are much sought after as companions, and the value of our gift is cultivated with purpose by our children.

Many are eager to leave Sanctuary Bay and begin the mission of the Nahtow. They honor and respect our heritage and the faith of our father Lehi. However, there are others who possess great memory who do not care for the mission of the Nahtow or our faith. They desire to leave, that they may seek greater knowledge among men—to become leaders and rulers. I mourn for these children. The spirit tells me their gift will leave their children and only those who are faithful to our mission will retain the gift of long memory and the light of understanding.

It is my final prayer, as I am about to depart this life, that the hearts of my posterity will be drawn to the mission Elan and I were given. It will be their honor to accept and embrace this great work as they go forth from this place, which has given us safe harbor for so long.

6

As Kedra led Jack out of the kitchen, he experienced an acute pang of disappointment. It was obvious she wanted to be rid of him. But if he'd been given the choice, he would have stayed in the kitchen, instead of going to meet her father.

He hadn't been allowed to look into her hypnotic gold eyes nearly long enough. They reminded him of the string of tiger-eye beads attached to the spirit feather, and the one she wore. They were every bit as gold, their color shifting in tone and depth, reflecting her mood and expression. There was something hauntingly familiar about them too. Looking into them, he felt the shadow of a memory, elusive, yet discernible. Their effect on him was startling, and at the moment incomprehensible, but undeniable. The inescapable truth was . . . he found Kedra Moore stunningly beautiful and *very* intriguing.

Despite the color of her eyes, she was an Indian. Her square face, high cheekbones, and olive skin told him that. Although her skin was light enough for Jack to have seen her blush. That would have told him she wasn't a full-blooded Indian, if her eyes and her last name, Moore, hadn't already.

He watched her hip length braid, which was liberally powdered with flour, swing back and forth with the gentle sway of her hips as she led him down the hall. Her trim hips were outlined by the buckskin trousers she wore, and their sway was accentuated by the motion of her braid. In the few places that had escaped the flour, her hair was blue-black. He liked the color and her sensible braid better than the puffy, swept up hairdos that were so popular with women and made them all look alike to him. He also found the grace with which her long lean body moved nearly as intoxicating as her eyes. It made him even sorrier that she didn't seem to want to spend any more time with him.

She walked by the backdoor and turned down the corner in the opposite direction from what he'd done when he came in. That had been his mistake, one he now couldn't regret.

Before they came to a stop in front of a closed door, the sound of angry voices reached them.

"You've got a lot more to lose than I do!"

"If you cross me, you'll find out how wrong you are!"

There was an ugly laugh, and the door jerked opened before Kedra could knock.

A man in his late twenties—by Jack's estimation—pushed Kedra aside. He had the same skin tone and blue-black hair as she did, was a shade taller than she was and every bit as slender.

Jack's hackles rose. He couldn't abide men who treated women like that. He glared into the man's startling ice blue eyes for a moment before the man stormed off down the hall.

"Don't pay any attention to Isaac."

"Isaac?"

"My brother—he's always in a foul mood." Kedra tisked and stepped into the office. "Papa, there's a man here to see you."

She motioned for Jack to come in.

Feeling unaccountably relieved that Isaac was Kedra's brother and not her husband, Jack ducked his head, and stepped into her father's office. He took in the pine-paneled walls, the oak desk and brown leather chairs in a glance, but took his time assessing Mr. Moore.

Kedra's father was a bear of a man, barrel chested and heavily muscled. He was a couple inches taller than Kedra, had thinning gray hair, a bushy mustache, and blue eyes, which at the moment sparked with anger.

The anger died as he looked Jack over. A broad smile replaced his scowl when Jack removed his hat.

"This is Jack Garrison, Papa. He got lost looking for your office. Now that I've shown him the way, I'll leave you two to discuss his business." Kedra backed out the door, closing it after herself.

Eli Moore came around the big oak desk with an out stretched hand. He gripped Jack's hand harder than polite manners dictated. Jack saw it as an attempt to immediately establish his dominance, and wondered why he felt the need to do so.

"I'm Eli Moore, Mr. Garrison. What can I do for you?"

Jack refrained from getting into a contest of strength and said, "Call me Jack."

"All right, Jack—I'm Eli." He gestured for Jack to sit in a leather chair in front of the desk and sat down again behind it. "I don't think I've seen you around here before. Where are you from?"

"Texas . . . mostly."

"I hear everything is big down in Texas," Eli said with a grin.

"And it's hot and flat too."

Eli laughed. "Is that why you're up this way?"

Jack leaned back in the chair. "I definitely need a change of climate and scenery."

"Are you looking for a job?"

"Maybe, but what I'm really looking for is a ranch."

"What kind of a ranch?"

"That's just it. I'm not sure. I like this area, so I thought I might stay a while and visit some of the ranches. See what it takes to run a successful operation around here. I expect the climate and the altitude makes a big difference in how a cattle ranch is run. I heard about your ranch and decided to come take a look—if you don't mind."

"Who told you about my ranch?"

"I met Hank and Trent at Maggie Allen's boardinghouse. What they told me about your logging enterprise intrigued me. I understand you have a contract with the government to cut lumber in the White River National Forest. I wondered how hard it was to get that contract and how profitable it is."

"I can certainly answer your questions and give you a tour of my operations, but it's a shame you're not looking for work. I could use a man of your size and strength right now—especially if you know how to handle an ax."

"I do, and I may need a job. I can't afford to whittle away my money on a boardinghouse while I decide if I like Glenwood Springs enough to stay. It might be better if I found a job while I make up my mind whether or not to buy a ranch around here."

Eli opened his pocket watch. "There's about thirty minutes before lunch." He paused. "You will stay for lunch, won't you? After lunch I'll show you my logging operation."

"Be my pleasure."

"Before we eat, I think there's just enough time to show you my cattle pasture."

After Eli appraised Soldier and pronounced him a perfect fit for Jack, the two rode off up a path, lined with pinion pines, southeast of the house. About half way up the sloping trail, Eli pulled his gray mustang to a stop and wheeled the horse around.

"Take a look." He waved at the vista in the valley below. "That meadow is where I run my cattle." He pointed to the southern end of the meadow. "See that small lake? The stream that runs out of that lake waters the meadow and the cattle."

"Nice setup," Jack said, looking down on Eli's herd, grazing in the deep grass of the meadow. "How many head have you got?"

"About two hundred. It's not a big operation, but my land won't support more than that." He gave Jack a sideways look. "I'm betting you worked on a ranch in Texas."

"I did."

"How many head did it run?"

"Three thousand."

"Then you must know your way around cattle."

Jack leaned on his saddle horn. "I know cattle ranching inside and out. What I don't know is the kind of logging that's done in Colorado. As you said, this country can't support the kind of herds I ran in Texas. I may need to consider what else I can do to make ranching here a profitable venture."

"You say *you* ran the herds in Texas. What does that mean?"

"I was the ramrod for the Canyon Rim Ranch, near San Antonio, for five years. They were good years, and my boss, George Decker, paid me well. That's why I'm now in a position to start up my own ranch."

"If I hire you, I'd need you to work both sides of my operation."

"I'll work whatever you want. But I'd only be willing to hire on as a part time, temporary hand. After all, my main business here is to look over the country."

"I take your point, and what I need right now is a temporary replacement for Josiah Blue, my regular jack-of-all-trades, while he's laid up with the gout," Eli said, turning his horse back down the trail.

"What exactly does Josiah Blue do?"

"Why don't we discuss that and nail down terms we can both agree on over lunch," Eli suggested.

Lunch was a disappointment. The food was good and there was plenty of it, but Kedra didn't join them, neither did Isaac. Jack had hoped to see Kedra again, before he left the ranch. He'd also been intrigued by the small snatch of conversation he and Kedra had overheard between Eli and Isaac. Instinct told him Isaac was someone he should assess more closely.

"Well, Jack," Eli began as he set aside his napkin, "I never hire a man to work my cattle or in my logging operation until I've seen him in action. I don't need to see you bulldog steers. A call to your previous employer will tell me all I need to know about that. But if you aren't in any hurry, how would you feel about showing me what you can do with an ax, after we tour my logging operation?"

Jack pushed back from the table. "I'd be happy too."

Eli's logging business turned out to be a simple affair. The trees were inspected and marked for cutting. Eli explained that his contract with the government only allowed him to cut down a certain number of trees in any given acre. Once cut, the trees' branches were removed and the trunks were cut into measured lengths. Then they were loaded onto a wagon or sled and taken to a chute that ran down the mountain to the train tracks. There they were loaded onto the train and sent to either Denver or Grand Junction.

Jack took in the whole operation with genuine interest. He considered the way Eli ran his logging business out dated and dangerous, but kept that opinion to himself. He complimented Eli on the operation as they rode back to the house.

He was no stranger to lumberjacking. One of his cases had taken him into the Great Northwest, where logging was big business and the operations there were complex, fine-tuned enterprises. Jack had spent four months as a lumberjack, gathering evidence in the illegal cutting of timber from both private and national forests. The lumberjacks he worked with had taught him the trade. His size and strength turned him into one of the best jacks in the Big Piney logging camp.

The wind was picking up by the time he and Eli got back to the ranch house. Buck took their horses, and they walked over to a tall ponderosa pine, swaying in the breeze.

"As you can see, the size of this tree has made it a danger to the house. A strong wind could bring it down on the roof."

"Where do you want me to drop it?"

Eli drew a line in the dirt. "Drop it within a foot of this line and you've got yourself a part time job—if you want it."

Jack took off his jacket, dropped his hat on top of it, and rolled up his sleeves. He'd had the foresight to put his gun in his pocket, instead of wearing it in a shoulder holster, and leave his sleeve gun locked in his room at the boardinghouse.

He took the ax Eli handed him and walked around the tree.

Kedra stopped washing dishes when she heard the *whack* of steel bite into wood. She looked out the window over the sink and watched Jack Garrison repeatedly swinging an ax. He made it look effortless.

"What are you gawking at?" Effie demanded as she put more dirty dishes into the sink. "You've seen trees cut down before, and that one has needed to go for a long time." She studied Kedra and smirked, "Unless of course it's not the tree you're interested in, but the man cutting it."

Kedra felt the unstoppable blush burn up her face. Dropping her eyes, she quickly went back to washing dishes. She looked up again when she heard the *crack* that told her the tree was about to fall.

It came down with a resounding crash.

Her father whooped, and said, "Right on the mark. You've got a job, Jack—if you want it."

Kedra's stomach turned over. She didn't want Jack Garrison on the ranch, and for more than one reason.

The wind carried Jack's response to her father's offer. "I appreciate the offer, but I'll need a day or two to think it over. I'm not sure I want to tie myself down just yet."

"Good!" she said out loud, before she could stop herself.

"What's good?" Effie asked, bringing over the dirty pots.

Ammon Nahtow—AD 450: My father, Nahtow, and my mother, Elan, have gone the way of all the earth. I am now the chief of the people called Nahtow. We have filled Sanctuary Bay and spread out along the more fertile parts of the western coastline of this land.

In this year, the land bridge, which led our parents here, has again emerged from the sea. It is the sign my father told me to look for. It is now time for us to go forth from the isolation of this place and begin our mission among the lost children of Lehi.

I have sent my son, Talon, a man of faith, with others mighty men of strong faith, to find a place for our people to settle, while we learn the ways of the land and its inhabitants. There are those who fear the land bridge will disappear before the men return. Those who fear are without faith, but they are few.

7

Luke Laramore was a U.S. Marshal from the top of his bald head to the bottom of his flat feet. Being a marshal was his life's breath. He possessed the unfailing instincts of a bloodhound and the tenacity of a crusader. When it came to getting his man, Luke was a fanatic. He never allowed anything, or anyone, to get in his way.

Jack felt the steel in Luke's gray eyes bore into him as he came through Tate Hadlock's back door.

Not bothering with greetings, Luke said, "I wish I had more to tell you."

Jack pulled out a chair and sat down at the pine-planked kitchen table across from Luke, shaking hands with the gruff marshal. "Then you *did* learn something?"

Luke smacked the table. "Precious little."

"I need anything you can tell me."

Tate Hadlock broke in. "Before we get started, would either of you like a drink?"

"Jack doesn't drink, and the doc made me give it up—said my liver was going to quit on me if I didn't." He glowered at Tate. "That's why I'm so ornery. I've got nothing to sooth my temper anymore."

"Not that he was soothing to be around when he was drinking," Jack said. His green eyes laughed, but his face was stoic. "Most of the time, he was even ornerier when he drank."

The corners of Luke's shaggy mustache quivered, but he killed the smile before it could form. "Let's get down to business." He took off his worn black bowler and propped his elbows on the table. "Tate, go over the sequence of events Jack asked us for."

Tate pulled a sheet of paper out of his pocket, and sat down.

Jack leaned forward.

"The morning of the Robbery I received a wire from Grand Junction requesting two officers meet the train. I sent my deputies, Buster Smith and Quinn Rawlins. Marshall Forbes put them in charge of giving Haru Ito a little exercise. They shackled him and walked him up and down the tracks for about twenty minutes. Both were carrying shotguns."

"Who was in the express car when your deputies arrived to give Ito some exercise?" Jack asked.

"Both marshals—Quinn heard Marshal Forbes tell Marshal Walsh he was going to go reassure Señor Ortiz that his property was safe."

"Will didn't say what the *property* was," Luke put in. "So as far as we know there still wasn't anyone in Glenwood Springs who knew the emeralds were in the express car."

"Marshal Forbes also told Marshal Walsh that he was going to send a wire to Denver."

"The wire was sent to me," Luke said. "Will wanted me to guard Ito and the emeralds for twenty-four hours, while he and Harry took a break. I agreed to meet them when the train came in and take Ito and the emeralds into my custody."

"Did Will leave the car before or after your deputies took Ito out for a walk?" Jack asked Tate.

"He left just before my deputies took Ito out for his walk."

"So Harry was left alone in the car," Jack said.

"No. As my deputies were taking Ito out, a couple of mail carriers were waiting to come aboard to pick up the Glenwood Spring's mail and load the mail bound for Denver."

"Your deputies didn't by any chance see the mail carriers leave?"

"I'm afraid not. They were gone by the time my deputies brought Ito back to the express car."

"Was Marshal Forbes still gone?"

"Yes."

"Then Harry was alone in the car when your deputies brought Ito back."

"That right, but it couldn't have been for too long." Tate consulted the paper he was holding. "According to Drew Ellis, Marshal Walsh came into the dining car about ten minutes after Marshal Forbes left it, which was about thirty minutes before the train was due to leave. Marshal Walsh asked Ellis to bring some coffee to the express car for Marshall Forbes and Ito."

"Who brought the coffee?"

"Ellis did," Tate said. "When I talked to him, he told me Will and Ito were alone in the express car when he came in with the coffee. Ellis returned to the express car about five minutes before the train was due to leave to pick up the coffee tray. He told me Marshal Walsh came back just as he was leaving the car," Tate said, dropping the sheet of paper he'd been referring to on the table.

Jack sat back, tapped the table with his long fingers and summed things up. "The train was in Glenwood for a little over an hour. During that time both Will and Harry left the car, in rotating shifts, for about twenty-five minutes each. When Harry was left to guard the emeralds, the deputies and the mail carriers came and went. During that time he might have been alone in the car for about . . ."

"I'd say no more than five or six minutes," Luke said.

"Okay. And while Will was guarding the emeralds, Ito was in the cell the whole time and the dining car steward came and went. So . . . the only people that are known to have entered the car while it was in the station were those on official business or those who were asked to come by Will or Harry."

"None of the porters we talked with saw anyone else come or go from the car," Luke said in an exasperated tone.

"What were you able to learn about Drew Ellis and the mail carriers?"

"Both mail carriers have been with the post office for years. According to their boss, both are stellar employees," Tate reported.

"And Ellis?"

"He lives in Denver and has worked for the D&RGW Railroad for ten years. He's worked his way up from luggage porter to dining car steward—working the Denver to Grand Junction run."

Jack exchanged a look with Luke. "Do a background check on the mail carriers, Ellis, and"—he turned to Tate—"I'm sorry, but your deputies too, just to be safe."

Luke nodded.

Jack's fingers tapped the table. Unless the background checks turned up something or he figured out where the pendant in Will's hand had come from, and what it meant, he was pretty much at a standstill. "Please tell me one of the passengers you interviewed today saw or heard something."

Luke grinned. "As a matter of fact—someone did."

"But don't get your hopes up too high," Tate warned. "It may just be a youngster's over active imagination."

"Tell me," Jack said, straightening in his chair.

"Mrs. Grace Gentry and her son, Frankie, were going to Denver to visit Mrs. Gentry's parents," Luke said. "As Tate told you yesterday, when the train stopped all the people crowded around the windows on the mountain side of the tracks, watching the conductor bang on the side door of the express car, trying to get someone to answer him from inside it—before he unlocked the door and went in."

"Frankie lost interest when he couldn't get close enough to see out the windows and went back to his seat on the riverbank side of the train." Tate paused and looked doubtfully at Marshal Laramore. The marshal nodded and Tate, reluctantly, said, "Frankie swears he saw an Indian come out from under the train and slide down the riverbank."

"How old is this kid?" asked Jack, his heart jumping.

"Frankie is eight, and according to his mother, he has a very active imagination. He particularly likes dime novels and the Pluck and Luck Magazine stories about cowboys and Indians," Tate said.

"So the whole thing could just be a tall tale."

"That's what his mother thought, when he told her," Tate said. "When he repeated the story to us, I thought so too."

"What about you," Jack asked Luke, trusting Luke's instincts.

Luke shrugged. "There's certainly room for doubt, but I'm inclined to believe the kid's story."

Jack's brows contracted, thoughtfully. "Okay. Maybe Frankie made the whole thing up, but let's say—for the moment—that he's telling the truth, and he did see someone crawl out from under the train and slide down the riverbank. . . . And how did he know the person he saw was an Indian?"

"He said the Indian was wearing buckskin clothes and had a long black braid with some feathers attached to the end," Luke said.

"Were the feather's white?" Jack asked, tight jawed.

Luke's eyes turned a cold steely gray. "Have you seen an Injun that wears white feathers at the end of his braid?"

"Her," Jack corrected, grimly. "I went out to Eli Moore's ranch today. I met Kedra Moore, Eli's daughter. She's part Indian and parades around in buckskin trousers, is as tall as a man, and wears her black hair in one long braid, which just happens to be ornamented with two white feathers."

Tate's hand shot up like a stop sign. "Hold on—Miss Moore is well known for flaunting her Indian heritage. Almost everyone in town has seen her in buckskins, wearing those white feathers. That's what convinced me Frankie Gentry was either telling a tall tale or just enhancing what he saw by describing the only Indian he's probably ever seen."

Something in the tone of Tate's voice as he defended Kedra Moore made Jake ask, "You sweet on her?"

A slight flush heightened the sheriff's ruddy cheeks. his eyes shifted from Jack to Luke and back again. "I asked her to step out with me about six months ago, but she wasn't interested—said there was someone else, and that was the end of it."

Jack felt relieved that Kedra Moore hadn't been interested in Sheriff Hadlock. It somehow made his defense of her more credible, while adding yet another question to Jack's growing list. *Who is Kedra Moore involved with?* His mind jumped to the white spirit feather he'd found in Marshal Walsh's pocket. *Could it be Harry?* He was about to propose that when a thought suddenly struck him. *Tate's knowledge of Kedra Moore might conclusively implicate her or eliminate her as a suspect.*

He pulled the pendant from his pocket and laid it on the table. "Does this belong to Kedra Moore?"

Tate made no move to pick the pendant up. Instead he seemed to draw back from it. He stared down at it with a puzzled expression, then up at Jack. "It's hers, but how did you—"

"Are you positive?" Jack shot the question at him before Tate could finish his own inquiry.

"Yes. But when she wore it to the New Year's Eve dance at the Hotel Colorado, it was attached to a heavy, and very unusual, gold chain. The necklace was so unique—I asked her about it."

"What did she tell you?" Jack asked, a sick feeling growing in his gut.

"She told me it an heirloom given to her by her Nahtow mother and had been in her mother's family for generations untold. Her father gave it to her when she turned sixteen, along with a matching set of earrings."

Luke picked up the triangular pendant with gold scalloped edges, fingering the broken holding loop at the top of the pendant. "Where did you get this, Jack?"

"In was in Will's fist," Marshal Garrison said coldly.

"I can't believe it," Tate murmured, stunned.

The fingers of Luke's rough hand curled around the pendant, forming a fist. "I think we can safely assume Frankie Gentry was telling the truth. When do we go get her?"

"We don't."

"What?!" Luke bellowed.

"If Kedra Moore is involved, she had help," Jack said thinking of the spirit feather and the argument he'd overheard between Eli and Isaac. "I want the whole snake, not just the head or the rattlers. Until I know who helped her and where the emeralds are, I'm not going to bring Kedra Moore in. I'm not going to tip my hand until I can hang everyone involved in the murders of William Forbes and Harry Walsh."

"So how are you going to play this?" Luke demanded.

"I want you to find out everything there is to know about Eli Moore and his son, Isaac. If either of them had a hangnail ten years ago, I want the details. And"—he pulled the spirit feather from his coat pocket—"I want to know who gave this to Harry."

Tate's eyes were as round as saucers.

Luke's were as narrow as a cat's. "Did you get that off Harry?"

"I did, and I have an ugly feeling Kedra Moore gave it to him." Jack shifted his icy green gaze to Tate, who still wore a stunned expression. "I think we have enough probable cause for a search warrant. Get me one, Tate, so I can legally poke around the Moore's ranch."

"It might take a day or two," Tate said.

"That's okay." Jack leaned forward. "Now, tell me everything you know about Kedra Moore."

Loc Nahtow—AD 500: I am the great grandson of Nahtow. I have led my people to Cumorah, the place where our first parents were given their mission. We have stayed together as a people, growing stronger and stronger, perfecting our gift and learning our mission. I have sent forth men to befriend the many tribes that live in the land. We are now known by our totem, our gold eyes and our exceeding height.

The people of the land know not the names of their first ancestors. They neither read nor write. In them there is suspicion, superstitions, and great ignorance. They worship the earth and the heavens, not the Creator of all things. We do not try to change them, yet we learn their traditions and write their genealogies as far back as they can remember.

Because we do not seek land or power, they have accepted us and allow us to hunt on the land. In exchange, we listen to their stories and histories. We recite them and they marvel at our ability to remember everything they tell us. Many of the tribes now come to us to make agreements, because they know the agreements will stay in our minds and we will write them, so there can be no disputes among the tribes. In this way we have been the instruments of brings a measure of peace to this area, but we know we must extend our reach. The tribes tell us of many others beyond their borders. We will go farther south and west, as our strength permits.

As we associate with the tribes of Lehi's children, I have seen that it is as our father Nahtow foretold. The Nahtow who take spouses from other tribes have found that their children do not possess the gift. This is known and my children and grandchildren are now careful to marry within the tribe of Nahtow.

8

Friday, June 12, 1908

After listening to the windup clock on the dresser tick away the night, Jack got out of bed in the wee hours of the morning, pulled the chair over to the open window, sat down, and stared out into the darkness, listening to the crickets.

He told himself for the hundredth time that he should feel elated to have two such solid, collaborating pieces of evidence against a suspect and one more piece he could probably tie down in the next couple of days. But he just couldn't reconcile the evidence, which clearly labeled Kedra Moore as a cold-blooded killer, with what Tate knew about the girl.

He'd been startled to learn that Kedra was a Mormon, and according to Tate, a good one. She didn't smoke, drink, gamble, swear, lie, cheat, or keep company with men of questionable morals. She was kind, involved with charitable causes, and well liked by everyone who knew her.

Assessing people was part of Jack's job. He usually had to make on the spot decisions, and was rarely wrong. His initial impression of Kedra Moore had been good. He smirked. *That's putting it mildly.* He'd seen her as proud of her Indian heritage, confident in her own abilities, naive as to the ways of the world and largely sheltered from its cares.

That kind of woman would hardly commit a triple murder and jewel robbery. Either she's the best actress I've ever run into—and he'd run into a few in his years as a marshal—*or something is completely out of focus right now.*

The first birds began to chirp as the sky lightened. Jack pulled his shaving gear from his satchel, grabbed a towel from the washstand and headed for the bathroom down the hall.

He didn't want Kedra Moore to be guilty. *How could anyone as lovely as she is, do something so despicable?* He could still feel the effects of her exotic beauty and hypnotic eyes. His whisker roughened jaw hardened, along with his heart. *Maybe that's how she gets away with anything she wants.*

Most men, after meeting her the way he had, wouldn't believe she was capable of any kind of criminal wrongdoing, no matter what the evidence said. *Shoot, I'm even having trouble believing the evidence.*

The sight of Will lying on a cold slab in the morgue came back to him. *If you are guilty, Miss. Moore, all your pretty ways won't keep me from seeing you hang.*

Eli shook hands with Jack. "I'm mighty pleased to have you on board until Josiah is better. I hope you're as good with a hammer and wrench as you are with an ax, because things have a way of breaking down around here."

"I'll do my best," Jack promised and asked, "So where do I start?"

"First, you better go over to the Blue's cabin—it's the one nearest the house—and have a talk with Josiah. He'll tell you what needs doin' for the next few days. It shouldn't be too much, and after you get done, you'll have some time to pursue your own interests. I'll introduce you to my crew at lunch. After lunch, Buck Gilbert, my cattle foreman, can show you how we do things on a Colorado ranch. On Tuesday, I'd like you to work with my logging crew for half the day. Rory Tralain is in charge up there—he'll tell you what's expected." He paused. "And of course you'll always have Sundays off."

Jack stood up. "I best get started. Thanks for taking me on, and let me know if I'm not doing things the way you want them done."

Eli laughed. "I won't have to. Kedra and Effie will do that. They make it their business to keep things up to par around here."

"I'll keep that in mind," Jack said, putting on his hat.

Jack ducked through the door of the Blues' home. He looked around the small cabin with the blue gingham curtains and rag rugs and liked what he saw. The place was clean and tidy—homey. It radiated with the warmth he felt from the Blues.

"Nice place," he said sincerely.

"This cabin was the original house built on the ranch before Eli Moore won the property in a card game in Leadville over twenty years ago," Josiah Blue confided from across the room.

"He won it just three months after Kedra's mother died," Effie added, ushering Jack over to the sofa where Josiah sat with his left foot propped up on a footstool.

Jack reached for Josiah's extended hand and found it impossible not to return Josiah's infectious smile. He was a solidly built man with gentle brown eyes and a heavy beard that matched his thick gray hair. Jack judged him to be about ten years older than Effie.

"Sit here," Effie said and went into the kitchen.

"I'm mighty glad you took this job," Josiah confided. "Miss Kedra has enough to do without taking over my jobs while this darn foot gets better."

"Sorry about your gout. I've heard it's real painful, but I'm glad to have this temporary part time job," Jack said. "It will save me the cost of room and board while I look around the area to see if I like Glenwood Springs enough to settle down here."

Effie came out of the kitchen and handed him a glass. "It's just lemonade, but at least it's cold."

"Thank you," Jack said and took a sip.

Josiah drank deeply out of the glass she handed him. "Good as ever," he pronounced. He shifted his sore foot. "I understand you're from Texas and in the market for a ranch."

"I am, but before I buy one I need to see a few successful outfits and learn more about raising cattle in the Rocky Mountains."

"Now that's smart." Josiah nodded his approval. "It's different than raising them in Texas. The winter months here can be hard and unless you know what you're doing you could lose a whole herd."

"That's why I need to talk to the ranchers around here."

"Well then, I suggest you go see the Bowles' place. They've been here longer than the Moores, and they know everything about running a successful outfit in these parts."

"And there's a real nice place that's up for sale a few miles south of town," Effie added.

"That's right. Sylas Beck is selling his ranch, and it's a beauty."

"Thanks for the tip. I'll be sure and go look the place over."

"Can I get you more lemonade?" Effie asked when Jack set his empty glass down.

"No, thank you, ma'am."

"Ma'am? I'll thank you not to call me that. My name is Effie," she scolded. "Calling me ma'am makes me feel like I'm in my dotage, and I can assure you, I'm not there yet."

Effie Blue was just starting to get that faded look, which Jack had noticed often afflicted women over forty. But he could also still see the pretty woman she'd been, even though her blond hair was going gray and there were lines around her eyes.

"I'll remember that—Effie," Jack said humbly. He turned to Josiah. "So what are my daily chores?"

"Nothin' that should tax a great big feller like you." Josiah ticked off the jobs on his fingers, pausing to answer Jack's questions. When he finished he snorted, and said, "I expect you'll have everything done in half the time it takes me."

"Well I'll do my best to live up to the Moores' expectations."

"If-in you don't, Miss Kedra, or my Effie, will straighten you out."

"That's what Eli told me."

"And you can bet on it. My Effie rarely gets her dander up. When she does, it's with good reason, and she ain't shy about speaking her mind."

"Neither is Kedra," Effie warned.

"I'll watch my step," Jack said through a grin and relaxed back against the upholstery of the well-worn chair.

It was easy to see that the Blues were a warm talkative pair, eager to share what they knew about the ranch and everyone who lived there. Jack decided he could afford to spend another few minutes with the Blues and lined up some leading questions.

"So, how long have you two worked for Eli?" he asked.

"Well now, I've been working for him for nigh on twenty years, and Effie here has been working for him even longer," Josiah said, shifting the pillow his gout afflicted foot rested on.

"That's right. I started working for Eli the day Kedra's mama died."

"What happened to Mrs. Moore?"

"She was in a buggy accident. I don't know the details, because Eli doesn't like to talk about it, but it put Mrs. Moore into labor and brought Kedra early. She didn't have the strength to nurse Kedra. In fact she died less than twenty-four hours after Kedra was born."

"Does Kedra look like her mother?"

"Well now, I s'pose she must—she sure don't favor her papa, but I never saw her mama. I only know she was a Nahtow Indian."

Jack set his glass down. "Nahtow," he said more to himself than to the Blues. *Now why does that sound familiar?*

"If it wasn't for my Effie, Kedra wouldn't have lived," Josiah said.

"Well I s'pose that's so," Effie said, giving Josiah a fond smile. "You see," she explained, turning to Jack, "I gave birth to a stillborn baby boy the day Kedra was born. The doctor who delivered me also delivered Mrs. Moore. He knew I was heartbroken about my baby because he was all I had left of my first husband."

"Effie's first husband was a ranch hand on a real nice spread up in Wyoming. He went and got his-self killed in a range war, when the ranch he was on got into a land fight with another ranch."

"That was six days before I went into labor. When my little Toby was stillborn, I was beside myself with grief, but then the doc brought Kedra to me to nurse, when her mama died, and it soothed my heart."

"So of course when Mr. Moore asked Effie to come with him to be Miss Kedra's nurse—"

"I said yes, and the very next day Eli packed us all up and we got on a train to Colorado."

Jack's brows furrowed. "Where were you?"

"In Douglas, Wyoming."

An old, forgotten fear crawled over Jack. He sat forward. "What year was this range war in?"

"In '86—why?"

"My own folks were killed in a range war near Douglas in '86."

"Well I'll be—how old were you?" Josiah asked.

"I was almost . . . five," Jack murmured, the shadows of lost memories hovering around the edges of his mind.

"Could be, you and my husband got caught in the same range war."

The growing chill, creeping along Jack's spine, invaded his chest. It was eerie to run across someone, after so many years, who might know something about that terrible day. Jack had closed out and forgotten his own memories of it, but as a child he'd suffered from nightmares for a few years after it had happened. He stared into Effie's wide eyes, his heart beginning to pound as some of those long repressed memories tried to touch his conscious mind.

A knock on the front door almost made him jump out of his chair.

Effie got up and opened the door.

"I mixed a poultice, I just found in a"—Kedra stopped abruptly when she saw Jack—"chemistry book Sarah gave me," she said, looking at him sternly.

Jack stood up. "I better get started on my jobs. I wouldn't want the boss to think I'm loafing around on my first day." He shook Josiah's hand and bobbed his head. "Ladies," he murmured, put his buff colored Stetson back on his head and ducked out the door.

As he closed it, he heard Effie say; "Now just what have you got against that young man. The look you threw at him could have dropped a gunslinger."

Jack paused on the other side of the door to listen to Kedra's reply through the open living room window.

She raised her voice, as though she knew he was listening, and said, "We don't need a saddle tramp hanging around here. That line about wanting to buy a ranch is just nonsense. I don't trust him, and I intend to keep a close eye on him."

"Which is exactly what I intend on doing to you, Miss Moore," Jack growled under his breath as he walk toward the barn.

The hours flew by rapidly as Jack mucked out the barn, put clean straw in the stalls for the ranch hands' horses, straightened up the tack room, gathered the eggs, and cleaned out the chicken coop. He found himself smiling or whistling as he went about his chores. This was definitely the life for him and he was itching to get on with it. But first he had to bring a deadly bandit to justice, and he might have taken a step closer to doing that if Kedra hadn't interrupted his conversation with the Blues.

He felt both sorry and grateful for Kedra's interruption. Sorry he hadn't been able to ask the questions he felt sure the Blues could answer for him about Kedra, but grateful not to have gone into the details of the range war that killed Effie's first husband.

The eerie sensation that had come over him when Effie told him about the range war, and the certainty that it was the same one that had killed almost everyone in the pioneer group his family had been with, had hit him hard. Finally, he'd found someone who might know more about what had happened that day, but asking would bring back memories and feelings he'd buried—a long time ago. He was sure Effie would bring the subject back up, whether he wanted to talk about it or not. Kedra's timely interruption gave him the chance to prepare himself for whatever Effie knew about that tragic day.

Pulling his mind away from the massacre that had killed his folks, Jack began chopping wood for the kitchen and all the fireplaces the house contained. Even though it was June, the nights up at this high altitude were still cold.

As he split logs he mulled over what he'd learned about Kedra Moore and her family. It wasn't much. He needed more solid evidence, because not only was he still struggling with his first impression of Kedra and the contradiction the evidence, so far, forced him to believe, but also because he felt certain there were more people in on the crime than just Kedra Moore.

The thing that kept grating on him was the growing probability that someone, either Will or Harry had been in on the crime. On the face of it, that seemed wrong, considering both Will and Harry had been killed. Still, Jack couldn't get the notion out of his mind.

Harry's holstered gun bothered him. The fact that Will had obviously tried to use his gun even bothered him. *It's backwards. Why didn't Harry shoot the bandit while the bandit was shooting at Will? And if the bandit shot Harry first, which is what must have happened . . . then the bandit's back must have been toward Will. That should have given Will enough time to draw and shoot the bandit. So why didn't he?* Jack shook his head, perplexed. *But the thing that's really wrong here is . . . if I was going to commit a robbery, the first thing I'd do would be to make everyone drop their weapons and be sure all of them were well out of anyone's reach. So why didn't the bandit do that?*

Jack gathered up an armload of wood and headed for the house. He slowed as the sound of voices reached him. Pausing near the open window of Eli Moore's office, he listened to the Moores' discussion.

"Just tell him you've changed your mind and that we don't need him, Papa," Kedra pleaded.

"For once I agree with Kedra. We don't need a stranger hanging around the place," Isaac Moore said.

"And just who is going to do Josiah's chores?" Eli asked. "You?"

"No," Isaac replied bluntly. "You know I abhor menial labor."

"Yes, we all know *that*," Eli snapped. "It's a wonder you're still here. Why are you still here?"

"I won't be for long, don't worry about that, old man."

The sound of a chair being pushed back hard, screeched through the window.

"Papa, no!" Kedra exclaimed, loudly.

"Watch your mouth or you'll find yourself out on your backside before the day is done," Eli growled.

"You wouldn't dare," Isaac sneered.

"Papa—Isaac, please," Kedra's voice was pleading. "Who does Josiah's jobs isn't worth quarreling over."

"You're right," Isaac grumbled. "But I don't like that overgrown stranger lurking around here."

"Neither do I," Kedra agreed. "Please send him away, Papa. I can do Josiah's chore until he's better."

"Did it ever occur to you two that I might have my own reason for wanting Jack Garrison here?"

"Oh, and just what would that reason be?" Isaac asked.

"He's looking to buy a ranch and if *we* can convince him that this is the spread for him, I'm going to sell it to him."

"Papa, you wouldn't!"

"Well, what d'ya know? Reason has finally prevailed," Isaac said. "Don't worry. I'll do my part to make this worthless place seem like the best deal Garrison could ever make. Now, if you'll excuse me."

The study door opened and closed.

"Kedra, I want your word that you'll be nice to Jack and talk up the ranch every chance you get," Eli said.

"No. I won't give you my word. I won't help you sell our home to Jack Garrison, not when I've already put in motion a plan to save it."

"What? What have you done?"

The sound of Effie hollering his name from the back door sent Jack scurrying toward it, grumbling over his luck.

Teroc Nahtow—AD 700: I am a direct descendant of Nahtow. My blood and that of my wife Siree is pure. We, and our children, hold in our minds all the knowledge of our fathers, as do many others of our blood. We live in the land of the Lenape people near the eastern sea.

In my first year as chief of the Nahtow, I decreed that our people should go forth by families, both to the west and to the south. I instructed them to seek out the inhabitants of the land and learn of them. After two years, we will meet at Cumorah to share the genealogies each family has gathered and write them on plates of ore, which I will prepare.

9

Sunday, June 14, 1908

Sunday morning Jack had the buggy ready when Kedra opened the back door dressed and ready to go to church. She stopped pulling on her gloves when she looked up and saw him standing beside the buggy.

The surprise Jack was about to deliver backfired on him as she stepped warily into the sunlight. He gaped, unable to look away from her. This was the first time he'd seen her in women's clothes, and she was stunning.

Her emerald green, fitted suit featured a long jacket and a narrow skirt, which were embroidered on the lapels, cuffs and hem, and then trimmed by a row of gold braid. The gloves she wore were the same dusky gold as the braiding on her suit and the band around the straw hat she wore.

Unlike the hats, now in fashion, which seemed to Jack to be as large as laundry baskets and as festooned as Christmas trees, Kedra's hat was a simple low crowned, short brimmed creation that sported nothing more elaborate than her silver clasp with the white feathers, which had been attached to the band.

The sun shimmering in her gold eyes put the braid on her suit to shame. Her shiny black hair hung in a cascade of ringlets over one shoulder and she carried a small handbag.

The tiger-eye beads, attached to the silver clasp and white feathers, flashed in the sun and caught Jack's attention.

His jaw tightened.

"What is your horse doing tied to the back of my buggy?" she asked, her gold eyes boring into his.

Would he ever be able to look into those eyes and not be pulled in by their hypnotic tug?

He cleared his throat and said, "Good morning, Miss Moore. As we are both going to the same church meeting, and since I don't know where that is, I thought you wouldn't mind if I came with you."

"What? . . . What do you mean; we're both going to the same church meeting?"

"I'm saying, I'm a Mormon—I was told you are too. I'd be obliged if I could accompany you, and learn where the Saints in Glenwood Springs meet."

Her mouth dropped open. "*You* are a Mormon?"

"Born and bred."

He was grateful for her incredulous expression. It kept him focused. She was so intoxicating it was all he could do not to lean down and kiss her. *Kiss her?* His mind jeered. *Hold on to your wits Garrison. She's a cold-blooded killer—for all you know—and you better keep that in the front of your mind.*

He watched the conflict in those hypnotic eyes and quickly said, "I hope you won't mind if I don't drive you home. I'm bringing my horse so I can go see more of Glenwood after the meeting."

And there it was—a look of relief, followed by reluctant resignation. Jack suppressed his triumph and the unexpected twinge of hurt he felt, pressed his lips together and waited.

"I . . . suppose since we're going to the same place . . . you might as well accompany me."

Before she could change her mind, Jack helped her into the buggy and raced around to the other side. He jumped in, immediately setting the horse, Molly, in motion, feeling grateful he didn't know the road well enough to take his eyes off it. *If I look at her . . . I'm sure to run us right off the road.*

The confines of the buggy put their sides in contact from shoulder to knee. He felt her slide over as far as possible, but his size didn't give her any escape room.

Her discomfort was palpable.

In an effort to put her at ease, which would expedite his job of pumping information out of her, he said, "I appreciate you letting me come with you. How many members of the church are there in Glenwood Springs?"

"There are only three families—plus me. Altogether there are twelve members . . . you make thirteen."

"Where do you meet?"

"In the Powell's home—Sarah and Jacob teach English, history, math, and science at the high school.

"And the other members?"

Rosina and Joel Stauffer own a laundry and a combination barbershop-hot spring's bathhouse. They have two children, Julia and Jefferson. Oliver and Mary Dukes have three children, Olivia, Florida, and Alfred. They live on a farm north of the river, west of town."

"Don't the Powells have any children?"

"Sadly, they don't. It's particularly tragic because they love children and would make wonderful parents."

Jack felt her begin to relax as she talked about the church members. He glanced over at her, caught sight of the earrings she was wearing and stared. Like the pendant he'd found in Will's hand, they were made of the same translucent green jade. *"Almost identical in color to an emerald . . . I wonder if the color is what tempted her to steal the emeralds.* He looked at her emerald green suit. *If she has some kind of an obsession with green . . . then maybe if I bat my eyes at her, she'll tell me what I want to know.*

He studied the earrings, which were also framed in gold, noting their scalloped edges were concave, not convex like the pendant's scallops. The Jade was cut in an elongated diamond shape. The gold scallops made the earrings look like leaves spinning in the breeze.

"Watch where you're going!" Kedra reached over and yanked on the reins, just in time to keep Molly from plunging off the trail.

"Sorry," Jack apologized, "I couldn't help admiring your earrings. I've never seen that color of jade—it is jade isn't it?"

"Yes."

"They're very unusual. I've never seen gold inlaid in jade."

Onti Nahtow—AD 800: In my days as chief of the Nahtow, my people have gone into all quarters of the land. Some go away for many years before they return, to the mountains we now call home, to tell the genealogies they have learned.

One of my sons, Tanar, traveled west and then far to the south. He found a people who possess greater learning than any we have seen so far upon the land. But they are a barbaric people and practice human sacrifice. From their land my son has brought rare stones of clear and vibrant green. They are gifts sent to us from the people among whom my son has lived. Tanar has gained the respect of these people, called Mayans. He has learned their tongue and their writing and has acquired all their understanding, wisdom, and history, which we now possess.

Albec Nahtow—AD 1,000: I will tell you of the meeting of my people on the Footstool of God and the reading of the genealogies upon the Great Altar. For thirty days we celebrated and danced. We sang the old songs of our fathers and recited the genealogies without ceasing. It was a time of renewal and recommitment to our mission. It was a time to share all the knowledge we have collected.

During this time, the spirit led me to a place where I will store all the genealogies that have been written since Ammon Nahtow left Sanctuary Bay. The records have multiplied exceedingly. The spirit has whispered that the records must have a safe place to rest. However, only my son, Nolac, will know of the place.

Nolac is a cunning artist in stones and gold, I have trusted him to make a map on the green stones that have been handed down through the chiefs of the Nahtow since they were brought from the land of the people called Mayans by our ancestor Tanar and given to his father Onti.

The map is in three parts. Two of the stones have been made into earrings to be worn by the wife of the chief. They form two parts of the triangular map and depict the Footstool of God and His altar, which are near our tribal home. These are two of the landmarks leading to the library. The third stone has been made into a triangular pendant. On it is the location of the library. Only the chief of the Nahtow and his heir will wear this talisman, and it will not be seen. It will hang from the heavy gold chain of power, which was handed down from our father Nahtow. The chain will be seen around the neck of the chief, but the pendant will be worn under a shirt. This is wisdom, for there are those, even among the Nahtow, who would sell the plates we write upon for money and betray our mission for wealth and power.

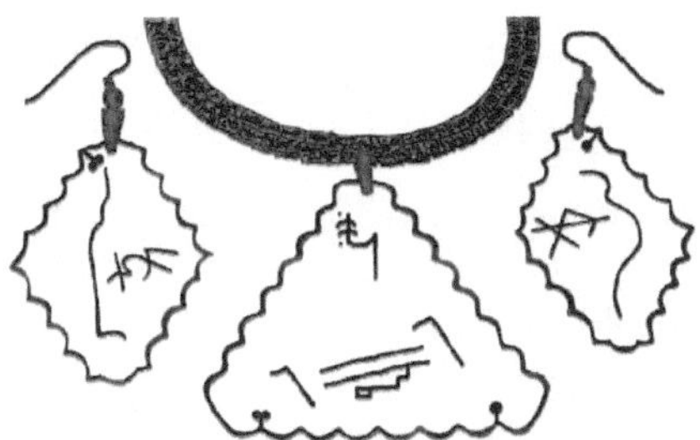

Kedra stilled her twirling earrings that spun with each bounce of the buggy. "These earrings are priceless to me. They're Imperial Jade, the rarest kind of Jade, and were left to me by my mother. She was a Nahtow Indian—the last of her people. My father told me these earrings have been handed down through many generations in my mother's family."

"Do you know what the symbols on them mean?"

"No, unfortunately, my mother didn't teach my father the Nahtow language, so the meaning of the symbols has been lost."

Jack glanced over at her again. Her face wore a tragic expression.

She said, "At least I have the earrings to remember my mother by and something of her culture and heritage."

"Are the earrings all you have of your mother's culture?"

"No." She touched the white feathers on her hat. "My father says all the Nahtow wore silver clasps with tiger-eye beads and white feathers. This particular symbol has also been handed down through the generations of my family. It's my tribe's totem."

She frowned.

"What?" Jack asked.

"It's nothing."

Jack risked another glance. "It must be something or you wouldn't look so sad."

She looked down at her gloved hands, clasped together in her lap. A tear hung on her black lashes. It tugged at Jack's heart in spite of what he suspected her of doing.

"I have so little of my mother. She died right after I was born, and, this morning, the pendant that matches these earrings, wasn't on its chain." She expelled a frustrated groan through her teeth. "I've racked my mind, but I can't imagine how I lost it."

Jack's heart rate pick up. "Do you remember the last time you wore it?" he asked, casually.

"Yes, I always wear it to church, and I did last week."

"Are you sure you took it off when you got home from church last week? Maybe you left it on and it came off during the week while you were working around the ranch."

"No. I took it off, and I *know* the pendant was on the chain when I put it away."

"You sound very sure."

I *am*. I can remember everything. I can even go back and relive it."

Jack gave her a dubious look.

"Never mind," she sighed. "I don't expect you to believe me about my memory— Go down 7th Street until you come to Blake Street then turn left."

Reining Molly in, Jack walked her down the steep part of the hill and onto the dirt streets of the city.

"Does the pendant look exactly like the earrings?"

"No," she said and described in detail the pendant Jack had found in Will's hand. "I can't imagine how Swindler got into my jewelry box. I always lock it because of his thieving ways, but that's what must have happened . . . unless—"

"Unless what?"

"Never mind."

Jack's gut felt as tight as the tie around his neck. Out of her own mouth she'd admitted the pendant was hers and she'd worn it last Sunday—the day before the murders. The probability that she had simply forgotten to take the pendant off last Sunday was high. In his mind, Jack could envision her struggle with Will. *He must have ripped the pendant from the chain in the struggle—that how it ended up in his hand.*

He looked over at Kedra's neck, expecting to see scratches or bruises, resulting from the scuffle. Nothing of her neck or throat was visible. It was covered by a high lace collar. Disappointed, he came back to the subject of Swindler.

"I'm surprised you allow Swindler to have free run of the house."

His tone must have been accusatory because she snapped, "I don't! I've even ordered window screens to keep him out of the house. The ones for the bedroom windows haven't come yet. The ones for the ground floor windows came, but not even the screens seem to keep him out. Swindler thinks he has a right to be in the house, because I kept him in my bedroom when he was a baby. He was orphaned and grew up running around the house with me . . . that is until he started stealing things and tearing things up."

"Just being a raccoon, you mean?"

"Yes— It's the next house on the left."

Jack pulled the buggy to a stop in front of a modest green Victorian house with a single gable in the front. A roofed porch covered the lower story along the front of the house, shading a picture window. The porch roof was supported by yellow-spindled columns, and a red balustrade enclosed the porch.

By the time Jack helped Kedra out and had gone to unhitch Soldier from the back of the buggy, three little girls and two little boys were running down the front steps.

"Oh, Sister Moore, come listen to me play my piece before the meeting starts," the oldest of the three girls said with a wide smile, displaying two missing baby teeth.

Jack watched her smile die as she spotted him walking Soldier over to the hitching post. She caught the other two girls by their arms and drew them back, taking in a sharp breath, but the boys barreled on, heading for Jack and Soldier.

Kedra intercepted them. "Let's all go into the house and listen to Olivia play her piece," she said, herding the children up the steps of the house amidst voices of protest from the boys. She paused in the doorway. "Just come in when you have the horses settled," she said to Jack and closed the door behind her.

After quietly advising the Powells about Jack Garrison, Kedra went over to the piano with Olivia. She sat down next to the girl on the piano bench and asked her to start playing—before anyone else had the chance to ask her about Jack. As Olivia played, she tried to keep her mind on the girl's performance, but couldn't block out the other children's voice as they told their parents about the giant outside who had come with Sister Moore.

Kedra glanced over her shoulder and found all the children, who ranged in age from three to six, had their noses pressed against the front window. The adults were no better. They too were peering out through the lace curtains.

This is going to be a nightmare! Their faces told Kedra they already had the wrong idea. She looked heavenward. "Help," she whispered.

Olivia finished her piece. Kedra was complimenting her when suddenly everyone in front of the window scattered and sat down in their usual seats.

Brother Jack Garrison ducked through the door and stopped.

Kedra got up from the piano stool and, with polite formality, made the introductions.

When she came to Alfred Dukes, who had just turned four, he asked Jack, "Are you Goliath?"

Jack smiled, and it was just as Kedra had feared. She was trying to ignore and dislike Jack Garrison. The less she saw of him the easier that was. Her mind went back to the buggy ride. Sitting so close to him she'd been painfully aware of how broad his shoulders were and had felt the ripple of his muscles beneath the jacket of his well-cut dark brown sack suit as he held Molly to a steady pace along the trail. He smelled of soap and a hint of peppermint.

She reminded herself that she simply couldn't afford to like him. Yet, she couldn't seem to keep from wondering about him. She'd had the absurd notion that if, and when, he ever chose to smile, the female population of North America would swoon, and she'd been right. His vivid green eyes danced and his smile transformed a handsome face into a knee buckling one. She knew almost intuitively that Jack was born to smile, but rarely did, and she wondered why.

Jack looked at her, and his smile widened.

Her head spun and she felt the blush creep up her cheeks.

The eyes of her friends flew back and forth between her and Jack and then consulted each other.

You don't understand! she wanted to shout. *I don't even like him!*

She'd been afraid he would always make her feel childish, after their embarrassing introduction, but he hadn't. He'd never even referred to it. Since starting work on the ranch, he'd been polite, respectful, and, she had to admit, hard working. She would never say it to Effie and Josiah, but the barn, the tack room, the bunkhouses, the chicken coop, and the garden had never looked so good.

Buck Gilbert had come back from working with Jack yesterday, singing his praises. It seemed as though there wasn't anything Jack Garrison didn't know how to do on a ranch.

Well, we'll see how he fares as a lumberjack on Tuesday. There again, she had a nagging suspicion, after seeing him fell the tree in the yard, that he would turn out to be better at logging than all the rest of the men put together.

Jack Garrison is just too good to be true. That means there's something phony about him—if only I could spot it. But if there was, over the next few hours she failed to find it.

Jack dropped to his hunches and said to Albert, "I can't be Goliath, because I'm a good guy, not a bad guy."

He held out his enormous hand to Albert. The boy's eyes grew round as he put his small hand into Jack's.

"My name is Jack, and I'm just visiting Glenwood Springs."

Albert's face fell. "You don't live here?"

"Not yet."

"Do you want to?"

"Well, partner, I intend to look around . . . then we'll see." Jack ruffled Albert's hair and stood up.

Jacob Powell called the meeting of the Glenwood Saints to order as Jack took a seat. Kedra took her place at the piano and Sarah stood up to direct the opening song. As the little group sang the first line of "Come, Come, Ye Saints", Kedra almost stumbled over the keys.

A deep bass voice rang with tones so clear that the piano seemed out of tune. Jack sang the bass line, and the compliment it was to the company as they sang the melody forced Kedra to concentrate hard on the keys, something she'd never had to do before. When the song ended, she turned around on the piano bench and listened to the prayer. After the prayer, she looked up and found Jack's eyes on her. He gave her a lazy grin that made her heart skip a beat.

Through the rest of the Sunday service, Kedra struggled to stay focused. Jack was sitting directly across the room from her. She glanced at him from under her heavy lashes. *I haven't been able to stop thinking about Jack Garrison since he found me on the kitchen floor. So what does that say about my fickle heart?*

She and Morgan had been exchanging letters for six months. They'd met when Morgan, a traveling salesman for a men's wear company, came through on the train. She'd dropped Isaac off at the train and started driving off when she noticed his briefcase was still on the seat of the buggy. Trying to catch Isaac before he boarded the train, she'd collided with Morgan.

The collision had been Morgan's fault, but as soon as she looked into his blue eyes, her annoyance had evaporated. His hair was black and wavy. He was an inch taller than she was and almost too handsome. He'd talked her into having a cup of hot chocolate with him after she delivered the briefcase to Isaac, and they had been writing ever since.

Admittedly, she'd had reservations. Morgan wasn't a member of the church. Sarah had discouraged her from getting involved with a non-member, even though she'd only spent a couple of hours with him over the course of six months. But whenever she talked about him, Sarah always told her, all she really knew about Morgan was what *he'd* told her. Whether or not he was telling the truth was another matter.

She knew Sarah was right, but Morgan was such a romantic figure that she'd let herself enjoy his attention and the small gifts he'd sent her. Now, as she looked at Jack, she couldn't seem to bring Morgan's face into focus and that was, well, unheard of for her. With an effort, she brought Morgan to her, admitting there was nothing more than friendship there, at least on her part, something she'd tried to convince Morgan of the last time she'd seen him.

She kept Morgan visible in her mind's eye, to hold thoughts of Jack at bay as she participated in the rest of the service, impressed with Jack's contributions to the meeting, in spite of her grave doubts about him.

When church ended, she realized for the first time since she'd joined the church, when her father finally agreed to let her get baptized at the age of fourteen, that she was grateful the meeting was over. She shrugged it off and began to relax. Jack would leave now and she could enjoy lunch with Sarah and Jacob.

"Kedra always stays for lunch after church," Sarah was saying to Jack. "Why don't you join us too?"

Jack's eyes found hers. She tried to keep the dismay out of her expression and knew she'd failed, when Jack's eyes laughed at her. The sensation those laughing eyes had on her made her immediately turn away.

She cringed when he said, "Thank you, Sister Powell, I'd love too."

Albec Nahtow—AD 1002: In this year, I have started a new tradition to keep the memory of the Nahtow strong. During our annual gathering, when we speak the genealogies of our brethren upon the Great Altar, we now also use this time for courtship and contest. The young men and women, who have come of age to marry, engage in many contests of the mind on the Footstool of God. They show forth their excellence in mind and spirit. They dance and sing and choose companions from among those who seek to marry. In this way, the memory of the Nahtow will remain strong and vibrant.

10

Jack got to know the Powells over fried chicken and dumplings. At first he thought they were an oddly matched pair. Sarah was tall and almost painfully thin. Jacob was a couple of inches shorter than Sarah was and quite round. However, as the meal progressed Jack saw that they were kindred spirits. They could practically read one another's minds and often finished each other's sentences. Jack couldn't help but envy the tenderness they continually demonstrated toward one another. It was something he longed to find.

He glanced at Kedra. The attraction he felt for her was undeniable, but that wouldn't keep him from doing his duty. Her blush, when he'd smiled at her, told him he was having an effect on her too. *Now if I can just use her interest to find out what I need to know.*

Sarah touched his sleeve and he realized he'd missed what she'd just said to him. "I'm sorry, what did you say?"

"I was wondering how long you've been in Glenwood Springs."

"I got here Wednesday."

"Then you missed all the excitement," Jacob said, passing him a bowl of fresh peas.

"What excitement?" he asked, dishing himself a second helping of peas.

"There was a triple murder and a jewel robbery inside the Jackson tunnel on the train headed for Denver, last Monday," Jacob said, helping himself to another hot roll.

"Yes, and two of the men who were murdered were U.S. Marshals," Sarah said, offering Kedra the basket of rolls.

Kedra shook her head and looked down at her plate.

Jack put down his fork, and feigned shock. He couldn't have asked for a better opening. "I'm surprised I haven't heard about this. Did the bandits get away with it?"

"Yes, they did," Kedra said softly, her attention still on her plate.

"It must have been quite a gang, if they managed to kill a couple of U. S. Marshals. Who was the other person that got killed?"

"That's one of the mysterious elements about the crime. Not only don't we know who the third man was, but we don't even know the names of the marshals," Sarah said.

Jacob selected another piece of chicken from the platter in the middle of the table. "The Department of Justice sent another U.S. Marshal out here to investigate the crime."

"I believe the newspaper said his name was Laramore," Sarah said thoughtfully.

"He's going to hold a news conference tomorrow and finally tell us what happened and what he's learned so far—if anything," Jacob said, doubtfully.

"Sheriff Hadlock has been interviewing everyone that was on the train, but no one has heard if he's learned anything. I think that's strange too," Kedra said.

"So the train was brought back?" Jack asked.

"Yes and the whole town was in an uproar for most of the night," Sarah said, shaking her head. "I think half the town went down to the station just to gawk."

"And get in the way— Poor Sheriff Hadlock had to deputize over two dozen men just to keep the peace," Jacob said.

Kedra took a sip from her water glass. "I'm glad I left town before news of the robbery reached Tate . . . that is Sheriff Hadlock."

"I didn't know you were in town that day, dear," Sarah said.

"I—I wasn't here for long, I just came in to . . . see a friend. I didn't hear about the robbery until the next day."

Jack considered Kedra's stiff posture and averted gazed. It had guilt written all over it. *So you were in town that day, were you? Just who did you come to meet Miss Moore?* Jack's eyes narrowed. *I'm going to make it my business to find out.*

Jack laid aside his napkin and sat back. "I have to admit, I'm interested in knowing what the Marshal Laramore has to say. Having something like this happen kind of makes me wonder if the west has really been tamed."

"What the west needs is to have Teddy Roosevelt send the Rough Riders out here. They would soon put an end to the lawlessness, out here," Jacob declared.

Jack grinned.

"What?" Kedra asked. "Don't you think Roosevelt's Rough Riders could clean up the untamed west?"

"It's not that, it's just—"

"It's just what?" Kedra asked.

"It's just—I was one of Roosevelt's Rough Riders."

"You?" Kedra exclaimed.

Sarah's brows rose. "You don't seem old enough to have been one of the Rough Riders."

"Actually, I was only sixteen, but because of my height, and, undercover of a somewhat scruffy beard, I joined up, and no one ever knew how old I was until after the troop was disbanded."

"Remarkable," Jacob said. He leaned forward. "I'd love to hear about that battle from someone who was actually there, if you don't mind talking about it."

Over dessert, Jack recounted the battle from his perspective, answered numerous questions, and noticed Kedra glanced at the mantle clock several times. After he finished off his second piece of chocolate cake, he thanked the Powells for their hospitality, said he had an appointment to see a ranch south of town, and regretfully admitted he should probably get going.

The relief on Kedra Moore's face was priceless.

Enjoy your reprieve from me while you can Miss Moore. Jack favored her with a dashing smile as he left. *You may have inadvertently given me one more nail for your coffin today.*

Kedra made her own excuses and left shortly after Jack. Normally she spent the whole day with the Powells. However, she needed some time to think about Jack Garrison and that smile he'd given her before he left—among other things.

Admittedly, the first smile he'd given her had dazzled her, but that last smile, as dashing as it was, had sent a chill down her back. She replayed it in her mind, examining it carefully. *There was a decidedly cold undertone to it, but why? What could he possibly have against me?* That smile made her feel as if he'd just walked over her grave.

She shivered and thought about Jack becoming a Rough Rider at such a young age. In her mind it added up to just one thing. *Jack Garrison is a dangerous man. He's too watchful and perceptive. He sees things other people miss. He knew I slipped up when I said I'd been in town and met someone. He knew I regretted saying it.*

She urged Molly to pick up her pace as they neared the ranch.

Who are you Jack Garrison? . . . And what do you want? I'd better talk to Isaac about him. Isaac has instincts about people, which I don't—no that could backfire on me. Isaac would much rather hurt me than help me, besides he wants Papa to sell out. He'd like nothing better than to move to Denver.

Her shoulders drooped. If she was honest, she was afraid that was what her father wanted too. Over the last couple of years, her father's restlessness had become more and more apparent. He spent longer periods of time in town at the saloons, and made more trips to Denver.

She'd begun to suspect that there was a woman in Denver, but couldn't figure out why he didn't just say so. If her father wanted to get married again, she wasn't against it.

What she did mind was losing her life on the ranch. *How can I keep Isaac and Papa from convincing Jack to buy the ranch—if that's actually what he's doing here? If it's not, then how can I find out what he's really up too?*

She went back in her mind and replayed the ride to church, watching each express on Jack Garrison's face. His face told her very little. It was his expressive green eyes that told her what she wanted to know.

A slow smile grew on her lips. *He's attracted to me!* Again, she went through the ride to church and the first smile he'd deliberately shot her way.

She wasn't mistaken.

Pulling back on the reins as she came through the ranch gate, she drove Molly around the house, to the barn, and pulled her up.

"I'm no fem-fatal, but I can learn."

"What?" Trent Wade asked.

She conjured up a beguiling smile and hit Trent with it as she tossed him the reins. His reaction was everything she'd hoped. The young cowboy missed the reins and had to chase Molly for a few steps before he got the horse stopped. He blushed as he helped her out of the buggy—smiling at her like a drunk the whole time.

Oh yes—I can learn!

11

It was dark by the time Jack got back to town. His visit to Sylas Beck's ranch had given him a lot to think over. The ranch was everything he wanted, well, except for the house. It was an old, run down log cabin with a single bedroom and a loft, overlooking the living area. Sylas hadn't even put in electricity or indoor plumbing, but those things were incidental.

Jack pulled Soldier up behind Sheriff Hadlock's house. Soldier always drew people's attention because of his size, like Jack did. It wouldn't do to leave him tied up to the hitching post out in front of the sheriff's house. Leading Soldier into a stall in the small stable behind Tate's house, Jack made sure he had water and oats before he closed the stable door and knocked on Sheriff Hadlock's back door.

Tate opened the door and Jack ducked through it. He took a seat across the kitchen table from Luke.

The feisty marshal was eating bread and cheese. He eyed Jack's Sunday suit. "Well aren't you as dandy as a daisy."

"Can I get you a plate?" Tate asked, opening a cupboard.

"Please," Jack said, cutting a thick slice of bread and dropping it on the plate Tate put in front of him. He topped it with a slice of cheese and took an apple from a bowl in the center of the table.

Luke leaned across the table, brandishing a knife. "Let's get started. I want to get to bed before midnight."

"What do you have to tell me?" Jack asked.

Tate looked at Luke, he nodded and Tate said, "We haven't been able to find anyone else that saw an Indian—or anyone—leave the train after it stopped outside the tunnel."

"Have you finished questioning everyone?"

"We have," Luke said, peeling an apple with the knife he held. "Frankie Gentry was the only one who saw anything."

"Okay. What did you learn from Señor Ortiz?"

"He said Will met him in the dining car shortly after they arrived here. According to Ortiz, Will was with him for about fifteen minutes, and they had a cup of coffee together."

Jack frowned. "If Will had coffee with Ortiz, why did Harry have Ellis bring more? Will wasn't a big coffee drinker—that I know of."

"Maybe the coffee was for Ito," Tate suggested.

Jack shrugged. "Did Ortiz tell you what he and Will talked about?"

Luke brushed breadcrumbs from his mustache. "Mostly, Will tried to reassure Ortiz that the emeralds were safe. He told Ortiz about the twenty-four hour layover in Denver, which he and Harry were going to take, and that I would guard the emeralds while they were there. Ortiz admitted they argued about the layover. He wanted to just keep going. Getting the emeralds into the hands of his buyers as soon as possible was all he could think of. That poor fella kept wringing his hands and saying over and over, 'I was afraid this was going to happen.'"

"Was he fearful enough to keep his mouth shut about the emeralds to the other passengers?" Jack asked.

"No one I talked to in the last couple of days, and no one we talked to today, knew what was in the safe," Tate said.

"Okay." Jack leaned back, staring at the wall over Luke's head. "What else have you learned about Harry's movements?"

"After he ordered a coffee tray for Will in the dining car, he went through the station and was seen by one of the porters walking west toward the Von Rosenberg Bridge," Tate said, taking a handful of strawberries from another bowl on the table.

"I wonder if he went across the bridge."

"He didn't," Tate said, popping a strawberry into his mouth. "Interestingly, Ortiz saw Marshal Walsh from the rear observation car. He met a lady under the bridge."

"Did Ortiz get a look at the lady?"

Tate shook his head. "He only got a glimpse of a pale yellow skirt and a big straw hat before Marshal Walsh and the lady disappeared into the shadows of the bridge."

"You need to find that woman," Luke said, biting into the apple he'd just finished peeling.

"I'm surprised she hasn't come forward. She must know Harry is one of the U.S. Marshals that were killed on the train just minutes after she saw him," Jack said.

Luke set his apple down and wiped his lips. "That bothers me too. But you *know* Harry—that woman may have been married. If that's the case, I can understand why she hasn't come forward. Still, I'm going to ask her to come forward tomorrow at the press conference. We need to know her connection to Harry and how long she was with him."

"Agreed." Jack drummed his fingers on the table. "Since she hasn't already come forward, I don't think she will—especially if doing so will compromise her. You need to ask if anyone in town saw Harry with a woman under the bridge." He paused. "I want you to give the press pictures of Will and Harry, along with their names, and the detailed description of the emeralds, Ortiz furnished us with."

"Okay— I'll also ask if anyone saw a small boat on the river at the time the train was stopped."

"That reminds me," Jack said turning to Tate, "Do you know if the Moores have a small boat? . . . Or if they have recently rented one?"

"I don't know if they have a boat, but I can ask Gordon Downing if the Moore's have rented one recently. He has a number of boats he rents out to tourists who want to fish."

"Good. One thing I forgot to ask you, Tate. Was there anything else in the safe besides the emeralds?"

"There was a pearl necklace and earrings, belonging to Mrs. Eunice Capshaw. She was on her way home to Denver from San Francisco, where she purchased the set, and was very upset about losing them." Tate smiled at Luke. "I told her the U.S. Marshal in Denver would be in touch with her."

"I'll get in touch with Mrs. Capshaw when I re-interview the people on the train and the crew who live in Denver. If I find out more than Tate did, I'll wire. But don't hold your breath, Jack. I think if anyone saw something they would have told Tate before they left Glenwood."

Jack acknowledged that probability with a nod. "I want you to grill Drew Ellis." He pulled the slip of paper he'd taken from Harry's notebook and gave it to Luke. "The D.E. on this paper could refer to Drew Ellis, the dining car steward. I want to know why his initials are in Harry's notebook."

"They could be the initials of the lady he met," Tate suggested.

"Maybe, but if Harry had a connection with Drew Ellis before this trip, I want to know. The train schedule from Grand Junction to Denver is on that slip too. It's the route Ellis has run for the past seven years. Find out if he—or any other member of the crew—was working on the train when it was robbed near Eagle, six years ago."

"I'll lean on him and see what I can squeeze out," Luke promised.

"Now, just a couple more things and we can all find our beds." Jack hesitated. His heart felt like a dead weight in his chest as he said, "Kedra Moore was in Glenwood on the day of the robbery. She told me she left town just *after* the train left. Tate, I want you to find someone who saw her in town. Find out what she was doing here and . . . what she was wearing. Also, find someone who saw her leave town—and I mean actually saw her ride out."

"I'll do my best. But you know once I start asking about Miss Moore's whereabouts on the day of the robbery, people are going to start talking."

"That can't be helped. She's still our main suspect and anything we can do to collaborate what Frankie Gentry saw, or refute it, is important." Jack huffed out a breath and told them about seeing the earrings that went with the pendant, Kedra's genuine distress over losing it, and her admission that she'd worn the pendant the day before the robbery.

"Now we're getting somewhere," Luke said setting his bowler hat on his head. "We now know that the pendant was in her possession the day before the robbery. So are you ready to arrest her, Jack?"

"No. I still think she had help, and I hate to say it, but I believe she had inside help."

"Are you saying you think Will or Harry was in on this robbery?" Luke asked, astounded. "That doesn't make any sense, Jack. They both got killed."

"What I'm saying is that someone on that train was in on the robbery. My bet is on Drew Ellis. He's the one that stopped the train and, conveniently, just at the place where a boat was tied up. I want to know if Ellis, and anyone else, was in on this crime. I want to find Ortiz's emeralds and Mrs. Capshaw's pearls. If I arrest Miss Moore now, without knowing who helped her, it's a good bet the people who did will just disappear and we won't ever see the emeralds or pearls again. I need some time to find out where the emeralds are."

Luke glowered at Jack, but nodded his head. "Now can I go to bed? My press conference is set for seven o'clock. The newspaper asked me to do it early. They want to put out a special edition tomorrow morning. That suits me fine. I'll be done with the press conference by eight and on the train back to Denver by nine."

"If you find out anything in Denver, call Tate. He'll let me know." Jack stood up and extended his hand to Tate. "Any word on my warrant yet?"

"I should have it no later than Wednesday," Tate replied, shaking Jack's hand.

"As soon as you do, I'll come get it."

"How can I get word to you about it?"

"Fortunately, Eli Moore put me in the guest room on the ground floor of the house. His office is only a couple of doors down and there's a phone there. I'll either call you tomorrow night, or show up at your back door after dark. I intend to come into town every couple of days to keep you informed of my progress and find out what else you've learned."

"If I'm not here, I'll leave the warrant on the table and the back door unlocked so you won't have to be seen with me on the street."

"Thanks, I'll be in touch," Jack said and went out the back door with Luke.

They paused at the door of the stable.

Luke peered up at him. "Don't go soft on me, Jack."

Jack stiffened. "What do you mean by that?"

"I mean, Tate told me what a dazzler Kedra Moore is. He said she *appears* to be as sweet and innocent as a kitten. Don't be fooled by her. The prettier and sweeter they appear, the more deadly their claws are."

"I gave President Roosevelt my word of honor that I would bring Will and Harry's murderer to justice. A pretty face and an innocent air aren't going to keep me from doing that," Jack growled.

"That's all I wanted to hear," Luke said and started to walk off.

Jack took hold of his arm.

"One more thing—Eli Moore has a contract with the government allowing him to cut timber in the White River National Forest. I want to know the terms of that contract."

"I'll wire Tate with the information," Luke said and disappeared into the darkness.

12

Monday, June 15, 1908

Isaac Moore pulled his black mare up in front of the Post Office and stepped down. The streets were unusually crowded for so early on a Monday morning. Then he remembered the state was holding its Democratic Convention in Glenwood and it started today. Still, it didn't account for the emotional current that filled the air. He found himself engulfed by boisterous exclamations and murmured whispers of shock. Sparks of outrage and grief flashed around him like an electrical storm.

Above the noise of the crowds he heard the newspaper boys advertising a special edition of the Glenwood Avalanche.

Waving the paper, they shouted, "Extra, Extra, read all about it! U.S. Marshals killed in the train robbery—named! Bandit gets away with rare emeralds! Get all the details right here! Extra, Extra . . ."

Isaac drew a coin from his pocket and bought the single sheet edition. He turned to go into the post office, intending to read the paper while he waited in line for the mail. As he started to tuck it under his arm, his eyes fell on the photographs of the slain U.S. Marshals.

Like many standing on the streets reading the paper, he stopped and stared at the faces of the marshals, and then began to read.

U.S. Marshal, Luke Laramore, sent by the Department of Justice to investigate the murders and the robbery, had shared the scanty information he'd uncovered about the crime. He'd also admitted that nothing, as yet, was known about the bandit.

Isaac brushed over the life sketches of the marshals, turned the paper over, and read the description of the emeralds that had been stolen on the back. A hint of a smile hovered on his thin lips as he finished reading. *I wonder how Kedra will react when she see this?* He folded the paper up, put it in the breast pocket of his coat, and went into the Post Office.

Waiting in line always irritated him, but this morning he enjoyed the morbid snatches of conversation buzzing along the line about the murders of the marshals as he moved up the line toward the counter.

The moment the postmaster handed him the mail, he shuffled through it and found the letter he'd hoped would come. As he left the post office, he inhaled the soft fragrance of the envelope, read the note, pocketed the letter with the newspaper, and stashed the rest of the mail in his saddlebag.

Back in the saddle, he rode toward Cohn Grocers and Meat. This was the only part of volunteering to come into town this morning that he hated. He cheered himself that Cohn had a very pretty brunette daughter, who would undoubtedly be behind the counter. She would be more than willing to fetch everything on the list for him for nothing more than his smile.

Grace Cohn filled Isaac's order, repeatedly glancing at him from beneath the dark lashes of her lovely hazel eyes.

He bathed her in his warmest smiles as she put each item on the list into his saddlebags with nervous, clumsy fingers, blushing each time she looked at him. *She's as eager to please as a puppy.*

"That's everything," Grace said, reluctantly handing him the bill.

Isaac took her hand as he gave her the money. She gasped softly, looked at him worshipfully, and went to make change.

When she offered him his change he held up a hand. "Strawberry Day is almost here. Keep the change and buy yourself some new ribbons for your bonnet."

"Oh, thank you, Mr. Moore. I will." She dropped her eyes, blushing brightly. "Are you going to attend one of the dances?"

"Certainly."

Grace's face lit. "Then, perhaps I can show you the ribbons I buy."

"What color will they be?"

"Red—like the strawberries."

"Of course." *I should have known she wouldn't have any more imagination than that.* "I'll look for your red ribbons and perhaps we can dance," Isaac suggested, knowing most the girls in town would be sporting red ribbons on their bonnets. *With any luck I won't run into Grace and her red ribbon bonnet.*

"Oh! That would be lovely."

Listening to her sigh, he went out the door. She was far too innocent for his taste. He smirked, thinking of the new chorus girl at the opera house. *Now there's a scrumptious little strumpet. What is her name? Lucy . . . no . . . Lillian.* He planned to run into her and very soon, tonight in fact. *It should be safe to return to the opera house now.*

He'd broken up with Ada Reese, the star of the opera, over a month ago. She'd turned out to be surprisingly dull company and he'd tired of her quickly. *Surely, Ada has found a new love interest—poor devil—and I'll be able to show my face back stage again, as long as I tread carefully.*

In the past year he'd gone through every desirable girl in the chorus. *It's too bad the chorus doesn't change over more frequently.* He disliked patronizing the town's few remaining bordellos, unless it was absolutely necessary. Those women were too well used. He preferred the fresh young girls who came to town starry-eyed, sure they were going to make a name for themselves on the stage and end up the star of a big theater in San Francisco or New York. *They're all little fools, but at least they're fresh little fools.*

Noticing a flower stand on the corner, he stopped and bought a nosegay of wildflowers. He wrote Lillian a pretty note, inviting her to a late supper after the show, and paid the girl to deliver the bouquet in the next hour.

No doubt when my bouquet arrives some of the other chorus girls will warn her, but they will also point me out when I go to see the show tonight. He always sat right up front. Once Lillian saw him, the date would be in the bag. It always fell out like that for him. It seemed the more women warned other women about him, the more intrigued his prey became.

His last stop was at B.T. Napier & Company. He inspected the new blue striped waistcoat he'd order, tried it on, found the style and cut to be even better than he remembered, and had the clerk wrap it carefully in paper and box it.

"How do you wish to pay for this, Mr. Moore?" The stuffy little clerk asked.

"Just put it on my father's tab," Isaac said airily. *The old man will be furious, but what can he do?* Isaac chuckled to himself.

Eli had gone on a drinking binge a year ago. What he'd disclosed to Isaac while he was heavily inebriated was a gift that just kept on giving. At first, Isaac was furious, ready to expose his father. However, after some reflection he'd seen the endless possibilities keeping his father's secret would bring him—he hadn't been wrong.

The new waistcoat was an investment even his father should appreciate. After all, being handsome wasn't all it took to engage the interest of an heiress with Goldie Yates's fortune. If he wanted to keep her interest, he also had to look the part of a man with money. Surely his father could appreciate the wisdom of not being seen in the same waistcoats over and over. He couldn't afford to let Goldie think he only owned two waistcoats. That wasn't the way to impress the girl, or her family.

Tucking the package under his arm, he left the store—smiling. He'd be in Aspen, where Goldie was visiting her aunt, next Sunday. *If only I didn't have to come back to this provincial place,* he fumed. *But that time is coming,* he consoled himself as he rode out of town.

Lunch was already in progress when Isaac entered the dining room. The family always ate lunch early so Effie and Kedra could prepare lunch for the ranch hands and deliver it between noon and one.

Isaac slid into his seat, laid his napkin in his lap, and began filling his plate from the covered dishes in the center of the table.

"Did you get the mail?" Eli asked with his mouth full.

Isaac rolled his arresting blue eyes over his father's crude behavior, finished selecting a slice of cold beef, put the cover back on the platter, and said, "The logging contract renewal is on your desk. The rest was incidental."

Eli grunted and continued to eat.

Once Isaac finished selecting his sparse lunch, his appetite for this plain country fare was never very good, he said, "There was quite an uproar in town when I arrived." He drew the special edition of the Avalanche from his pocket and unfolded it. "Would you like me to read to you about the emerald robbery and the murders of two U.S. Marshals?"

"I don't think it's a topic of conversation I'd enjoy with my lunch," Kedra said from across the table.

Isaac's eyes moved on to Jack. He didn't like this part-time employee eating with them and using the guest bedroom, but if it led to the saddle tramp buying the ranch he could endure it.

"Do you feel the same way?" he asked Jack.

"If it troubles Miss Moore, I can wait to read about the robbery."

Eli laid down his fork and snatched the paper from Isaac's hand. "I'd like to read about it, but we can wait to discuss it—if there's anything to discuss—until after lunch."

Holding the paper in one hand and eating with the other, Eli read in silence, his face growing grim as he read.

With a shrug, Isaac began to eat, while engaging Jack in light conversation about the ranch. He noticed the big man gave him evasive answers when he asked what Jack thought of the ranch. The saddle tramp seemed to struggle to find anything about the ranch to compliment. Isaac pressed Jack, enjoying the game, until Eli turned the newspaper over.

Kedra suddenly began to choke.

"Drink some water," Jack said, picking up her glass.

She shook her head and got up. "Excuse . . . me," she managed to gag out and rushed out of the room.

Isaac sat back in his chair, grinning broadly. He doused the grin when Jack looked across the table at him.

"I wonder what happened," Isaac said, innocently.

Kedra ran out of the house and into the barn, still coughing and gagging. Her head was spinning and she wondered if she might pass out. She stopped at the back of the barn, holding onto the railing of a stall, trying to steady herself, until the coughing subsided. *He didn't have to bring out that newspaper. He did it on purpose, but why? He doesn't know, I'm sure he doesn't, but then neither did I!*

The sound of someone entering the barn made Kedra whirl around. Trent Wade, the youngest of her father's hired hands, came into the barn, leading a sick looking cow.

Kedra stood still, hoping he wouldn't see her. She was too upset to want to talk to anyone right now.

Trent put the cow in a stall, turned toward the haystack, and spotted her. "Miss Moore . . . is somethin' the matter?"

"It's nothing, I'm all right."

"You don't look all right," he said, ambling over to her.

Kedra tried to compose her face and stop trembling.

"I'd like to help," he said, stepping closer.

She put her hand on his arm as much to reassure him she was fine as to ward off his advancing steps. "I'm just a bit upset. I'll be—"

His arms were around her in a flash. Holding her tight, he murmured endearments.

Kedra pushed against his chest.

His embrace tightened.

"Trent, let me go!" she struggled to escape his arms.

"It's all right, I won't tell no one," he whispered hoarsely, brushing her brow with an awkward kiss.

The smell of whiskey assaulted her. She jerked backwards as hard as she could to avoid the kiss he aimed at her mouth. They fell into the haystack, landing in a cloud of hay. He had her pinned underneath him.

"Stop it, Trent," she cried, more angry than afraid. Turning her face away to avoid his kiss, she worked her hand loose from between them and doubled up her fist.

Suddenly, Trent was lifted off of her.

Jack threw him across the barn by his collar and the seat of his pants. The set of Jack's jaw and the look in his eye made Kedra fear for Trent's life.

Jack took a step in Trent's direction.

"No, Jack!"

Trent staggered drunkenly to his feet. "I didn't . . . *do* . . . nothin'."

Jack took another step, his big fists closing.

Trent clutched his head, turned, and stumbled out of the barn. Kedra's heart pounded in her ears.

Jack reached out a hand to help her up.

She didn't want him to know how upset she was. *As soon as he touches me he'll know.* She avoided his hand and tried to sit up.

He didn't wait for her to get up on her own. He scooped her up and set her on her feet, his eyes both concerned and angry. Abruptly, he turned his back on her and took off his jacket. Without turning around, he handed it to her.

"Your blouse is torn."

Her face went hot as she looked down at her blouse. The buttons had been torn off in the struggle, leaving her undergarments exposed.

She snatched the jacket from Jack's hand and slid her arms into the sleeves. The jacket held the warmth of Jack's body, and immediately diminished her shaking. She again inhaled the faint hint of peppermint that clung to Jack. Wrapping the huge jacket around herself, she tried to understand what had just happened. Then it hit her—fem-fatal.

This is my fault. He took that smile I hit him with the other day as an invitation. The smell of whiskey told her he'd been drinking during his all night shift with the herd. *When he saw me in distress, he just tried to comfort me in the way he thought I wanted him too.*

"Jack," she said, forgetting to call him Mr. Garrison. "Please don't say anything about this."

"Your father should know what kind of man he's hired."

"Trent thought I was upset. He was just trying to comfort me, and he got carried away—that's all. He's had a crush on me for a while." She touched Jack's arm. "He's just a kid, and I'll bet, after what just happened, he'll steer clear of me for a month." She laughed brokenly. "After a run in with you, I'm sure he'll be on his best behavior."

He searched her eyes.

She held his until they softened.

"I'll have a little talk with him," Jack insisted.

"No! Um . . . please don't. I'll talk to him. He probably thinks I intend to have him fired. I better go find him before he packs his things and rides out of here."

"You shouldn't be alone with him."

She flapped the sleeve of his jacket, waving his concern aside, her hand lost in the long sleeve. Looking at his jacket, which hit her at the knees, she said, "I can't go like this. Would you go to the kitchen and get an apron for me. There's a big white one behind the door."

"If that's what you want."

"It is, and, Jack, don't let anyone see you, please."

A hard look across his face, but he nodded and left the barn.

Kedra's legs suddenly gave way. She dropped down into the hay. She was more shaken up by the incident than she'd admitted to Jack. Trent's advances were as unexpected as the shock at lunch was. Her photographic memory brought the newspaper pictures of the dead marshals to her in vivid detail. She burst into tears. *Morgan how could you? I trusted you.*

Helm Nahtow—AD 1200: I am a direct descendant of Nahtow, but I am not the first born of my father, Jedro. My older brother, Lamah, rebelled against my father. He killed my father in the Nahtow library, after my father gave him the pendant of knowledge and leadership.

When they did not return at the appointed time from the library, my mother, Talla, told me where to look for my father, for he had shown her how the earrings and pendant fit together to form a map to the library.

I went to the library to find my father. My coming surprised my brother and he didn't have time to hide his crime. He confessed that he cared nothing for the mission of the Nahtow or the simple manner in which we choose to live. His perfect memory has made him proud and vain. He tried to persuade me to take part in his plan to steal the book of Nahtow, sell the ancient artifacts of our forefathers, and go beyond the narrow neck of land to the south. There he thought to establish a kingdom for himself by the cleverness of his mind. His intent was to acquire the riches of the earth by the subjugation of the innocent and ignorant of our brethren, ruling over them and living as a mighty king.

When I refused to take part in his plans, we fought on a narrow land bridge. I overcame Lamah, for I am a very large and powerful man. I took from him Nahtow's gold chain with the pendant of leadership and knowledge. Then I threw Lamah into the abyss. I entombed my father inside the library and put the book of Nahtow back in its place.

In the year since my father died, I have become the chief of the Nahtow. It is in my heart to fulfill the mission of the Nahtow.

13

When Jack walked back into the barn with the apron, he found Swindler sitting in Kedra's lap. Their affection for each other was obvious, so was the fact that Kedra had been crying. As he approached, she buried her face in Swindler's fur.

Jack stopped and silently waited for her to brush away any lingering tears and regain her composure. He knew better than to mention her tears or question her about them. It was reasonable to assume they were due, at least in part, to Trent's rough advances. Still, Jack couldn't help wondering about Kedra's sudden departure from the table at lunch after she saw the pictures of Will and Harry, or the vicious smile Isaac sent after her.

"Sorry it took so long. I had to wait for Effie to leave the kitchen," he said, handing her the big coverall apron.

"Thank you," she said, standing up.

Jack turned his back and took his jacket from her when she pressed it into his hand. As he put the jacket back on, he inhaled the soft scent of clovers—Kedra's scent. Sunday's drive had made him familiar with the scent, but he was unprepared for the way he felt as it engulfed him. The irrational desire to prove Kedra's innocence collided with the stark evidence of her guilt. The more he saw of Kedra the more convinced he was of her naiveté. He turned toward her as she began to speak, more confused than he'd ever been in his life.

"I'd better go, if I want to catch Trent," she said, stepping around him. "Thanks again," she called as she hurried out the barn door.

He watched her cross the barnyard then looked down at Swindler, handed him the carrot he'd meant for Soldier, and confided, "If I don't become immune to that woman very soon, I'll have to take myself off this case."

His expression sobered as he went back over the irrefutable evidence against Kedra Moore and what Luke had said about the deceptiveness of a woman's beauty. *I'm not going to let you confuse me, Miss Moore. I'm going to come up with more solid proof. I'm going to find those emeralds, figure out who else was in on this crime with you, and how it was committed.*

He looked down at Swindler. "If only you could talk."

The raccoon finished off the carrot and pulled on Jack's pant leg.

"I already gave you something, now it's your turn. Tell me where she put those emeralds."

Swindler squeaked when no more food was forth coming and climbed up the ladder to the hayloft.

Kedra went to the cabin Trent shared with three other ranch hands. He opened the door on her first knock and invited her in.

She politely declined—Trent was alone in the cabin.

Standing on the doorstep she accepted his effusive apology, told him he shouldn't drink while he was tending the cattle, assured him neither she nor Jack intended to say anything to her father, and told him to get some sleep.

His gratitude was embarrassing.

She listened to as much as she could bear, before excusing herself and hurrying away.

Effie would be wondering where she was, but she still needed a little time to gather her composure, especially if she didn't want Effie to see how upset she felt. She stopped at the hen house and quickly gathered a dozen eggs into the deep pockets of her apron.

The faces of the two slain marshals intruded on her until she thought she'd go mad. None of the tricks she usually used to clear her mind banished them. With growing dread she knew she had to get a hold of that newspaper and read what Marshal Laramore had told the press about the train robbery.

Normally, she would have just gone into her father's office and asked him for the newspaper. They might even have discussed the event together. But she couldn't bring herself to do that. She couldn't even go into his office and ask for the paper. No, she would have to wait until he went out.

Hurrying upstairs to her room, she changed her blouse and tied the egg-filled apron back around her waist. When she went into the kitchen, she used the eggs as an excuse for being tardy.

Effie gave her a look and then said, "Well, I'm glad you went and got the eggs. We'll need them for the custard tonight."

Kedra congratulated herself on her successful ploy and tried to pay attention to Effie's chatter as they packed the ranch hands' lunches.

It took forty minutes to deliver the lunches to the cowhands and lumberjacks. During that time she shut her mind down to everything else. When she was done, and again in the saddle, she gave Flyer his head and let him run. She turned her face up to the sun and let the breeze whip her braid out behind her.

The joy she felt at just being in the saddle, riding across the rugged plateau, momentarily freed her from all her cares. Out here she was Nahtow, wild and free, unbridled from the rules and restrictions of her father's society.

Her urge to roam the land beat inside her breast with a yearning she knew came from the generations of her Nahtow ancestors. She longed to know more about them, wished she'd known her mother and her Nahtow kin, wished she'd had a choice in the life she was living. If her mother had lived, she might have been given a choice, whether to grow up in the white man's world or the Nahtow's world. Her heart wanted to claim her Nahtow heritage and its freedom, but her mind longed for the knowledge locked away in the white man's universities and libraries.

She pulled Flyer up and stopped on the ridge overlooking the Colorado River. Below her she saw the train tracks. In the distance she heard the sound of the train blowing its whistle as it approached the Jackson tunnel from the east. Urging Flyer along the rim of the ridge she found a better vantage and watched the train clatter over the tracks and enter the tunnel. The travelers coming back to Glenwood Springs were almost home.

Home! Effie! Dinner! What time is it? How long have I been out here? The questions ran through her head as she turned Flyer and urged him to reminder her why she'd given him that name.

Effie was muttering when Kedra raced into the kitchen.

The older woman gave her an exasperated look. "Well look who finally decided to come home and help!"

"I'm sorry, Effie. I lost track of the time. The plateau is so beautiful with all the new summer growth that I couldn't help enjoying it."

"You be sure to share that pretty speech with the hands when they wonder why dinner is late," Effie snapped. "Now if it isn't too much trouble, will you please peel the potatoes and put them on the stove?"

Kedra ran water in the big porcelain sink, and dumped a sack of potatoes into the water. She was half way through peeling the potatoes when she looked out the window and saw her father walking across the barnyard with Buck. This was the chance she'd been waiting for. It would take less than a minute to get the newspaper out of her father's office, where she was sure it had ended up.

She glanced at Effie, browning pork chops on the frying grill. Effie's back was to her. If she was fast and quiet, Effie might not even know she'd left.

Thankfully she was wearing moccasins today. Laying down her knife she crept across the floor to the door and slipped out. She bolted down the hall, rounded the corner, and dashed through the door to her father's office.

The office was dimly lit by the fading rays of the late afternoon sun. Kedra glanced around room, but didn't see the newspaper. She moved into the room and searched the top of her father's desk.

Nothing.

Her time was running out when she saw the newspaper crumbled up in the wastepaper basket. Snatching it out, she straightened the sheet of paper, folded it, put it into her apron pocket, and ran out the door—straight into Isaac's arms.

"Did you find it?" Isaac asked with a humorous smirk, his hand running down her long braid.

"I don't know what you're talking about," Kedra said, jerking away from him and walking quickly down the hall.

"Oh I think you do, but it won't bring you any comfort," he called after her as she turned the corner.

She slipped back into the kitchen without Effie being any the wiser. The longing to read the newspaper grew with each potato she peeled. *I'll just have to wait until I go to bed,* she told herself firmly.

Hours later, when Kedra finally retired to her bedroom, instead of immediately looking at the newspaper, she sat in the big chair under the window, leaving the paper in the pocket of the apron. During the evening, an odd reluctance had overcome her desire to know what the paper contained. As the minutes of indecision grew, so did the dread that pressed against her heart. *I have to face this—I have to.* Reluctantly, she pulled the newspaper from her pocket, inhaled a slow breath, let it out even slower, and unfolded the newspaper.

She stared at the pictures of the marshals, wondering if she could ever become immune to the guilt their faces imposed on her soul.

When their faces started to blur, she realized she was crying. Soundless sobs racked her for a long time before she regained control of herself and read about Marshal William Forbes and Marshal Harry Walsh.

Marshal Forbes had been about to retire. His wife, Emily, his four grown children and his nine grandchildren were brokenhearted.

Her eyes burned and her jaw hardened as she read about the rich young heiress Marshal Walsh was engaged to, the couple's coming nuptials, and how inconsolable the bride to be was.

She tore her eyes away from the pictures of the slain marshals, focusing instead on Marshal Laramore's account of the dining car attendant who had alerted the conductor to the trouble. Her heart seemed to pound with each word she read. It accelerated with the passengers' accounts of the gunshots they heard as the train entered the tunnel, and their reactions when they learned everyone in the express car had been murdered. Marshal Laramore admitted the law was baffled by how the bandit could have entered and left the locked express car unseen.

Kedra dropped the paper into her lap and let her head fall back against the cushioned chair, waiting for her heart to stop racing. After several minutes, she found the courage to pick the paper up again. She finished reading the few remaining details Marshal Laramore revealed at the news conference about the robbery and murders.

When asked why he thought everyone had been murdered, the marshal held up a flour sack mask and speculated that it had been pulled off by one of the marshals. The bandit then killed everyone to keep his identity secret. The frustrated marshal admitted his investigation hadn't turned up any solid leads as to the identity of the bandit—so far. He announced Sheriff Hadlock would take charge of the case, while he escorted the bodies of the slain U.S. Marshals to Denver.

Kedra took an exhausted breath, as though she'd just finished a long uphill climb. She scanned the page looking for anything she might have missed and bolted out of the chair. Her hands shook as she read the notice near the bottom of the page. It was a request for the woman Marshal Walsh met under the bridge, on the day of the robbery, to come forward. It described the woman as wearing a pale yellow skirt and a floppy straw hat. The public was asked to get in touch with Sheriff Hadlock, if they'd seen the woman or knew her identity.

What if they find out, what if they already know? What if someone—the spirit feather! It will lead them to—me! What can I do?. . . I can't come forward!

Trembling on the edge of panic, she turned the paper over, read the descriptions and looked at the drawings of the emeralds that had been stolen. *How long will it be before some U.S. Marshal comes here to question me about those emeralds?*

14

Tuesday, June 16, 1908

Jack noticed that Kedra looked a little ragged around the edges the next morning at breakfast. As usual, her long black hair was braided down her back, her tribes' totem attached to her braid. But instead of buckskin pants, today she wore a split leg riding skirt with a white blouse tucked into a trim waistband. It made her look very feminine. Only the weariness in her eyes and a slightly pinched expression told Jack about her sleepless night. Her lack of appetite and conversation told him something was weighing on her mind.

Twice her father spoke to her and had to repeat himself. Finally he asked, "Are you feeling well, Kedra?"

"What . . . Oh, yes—I'm fine. I'm just thinking about what needs to be done today."

Effie came into the dining room in time to hear what Kedra had said. She refilled Eli's coffee cup and asked if anyone wanted more eggs. When no one took her up on her offer, she reminded Kedra of her promise to clean the front parlor.

"I'll go clean it right after the dishes are done," Kedra promised, laying aside her napkin.

"Then let's get started on the dishes."

Kedra picked up her plate and followed Effie out of the room.

Jack pushed back from the table.

"Are you ready to spend the morning logging?" Eli asked him, setting his empty coffee cup aside.

What I'm ready for is to find some answers. "I am," he said, standing up. "I better go find Rory. I wouldn't want to hold the crew up while they wait for me to finish breakfast."

The logging crew rode off into a clear, cool morning. The air was crisp and so fine that Jack found himself drinking it in like a thirsty man. He and Soldier followed the logging crew, which consisted of Rory Tralain, Flint Dawson, Sloan Adams, Royce James and Cash Naylor, up the narrow logging trail.

As the trail wound around, Jack was able to observe the logging crew. Without exception, all the men's faces were adorned by varying kinds of whiskers. From handle bar mustaches to complete beards, they displayed the style of whiskers favored by cowhands.

Jack looked them over with concern. All of them wore cowboy boots, not the best footgear for logging. It made Jack wonder about their skills as lumberjacks.

Rory teamed Jack up with Cash, a young man in his early twenties. They were given the task of cutting the already marked trees with a two-man crosscut saw. Cash was friendly, intelligent, and talkative, which meant he was out of breath and spent by the time they dropped their first tree.

Jack took the saw and walked over to the next tree.

"Give me a minute and I'll be ready to go again," Cash said, drawing in deep breaths.

"Would you be offended if I showed you a few things that will make this job easier for both of us?" Jack asked.

"Like what?"

Patiently, Jack taught Cash how to get the most out of the crosscut saw, how to establish a rhythm, how to use his body and muscles to move with the blade, how to breathe and to save the talk for their lunch break.

The next tree went down easier. Cash whooped as it crashed to the ground. After that, they fell into a comfortable push and pull rhythm with only the sound of the saw to mark their presence. That constant rhythm allowed Jack to think about the case, and Kedra Moore.

He needed answers from her and decided; *maybe the best way to find out what I want to know is just to ask.* If he could find a way to innocently ask a few questions, he might be able to find out who else was in on the robbery. *Primarily, the man she told Tate she was involved with, six months ago.*

The day began to heat up. Jack wiped his face with his neckerchief as he and Cash brought down their tenth tree. Between his strength and knowhow and Cash's enthusiasm and ability to learn, they cut down more trees by lunchtime that the other two teams combined.

Jack and Cash stopped when they heard Rory call the logging teams in for lunch. They gathered under the shade of a grove of pinion pines, where their horses were tied up, hungry and ready for a break.

Kedra was unloading a big hamper strapped to her saddle. She handed out cold chicken sandwiches, potato salad, pickles, and apples from the root cellar—in back of the barn—and freshly baked oatmeal raisin cookies.

"Thank you, Miss Kedra," Rory said.

The sentiment echoed through the men like a chorus.

Jack wiped the sweat from his face with his sleeve. "Do you always bring the men their lunch?"

"Most days," Kedra said, refilling his canteen. "It's more time efficient than having the men come back to the house for lunch."

"I see your point, and thank you. It looks delicious."

"You're welcome," Kedra said and moved on to refill the other men's canteens.

She spoke to Rory for a moment, mounted Flyer, and gave the men a wave.

Jack noticed a rifle strapped to her saddle as she wheeled Flyer around. He watched her until she disappeared beyond a cluster of pines.

"You know," Flint Dawson said, following his gaze, "I never thought I could work for a woman, but if Miss Kedra Moore took over running this place, I believe I'd stay on."

"So would I," Slone Adams said. "You've got to admit she's the prettiest thing in these parts."

"Prettiest gal I've ever seen," Cash put in, and bit into his second sandwich.

Royce James fixed Jack with an inquisitive eye. "As you can see every cowpoke on this ranch is sweet on Miss Moore. How about you?"

"I just met Miss Moore a few days ago," Jack said, sidestepping the question. "I don't know much about her yet."

"And you won't get to," Royce said sourly. "She's strictly off limits!"

"I sometimes wonder if Mr. Moore sends her up here just to keep stringing us along," Flint said, helping himself to more potato salad.

"What do you mean?" Jack asked.

"You might as well know," Rory said regretfully, "because if we don't tell you, the cattle crew is sure to."

Jack scanned all the solemn faces. "Tell me what?"

Slone tossed an apple core into the trees. "Eli Moore is flat broke."

"We haven't been paid in two weeks," Cash said, brushing cookie crumbs off his shirt.

"The men think Eli is keeping us from walking off the job by sending Miss Kedra to feed us extra good meals and reassure us that we'll get paid real soon," Rory explained.

"It's harder to walk out on a pretty face and a fine turned ankle than a gruff old man," Flint said. Then sighed, "That filly has a way of making a man stay put even when he knows he should be looking for another pasture."

Jack leaned forward. "How long has the ranch been in financial trouble?"

"Ever since Isaac got back from college," Flint said, and spit.

The gesture wasn't lost on Jack. "How long ago was that?"

"Well, let's see," Slone brushed a hand over his mustache flicking out cookie crumbs. "Seems like it took Isaac a couple of years longer to get through college than it takes most kids, so he didn't come home until about three—three and a half years ago."

"I'd say that's about right, but things didn't start going downhill fast until about a year ago," Flint said.

"It started after Mr. Moore came home from a weekend bender. Drunk as a skunk he was," Royce said.

Rory stood up, brushed the crumbs off his tin plate and put it into the large hampers Kedra had left. "I think we better get back to work. We're beginning to sound like an old ladies' sewing bee." He looked at Jack. "What you ought to know is that most of us like working here. We're willing to ride the bronco for a while and hope things turn around for the Moores. Miss Kedra keeps telling us things will get better in a few months and all of us want to believe her."

"That's right, and as long as we've got room and board, we can afford to wait, at least for a while," Slone said.

"Not me," Cash said. "I told Mr. Moore last Friday, when we didn't get paid again, that if we didn't get paid this weekend, I'd have to go. I need the money for college in the fall. I can't wait indefinitely."

"We'll sure miss you kid. It's a shame you have to leave, and just when you've finally started to grow a respectable mustache." Flint grinned.

Cash took the teasing in stride, returning Flints grin. "To bad you won't get to see me wax and curl up the end of this manly handlebar mustache."

"Is that what you're hoping it will grow up to be?" Rory asked with mock astonishment.

Everyone, including Cash, laughed. Cash's manly mustache had a long way to go.

"Seriously though, I do think Miss Moore could turn things around on this spread. The problem is, the farther behind the Moores get, the more money it will take to set things right. As it is, I don't think they'll be able to find the money to do it any time soon, and I can't wait," Cash said sadly.

Jack clapped a consoling hand on Cash's shoulder, and put his dirty tin plate into the food hamper. As he went back to work cutting the limbs from the downed trees, he mulled over what he'd learned. He already knew the ranch was in trouble. Just looking at the operation with Eli on the day he first visited the ranch had given him that hint. *That's why he wants me to buy the place.*

The ranch was poorly managed. There were too many hired hands working the cattle, not enough experience among the logging crew, and there weren't enough evergreens on the plateau, which was covered mostly by pinion pine, to making logging a profitable venture. *If Eli is breaking even on the lumber deal, I'd be surprised.*

Jack braced his foot against the trunk of a tree and brought his ax down, severing a thick limb with one blow. *Could Kedra's love for her father, and this ranch, provoke her into committing such a terrible crime, just so her father could keep his ranch?* He knew first hand that many murders and robberies were committed by people whose motives were a lot more trivial than the loss of their home.

By the time he finished cutting the branches from the tree, he'd decided he needed to take a look at Eli's financial records. If the ranch was in as much trouble as the men said, then that provided a strong motive for stealing the emeralds.

Jack's ax bit into the branches of another downed tree. *But how did Kedra, or the Moores, find out about the emeralds, and are they on this ranch*?

He thought back over Kedra's reaction to the pictures of the marshals in the paper. It didn't make sense. *She killed them, and yet her reaction was one of acute dismay.* Jack knew shock could be feigned and women were often better at it than men were, but Kedra was the best he'd seen so far.

Then there was Isaac. From the moment Jack had laid eyes on Kedra's brother he'd thought Isaac was involved, somehow. *But how?* He'd intentionally upset Kedra yesterday at lunch, Jack was sure of it. *But why? For that matter, why didn't Eli react at all over the murders? He didn't even seem to notice Kedra's choking was a reaction to the pictures in the paper or that Isaac enjoyed her distress.*

Confusion grew as Jack continued to chop off branches. This case felt as though he'd been assigned to rummage through a vast junkyard for the pieces of a puzzle that had been tossed into a hard wind. Even if he managed to find all the pieces, he wasn't sure he could make them fit together.

At two o'clock, Jack put down his ax. He was only supposed to have cut lumber until noon. Staying for lunch had been enlightening, but now he wanted to talk to Effie and Josiah Blue. They were sure to have more insight into the Moore family than the cowhands and loggers. *Maybe they can help me piece this puzzle together.*

Rory thanked Jack as he saddled Soldier. Jack stepped into the saddle, waved a hand to the crew, and turned Soldier down the trail. The pine trees thinned out, replaced by pinions and sagebrush, as he rode out of the White River Forest and back onto Eli Moore's ranch.

It's got to be close now. He'd seen a pond on the day Eli brought him up to see his logging operation. A glimmer of water caught his eye, off to the south. The pond was thirty yards off the trail. It rippled in the sunlight with a cool invitation.

Cutting trees was hot, sweaty work, made even hotter by the sunny June day. Jack led Soldier off the trail and let the big stallion pick his way down a rocky hillside to the pond. He walked Soldier around the pond to a clump of dense bushes, with a good entrance into the pond.

Just ten minutes, that's all I want. Jack pulled off his boots and quickly shucked his clothes. He'd come prepared and took the towels from his saddlebag.

It was going to be icy cold, as all mountain ponds were, but that was what made the pond so inviting. Jack knew the best way to get into ice cold water was to do it all at once. He laid his towels on a rock that protruded out into the water. Not knowing how deep the pond was, he took a fortifying breath and launched himself out over the water, stretching his long body out horizontally. He splashed down, went under, and came up with a whoop. It was every bit as cold as he'd imagined. Four powerful crawl strokes took him out to where he couldn't touch the bottom.

The pond was about fifty yards long. He struck out across the water, stroking hard. When his feet again found the bottom, he turned and swam back. By then the water was beginning to feel a bit warmer and he was definitely feeling refreshingly cold.

Ten yards from the bank, he stood up in the waist deep water, shook the water from his hair, ran a hand over his face, and recoiled.

Kedra Moore was standing at the edge of the pond.

15

Kedra studied him through narrowed eyes. "I was thinking of going for a swim myself," she said, bending down to swish her fingers in the icy water.

Jack backed up until the water was chest deep. "I was thinking of getting out."

"Don't let me stop you," she said, walking out onto the rock where his towels were.

"I'm afraid you have me at a disadvantage."

"I thought that might be the case." She sat down on top of his towels. "I need to talk to you."

"Can it wait until I have my pants on?" he asked, goose bumps riddling him.

Swimming across the pond made the icy water bearable, being forced to stand in one place was making his feet go numb.

She pursed her lips and seemed to consider the idea. "A captive audience is always so much more attentive."

"Miss Moore, you are behaving in a very *unladylike* fashion."

She tilted her head in a considering way. "I suppose being a savage, or at least part savage, accounts for that." Her eyes gleamed. "Besides, how am I supposed to keep the savage side of my nature in check when you decide to take off all your clothes and go swimming in the middle of the day? I mean, you know how we savages feel about white men, especially one as white as you, Mr. Garrison." She laughed wickedly. "I have to confess, my *savage* inclination is to let you stand out there and find out if your skin will turn as red as your hair."

Taelon Nahtow—AD 1500: My people and I have come east, from our home in the great mountains. I must learn the truth of the rumors, which have come to me from my cousin, Calah, who is with the Lenape people. He sent me word that white skinned men have come from the east sea on large ships. Many have eyes the color of the sky and grass. Some have hair the color of corn silk or the fiery color of the sky at sunset. They wear strange clothes and have fierce weapons. My heart burned within me when I saw them, for their coming is prophesied in the Book of Nahtow. I must ponder on what this means for my people and our mission.

Jack felt his face flush. He hated the fair complexion that went with his red hair as much as he hated his hair.

She smiled mischievously and the effect it had on him was like a caress. It warmed him all the way down to his toes. *I'd be willing stand here and freeze to death, or broil in the sun, if she would just smile at me like that again.* His heart had never been so affected by a woman's smile. He clinched his jaws together to keep his teeth from chattering and reminded himself that Miss Moore, for all her beauty, was his only suspect in three cold-blooded murders.

His green eyes flashed ice.

She abruptly stood up, tied his towels together, and threw them to him. He caught them and held them above the water.

Turning her back on him, she jumped off the rock and walked over to her horse. "I'll give you thirty seconds to get into the bushes."

Jack quickly draped one towel around his neck, plunged the other one into the water, wrapped it around his hips, and trudged out of the pond.

He had just grabbed his clothes and made it into the bushes when she said, "Time's up."

"What do you want to talk to me about, Miss Moore?" he asked drying off and dressing as fast as he could.

"Are you really looking to buy a ranch?"

"I am." Jack was grateful he didn't have to lie to her. "Owning my own ranch has been my dream ever since I can remember."

"Why here—in Glenwood Springs? My father told me you were the foreman for a ranch in Texas. Why not buy a ranch there? You know how ranching is done in Texas, so why come up here?"

Jack walked out of the bushes bare foot, holding his socks and boots. "Texas is hot, dry, and too flat to suit me. I lived on a small farm in the Wasatch Mountains of Utah, when I was a kid. I liked the feel of being in the mountains."

The job often forced Jack to be less than truthful. However, it was always better to stick to the truth, whenever possible. Everything he'd just said was true. He had lived on a small farm in Huntsville, Utah. The place belonged to Hyrum and Jenny Creamer. The Creamer's had taken him and his brother, Jared, in, after their parents died, and tried to raise them. But Hyrum was a stern man and Jack had finally run off when he was twelve. Jared had stuck it out, married a neighbor's daughter and eventually bought a farm south of Provo, Utah.

"I thought I might like to be closer to the mountains and my brother—just not too close." He smiled ruefully.

Walking out onto the rock, Jack dangled his feet in the water, dried them off with his damp towel, put his socks and boots on, and stood up. He hopped down off the rock and faced Kedra.

She looked up at him, searching his eyes.

He felt her eyes hypnotic pull and tried to resist it, but she had the most incredible eyes he'd ever seen and he just couldn't seem to get enough of them.

"Are you interested in buying *this* ranch, Mr. Garrison?"

"I liked it better when you called me Jack."

He wanted her to feel more comfortable with him—drop her guard, treat him as she did the other ranch hands. Only then would it be possible to extract information from her.

Her distrustful gaze told him she wasn't going to do that, at least not yet.

"You didn't answer my question—Jack."

"Would it make you unhappy if I bought the ranch?"

"So you are interested in buying it." It wasn't a question. She stepped back, dropping her head.

She truly loves this ranch. Jack's expression hardened. *I wonder how far she would go to keep it. If I can make her believe I'm interested in buying the ranch, it might force her hand. She'd have to find a buyer and sell the emeralds right away. The only way she can keep Eli from selling out is to pay whatever debts he has, and then reorganize the ranch's operation. With the money from the emeralds, she could make this place profitable again.*

Jack opened his mouth to tell her he was seriously considering the ranch, but she looked so miserable, so vulnerable, he couldn't do it.

"I'm not interested in buying your ranch, Miss Moore."

Her head came up. She searched his face. "Honestly?"

"It's not the kind of ranch I'm looking for. I want more pastureland. I want to run at least a thousand head of cattle. This ranch can barely support the two hundred head your father is running now."

She exhaled relief. "Good!"

"Now that I've answered your question, may I ask one?"

"Okay— Wait! Don't move!" she hissed softly.

She slowly stepped backwards, turned slightly, and slid the rifle from its sleeve on her saddle. In one smooth motion she turned, brought the rifle up, pressed it into her shoulder, looked down the sight, and fired.

Jack spun in the direction of the shot in time to see a yearling elk drop on the other side of the pond.

"I get tired of eating beef all the time," she explained, putting the rifle back in its sleeve, and saddling up. "I've been tracking that elk for the last hour, that's how I happened to interrupt your swim."

"You're going to need some help getting him home," Jack said, mounting Soldier.

"Why do you think I intruded on you?"

"Just how long did you watch me?"

"Don't worry, white man, you were already on your way across the pond when I spotted Soldier."

Jack reflected on how efficiently she used a rifle as they rode through the brushes along the edge of the pond. She was not only good with a gun, she was fast. In his mind, he played over the robbery. He watched her kill Harry, then whirl around to shoot at Will.

It still didn't add up.

After seeing her in action, he decided she was fast enough to have pulled off the maneuver. *Except she wouldn't have just grazed Will, she would have killed him. Unless . . . her attention was on Harry and Will surprised her. If she was taken unaware, her aim might have been off. When Will fell back on the bed, she might have thought he was dead, and then shot Harry. But if that was how it happened, then why was Harry's gun still in its holster? The moment she fired on Will, Harry should have drawn his gun. Even if he wasn't fast enough to raise it before she turned back and shot him, there would have been enough time for his gun to have cleared the holster.* He gripped Soldier's reigns tighter. No matter how he looked at it, it didn't make sense.

He set the problem aside.

"Miss Moore, is the ranch in financial trouble?" He already knew the answer, but wanted to hear what she would say.

She pulled Flyer up. "Is that what the men told you?"

"They told me they haven't been paid in a couple of weeks." he said, pulling Soldier up beside her.

She sat straight and rigid in her saddle, her jaw set. "They'll be paid at the end of this week."

"Everything they're owed?"

"No . . . just for the week."

"You'll lose Cash Naylor."

"I know, and I'm sorry. But it will be better for him if he finds another job now, while he still has most of the summer to work." She urged Flyer forward.

Jack followed. "The men respect you, Miss Moore. They are of the opinion that if you were in charge, the ranch could get back on its feet."

"I *am* going to get the ranch back on its feet."

"How?"

They stopped their horses and stepped down a few feet from the dead elk. The bullet had hit it in the head.

"I'm glad it didn't suffer," she said, walking around the elk.

"Your horse or mine?" he asked.

"Yours is stronger."

"Mine it is."

"Which end do you want me to lift?"

"Neither." Jack pulled Soldier up beside the elk, squatted down, shoved his arms under the body of the elk, hoisted the elk onto his shoulders, stood up, and set it across his saddle.

"I've never seen anyone do that before," Kedra said, wide eyed. "That bull is only a yearling but he must weigh at least four hundred pounds, and its dead weight."

Pulling a rope off his saddle, Jack shrugged.

Together they strapped the elk on Soldier's back.

"Tell me how you plan to turn the ranch around."

"I'm going to teach school next fall."

Jack frowned. Was this what she'd meant when she told her father she'd already put a plan into motion.

"I don't know what school teachers are paid," he said, "but it won't be enough to pay the wages of more than a couple of the ranch hands at best."

"I'm going to convince my father to let some of them go. He doesn't need the number of men he's got running the cattle. As for the logging, he needs to give that up. You saw it for yourself. There aren't enough pines on the plateau. Every week he has to go farther and farther into the section of White River Forest his contract covers to cut trees."

"You're right. The farther your father has to go to cut the trees, the longer it will take to get the lumber out and the less he'll make."

"That's what I've been trying to tell him for the past year. But you heard Isaac tell him the letter came to renew the contract. He told me he's going to write and ask if he can transfer the deal to the new owner, when he sells the ranch. He thinks having the contract will make the ranch more attractive to buyers."

"It might discourage more buyers than it attracts."

"That's what I've been telling him. If he doesn't renew the contract, we could let more than half the ranch hands go." She groaned. "I hate to do it, but if we did, and I went to work, we could put the ranch back on its feet. It would never make us rich, but we'd be okay."

They finished tying down the elk. Jack inspected the job and said, "We'll have to ride double—I don't intend to walk back.

He watched that realization dawn on her. He wasn't crazy about the idea either. Just being around her was getting to him. Being as close as sharing a horse with her was going to be . . . uncomfortable.

"All right," she finally said, and swung herself up into the saddle.

He took the arm she offered, as he stepped into Flyer's stirrup, and seated himself behind the saddle, holding Soldier's reins.

"We best take it slow and easy," he said, slipping his arm around her waist.

She stiffened.

"For balance," he said, holding onto her, loosely.

With a tap of Kedra's heels, Flyer started off at a slow walk.

To take his mind off the feel of his arm around her, Jack said, "What does your father think about you going to work as a school teacher?"

She kept her face forward. "He won't discuss it. He says it would leave Effie all alone to do the domestic chores. But he could hire the Blue's daughter, Dora, to come and help part time. I'm sure she could use the work. Her husband is a clerk at the bank and they don't make a lot of money."

"If your father has to pay someone to work part time to help Effie, then less of what you earn will go toward the ranch hands' pay. Maybe that's all the help the ranch needs, but what about you Miss Moore? What about your life? Do you intend to spend it teaching school so your father can keep a ranch—I've gotten the feeling—he doesn't want anymore?"

The ranch came into view below them. At that distance it looked like a picture post card with the big log house and the little log cabins, backed by the barn and corrals, sitting on the edge of a green meadow.

Kedra swept her hand over the panorama. "That's my home, and I love it. I'll do whatever I have to, to keep it."

Including robbery and murder? Jack couldn't help wondering.

Enoch Nahtow–1621: Long has it taken the white man to begin to prosper in the land. As chief of the Nahtow, I have sat with them and eaten of their first harvest in the land, which they call Massachusetts. They have been helped by the Wampanoag. The great chief of the Wampanoag, Massasoit, has eaten with them in peace.

These white men carry a book that contains an account of the first man and woman, placed upon the earth by the hand of God. They call themselves Christians. It is a name we too go by, but have not spoken in many generations. It is one more sign prophesied by our father Nahtow. We know that the great God will give the land into the hands of these white men, and we wonder how much longer our mission will continue.

16

Wednesday, June 17, 1908

Jack stood in the door of the barn holding Flyer's reins and watching Eli and Buck Gilbert ride out. They were headed for the pasture. The cow Trent had brought in the other day was definitely showing signs of some kind of intestinal disorder.

It was one of a dozen young cows Eli had bought two weeks ago. Buck had told Eli last night that he thought a couple other cows, from that same group, were beginning to show signs of illness.

After looking over the cow in the barn with Jack, and asking for his opinion, Eli decided he'd better go look at the other cows he'd bought. Jack told him if those cows had brought an intestinal infection with them, then they had to be cut out and kept away from the rest of the herd until the problem could be diagnosed.

Jack was worrying over the problem when the backdoor opened and Kedra came out in a buff colored riding skirt and jacket. Uncharacteristically, her hair was wound into a bun at the nape of her neck. On her head she wore a very becoming slouch hat with a narrow brim, her tribe's totem adorning the hatband.

She pulled on a pair of riding gloves as she walked across the barnyard, a leather satchel slung over her shoulder.

Jack sighed before he could stop himself. *If only she had a devious look about her—more coarse, more criminal, more . . . guilty.*

"Did you enjoy your elk steak last night?" she asked.

"Very much."

She smiled and he admitted to himself that he would never become immune to her smile. It was like her eyes, they had a power over him he'd never encountered. *But I'm going to fight it with everything I've got.* To that end, he thought of Emily Forbes, living the rest of her life without Will. His heart immediately hardened, along with his face.

She lifted and inquisitive brow. "You don't look like you enjoyed it," she said, taking Flyer's reins from him and slipping a booted foot into the saddle's stirrup.

"Sorry, my mind was on something else."

"Must be something pretty bad, you look like someone just died." She settled herself in the saddle. "Maybe Effie's elk stew for lunch will take your mind off your troubles."

Someone I loved did die, and, everything, so far, points to you as his killer. Until I know exactly what happened, nothing is going to take my mind off my troubles. Aloud, he said, "Won't you be back for lunch?"

"No, I've got a busy schedule today. It's the last meeting of the Strawberry Day committee, and I've got loose ends to tie up."

"The Strawberry Day committee?"

"You don't know about Strawberry Day, do you? I'd explain it, but I'm already running late. Ask Effie." She nodded at the back door as Effie flew through it.

"I almost forgot!" She handed Kedra a list. "You be sure to get these things, or I won't be able to make my best strawberry pies."

Kedra pocketed the list and lightly kicked Flyer's flanks with her heels. The mustang leaped forward, fresh and ready to run.

Jack watched her until she was out of sight.

"She sure is something to see, especially when she gets gussied up like a lady, instead of running around looking like a savage."

"She's very proud of her Indian heritage. I admire her for that."

"I do too, but she's also white. She needs to be proud of that as well. Besides, she's living in the white man's world. It would be to her advantage to learn what that heritage can do for her."

"It must be hard for her—trying to live in both worlds. It's like two different people inhabiting one body."

Effie scoffed. "That's quite a piece of philosophizing. What she needs to do is accept the side of herself her bread is buttered on and just get on with her life."

"And speaking of getting on with life, I'd better get on with my chores. Spending yesterday afternoon butchering that elk has put me behind."

"Why don't you start in the garden? I'll come with you and we can see if anything has grown up enough for me to use in the stew I'm fixin' to brew."

"There might be some carrots, but they'll be small."

"That's fine, they're better when they're small. I'll go get my basket and my bonnet and come right back. I need to check the strawberries too," she said and strode briskly toward her own cabin.

Jack went into the barn and came out with a basket and a hoe. Effie met him a minute later with her bonnet on to shade her face from the bright sun that shone down on them from a cloudless sky.

"I hope it's this nice for Strawberry Day," she said, leading the way to the strawberry patch. She paused and surveyed the plants. "Oh my, this patch is plum bursting with berries. We best pick a couple buckets full, and I'll make pies to go with supper."

"What is Strawberry Day?" Jack asked, following Effie as she walked along a neat row of strawberry plants to the back of the patch.

"Why it's the biggest annual event this town has. Not even the fourth of July is as big a celebration."

"When is it?"

"This Saturday will be the eleventh annual celebration, and, according to the newspaper, it's going to be bigger and better than ever."

"Just what goes on at this celebration?"

"Kedra could tell you more about it than I can. She's on the committee that Ed Wallace is heading up to organize the celebration." Effie bent down, plucked a big ripe berry, and put it in her mouth. "Hmm! Pure heaven— Now where was I . . . oh yes—the celebration. It will start Friday evening when they open the big hot springs pool for free swimming. That will go through Saturday morning, until noon. Then everyone will feast on strawberries. There will be cream and sugar, cakes and pies and everyone will eat until they're plum sick. Kedra told me there will be four hundred crates of berries this year—fifty more than last year."

"So everyone eats strawberries until they're ready to bust," Jack said, dropping to his knees. He picked the big red berries, inhaling the sweet scent as he crawled along the row.

"Yes! Then there's a baseball game between our own Hot Water Boys and the team from Grand Junction. We've already beat them twice this season, but we want to trounce them again. After that, there are band concerts and two free dances in the evening." She sighed. "I wish Josiah's foot was better. I love the street dances."

"Street dances?"

"One's being held on the corner of Grand Avenue and Eight Street. The other will be at the corner of Cooper and Eight Street. Kedra helped recruit the bands and orchestras that are going to perform."

"How many are coming?"

"Let see now"—Effie started ticking them off on her fingers—"from Leadville there will be the Redstone Elks Band and the Schiller Orchestra. From here there will be The Grand Valley Band and the Rittmayer Orchestra. Oh, how I'd love to dance to the music of the Grand Valley Band on one of those big canvas floors they put down on the street— I think we've picked enough strawberries for today."

Jack stood up with two full buckets of berries. "Strawberry Day does sound like fun. Will everyone from the ranch go?"

"I should say so! Eli always gives the ranch hands some time off to go and enjoy the celebration," Effie said, leading the way to the rows of carrots.

Good. With everyone gone to Strawberry Day, I'll be free to poke around in the living quarters of the house. If the emeralds are in the house, I'll find them.

"Do you know how to dance, Jack."

"I can when the occasion calls for it" he said, warily. "But I doubt I'll go to the Strawberry Day dances."

Effie shrugged and sighed as they stopped in front of the rows of carrots. "I was just thinking that maybe you could take Kedra to one of the dances. I don't think anyone has asked her yet."

"That surprises me," Jack said, pulling up a carrot and brushing the dirt off for Effie's inspection. "I would think Miss Moore would have many invitations."

"Oh it's not that she has ever lacked for invitations, it just . . . she always has some excuse not to accept them. I think that's finally caught up with her. Now the invitations don't come as often." Effie took the small carrot Jack handed her and put it in her basket. "That's a good size for the stew. I think about two dozen will do."

Jack went to work pulling carrots from the ground. *So Miss Moore has scuttled her own social life. Does that mean she isn't seeing the man she told Tate about anymore? I wonder if she's decided to dedicate her life to taking care of her father and his ranch, instead of getting married and having children—what a waste.* He scowled. *But then, she decided to waste her life when she committed grand larceny and three murders.*

Kedra walked out of the city council room with Ed Wallace. He was a pillar of the community. A man more interested in promoting the common good than receiving accolades for the things he did to improve life in the Glenwood Springs area.

"Thank you, Miss Moore, for heading up the music this year. Arranging for additional musical groups will add to the festivities, and having two dances will give everyone a choice."

"Hopefully, it will spread the people out so neither dance will become too crowded," Kedra said, stopping beside the hitching post where Flyer stood.

"Which dance are you going to attend?" Ed Wallace asked.

"I—I haven't decided yet."

"Well, which ever one you attend, I'm sure it will draw all the young men." Ed smiled, squeezed her hand and hurried away.

Kedra watched him walk away with a frown. *I've chased off all the eligible men in this town and now I don't have a date for the dance.*

"What am I going to do?" she asked Flyer, stroking his nose. "Everyone knows I'm the head of the music committee. I have to show up for the dances. If I don't go, people are going to wonder why. And if I show up without an escort, no one will spare my feelings by not asking why I'm alone. What am I going to say? That no one wanted to take me."

Flyer snorted.

"It not the truth, you know."

John Gray Wolf, an old Ute brave, stopped suddenly, his slow progress through the streets of Glenwood arrested by the sight of a totem he knew. He hadn't expected to see another Indian and certainly not one that wore the Nahtow totem.

It adorned the hatband of a girl with black hair. He was quite astonished by her height. She was taller than he was by at least six inches. The girl was talking to her horse in a low voice. He realized she was about to mount and tried to hurry toward her.

"My sister," he called, but she was in the saddle and riding away before he could reach her.

If he had been younger, he would have chased her down, but his old legs didn't have the strength any longer. Instead, he watched her ride down the street, his sharp eyes fastened on her totem.

He'd only seen the Nahtow totem worn by one person, and, as far as he knew, no else had the right to wear it. *Could she actually be a Nahtow Indian?* It seemed very unlikely.

Stopping the first man that crossed his path he asked, "Forgive me, sir, but are there still Indians in Glenwood Springs? I thought I saw one just now."

The man wore the coat and tie of a gentleman. He looked down his long nose at Gray Wolf. "I didn't think Indians were allowed to roam about anymore. Aren't you supposed to be on a reservation?"

"I am here to visit the place I, and my ancestors, once lived. You need not worry, my people, the Utes, are still held captive on a reservation in Utah. After I have said a final farewell to this sacred home of my ancestors, I will return to the reservation."

"See that you do," the man said and walked away.

Gray Wolf tried again, this time stopping a man in work worn clothes. He repeated his question about other Indians, and added, "Could you also tell me where I could send a telegram."

The man eyed him with suspicion, but said, "There's only one Indian I know of that lives in Glenwood, and she's a half breed."

"Do you know her name?"

"Moore . . . I think. I don't know her personally."

"And the way to the telegraph office?"

The man gave Gray Wolf directions to the telegraph office.

"Thank you," Gray Wolf said and hurried toward the Western Union office.

Kedra set off down the street, on her way to return a book she'd borrowed from Sarah Powell. Flyer wove in and out of the heavy traffic on Pitkin Street, while she returned numerous greetings from friends with an effort, her heart a dead weight in her chest, her mind troubled by an unanswerable question. *Will I ever know why, Morgan? There's no one I can ask, even if I dared to.*

Flyer automatically turned left at tenth street and then again at Blake street. He stopped in front of the Powell's house. Kedra came back from her unhappy reflections with a start.

"Thanks." She patted Flyer's neck. "At least one of us knows where we're going."

She tied Flyer to the hitching post, took a book she'd borrowed from her saddlebag, and firmly reminded herself, *I must go to the market and get home in time to help Effie prepare supper. I must keep control of myself, and not get book greedy.*

Enoch Nahtow—1650–1653: I sent my son, John, to the school of the white man. His mind is ever hungry, and the white men marvel at how quickly he can learn. They have accepted him in the school called Harvard University. In this school they study the Bible, the book the white men brought with them from across the sea. The whisperings in my heart tell me the Nahtow should know what is in the Bible and learn all they can of the white man's knowledge.

The minds of the Nahtow are always hungry for knowledge. John has taught the Nahtow, at our annual pow-wows, all he's learned in the school of the white man. Many of us now carry this Bible with us, in our minds, though we do not believe all the ideas John was taught by the white men.

Sarah answered the door a few moments after Kedra knocked. "I wondered if you would stop by," she said ushering Kedra into the Powell's floor to ceiling library.

Every wall was lined with shelf after shelf of books. There were new ones, old ones, classic and contemporary, fiction and nonfiction, famous authors and relatively unknown ones. There were books on science, history, mathematics, English, art, and every book the Church of Jesus Christ of Latter-day Saints had published. It was as close to heaven as Kedra thought she could get.

"I finished this book on irrigation, but I'd like to keep the chemistry book a little longer," Kedra said, handing the irrigation book to Sarah as her eyes eagerly began scanning the shelves.

"Did you find a study on irrigation helpful?"

"Oh, yes. An irrigation system could possibly double the size of our meadow."

"So how soon are you going to start building it?" Sarah asked with an amused laugh.

Kedra had been the driving force behind all the up-to-date conveniences on the ranch. Once she read about something, and understood how it worked, and how to build it, she sent for the equipment and parts and set the men to work. So far she'd installed indoor plumbing, electricity, a phone, and a modern kitchen in the house. It had also been her idea to create the logging slide down the side of the plateau to the train. That one idea had kept her father's logging operation profitable, at least for a while.

"Do you have a book on medical procedures?" Kedra asked ignoring her friends teasing.

"Several—over here, I believe." Sarah walked over to the shelf next to the window and started running her fingers over the spines of the books. "Here's the newest one I have. It's by far the best medical book I own." She pulled it from the shelf and asked, "Who are you going to treat, Dr. Moore?"

Kedra thumbed through the index of the book. "I'm hoping to find a better treatment for Josiah's gout." Her finger stopped. "Good it has one." She closed the book without looking up the entry and smiled. "Now I'd better get out of here before I get greedy and lose track of the time—again."

Sarah grinned. "All right, I won't dissuade you with temptation."

"Just walking into this room is an overpowering temptation."

"Yes, but I didn't show you the book on Ute culture and folklore I just received."

"*Oh!* You shouldn't have told me. Now I'll *have* to see it. I think it's tragic that the Utes were driven out of the Glenwood Springs area."

"I was going to save the book and give it to you as a birthday gift, but I think you should have it now. After all, your birthday is less than two weeks away. When you've finished it, call me. I'll invite you over for cake and we can talk about it."

Sarah went and got the book. She squeaked when Kedra crushed her in a bear hug.

"Thank you so much. You are my dearest friend!"

"I'll appreciate that compliment as soon as I can breathe again."

Kedra laughed and hugged her again.

Arm in arm they walked toward the door. As Sarah opened it she asked, "Will we be seeing Brother Garrison again this Sunday?"

"I suppose so. He isn't leaving until Josiah's foot is better."

"Is that why you wanted the book—so you can cure Josiah and be rid of Jack Garrison?" Sarah asked with uncanny insight.

"Yes. He makes me very uncomfortable."

"How?"

"He's—he's just so good at everything he does."

"And that's bad?"

"No, but it make everyone around him appear second rate, if you know what I mean."

"Does he treat people like they're second rate?"

"No, and that bothers me too. He so . . . so understanding, patient, and kind."

Sarah laughed, "No wonder you want to be rid of him, who'd want a man like that around."

Kedra's gold eyes flashed. "He's too good to be true and that means there's got to be something phony about him. Besides he's too watchful. I feel like I'm under a microscope every time he looks at me. It's as though he knows something about me that I don't know."

"That doesn't make any sense, Kedra."

"I know and that's what's bothering me. He's also very inquisitive about Papa, Isaac, and the ranch. I don't like it. My family's problems and shortcomings are our business, not his. I don't want him poking his nose in where it doesn't belong."

"Are you afraid he knows how bad things are on the ranch?"

"I'm sure the logging crew told him some of it. Now it's only a matter of time before he figures out the rest."

"Well then, I hope you find a cure for Josiah's gout soon."

"So do I." Kedra looked down at the medical book in her arms. A lace bookmarker was sticking out of the book. She started to pull it out, intending to return it.

Sarah's hand covered hers. "Keep it as a reminder of who the book belongs to." She laughed. "I'm afraid once you start reading about medicine, you won't want to give the book back."

Kedra grinned. "Aren't you afraid for the chemistry book too? I've had that one for over a month."

"Yes, but remember this librarian knows where you live. The medical book you can keep indefinitely. The chemistry one, I'll need back before school starts."

"I'll remember," Kedra said, starting out the door.

Sarah stopped her, laying a gentle hand on her arm. Hesitantly, she asked, "Are you still writing to Morgan?"

"No," Kedra said and quickly turned away. "That's all over—now."

"Kedra, what—"

"Please don't ask me to explain. You never wanted me to get involved with him, and . . . you were right. He wasn't who I thought he was." Kedra pulled away from her friend. "I better go. Effie will need help getting supper on."

Enoch Nahtow—1660: I have come east to await the return of my son, John. After he taught us all he'd learned in the school of the white man, he was desirous to sail across the sea to the land of England. Five years he has been gone. I long to see him before I die and hear all he has to tell about the white man's land.

John Nahtow—1670: I have succeeded my father as chief of the Nahtow, a year after I came back from across the great sea, where I saw the mighty civilization of the white man. Their ways are complicated and strange. Their knowledge in many things exceeds that of the Nahtow. I have learned much that is of worth, which I have taught to my people. However the whites are also full of wickedness and corruption. I have not told my people of their evils.

During my time in England, I learned about a book called a diary. It is a book of blank pages. They are used by many to record life events and feelings. I acquired several cases of these books, and I have continued to acquire more, as they are needed. The Nahtow now write the genealogies we collect in these books. This is easier than making metal plates and engraving our language on them. Still, the book of Nahtow will always be engraved on plates.

17

After supper, Jack went to the corral with Eli to examine the cattle Buck had brought up from the pasture. More of the cattle Eli had purchased two weeks ago were beginning to show signs of illness.

"Does Glenwood have a veterinarian?" Jack asked Eli, after looking the cattle over.

"Yes. Dr. Pell lives on 9th street."

"I'm headed into town tonight. Do you want me to stop by Dr. Pell's house and ask him to come out in the morning?"

"No need. He has a phone. I'll go give him a call. Have a nice evening in town," Eli said distractedly, leaving the corral.

The evening shadows were growing by the time Jack hit 7th street. The sun had disappeared behind the western plateau, but it would be light for another hour. An hour Jack needed to kill.

He turned Soldier toward Maggie Allen's boardinghouse, deciding it might be a good idea to hear a little of what was being said by the town's people about the robbery and murders. Mory Young and Professor Falkner were sure to be good sources for town gossip.

"Nice to see you, Jack," Mory said as Jack walked up the steps and joined him on the porch.

"You too," Jack said, taking a seat next to the elderly man.

"Lovely evening to sit outside and just watch the neighbors go by." Mory waved to some young boys meandering down the street.

They sat in comfortable silence, watching people go up and down the street. Every so often Mory exchanged greeting with someone.

When there was a lull in the street traffic, Mory asked, "What brings you to town on this fine evening?"

"Just thought I'd catch up on what's going on. I don't hear much news up on the plateau."

"You ought to be glad you're out of the hustle and bustle of town. It's been quite a week down here."

"Oh?"

"All those *democrats* showed up for the state convention on Monday and Tuesday. The town hadn't recovered from all the politicians before a whole train full of *druggists* came in this morning for a convention that goes through Friday." Mory's opinion of the visitors was apparent by the disgust in his voice and his wagging head. "No doubt half of them druggists and salesmen will stay over for Strawberry Day."

"Is Maggie full up?"

"Has been since last Saturday, when some of them politicians rolled in."

The door to the house stood open, allowing the evening breeze to cool the house. Through the screen door, Jack heard the phonograph begin to play. The boisterous voices of men singing instantly joined in.

"Sounds like the druggists are enjoying themselves." He glanced at Mory's sour expression and jerked his head toward the screen door. "Are they the reason you're out here."

"Them fellers make weekends with the miners seem peaceful by comparison. I don't mind telling ya, that I'll be happy as a June bug fluttering around a gas light when they're gone."

Jack clapped his shoulder with a sympathetic hand.

"It wouldn't be so bad if they were all druggists—them fellers are pretty quiet. But half the fellers in the parlor are salesmen trying to get the druggists to buy all sorts of newfangled products."

The screen door opened and Maggie came out onto the porch. She dropped into her rocking chair with noticeable exhaustion. "I thought I recognized your voice, Jack."

"I'm surprised you could hear him over all the racket going on in the parlor," Mory grumbled.

"Mory tells me you have a house full of druggists and salesmen," Jack said.

"My house is filled from the basement to the rafters with them. They have driven poor Norman to his bed—his ears stuffed with cotton," she disclosed, a note of humor creeping into her voice.

"Jack's lips twitched. "Poor Professor Falkner."

Maggie began to rock gently back and forth. "Have you come to collect the refund I owe you for the five nights you didn't stay?"

"No, you keep it. I'll let you earn it—one of these days. Right now I'd like to know if I can leave Soldier in your stable for a couple of hours. I have a call to make and I think he'll be more comfortable here than tied to a hitching post."

"That's fine with me." Speculation danced in Maggie's eyes. "Are you going to see a girl? You know there are two dances in the evening on Strawberry Day. If you haven't asked anyone already you better do it tonight... before all the pretty girls are spoken for."

"You're the second woman to tell me that today. I guess I'd better quit fighting the tide and find a girl who will go with me. Got any ideas?"

"How about taking your boss's daughter? Now there's a rare beauty. But I suspect she's already been spoken for."

"Maybe"—Jack rubbed a hand over his jaw—"but I just might try my luck and see."

"Better go home and get it done tonight, or you won't have any luck at all, I'm thinking," Mory said.

Jack leaned forward and changed the subject. "I saw the special edition of the Avalanche about the two U.S. Marshals that were killed and the emerald robbery. Does the sheriff have any leads yet?"

"Nothing I've heard about," Mory said.

"I haven't heard anything either. Having a house full of guests has kept me on the run. I haven't picked up a newspaper since that special edition of the Avalanche came out."

Jack stood up. Twilight had fallen, and the moon was rising. Darkness wouldn't be far behind. He needed to get Soldier settled into the stable and be on his way. It was a shame that both conventions had come to town this week. They had taken the focus of the boardinghouse off the murders. Disappointed, Jack excused himself and led Soldier around to the stable.

Darkness blanketed Glenwood by the time Jack left the stable. He stepped out into the night, anxious to complete his errand. He'd telephoned Sheriff Hadlock late last night and learned the search warrant for the High Peak Ranch was ready.

Sheriff Hadlock's house was dark when Jack reached it. He went around to the back door and knocked. When Tate didn't answer, he opened the door and switched on the kitchen light. Lying on the table, on top an envelope, was a note with his name on it.

Pulling out a chair, he sat down and started to read.

Jack,

Here's what I've learned so far: The Moores do own a small blue fishing boat, which Gordon Downing keeps and maintains for the Moores in exchange for allowing him to rent it out to fisherman. Mr. Downing told me the Moore's boat disappeared a day before the train was robbed. He didn't report it because his son sometimes takes the boat out, without telling him, when he lines up a last minute fishing excursion. He always keeps the boat and cleans it up before he returns it. When Mr. Downing found the boat back in its spot by the dock the morning after the robbery, he forgot about the whole thing. I had him ask his son if the boat was in his possession on the day of the robbery. His son denied having taken it.

Next, I can't find anyone who saw Miss Moore in town on the day of the robbery— I'll keep looking. We know she was here, so I'm sure someone must have seen her.

I got a call from Luke yesterday. The Denver passengers haven't been any help. He also hasn't been able to find out if Drew Ellis was working on the train when it was robbed near Eagle, because the D+RGW doesn't keep records over five years. He also hasn't been able to catch up with Ellis. The D+RGW railroad told him Ellis left on his regular run from Denver to Grand Junction this evening. Ellis has a twenty-four hour layover in Grand Junction on Friday and will be back in Denver Sunday morning. Luke plans to meet the train and talk to him.

Luke also told me he's hot on the trail of something interesting in Eli Moore's past. He wouldn't go into detail, but said it might have a bearing on the case. As soon as he's tracked down that lead, he'll come back to Glenwood and fill you in on everything—including his interview with Drew Ellis.

One more thing, I've been racking my brain since you showed me that spirit feather and I finally remembered where I'd seen another spirit feather like the one you found in Marshal Walsh's pocket. Miss Donna Parlee lives across the street from me. A few months back, I saw the exact same spirit feather lying on top of her piano. Unfortunately Miss Parlee is in Toronto attending the funeral of her grandmother right now, or I would ask her where she got the feather. One thing I do know—she's given piano lessons to Miss Moore for five years.

"I'm going to be busy the next couple of days, because of Strawberry Day, but if you can drop by on Sunday night, we can exchange any more information I get by then. I'd also like to know what you've found out.

Tate

P.S. The search warrant is in the envelope.

Jack looked the search warrant over, and put it in his pocket. Leaving his own note on the backside of Tate's note, he agreed to meet Tate on Sunday night, turned out the kitchen light, and left the house.

It was nearly ten o'clock when Jack rode out of town. The stars over the dark plateau were spectacular. In a remote corner of his mind, Jack admired them, but even their beauty failed to distract him.

Everything keeps leading me to Kedra Moore. He groaned out loud and admitted he didn't want her to be guilty. More than that, he couldn't accept her guilt. *It just doesn't feel right.* His gut instincts were rarely wrong, but it was impossible to argue with the mounting evidence, and yet, the evidence didn't make sense.

Or did it?

Jack rocked from side to side, the reins held slackly in his hand as Soldier took them back to the High Peak Ranch. The ugly suspicion still lurking in the back of his mind pushed its way forward. *Harry always did seem to live in excess of a marshal's salary.* Jack had heard a rumor that the Justice Department was thinking of investigating

Harry. *If Harry was the inside man, it could explain how Kedra Moore got into the express car.* He considered Kedra's effect on him and sympathized with Harry. Handsome Harry was, after all, a ladies man. But picturing Kedra as a ruthless temptress was a hard sell. *She's just too innocent to pull off that kind of act, besides, where could she have met Harry?*

"Think Marshal!" he chided himself. *It's much more likely that Kedra knows Ellis. He comes through Glenwood all the time on the train. What if Kedra and Ellis were in cahoots? Maybe he's the man she's been seeing. Yes, and if Ellis was also Harry's friend, he could have introduced Harry to Kedra. Harry must have told either Kedra or Ellis about the emeralds. They planned the robbery, and Kedra convinced Harry to go along with it. But then . . . Harry's murder makes no sense . . . unless Harry was just the sucker Ellis used to get information about valuable cargo and access to the express car.*

When Jack compared it to the facts, it made sense. *That has to be it. Harry got Kedra into the car. When the train entered the tunnel, Kedra came out of hiding and Harry opened the safe. Somehow, Will surprised them and Kedra was forced to shoot him. That's when everything went wrong. The shot inadvertently signaled Ellis to come bang on the door of the car. Kedra opens the door, nearly hysterical about shooting Will. Ellis comes in and shoots Harry just as Will comes to and attacks Kedra, pulling off her mask and the pendant. Ellis intervenes and kills Will and Ito—now that I can buy!*

Mulling over Kedra's reaction to Harry's picture in the newspaper took his scenario one-step farther. *I'll bet Kedra had no idea Ellis was going to kill Harry, but when he thought Kedra had killed Will, he decided it wouldn't be safe to leave anyone alive. It would also give him more of the loot, but then . . . why didn't he kill Kedra and take it all?*

Jack straightened in the saddle. *Because he needed Kedra to take the emeralds off the train! If I'm right, then the emeralds are still in Kedra's possession. But I'll bet they won't be for long.*

He reviewed the timetable Tate's letter had outlined for Ellis's trip to Grand Junction, calculated Ellis's twenty-four hour layover, and when he would come back through Glenwood Spring. *On Saturday evening—Strawberry Day! I've got to keep Miss Moore from handing off the emeralds to Ellis!* Jack's heart started drumming a hard staccato rhythm. *As soon as she does—he may kill her! I've got to keep my eye on her from the moment the train arrives until it leaves. And I think I know how I can do that.*

His hand tightened on the reigns. "Let's move," he said to Soldier.

The stallion picked up his pace.

If I'm lucky, Kedra will follow her nightly routine and be in the barn feeding Swindler the leftover scraps from supper.

Soldier galloped through the gates of the ranch and around to the barn. Jack jumped off his back and grinned when he saw the dim light of an oil lamp glowing through the open door of the barn.

"Miss Moore, are you in here," he called as he entered the barn, not wanting to frighten her.

"Yes. I'm just giving Swindler a snack."

Jack found her in the back of the barn and smiled. "If you keep feeding him snacks, he's going to get fat. He needs to spend the night foraging. That will keep him lean."

"I've been cutting his treats down, over the last couple of weeks." She patted the raccoon's head after he finished off his snack and begged for more. "That's all there is, my friend," she said and started to pass the lantern to Jack.

"Would you mind holding the lantern while I unsaddle Soldier?"

"Sure."

She held the lantern up as Jack opened the gate to Soldier's stall and led him in.

"I'd like to ask you something, Miss Moore," Jack said, unbuckling Soldier's saddle and setting it on the railing.

"What," she asked warily.

"Effie told me about Strawberry Day this morning. She said there are two dances in the evening, and I was wondering if you would go with me to the dance of your choice."

She blinked, staring at him as though he'd just grown a set of horns, her gold eyes molten in the light of the lantern.

He was prepared to beg and even plead, but one way or another he had to get her to spend the evening with him.

Her reluctance was evident as she continued to silently stare at him, but the fact that she hadn't said no, right away, gave him hope.

"I know it's rather short notice, but would you consider showing an outsider around and introducing me to people. If Glenwood Springs is going to be my home, I'd like to meet some of the residents. Having you introduce me would give me a leg up."

A struggle played out in the depth of her eyes. The look she fixed him with made him feel sure she was going to reject his proposal. He started mentally preparing more reasons she should go with him.

"Okay," she said abruptly. "I'll go with you and introduce you to the people I know."

"Thank you, Miss Moore, having you accompany me means a lot to me," he said, genuinely surprised, and, he couldn't deny it, pleased by her acceptance and the prospect of spending an entire evening with her.

18

Thursday, June 18, 1908

Isaac followed his father into his father's office after breakfast. He closed the door to ensure the entire house wouldn't be privy to their conversation.

"I'm going to Aspen on Sunday night," he said, flopping down in one of the leather chairs in front of his father's desk.

"What for?" Eli asked, sitting down behind his desk.

"I have a rather important engagement with a lady."

"A wealthy one—no doubt."

"Certainly, and this particular lady is extremely wealthy. In fact, she is going to be your salvation."

"What do you mean?"

"I mean if everything goes as I've planned, I'll be moving to Denver in a matter of weeks, which is why I need some money."

"I don't have any to give you."

Isaac's haunting eyes burned with bitter coldness into his father's eyes. "Now that is truly a pity." He got up and strolled toward the door. "I guess I'll just go find Kedra and have a *brotherly* chat with her." He reached for the doorknob.

"Wait!" Eli's jaw worked out his anger as he pulled out his wallet. "I've got fifty dollars, that's all I can give you. I don't have any more cash in the house."

"Just think of this as an investment in your freedom." Isaac took the money from his father's hand. "It's pitiful what a man will do to keep an illusion alive," he sneered, pocketing the money.

Eli Moore sat at his desk, running his hands through his thinning hair. Up until this morning he'd hoped he could turn things around. Now he knew that wasn't possible. His luck had finally run out.

Trent Wade, who brought in the first sick cow, had been assigned to keep a close eye on it. He'd checked on the cow every couple of hours throughout the night. The animal had died two hours ago.

The phone on the desk rang. Eli picked it up.

"Mr. Moore, this is Dr. Pell. I wanted to let you know that the infection in the cows you bought isn't contagious. Your other cattle won't get it. It was caused by the feed those cows were eating before you bought them."

"The first one that got sick just died."

"I'm sorry, I'm afraid you can expect to lose between thirty and a hundred percent of those animals."

"At least the rest of the herd won't get it." Eli said, thanked the vet, and ended the call.

Losing those cows would put him under. He'd planned to fatten them up for a few weeks and then sell them down the valley to one of the mining camps. He thought he could get top dollar for the cattle because they were young and tender, and because most the beef in the valley wouldn't be for sale until the fall. The ranchers in the area usually sold their herds to the big butcher houses back east.

He'd planned to use the money he made on the cows to pay the ranch hands everything he owed them. Then he intended to let half of them go, something Kedra had been after him to do for months.

His fists slammed against the desk. *How can I keep things going now? Not only am I going to lose those cows, and the ability to pay off the men, but I also have to pay Dr. Pell for telling me they might all die.*

Eli jumped up and paced the space behind his desk, from one wall to the other. *Who would have believed my own son would be the one to take me down.* He couldn't delude himself into believing Isaac had anything else in mind, and he had to admit Isaac had cause.

"But I did everything I could for him. He wanted to go to college to become a man of business, and I financed it, although I could ill afford it. I laid the best opportunity I could give him to create the life he wanted right in his lap. And what did he do? . . . He took two years longer to finish and barely graduated," Eli recited his failed efforts with Isaac as he paced back and forth. He groaned and admitted, "I should have sent Kedra to college instead of Isaac. She would have graduated in half the time—and with honors. Then in my old age, I wouldn't have to worry about anything. She would gladly support me." He laughed sardonically. "Even now, Kedra is willing to step in and support me."

He sat back down and held his head in his hands. *Why didn't I listen to Effie and Josiah?* He asked himself, and then answered; *because I refused to believe my own son was a muckraker, a freeloader, a waster.*

The laugh that burst out of him was ironic and self-accusatory. *Isaac is just a chip off the old block. Only he's smarter than I ever was. He could have told Kedra everything and gotten his revenge, instead he's held what he knows over my head and is bleeding me dry. He won't be satisfied until Kedra and I are begging on the street corner in rags.*

A knock on the office door, lifted Eli's head.

Kedra came in. "I went into town and got the mail." She put several letters on his desk, hesitated, and then sat down across from him. "Are things that bad?"

"I never could hide how I feel from you," he said, holding out his hand to her.

"What's the matter," she said, taking his hand.

"I don't have the money to pay the men again this week."

"No! Papa, what happened?"

"The veterinarian bill for the sick cows is what happened."

"Can't we even pay them part of what we owe them?"

Eli smiled sadly. He loved her for saying "we", including herself in the financial responsibility to pay the ranch hands.

"I intend to pay Cash Naylor his full wages and then let him go. The rest I can give a few dollars too, but I can't afford to pay them in full."

"Papa, why don't you sell some of the heathy cattle? Pay the men and then let most of them go. We can reorganize and in a few months we'll be back to making a profit again."

His eyes dropped to the mail. On top was an envelope from BT Napier & Company. It could only mean one thing. Isaac had bought something. No doubt it was expensive and he was expected to pay for it. He shook his head. There was little left that he could do.

His shoulders sagged. Then he remembered the vow he'd made when Kedra was born. *I won't let her down, even if that means being sucked dry by Isaac and then starting over again—after he's forgotten about me. Kedra will forgive me for losing the ranch, what she won't forgive is my past and the choices I made back then.*

He squared his shoulders. "We are going to reorganize. The logging contract isn't being renewed. The letter I received Monday from the Forest Service told me they don't want to renew the contract. It will expire at the end of the month."

"I'm sorry—but it's for the best, Papa."

"I know, but I can't let the men go until I can pay them."

"How are we going to do that?"

"I'm going to sell the entire herd. I'll pay the men off and we'll let everyone but the Blue's go. The ranch can support us if we live simply."

"What you're saying is, no more new clothes or piano lessons or any of the other silly things I spend money on, and that's fine with me." She took a breath. "I'll take the teaching job. It will help get us through the winter and after that we can start rebuilding."

Eli nodded, and kissed her hand. "I want your promise that what I'm going to do will stay between you and me."

"I promise," she said, leaned over the desk and kissed his cheek.

John Nahtow—1685: The white man is pushing westward, driving out the children of Lehi, who they call Indians. There is growing animosity between the whites and many of the Indian tribes. Both have committed atrocities, resulting in distrust and fear.

Mathias Nahtow—1735: In my time as chief of the Nahtow I have seen growing turmoil in the land among the whites. Many of them want to claim this land as a new nation, free from the nations from which they came. Others are here to keep them subjugated to their native lands. The children of Lehi have been caught up in this struggle and many have become confederate with one side or the other for money and gifts given to them from the white men. My heart whispers that the Nahtow must withdraw from the eastern lands, before there is war among the whites and we find ourselves entangled in it.

19

Trent Wade felt as sick as the cows he was watching. He still couldn't believe what he'd overheard when he went to check on the cow in the barn last night. That hulking cowpoke had gotten Kedra to agree to go to one of the Strawberry Day dances with him—something Trent had been trying to get the courage up to do all week.

She'd forgiven him for his drunken advances, and hadn't told her father. He'd taken that as a sign. She must really like him or she would have squealed on him. All he had to do was take things slow and treat her right. Taking her to one, or both, of the dances would have given him the chance to make up for his behavior and prove he could be a gentleman.

He kicked the ground with the toe of his boot. Dirt and rocks flew.

"Hey! Watch what you're doing. I just had these pants washed," Isaac said, brushing off the leg of his trousers.

"I'm—I'm sorry. I didn't see you."

Isaac's frosty eyes bore into him. "What's bothering you, Trent?"

"It's nothing—really."

"Must be something or you wouldn't be moping and kicking up the dirt. I owe you a favor for getting me out of that scuffle in town last month. If you'll tell me your troubles, I'll try to help you."

"Well," Trent began, his face growing warm, "it's just . . . well . . . I was hoping to take Miss Moore to one of the Strawberry Day dances."

"And you're afraid to ask her. Why don't I go ask her for you?"

"It won't do any good—that big gorilla asked her last night. I heard him ask her, and she said yes."

Isaac's brows rose with surprise then contracted in thought. "I didn't think she liked him."

Trent had thought that too, until the big brute had thrown him across the barn. *She probably changed her mind about him then,* he decided. *Girls like men who rescue them.*

"She must like him if she's willing to go to the dance with him," Trent said miserably.

Isaac stared through Trent as though he wasn't there. His face took on a devious look. He nodded to himself and smiled.

Trent took a step back. He knew enough about Isaac to be afraid of that particular look. It always spelled trouble.

"How would you like to be the one to take Kedra to the dance?"

"I would, but what about Garrison?"

"If you do what I tell you to do, I think she'll change her mind and go with you?"

"What would I have to do?" Trent asked cautiously.

Isaac's grin sent foreboding down Trent's spine, but by the time Isaac explained what they were going to do, Trent was smiling broadly.

Kedra came out of the Blues' cabin, after packing Josiah's foot with the new poultice she'd found in Sarah's medical book, her mind mulling over what Effie had just told her about Jack. If it was true, it was a bizarre coincidence.

It was a chilling discovery—knowing Jack parents had been killed in the same range war that killed Effie's first husband. It was puzzling too. Effie told her every time she tried to bring the subject up; Jack politely put her off. *Why would he do that?*

Nearing the corner of the house, her steps slowed as she tried to figure Jack out. She finally shook her head. *It's Jack's business, not mine—but maybe I'll ask him about it when he takes me to the dance.*

The dance! Relief drenched her. Going to the dance with Jack might stir up some uncomfortable speculation, but at least she wouldn't be ashamed to show up. Besides, what fun would it be to wear her new dress if there wasn't someone to admire it?

A hard pang of guilt, due to the cost of the fabric for her party dress, stopped her in her tracks. *No! I bought the fabric six months ago and finished the dress weeks ago—before I knew how bad things were,* she rationalized.

"Don't talk to me about Garrison and all his virtues," Trent's voice reached her from around the corner of the house.

Kedra pressed her back against the wall, held her breath, and listened intently.

"You have to admit, the guy can do anything he sets his mind to," Isaac said.

Trent's laugh was bitter. "Including, winning ten bucks from me."

"Oh? How did he do that?" Isaac asked.

"I told him Miss Moore wouldn't go out with the hired help—told him your pa wouldn't like it and she wouldn't go against your pa."

"True enough."

"Garrison bet me ten buck he could get her to go with him to one of the Strawberry Day dances. I took the bet, figuring it was easy money. Then last night, when I went to check on that sick cow, I heard him in the barn with Miss Moore, asking her to go with him."

"And?"

"You could have knocked me down with a flick of your finger when she said yes."

"I don't believe you!"

"Go ask him. He came and gloated over me this morning. I told him I wouldn't pay him until I saw him dance with Miss Moore."

"Why that no good—"

Kedra's heart beat in her throat. Her eyes filled. *I don't even like him,* she reminded herself. Then, in a sudden burst of honesty, admitted that wasn't true. She'd purposely fought against allowing herself to like him—mostly because of the humiliating way they'd met, coupled with her fear that he wanted to buy the ranch. Now she couldn't deny the attraction she felt for him, or that she had been looking forward to going to the dance with him.

Her instincts still told her there was something phony about him, even if she couldn't put her finger on what it was. *Isn't that what happened with Morgan too? And look how that turned out. That experience should have put me on guard.* Her chin trembled. *Am I doomed to always be attracted to the wrong kind of men?*

Morgan had deceived her and it had made her more angry and confused than hurt, but being used by Jack felt deeply hurtful. *It wouldn't if I didn't feel something for him.* Refusing to cry, she let anger replace the hurt. *I'm not going to let Mr. Garrison get away with this!*

She stormed around the corner of the house, "Jack Garrison isn't going to win that bet, Trent!"

"Miss Moore!" Trent's eyes went wide with shock. "I'm real sorry you heard that."

"I'm not." Kedra walked up to Trent. "What do you say we turn the tables on that saddle tramp?"

"How?"

"Would you like to take me to the dance?"

"Miss Moore, I'd be honored, but I don't want to lose all my teeth. You know Garrison will be mad as a grizzly when he hears you found out about the bet."

Kedra's eyes simmered. "He won't find out—at least not until it's too late." She looked at Isaac. "You won't say anything to him, will you?"

"Not a chance. I don't like the guy. Watching you take him down a few notches will be delightful."

"Good, now here's what I'm going to do."

20

Friday, June 19, 1908

Kedra went out of her way to be pleasant to Jack during breakfast, promising to come out into the garden and help him pick strawberries as soon as the dishes were done.

She made the mistake of glancing at Isaac and almost lost her composure. Normally he didn't allow his feeling to show on his face. Over the years Kedra had come to understand his moods and feelings by looking into his unusually piercing eyes. They were very large and a startling shade of pale blue. When Isaac was angry, unhappy, or frustrated they darkened in color, going hard like ice. When he was happy, amused, or things were going well, they would fade into the palest blue Kedra had ever seen—like now. He was amused by her subterfuge.

It was so unusual for her to share his amusement that she almost laughed. She coughed and kept her eyes off him.

Jack got up from the table.

"I'll be out to help you in about fifteen minutes," she said, smiling. That slow grin, which had the power to accelerate her heart, grew on his face.

She set her glass of milk down with a clunk; afraid she might douse him with it, and kept her smile firmly in place.

"I'll wait to pick the strawberries until you come," he said.

After he left, the warmth of his grin lingered in her mind, but she refused to let it touch her heart, reminding herself that all she meant to him was ten bucks and gloating rights.

"Don't expect me for lunch or dinner," Isaac said, wiping his lips with his napkin and getting up. "I've got business in town today."

Eli set down his coffee cup. "Could it wait until this evening? You know I've given everyone the day off tomorrow. That means there are extra chores to do today. I could use another hand to help bring up hay for the sick cattle in the corral."

Isaac fixed his father with an aloof gaze. "Then I suggest you get Garrison to do the extra work. He owes us far more labor than he's giving us—considering the way he eats."

Kedra watched her father's face darken and quickly said, "Papa, if you need more men to bring up the hay, why don't you have Rory and the logging crew help do it after lunch?"

"You see—problem solved." Isaac straightened his tie, brushed a crumb from his tailored made jacket, and left the room.

Eli threw down his napkin.

Kedra took his hand.

His angry expression melted away. "You always step in before I blow up. Thank you."

"The logging crew might as well help with the hay—"

"Seeing as how the logging is going to come to a sudden halt anyway"—he finished her thought and blew out a defeated breath—"and so are their jobs." He put a hand on Kedra's cheek. "But not today—today all the employees on the High Peak Ranch are going to get paid."

"How? I though you didn't have the money."

"There's just enough in the bank to pay everyone for this week. Dr. Pell's bill can wait. Monday morning I'm going to Carbondale to see Oran Kerr. With a little luck, I'll be able to sell the herd to him, pay off the men, and let everyone go by the end of next week. Then you and I will start over."

Kedra felt the tears build in the back of her throat, she swallowed and blinked hard, found her courage, and asked hesitantly, "Will Isaac let us rebuild, Papa?"

He looked out the dining room window, toward the meadow. "Once I have nothing left, he'll leave."

"But you'll still have the ranch."

"That won't do him any good, since I haven't got a buyer. I'll give him whatever is left over from the sale of the herd, after I pay everyone I owe money to."

Kedra put her arms around his neck. She knew Isaac was holding something over his head, blackmailing him, but she couldn't bring herself to ask about it.

"I'm sorry about Isaac," she said.

A tear ran down her father's weather beaten cheek. "Don't judge him too harshly, he has cause to feel the way he does about me."

"I'm not his judge. I just feel sorry for him. He's so . . . unhappy and angry. He'll never find happiness unless he lets go of his anger."

"That's what I'm afraid of, but more than that, I'm afraid his anger will lead him into real trouble someday."

Thirty minutes later, Kedra watched Isaac ride out, the handles of a valise looped over the horn of his saddle. For a moment she wondered about the valise, but her mind was too weighted down by the problems of her family to wonder for long.

Finished with the breakfast dishes, Kedra hung her apron behind the kitchen door. In her present frame of mind, she wasn't sure she had the courage to go through with her plan to get even with Jack.

The conversation between Trent and Isaac ran through her head in perfect, humiliating detail. She drew herself up, and went out to the vegetable garden.

She caught up with Jack crawling along a row of bush beans and stopped in front of him. *That's exactly where you belong, Jack Garrison—groveling in the dirt at my feet.*

He looked up, smiled, and got to his feet.

She returned the smile with an effort.

"I was afraid I'd have to start picking strawberries without you."

"Sorry, the dishes took a little longer than I thought they would."

He handed her a bucket. They walked back to the strawberry patch and started crawling along the neat rows.

Dropping a handful of strawberries in the bucket, she said, "I'm leaving for town in a couple of hours. As a member of the Strawberry Day committee, I have a number of things I have to oversee."

"Effie told me you're responsible for the music. What else are you responsible for?"

"Making sure everything is ready for the dances, which includes the decorations, the band stands, the canvas floors, the refreshment tables, and the refreshments."

"It sounds like a lot of work. Do you need help?"

"No. I have an army of help. I just have to ensure everything gets done. I'm telling you, because I'm not coming back to the ranch tonight. I'm staying at Sarah's house until Strawberry Day is over."

Jack's brows contracted, a look she couldn't identify flickered over his face. The unsettling feeling that he knew what she was up to ran through her mind.

"Is that where I should pick you up for our date?"

"Yes."

"What time?"

"About six-thirty."

Again, that strange look momentarily touched his face.

"If I picked you up around five-thirty, we could have dinner, at the restaurant of your choice, before the dances start. I'd like the chance to just sit and talk with you in some quiet restaurant."

Kedra searched a strawberry plant to keep him from seeing her disgust. *A dinner you think Trent will end up paying for, but I'm not going to let that happen. I've known there was something wrong about you since the day you showed up. You're exactly what I thought you were—just a no account saddle tramp. You may be a member of the church, but you aren't a good man. No good man would use a woman the way you want to use me.*

She put a delighted expression on her face, even though going to dinner was an unexpected twist, decided accepting his invitation would fit nicely into her plan, and said, "The restaurants are going to be packed. You better try to make a reservation before I leave for town. I'll need to know what time you're coming to pick me up."

"Tell me where you'd like to go."

"The Hotel Colorado—it's a lovely place to eat, the food is good, and it has some very quiet corners," she said, in what she hoped was an inviting tone.

"As soon as we finish up here, I'll call for a reservation and let you know the time before you leave."

The warmth in his eyes, when he smiled, ached through her. She dropped her head and briskly picked strawberries.

Jack knocked on the door of the Blues' cabin, holding a basket of fresh produce in his hand. The basket contained peas, carrots, the first picking of beans, and strawberries. Since his first day on the job, Jack had made a habit of checking in with Josiah. He consulted Josiah on the daily chores to ensure the older man felt needed, and make sure he was doing everything Josiah wanted done.

Effie opened the door and took the basket from him. "Right nice morning—isn't it?"

"Picture perfect," Jack agreed, ducking through the door.

"Isn't that always the way of it," Josiah said in a complaining tone. "I couldn't be laid up in the winter when I'd like to just stay inside. No, I have to be cooped up when the weather is the best we get all year."

"He's feeling a mite restless," Effie whispered to Jack.

"I don't blame him," Jack whispered back, and then asked Josiah, "How's the foot?"

Josiah shifted the position of his foot on the footstool and said, "It's feeling better, but it stinks!"

Jack noticed a pungent odor as he sat down in the chair next to Josiah. "Whew! You're right. What in tarnation have you got on that foot?"

"A castor oil wrap. Kedra found the instructions in a medical book," Josiah grumbled. "She's supposed to come back any time now and take it off."

"He's supposed to eat strawberries, too" Effie reported. "Kedra read that eating them will help."

"At least I can enjoy the strawberries—if I hold my nose."

Jack laughed and leaned back in the chair, trying to put a little more distance between his nose and the smell of the castor oil. "So what are the extra jobs that need doing today?" he asked Josiah.

"Nothing I can think of off the top of my head." Josiah scratched his beard. "What I could use, since you'll be able to get the usual chores done in no time, is some company—can you spare an old man a few minutes?"

Effie brought out a bowl of the strawberries Jack had just picked, washed and ready to eat. She set the bowl on a table between the men and sat down next to Josiah.

She sent Jack a smile. "I hear you finally came to your senses and asked Kedra to go to one of the Strawberry Day dances."

"I did," Jack said shortly, not wanting to pursue the subject. He could tell, by their knowing looks, that his motivation for taking Kedra to the dance wasn't what they thought it was—or hoped.

"Well you'll be taking the prettiest gal in town. She made herself a right pretty dress for the dance, a few weeks back." Effie's eyes did a jig. "I'm not going to tell you what it looks like, except to say its pale yellow with black trim. I talked her into wearing her hair up too."

"No doubt with the totem of her tribe as an adornment," Jack said.

"Well, yes. She always wears that, you know."

"I have noticed." Jack sat forward. "She's very proud of her Nahtow heritage. What about Isaac does he take pride in being Nahtow?"

"Oh my, I guess no one's mentioned it to you, but Kedra and Isaac had different mothers. Isaac's mother was a Cajun girl—French and Mi'kmaq Indian. Both of them take after their mothers. I once saw a cameo of Isaac's mother. She was a beauty, tall and willowy with black hair and pale blue eyes, just like Isaac. And from what Eli tells me, Kedra is the image of her mother. She too was tall and willowy, with black hair and those remarkable gold eyes."

Jack compared the sibling in his head and couldn't find anything of Eli in either one. He'd noticed that on the first day. *They both take after their mothers and it's their Indian heritages that make them initially appear so much alike.*

"What happened to Isaac's mother?" he asked.

"I don't know how she died, if that's what you mean. Eli only told me she died in New Orleans, about a year after Isaac was born."

"That must have been very hard on Eli—raising a baby by himself."

"He didn't. Eli gave Isaac to his wife's sister, Ursula. She too was living in New Orleans and had a son about two years older than Isaac. At the time, Eli thought it was the best thing he could do for Isaac."

"Wasn't it?

"It was, and Eli should have just left well enough alone," Effie said fiercely.

"It took Eli a few years after he won this ranch and built the house to get the ranch on its feet. Once he did, he sent for Isaac," Josiah said.

"Isaac was eight years old when he came here—"

"He hated the ranch the moment he saw it. Even at eight he was already an uppity little snob," Josiah said harshly.

Effie wrung her work worn hands, and confided, "He hated Kedra even more. Eli has always talked about Kedra's mother. Everyone knows how much he loved her, but he has never talked about Isaac's mother."

Josiah re-positioned his foot. "Not only did Eli love Kedra's mother more than he loved Isaac's, but everyone, including Isaac, knows Eli favors Kedra."

"I think that's why Isaac has always been so mean to her," Effie remarked, thoughtfully.

"Mean to her—how?" Jack asked.

Effie sighed. "When she was young he would take her favorite toys and break them, just to make her cry. He liked to hit and pinch her too, for no reason at all."

"And the more Eli whipped him, the worse he got," Josiah put in.

"After one terrible incident, I was told not to leave Kedra alone with Isaac," Effie said with a little shiver. She leaned into Josiah and confided, "Frankly, I don't like being alone with Isaac. He scares me."

Jack soaked in every word. It explained why Isaac always seemed so hostile and resentful. It also explained Isaac's smile after Kedra saw the special edition of the Avalanche and ran out of the dining room. *He was deliberately tormenting her, and watching her emotional reaction entertained him! But that means he must have known something in that paper would set her off. Could it be that Isaac knows what she did and is blackmailing her!*

He couldn't discount it. *It means Isaac could send Kedra and Drew Ellis to the gallows. If Isaac is blackmailing her—then he knows about the emeralds. But I'll bet he doesn't know where they are. The emeralds may be the reason he hasn't turned Kedra in. He wants his cut. I'd better keep tabs on Isaac. I need to know how far he'd go to hurt Kedra and what he's capable of doing.*

The mantle clock chimed the half hour.

Jack stood up. "I best be about my business."

"Thanks for sittin' a spell," Josiah said, holding out his hand.

"No trouble—" Jack took his hand. "It's been enlightening."

An hour later, Jack helped Kedra into the buggy. The clear cool morning promised to turn into a beautiful summer day. Placing Kedra's satchel beside her on the seat, Jack couldn't help wondering if the satchel contained half a million dollars in rare emeralds. If it did, he intended to intercept them and Drew Ellis, when the train came through.

He'd made up his mind to let Kedra meet the train and pass the emeralds off to Ellis. It was a dangerous gamble. If he wasn't close enough to catch Kedra in the act, he was afraid Ellis might kill her, eliminating the only person who knew how the robbery happened. But if he could apprehend her with Ellis, in the act of giving him the stolen gems, then he could close the case tonight. That was something he wanted to do as quickly as possible. Kedra Moore was beginning to affect his judgment. He didn't know how much longer he could take being around her. Not even knowing she'd taken part in Will's murder was helping him keep his growing feelings for her in check any longer.

She was a picture to look at in a dusky red tailored suit with black scalloped trim. Her heavy hair was braided in an intricate style. It started above her right ear, moved down and around the back of her head, ending under her left ear. The rest of her long braid was looped over her shoulder, the end secured behind her left ear with her tribal totem. The white feather's accentuated the delicate white lace on the high collar of her blouse.

Why must she be so beautiful? Jack wondered. Then had to admit it wasn't just her beauty that was wreaking havoc on him and his investigation. *It's everything about her. The way she treats the ranch hands, keeps her father and Isaac from coming to blows, her involvement in the community, and the obvious love the little group of saints feels for her.* None of it made any sense when he compared it with the evidence he had against her.

He couldn't refute the growing evidence. It made him feel as though Kedra Moore was two different people. *If she is living a double life, she's doing a superb job of it.* He'd never met someone that baffled him more than she did.

"Our dinner reservation is set for six-fifteen," he said, again finding himself captured by her eyes. "I'm sorry I couldn't get an earlier one. I'll pick you up at the Powell's house just after six tomorrow evening."

"You really should come into town tomorrow morning and indulge in the strawberry feast," she said, sounding sorry for him.

He'd volunteered to stay on the ranch, watch the sick cattle and do his own chores, while everyone went into town for the celebration. Eli was going to come back in the afternoon and spell him so he could go to the dance, something Eli said he didn't want to attend.

A wry smile lifted Jack's lips. "I can't eat another strawberry, Miss Moore. I've eaten so many over the last week that my hair has gotten even redder." He pulled off his hat, exposing his bright red hair.

Her musical laugh sent his heart racing.

"You—you may be right," she said still laughing. "I'll bet you never eat beets!"

"I wouldn't dare," he said, giving her a horror-stricken look.

She picked up the reins. "I better get going before I'm late."

"I'll see you tomorrow, just after six."

With a smile, that left Jack uneasy, she shook the reins and waved her hand as Molly started off at a trot.

Jack watched her until the buggy disappeared around a bend. *The train will pull in at five-thirty. I'll be there when it does.* Sorrow settled into his chest. Arresting Kedra Moore was going to be the hardest thing he'd done as a marshal. As soon as she was arraigned and he gave his evidence, he intended to leave the state of Colorado and never come back. He couldn't bear to be here for her execution.

21

Strawberry Day—Saturday, June 20, 1908

The jubilant ranch hands galloped through the gates of the High Peak Ranch, decked out in their best shirts and string ties. Their pockets jingled with a full week's pay, something that heightened Jack's suspicions.

Even Josiah went. He'd been reluctant, because walking around was still painful, until Jack suggested Effie take his chair, his footstool, and a small table along in the buckboard.

"If you don't want to get out, we can set you up like a king in the buckboard. You'll have a great view of the street, and I'll bring you anything you want. We can park the wagon right next to all the tables, so you can visit with folks and eat strawberries and cream until you bust," Effie told him.

Josiah's craggy face lit. "Okay, I'll go!"

Eli drove the buckboard. Effie and Josiah waved to Jack as they pulled out. When they were gone, Jack checked on the sick cattle, moved one more into the corral where the ones showing symptoms were being kept, and went into the house.

He called Sheriff Hadlock, hoping Tate could provide backup for him when the train came in. Tate had already told him how busy Strawberry Day was for him and his deputies. He'd even deputized an additional dozen men, just to keep order.

The phone rang five times before the receiver was picked up.

"Sheriff Hadlock," Tate said into the receiver.

"Tate, its Jack . . . I wonder if you could give me thirty minutes of your time this evening?"

"What's up?"

Jack explained his theory about Ellis and Kedra and what he thought might happen when the train pulled in."

Tate whistled softly through the receiver. "That's a different twist on things, but it does answer many of the questions we've been wrestling with. So what do you want me to do?"

"I need you to be at the train station at five-thirty, when the train comes in. I'll be there too. If Miss Moore is going to meet Ellis, she'll do it in the first thirty minutes, because she has a dinner date with me at six."

"Wow!"

"Just part of the job— I need your help to stake out the station. If I'm right, we've got to be close enough to apprehend Miss Moore and Ellis the moment the gems change hands. I believe Ellis will try to get her alone before the exchange is made. Once she gives him the gems, I think he'll kill her—as he did everyone in the express car. Miss Moore is the only one left that can connect him to the robbery."

"I'm still having a hard time accepting Kedra as a thief and a murderer."

"I would be too, except the High Peak Ranch is on the verge of folding, and that's strong motivation for Miss Moore. She loves the place. I'm going to use the search warrant you got for me to poke around while everyone's in town. If I come up with anything, I'll let you know."

In the background, Jack heard someone come into Tate's office and start talking excitedly, moments later other voices joined the first.

"Hold the line for a minute, Jack."

The line went silent as though Tate had covered the receiver. Jack waited patiently.

Tate came back on the line. "I've got to go, but I'll be at the station at five-thirty."

"Meet me in the alley across from the Manhattan Restaurant, between Blake Street and Cooper. I'll tell you how I want to handle this then. Thanks."

Jack hung up the telephone receiver and looked around Eli's office. On the corner of the desk there was a ledger and a bankbook. Jack meticulously reviewed them. He stopped at the entries made yesterday when Eli returned from town and paid the men. *He virtually emptied his bank account. Now he's broke. He's going to be forced to sell—unless he finds a new source of revenue—fast.*

A search of the rest of the room didn't turn up anything except a wall safe behind a painting of the Maroon Bells, a famous set of twin peak near Aspen, Colorado, and the cancelation of the logging contract. *That may be the final blow for this ranch.*

After being sure everything he'd touched was back in its place, he left the office and climbed the stairs. He hadn't been upstairs to the Moores' private living quarters before.

At the top of the stairs, there was a large sitting room with comfortable chairs surrounding a fireplace. A piano stood next to a large window. On both sides of the window, bookcases lined the wall.

The warmth of the room was all Kedra. He could see her in this tasteful, yet unpretentious room. The colors reminded him of her too—decorated in tones of rust and gold, accentuated by green. It was a family space, not a place any of the Moores would hide something.

He walked across it and stepped into the hall.

The first door he opened took him into Eli's bedroom. It was a very masculine room, with heavy pine furniture. Pictures of Kedra and Isaac were scattered throughout the room. Jack stopped to look at Kedra as a little girl. He watched her grow up as he moved around the room, the pictures bruised his heart. He finished searching the room, concluding that if Eli had anything incriminating it was locked in the office safe.

He stepped across the hall and opened the door to a large modern bathroom. It featured the most up-to-date toilet, a huge ball and claw tub, an ornately framed oval mirror over a porcelain pedestal sink, flanked by a double set of floor to ceiling cupboards.

Jack closed the bathroom door and tried the door next to it. It was locked. He inserted a small tool into the lock. A moment later, he turned the doorknob and entered. The room was an elegant boudoir, but not a female one. A canopy bed, hung with midnight blue velvet curtains, dominated the room. The furniture was inlaid mahogany as were the closet doors.

Jack opened the closet and examined several fashionable suits and multiple pairs of shoes and boots. In the back of the closet, he found a very expensive ladies overcoat. The coat's outer pocket contained a fake mustache. An inner pocket contained a gold-lamé evening bag. The bag contained a cake of rouge, a tiny attached mirror, five dollars in small bills, and a handkerchief. The handkerchief was monogramed with E.O. on the edge. He closed the purse, and put it back where he'd found it.

Behind the coat there was a black dress. Jack ran a hand over the silky fabric adorned with lace. He searched the shelf above the dress. Underneath a top hat, he found a woman's black veiled hat. It was a delicate creation, meant to obscure a woman's face. *I wonder if all this female attire belonged to Isaac's mother.* A different thought struck him. *Maybe they aren't keepsakes but gifts he intends to give to a lady.* Jack was no expert on women's fashions, but he could tell the items were all first rate.

Finished with the closet, Jack began a methodical search of the room. He stopped to look at a watercolor cameo of a woman set on a stand. The woman had to be Isaac's mother. She was every bit as beautiful as Effie had said, and it was astonishing how closely Isaac resembled her. The thing that struck Jack was how cold her eyes were. He'd seen that same look in her son's eyes.

Assuring himself that everything was back in its place, Jack closed the door to Isaac's room and relocked it, feeling disturbed.

Other than the cameo, there weren't any personal mementos of Isaac's life. There were no personal papers, letters or mementos from his college days, pictures of friends or even of his family. It was all very impersonal, almost as though Isaac didn't really live there, but was just stopping there for a few days.

Jack paused before entering Kedra's bedroom. He'd conducted hundreds of searches for evidence, but not with the feeling of dread that filled him now. *It has to be done.*

Automatically ducking under the doorframe, he stepped into the room. It was like looking beneath the surface of Kedra's beauty and into her heart. The room had an old fashion charm, with a braided rug on the floor and a patchwork quilt on the bed. The design of the quilt spoke of Kedra's Indian heritage in the geometric patterns and colors, as did the pictures on the walls. Her dresser was covered with photographs of her family. A small desk was stacked with books. A crowded bookcase stood next to the desk and a deep-seated chair sat near the window, a standing lamp behind it.

Jack searched the closet, her clothes were simple and yet they were up to date and well made. The vanity held only a hairbrush and pins for doing up a woman's hair. He moved on to a bedside table, opened the drawer and found a bible. He flipped through it and dislodged a small key, resting against the spine of the book.

The key unlocked a jewelry box on the vanity. In it, there was a heavy gold chain of unusual design and unique workmanship. An empty loop hung from the center of the chain. *This must be the Jade pendant's chain.* The only other things of interest in the box were the pendant's jade earrings. Jack carefully examined the earrings, something he hadn't been able to do when Kedra was wearing them, then relocked the box and put the key back in the Bible.

By the time Jack finished going through the chest of drawers, his fingers were scented with the delicate clove fragrance that always clung to Kedra. The fragrance was distracting. He went into the bathroom and carefully washed his hands, ridding himself of her scent, but couldn't rid himself of the guilt. For the first time in his career, he felt guilty about doing a search of a suspect's room. His guilt was exacerbated because, as yet, he'd failed to turn up anything.

Returning to Kedra's room, he went to the desk. Unlike the rest of Kedra's belongings, which were neat and orderly, the desk was cluttered.

A medical book lay on top of a stack of books, open to a page on gout. He read the instructions for the castor oil poultice Kedra had applied to Josiah's foot, and set it aside. Under the medical book was a chemistry book. As he picked it up, it fell open to where a newspaper had been place in it. His eyes fell on the special edition of the Avalanche, outlining the robbery and murders.

Harry's picture had been cut out of the newspaper. *Why would she cut out Harry's picture unless . . . it's some sort of sick memento?*

He was about to close the book when he noticed the subject of the page the newspaper had been stuck in. The entry read: Chloral Hydrate—a compound commonly called knockout drops. Its uses were outlined. Ways to compound the chemicals to minimize taste and smell were described. Common ways to further mask the taste were listed. Jack noticed that when added to coffee, sweetened with sugar, or alcohol it was almost undetectable. The effects of the drug were discussed. There were three primary reactions. A person given the drug could fall asleep. They might become delirious, or the drug could induce terrible pain.

Jack dropped into the desk chair, looking at the puzzle from a new direction. *That must be how it happened.* He reread the entry, his muscles tightening into knots from his fingers to his shoulders.

Replacing the newspaper, he closed the book, and put it exactly where it had been, setting the medical book on top. Anger pulsed through him as he began searching the desk drawers. In the first drawer he found nothing but desk paraphernalia. In the second drawer he found an address book and numerous letters, both professional and personal.

The bottom drawer was locked.

Again he employed his entry tool. He found a bundle of letters dating back over six months. All the letters were written in the same hand. He opened a few and found they were from a man named Morgan O'Shea.

That wasn't a name that figured into the crime—as far as he knew. He debated reading the letters then decided to read just the most recent one. The postmark dated it just few days before the murders.

He opened the envelope, pulled out the letter, and found the picture of Harry. Stunned, he started to read. Two sentences leaped off the page at him.

I'm looking forward to June 8th.

The day of the murders!

I'll meet you under the bridge as soon as I can get free. We'll talk about what we are going to do. Trust me, sweetheart. I'll do anything you want.

Jack's fingers began to curl around the letter. *She certainly made a sucker out of Harry.* He forced his fingers to stop. Laying the letter on the desk, he smoothed it out, re-inserted it and Harry's picture into the envelope, and put it in his pocket. He was about to shut the drawer when he realized the depth of the drawer didn't correspond with the depth of the drawer face. Removing the letters, he tapped on the bottom of the drawer and heard a hollow sound. A quick examination revealed a small notch at the back. He inserted his entry tool and lifted out the false bottom of the drawer.

A Webley Bull Dog pocket revolver lay in the bottom of the drawer. The short barreled, double-action revolver had a swing-out ejector rod and a short grip. It featured a 2.5-inch barrel and was chambered for five .450 Adams cartridges.

He swung out the barrel. There were four spent shells and one unfired round. *I know where the other bullets are. One killed Harry, one grazed Will's head, another is in his chest, and the last one killed Ito.*

Minutes slipped by as he stared at the lethal little gun, with its ivory grip. *Those gold eyes have blinded me and made me stupid.*

He rearranged the pieces of the puzzle. He'd been wrong about some of the facts. He'd even been wrong about how the events in the express car had happened. Most of all he'd been wrong about who'd killed Will and Harry.

A cold sweat broke out on his forehead. Carefully wrapping the gun in his handkerchief, he put it in his pocket. After replacing the false bottom, he put the letters back in the drawer and relocked it. The rest of the letters could be confiscated after he arrested Kedra.

Without suffering another pang of guilt, he finished searching the room, without finding anything else. *I must be right about the emeralds or they would have been in the drawer with the gun. She took them with her to pass off to Ellis. With any luck, I'll have them in my possession this evening.* His jaw tightened. *Then I'll arrest Drew Ellis and Miss Kedra Moore.*

22

Jack met Tate in the narrow alleyway across the street from the Manhattan Restaurant, between Blake Street and Cooper Street, just below the railroad station. They held a quick discussion on where to station themselves. There were too many ways to leave the station's platform. People could walk through the station, but they could also walk up the slopes on either end of the station to 7th Street, or walk along the bank of the Colorado River toward the bridge. With only Tate's description of Drew Ellis, Jack assigned himself to look for Kedra, and gave Tate the job of spotting Ellis.

The train whistle blew, announcing its imminent arrival from Grand Junction. Tate hurried down the alley toward Cooper Street. Jack came out of the alley on Blake Street and strode up the street to 7th. He crossed 7th and walked down the slope on the east side of the red flagstone station, positioning himself at the corner of the building. His height allowed him to see all along the platform to the west end.

The train came to a stop in the midst of a belch of steam. Uniformed porters immediately started unloading the arriving passengers' bags.

Jack searched the crowded platform for Kedra, looking for the pale yellow dress with black trim Effie had described. He felt sure she would have changed into her party dress before she met the train. There wouldn't be enough time to meet Ellis, get back to the Powell's, change her clothes, and be on time to go to dinner with him, unless she was already dressed.

Fifteen minutes later, most of the arriving passengers were gone.

Nothing! Jack's eyes shifted watchfully, his confidence waning. *It might not be wise to transfer the gems here. They can't afford to be seen together. Maybe they're waiting until things die down before Kedra gives Ellis the gems. But then why didn't I find them in Kedra's hiding place?*

Another five minutes dragged by. Jack knew if he didn't spot Kedra in the next couple of minutes, he would have to leave.

A dining car attendant, wearing a white jacket and bowtie, came out of the train. Jack studied him. He fit Tate's description of Drew Ellis. He was in his late twenties or early thirties, of average height and build, with a neatly trimmed mustache. His short blond hair was visible at the back of his cap. The steward walked purposefully into the station.

Scrambling up the hill, Jack hugged the side of the red sandstone building. Surveillance was a job he usually handed off to his deputies, because he just stood out to much. Peeking around the corner of the building, he watched the steward come out of the station, cross the street, and go into a saloon.

A saloon? That didn't figure. He was sure Kedra wouldn't go into a saloon. He followed the steward anyway.

Pushing through the swinging door, Jack paused to let his eyes adjust to the dim light of the bar room.

The man he hoped was Ellis, stood at the bar, talking with the bartender.

Could Kedra be using a third party to pass the emeralds? Jack wondered, sitting down on a barstool a few feet from the dining car steward. He was close enough to hear what the bartender said before he left the bar and slipped into the back room.

The steward tapped the top of the bar with impatience fingers.

The bartender returned. "Mr. Bosco says its okay."

Green backs changed hands.

"Thank Mr. Bosco, he saved my hide," the steward said.

"Who's going to pick the scotch up?"

"Do you have someone who can bring it?" the steward asked.

"For four bits, I'll bring it," Jack said, standing up.

The steward eyed him with an alarmed expression. "I don't—"

"I'm not going to rob you," Jack assured him. "I just need a little money for a drink."

The steward still looked skeptical.

"You better take him up on his offer. I don't have anyone right now who can bring the case over," the bartender said.

"Well—all right, but hurry, please," the agitated steward said.

Jack followed the bartender into the basement, which housed a busy brewery. He returned a minute later with a case of scotch.

The steward examined the case and nodded. "Let's go."

They stepped out of the bar and into the glaring sun.

"My name's Jack," the marshal said, conversationally.

"Thanks, for your help, Jack. I'm Fred," the steward said as they dodged horses and buggies, coming and going in front of the station.

"Nice to meet you, Fred," Jack said, disappointed the steward wasn't Drew Ellis. Still, getting aboard the train and actually laying eyes on Ellis would be a plus.

Fred held the door of the station open for Jack. He ducked and went through. They jostled their way across the terminal and exited the station. Departing passengers, and those saying goodbye to them, filled the platform. Porters assisted the departing passenger with their luggage and helped them find their assigned compartments.

"Do you usually restock your liquor supply enroute?" Jack asked, striding toward the train, forcing Fred to scurry to keep up with him.

"No—never—it costs too much. But Drew Ellis, our head steward, who was supposed to restock all the liquor while we were in Grand Junction, didn't get it done . . . among other things. In fact, he didn't even show up for work this morning."

"He didn't get on the train?"

"No, and the conductor and the cook are furious. He'll probably get fired," Fred said with satisfaction.

"Has he missed work like this before?"

"Never."

"Maybe he had an accident or got sick. Didn't anyone check on him?" Jack asked stepping aboard the train.

"No one knows where he stayed last night, and there wasn't time to search for him— Put it here." The steward indicated a shelf in the pantry of the dining car.

Jack set the case down and Fred gave him fifty cents.

"Thanks for your help."

"Glad to do it." Jack jingled the coins, put them in his pocket, and left the train.

He spotted Tate on the west side of the station, made eye contact, and jerked his head toward the street.

They again met in the alley.

"Drew Ellis didn't get on the train in Grand Junction this morning," Jack said, going straight to the point.

"Why?"

"Unknown, but I don't like it. Call the Grand Junction Sheriff, use Luke's name and authority—ask him to find Ellis. According to the steward I was with, Ellis has never done anything like this before."

"I'll see what I can find out."

"Thanks, Tate. Sorry to have wasted your time."

Stakeouts were always gambles, which frequently didn't pay off. This one hadn't paid off the way Jack had thought it would, still he'd learned something. What it meant wasn't clear yet, but the unsettled feeling in his gut told him it was important.

"It wasn't a waste for me," Tate said. "I saw a couple of trouble makers get off the train. I know their haunts and habits. I better get a couple of deputies on them." He shook Jack's hand and hurried away.

Jack made it to the Powell's house at five minutes after six o'clock. Before he reached the front door he saw the note tacked to it. His name was on the folded sheet of paper. The unsettled feeling, which had started in the train station, spread from his gut into his chest. He opened the note and read it through.

Jack,

A couple of unexpected things have come up, which require my attention. I'll try to get them done quickly and meet you at the Hotel Colorado, hopefully no later than six-twenty.

Thanks for your patience,
Kedra

Jack crushed the note in his hand. His instincts told him something besides Kedra's responsibility for the dances was the reason she wasn't here. He knocked on the Powell's door and waited.

No one answered.

He knocked louder.

Still no one came.

He looked down at the note in his fist. *Where are you Kedra?*

In the distance he heard the train whistle, warning the passengers there was just minutes before the train left.

His watch said six-ten.

He knew where both dances were being held. Again in the saddle he rode back up Blake Street to 8th, turned left, and rode for a block to the intersection of 8th Street and Cooper Street.

It was a flurry of activity. A huge canvas floor had been rolled out in the intersection and the band was beginning to assemble on the bandstand. Women were hurrying back and forth putting out bowls of strawberries, plates of sugar cookies, and jugs of water.

Jack walked Soldier over to the refreshment table, stepped down off his back, and touched an elderly woman's arm. "Excuse me, ma'am, but do you know where I could find Miss Kedra Moore?"

The white haired lady looked up at him with sharp brown eyes. She smiled broadly at him. "She was here a while ago, but I don't know where she's gone. You might try down the street—at the other dance site."

"Thank you, ma'am," he said, pulling on the brim of his hat.

He tried two other people with no luck.

It was six-fifteen.

The other dance site was straight down 8th street. *I can check it out and still be at the Hotel Colorado by six-twenty.*

The story was the same at the other dance site. Kedra had been there but no one knew where she was now.

Jack rode Soldier hard across the bridge, hoping Kedra was already at the hotel. A lackey held the big stallion's head as Jack stepped down. Tossing the boy a tip, Jack strode into the grandeur of the Hotel Colorado. He didn't pay much attention to the lofty ceiling and the broad carpeted hallway, staged with luxurious sitting areas.

Stopping at the desk, he asked to be directed to the outdoor dining patio. The maître d' took him there. A waiter showed him to his reserved table.

Kedra wasn't there.

"I'm expecting a lady to join me," he said to the waiter as he sat down.

"Then perhaps you would like to look at a menu or order a drink while you wait."

He ordered a glass of lemonade, and then shifted his chair so he could see the patio entrance.

People came and left, but not Kedra.

The dining patio of the Hotel Colorado sat in a garden outside the hotel's main wing, flanked on either side by protruding wings, facing south. If Jack hadn't been speculating about where Kedra was, he would have enjoyed the view of the hot springs pools, and the Colorado River.

The waiter brought his lemonade.

He took a sip and set the glass aside.

The minutes ticked by. His anxiety grew. The feeling that something was wrong intensified. Suddenly, for reasons he couldn't understand, he found himself praying that Kedra was all right. Even as he whispered the prayer, he acknowledged the irony. He intended to arrest Miss Moore and provide enough evidence to hang her. The prayer forced him to examine his feelings.

If Huck Finn was right and you "can't pray a lie" then he had to face facts. He cared about Miss Moore, more than he'd allowed himself to admit. He didn't want anything bad to happen to her. It was a hard admission, but once he'd made it the rest of what was in his heart spilled out too.

Kedra was everything he wanted in a woman. She could probably out ride him, could definitely shoot as well as he did, loved ranch life, and wasn't afraid of hard work, or caring for sick people or animals. Effie had told him Kedra made all her clothes too, because of how tall she was. She wasn't obsessed with fashion, or seeking all the pleasures of the world. She could cook, was involved in the community, and shared his faith. To top it off, she was the most beautiful woman Jack had ever seen. Her eyes alone would have stolen his heart.

His heart! *Is that what's happened to me? Have I let myself get emotionally attached to a murderer?* It was unthinkable. He faced the final truth and admitted his heart didn't believe she was guilty even though all the evidence pointed directly at her.

He glanced at his watch. It was six-forty-five. The train had left and he hadn't even heard the whistle blow. Disgusted with himself, he downed the lemonade, decided not to wait any longer, paid his bill, and left the hotel.

Maybe Kedra's troubles with the dances took longer than she expected. He would find her at one of the dances, and this time he'd look until he did.

23

Jack rode over the bridge to the sounds of an orchestra warming up. Stringed instruments joined the swelling tones of brass ones, with the start stop plucking that went with tuning the instruments. Soldier's ears turned back against the discordant and competing tones.

It wasn't until Soldier started down Grand Street that the ugly suspicion crept into Jack's mind. *Did she intentionally stand me up?* The more his mind lingered over the thought the more certain he was. *If she wasn't going to be able to keep our dinner date, she could have sent someone over to the hotel to tell me—it isn't that far. Come to think of it, she isn't the kind of woman who'd leave a man cooling his heels without letting him know why.*

His immediate hurt outweighed his anger. *She didn't have to go out with me. So why did she say yes? She has no reason to intentionally hurt me . . . not after I told her I wasn't interested in buying the ranch.*

Actually, he'd thought after the ride home from the pond that they had reached an amicable understanding, and were on their way to becoming friends. *Friends? I need to have my head examined.*

It was his job to get close to her, even deceive her, if that's what it took to enable him to compile enough evidence to convict her.

Honesty, would no longer allow him the lie of telling himself he was only getting close to Kedra to gather evidence. It also wouldn't allow him to escape the fact that he'd have to arrest her, once he found the emeralds.

The corner of Grand Ave. and 8th Street was already crowded with people. Laughter and music filled the air. The Redstone Elks Band began to play a popular tune. Couples crowded onto the canvas dance floor, moving like a wave to the rhythm of the music.

Jack sat on Soldier's back, overlooking the crowd. Most of the women were wearing shades of red in honor of the day. All the red would make spotting Kedra's yellow dress easier. He searched the crowd and the dance floor. It was hard work with the constant movement of the dancers and the people milling about.

He spotted Buck Gilbert step onto the dance floor with a pretty girl in a bonnet adorned with red ribbons. He watched the tall cowboy dance the girl across the canvas floor. Buck looked at the girl with open admiration. The girl smiled up at him, but Jack noticed her eyes wandered the crowd, a sure sign she was looking for another man.

Poor Buck.

Jack liked the High Peak's foreman and respected his judgment. Buck had confided that he'd advised Eli not to buy the cattle that were now sick, but Eli hadn't taken his advice.

After watching the crowd for fifteen minutes without any luck, Jack decided to try the other dance. Soldier plodded down 8th Street, while Jack searched it for Kedra.

He spotted her almost immediately as he reached the intersection of 8th and Cooper. Stopping behind the refreshment table, beyond the lights of the Chinese lanterns that lit the dance floor, he watched her, mesmerized.

Her hair was swept up in a way that showed off her long, slender neck. The light of the lanterns gave her skin a soft golden hue. Her gold earrings caught the light as they did their own dance, so did her totem. The feathers and beads, clipped in her hair, spun as she moved.

Trent Wade was dancing with her, his face an advertisement for a man in love. Kedra looked at the young cowpoke with, what Jack thought was, a tolerant smile.

The Grand Valley Band finished their rendition of "There Never was a Girl Like You".

Kedra and Trent walked toward the refreshment table.

Jack backed into the shadows and tied Soldier to a hitching post.

Kedra stopped to talk with some people.

Trent went on to the crowded refreshment table.

The Rittmayer Orchestra began playing, "Sweetheart Days", a slow waltz.

Slicing through the crowd at Kedra's back, Jack took hold of her hand, pulled her onto the dance floor and into the swirling dancers before she could utter a protest.

"I believe this is my dance, and *you* are *supposedly* my date."

Her face was inscrutable, but her eyes flashed with gold fire. "How dare you drag me off in front of my friends like that?"

"Since manners don't seem to mean much to you, I figured you wouldn't mind." He stared into her angry eyes. "If your responsibilities kept you from keeping our dinner date, you could have at least had the courtesy to send someone to tell me."

Her chin came up. "My responsibilities didn't keep me."

His chest tightened. "Then why did you stand me up for dinner? I didn't twist your arm to come on this date. If you didn't want to come with me, you could have just said no."

"I don't owe a man *like you* any explanations."

"A man *like* me?" Jack pulled her closer. "What do you mean?"

She pushed back, opening a gap between them, and hissed, "I mean you are a dirty, rotten, no count, saddle tramp, and I want you off the High Peak Ranch tonight—or I'll tell my father what you did."

"Just what am I supposed to have done?"

"The game is up, Garrison. I know about your bet with Trent."

"I don't know what you're talking about."

"Do you have the gall to deny you bet Trent ten dollars you could get me to come to this dance with you?"

"Did Trent tell you that?"

"No, I overheard him tell Isaac about the bet. Isaac couldn't believe I'd come with you. Trent told Isaac he thought you were just making the whole thing up and refused to pay you until he saw us dancing together."

They had all but stopped dancing. Couples whirled around them while they locked angry eyes on each other.

Another couple almost bumped into them.

Jack pulled Kedra back into his arms and moved into the flow of the waltz. Now he knew exactly what she thought of him, and it hurt.

"I'm not the kind of man that would ever use a woman like that," he said through his teeth.

"Oh, and I suppose I'm just expected to take your word for it, am I?" she asked sarcastically.

He reviewed the circumstances of how she'd learned about the bet and found them highly suspicious.

"How did you happen to overhear Isaac and Trent's conversation?"

"I was on my way from the Blue's cabin to the trash can outside the kitchen door. I had just unwrapped Josiah's foot and I wanted to take the used poultice directly to the trash, because of the smell. I heard them talking, before I got to the corner of the house. They didn't know I was there."

"Didn't they? Think about it, Miss Moore. Effie and Josiah told me some of the things Isaac has done to you in the past. Do you really believe it's outside the realm of possibility that he simply thought it would be amusing to sabotage our date? Or that Trent would go along with it? You know Trent is sweet on you and after what I did to him, he has every reason to want to get back at me."

A tentacle of doubt touched Kedra's face, and she admitted, "Isaac might, but Trent wouldn't go along with him. He wouldn't do that to me. Not after I forgave him for mauling me."

The song was coming to an end. As the last measures played, Jack noticed Trent standing at the edge of the dance floor, a murderous look on his face.

"I know how I can prove my innocence," Jack said hurriedly.

"How?" she asked suspiciously.

"Let's just dance over to Trent, and I'll demand my ten dollars. After all, I am dancing with you, and he's watching."

"Oh, so I'm supposed to let you win the bet, and that's how you're going to prove you didn't make it?" she asked, disgusted.

"I'm not going to prove it, Trent is. Just go along with me, *please*. Let me prove my innocence."

She glanced over at Trent and then back up at him. "All right, prove you're innocent."

They danced over to Trent on the last notes of the song.

"I'll take the ten bucks you owe me," Jack demanded.

Trent balked. He looked wide-eyed at Kedra.

"I'm afraid you will have to pay him, Trent. After all I did dance with him," Kedra said dejectedly.

Jack held out his hand.

"No . . . um . . . wait. I—I . . . um . . . don't owe you any money."

"You do if I made the bet with you, you claim I did."

Ten dollars was a lot of money, something the ranch hands hadn't seen much of in the last few weeks. Trent looked from Kedra to Jack and back again.

"Miss Moore, there—there wasn't any bet," Trent said in a rush. "I was just upset when I overheard you accept his"—he jerked his head at Jack—"invitation, because I wanted to take you. Isaac offered to help me break up the date and get you to go with me."

"Is that the truth, Trent?"

"Yes ma'am." The young cowboy hung his head.

Kedra looked up at Jack, shame faced. "I owe you an apology, Mr. Garrison. Please forgive me, I misjudged you. I'll understand if you don't want to spend the rest of the evening in my company."

"I liked it better when you called me Jack," he said, pulling her back onto the dance floor as the band began to play "I Love You So".

After dancing in silence for a few bars, Kedra said, "I—I feel like such a fool. You would think after all these years . . . I wouldn't fall for Isaac's tricks."

"Maybe it's just in your nature to trust people."

"Not Isaac. If he had told me about the bet, I wouldn't have believed it. Getting Trent to go along with him is what did me in."

"It's hard to always be on guard against someone, especially when they live with you."

"He hasn't played a trick on me in quite a while. I guess I thought he's outgrown doing that." Her face became indignant. "I'd love to get even with him—just once!"

Jack turned slightly and saw Isaac standing on the edge of the dance floor with a heavily made up young woman, scowling at them.

"You're getting even with him right now," he said.

"Right now? . . . How?"

"Look to your left."

Kedra glanced left. She started to scowl.

"The best revenge it to let him think you're delighted to be with me. It will drive him nuts." Jack moved them across the floor toward her brother.

Kedra gave Jack a spectacular smile, one her brother couldn't miss, and relaxed into Jack's arms. He pulled her close, leaned his head against the side of hers, and softly sang the love song the band played into her ear.

She felt like a dream in his arms.

They waltzed around the floor, under the glow of a hundred Chinese lanterns, and for a few minutes Jack forgot he was a U.S. Marshal, forgot the girl he held in his arms was his prime suspect.

When the dance ended, she said, "I can't imagine what you must think of me. First, I nearly collide with you on the trail and don't even stop to apologize. Next, you find me wrestling a raccoon, covered in flour, and I almost hit you with a pot. Then I intrude on your swim, trap you in that icy pond, and purposely let you stand there and freeze. And now I have accused you of being a—"

Jack put a finger to her lips. The sensation rocked him from head to heels. He quickly pulled his finger away. "Miss Moore, I think you are a very lovely young lady."

"I'd like it better if you called me Kedra," she said softly, blushing over his compliment.

"Kedra, I'm starved, would you like to come with me to find something besides strawberries and cookies to eat. Or did you have dinner with Trent?"

"He took me to one of the outdoor grills in the park, but I didn't feel much like eating. I know most of the old timers who make the barbecue and you're just as likely to be eating someone's horse as you are to be eating pork or beef."

Jack laughed, "I've been to a few of those kinds of barbecues myself. What do you say we go over to the Hotel Colorado and sit on the patio? You can have something lite, if you don't want a full meal, or just something to drink. I'm sure we can hear the music over there, and we could just talk for a while."

"That sounds wonderful. I'm about dead on my feet. It's been a crazy couple of days, just getting everything ready for these dances."

"Where's the buggy?" Jack asked, leading her off the dance floor.

"Trent took it back to Sarah's house, before the dance started."

"I'll take Soldier and go get it."

"No, let's just ride Soldier over to the hotel."

"That might be hard on your party dress, which is *very* pretty."

"That's nice of you to say."

They stopped next to Soldier.

"If you'll just help me sit side saddle, I think my dress will be safe."

He picked her up and set her sideways on the saddle. She looped her leg around the saddle horn, exposing a very shapely ankle. Jack swung up behind the saddle, his arms encircling her as he took the reins. Holding on to his feelings as tight as the reins, he set Soldier walking up the street toward Grand Avenue.

Jonah Nahtow—1784: In the eastern lands, a new nation called the United States of America has been born of blood and battle, between the whites who wanted the land for a new nation and those who wished to claim the land for their countries beyond the sea. I believe the white man's hunger for land will never be satisfied.

What it means for the children of Lehi has yet to be seen. But I fear that this new nation of liberty will attract many people from lands beyond the sea. This precious land will fill with inhabitants, who will drive the children of Lehi into the most remote and undesirable parts of the land. Even now the great Delaware Nation, which consists of all the Lenni Lenape people, and their tribes, have been pushed off their lands in the east by the white men. They have moved west, into the Ohio valley.

24

Jack settled Kedra into a chair on the dimly lit patio of the Hotel Colorado. They gave the waiter their order and sat back, listening to the music from across the river. At this distance they could hear the music from both dances. The bands and the orchestras traded off playing the popular tunes of the day.

Kedra sighed, "This is heavenly." She fixed Jack with a wry expression. "Next year I don't think I'll volunteer for the Strawberry Day committee."

"It does tend to limit the enjoyment when you're responsible to bring everything off according to public expectation."

"You have no idea." Kedra closed her eyes and swayed with the music of a slow ballad that drifted across the river. "When I got here, yesterday morning, Ed Wallace, the head of the committee, was almost beside himself. The second canvas dance floor hadn't arrived from Grand Junction on the Thursday evening train."

"Does having a canvas dance floor matter so much?"

"It does to the ladies and to Mayor Drach. He ordered Ed to send someone, on the city's private express train, to Grand Junction to track it down and get it to Glenwood."

"Who drew the short straw on that job?"

"I did."

"You were in Grand Junction yesterday?" Jack asked, stunned.

"Most of the day and half the night—I didn't get back to Glenwood until the wee hours this morning."

"It took that long to find the canvas?" Jack tried to make the inquiry sound interested, without sounding like an inquisitor, but his jaw was rigid. *If she was in Grand Junction last night, then the emeralds might already be in Ellis's possession, and that's why he wasn't on the train tonight.* His gut twisted. *Maybe Ellis and Kedra are more than just partners in crime. But if Kedra met Ellis in Grand Junction with the gems—then why is she here? Why didn't she run off with Ellis? Unless she only gave him a few of the gems to fence so she could save the ranch. If that's it, I hope the Grand Junction sheriff can find Ellis before he finds a fence.*

"It took a couple of hours to find out where the canvas floor was."

"Where was it?"

"The car carrying it got hooked up to the wrong train and it ended up fifty miles south, in Montrose. It took a lot of fast-talking and some threats to get it expressed back to Grand Junction. That took hours. Then I had to find men to load it onto the express train."

"It sounds like a miserable day. What did you do to pass the time while you waited for the canvas to come back from Montrose?"

"I slept in the express car."

"What about the engine crew?"

She gave him an odd look. "I don't know. They woke me up when the train from Montrose arrived." She covered a yawn and added, "We didn't get back until two this morning. I was up at four-thirty, and my crew had the floor laid by sunup."

"No wonder you're tired. We can make this a fast dinner and cut the evening short if you'd like."

The waiter arrived with their order.

"I love salmon," Kedra said, putting her napkin in her lap.

"So do I," Jack said, digging into a double order of the broiled fish.

They ate in silence for a while, content to listen to the music floating across the river, enjoying new potatoes and fresh asparagus covered in hollandaise sauce.

A few couples, also dining on the terrace, began to dance on the lawn. Jack and Kedra watched them as they finished eating.

"Would you like dessert?" Jack asked.

"Why don't we dance and let that be our dessert—then you can take me home."

The night was clear and getting cold. Jack felt Kedra shiver as he led her onto the lawn. He took off his jacket and put it around her. She snuggled into it, buttoned it up, and pushed up the sleeves until her hands came out of them. They danced under the light of the stars to "Some Day When Dreams Come True" and then to "From Your Dear Heart to Mine".

Jack never imagined he could feel so conflicted. He'd never felt for a woman what he felt for Kedra Moore. She was more than he'd dreamed of and everything his badge sought to fight against and destroy. He wouldn't compromise his honor or integrity for her. Yet, he couldn't keep his heart from trying to explain away all the evidence against her.

She laid her head against his chest. He tried to keep his heart from racing, but it was impossible. With each passing moment the desire to kiss her grew.

When the song ended she stepped back. "Jack, I want to apologize again for standing you up."

"There's no need."

"Yes, there is. I was too quick to believe what was said about you, because I was recently deceived by someone I trusted."

"Was it a man you had feelings for?" he asked as they sat back down at their table, feeling rotten about trying to lead her into disclosing something he could use against her.

"Yes, but not the way you think. I saw him as a friend. He was someone I ran into, literally, at the train station six months ago. We started writing to each other. He told me he was a traveling salesman. His letters were interesting, full of the people he met and the places he visited." She looked out into the darkness. "I enjoyed the little gifts he sent me."

"It sounds as though the relationship meant more to him than it did to you."

"He went out of his way to make me think I meant everything to him," she said bitterly. I was uncomfortable with how he felt and the last time I saw him, I told him all we could be was friends. He was upset and tried to get me to change my mind. When I wouldn't, he said he understood and left. Then, recently, I found out he wasn't who he said he was. All his pretty talk about his feelings for me were a lie." She looked directly into Jack's eyes. "I can't stand a man who lies about who he is and how he feels."

Is that why you killed Harry?

"It's the reason I was so quick to judge you. I thought you really wanted to go with me. Then I'm told all you want is to win ten dollars and bragging rights."

The word *louse* pounded in Jack's ears. He was everything she'd just said she hated in a man.

There were times, like now, when his job required subterfuge. It was just one of the tools of his trade. He didn't like using it, and most the time didn't have to, but this time, he had no choice. If he was going to find the emeralds and make good on his word to President Roosevelt, to bring Will and Harry's murderer to justice, he had to use whatever means he could legally find to flush out his prey.

"I can understand why you believed what you heard, and I accept your apology, so let's just forget about the whole thing," he said, hoping to end the discussion. He began to reach for her hand and thought better of it. "It's getting late, why don't I take you home," he suggested, growing anxious to escape her company. There were a lot of things he had to sort out, things she might keep him from seeing clearly if he spent any more time with her.

He pushed back his chair. "Are you ready?"

"I guess." The orchestra, across the river took up a slow instrumental number. "But could we have one more dance?"

She smelled of cloves and a summer evening's breeze. She felt like she belonged in his arms. With her head on his shoulder, she closed her eyes. He looked down at her long black lashes, dancing her across the lawn.

She moved with him as though they were one.

His arm drew her closer.

She came willingly.

His steps slowed.

The deep shadows of the garden hid them from everyone.

She lifted her head from his shoulder and looked up into his face.

He started to bend his head to meet hers. A trickle of sweat rolled down his back. He straightened suddenly.

She looked at him with a slightly puzzled expression as the song ended.

"We better go," he said, and led her back through the hotel.

Kedra was reluctant to end the evening when they pulled up in front of the barn. What had started out as an ugly trick had turned into a lovely evening. It even felt good to tell Jack about Morgan, although she'd refrained from saying Morgan's name.

"You know, I didn't keep my promise," she said, laying a hand on his arm, keeping him in the buggy a moment longer. "I didn't introduce you to any of the people I know."

"That's okay . . . perhaps some other time." He climbed out, helped her out of the buggy, and reached back in to get her suitcase.

He sounds distracted. Kedra frowned. *Maybe he didn't enjoy the evening as much as I did.* "I'll take my suitcase inside," she said, wishing he didn't have to settle the horses and could come in with her.

A sudden rush of embarrassment overtook her, and she wondered if she'd been too forward during the evening. *Have I made him uncomfortable?* Had her enjoyment of that last dance and the ride home been too obvious? She disliked girls who set their caps at men. *Is that what he thought I was doing, when I suggested that last dance and practically hugged him all the way home for warmth?*

She took off his coat and handed it to him. "Thanks, I should have brought a shawl."

He nodded, his expression unreadable, but she felt as though he'd closed her out.

Her embarrassment grew with his silence. "Thank you for dinner and a lovely evening," she said, quickly turning away.

He put a hand on her shoulder. "Thank *you* for believing me and spending the evening with me. I enjoyed it. Now, I should get these horses bedded down."

She watched him lead the horses away. His parting words sounded sincere, and made her heart smile.

Jack took his time bedding down Molly and Soldier. He was a drowning man with no hope of rescue. *Why? Why her . . . of all the women I've met. This country is full of beautiful girls, some with Kedra's talents too. I've met very attractive girls who are members of the church as well. Why didn't I fall for one of them?*

Kedra's gold eyes looked up at him, and he knew. Her hypnotic eyes had pulled him in like a whirlpool. Even now he couldn't get enough of them.

He tried to shut out her eyes. When he couldn't, he focused his mind on Luke Laramore, who'd be back in town tomorrow.

My time is running out. Unless I can find some evidence against someone else . . . no later than Monday night, I'll have no choice but to arrest Kedra. There is more than enough evidence to do it right now. He groaned, patted Soldier and left the barn. *If there was just something I could find to refute all the evidence against her. But how can I explain away the letters between her and Harry, alias Morgan O'Shea.* There was no doubt in his mind that they were one and the same. *Harry's letters, along with all the other evidence, ties Kedra directly into the robbery and murders.*

He closed the door to the small guest room and lay back on the bed. Kedra's room was right above his. Sometimes when she was in her bedroom he could hear her moving around.

The house above him was silent. *Sleep well, while you can, Kedra. Your time is running out.*

25

Sunday, June 21, 1908

Jack walked Soldier through the darkness to Sheriff Hadlock's house. It had been a miserable Sabbath. The Glenwood Saints had opened their hearts and homes to him. And how was he repaying their trust? He was deceiving all of them. Not by his faith, because that gift was ever his companion, but by his conduct.

All of the Saints had seen him with Kedra last night. Their knowing looks and gentle teasing during the Sunday meeting had made his face burn with shame. Kedra had taken the teasing with good grace, and that just made the whole thing worse.

Lunch with the Duke family had been uncomfortable, too. Alfred, the Duke's little boy, was relentless in his questions about Jack's interest in Kedra, no matter how Jack tried to distract him. Mary, his mother, finally told him to quit pestering Brother Jack. He used his appointment to visit the Bowles' ranch as an excuse to leave as soon as he politely could.

The Bowles were one of the first ranching families in the Glenwood Springs area. They ran an impressive operation. Jack absorbed a wealth of Rocky Mountain ranching information over the course of the afternoon from them. They kindly invited him to stay for supper. His appetite was much better at their table than it had been at the Duke's table. But now, supper felt like a rock in his stomach.

He settled Soldier into Tate's small stable, dreading the coming meeting. With the evidence he now had, he knew Luke would push for an immediate arrest. *I have to buy a little more time . . . but for what . . . the emeralds? Every piece of evidence I've turned up has put one more nail in Kedra Moore's coffin. Finding the emeralds in her possession would be like personally putting the hangman's noose around her neck.*

At the back door, Jack stopped and said a prayer for strength and guidance, but mostly for the courage to do his duty and the insight to see the truth. Reminding himself of his oath as a U.S. Marshal, and the one he'd made to President Roosevelt, he ducked through the door.

The smell of coffee filled the brightly lit kitchen. Tate and Luke were both eating strawberry pie.

"I would think after yesterday, you wouldn't have the stomach to look anymore strawberries in the eye," Jack said to Tate.

"As it turned out, I didn't get to eat too many strawberries. My hands were full all day with minor scuffles and disorderly conduct, something Mayor Drach wanted squashed and kept quiet."

Jack took off his hat and sat down at the kitchen table across from Luke, who continued to industriously shovel pie into his mouth. He nodded at Jack and kept shoveling.

Tate finished off his pie and pushed his plate aside. "I have a lot to tell you and none of its good."

"Me too," Luke mumbled with his mouth full.

"So, who wants to start?" Jack asked, stretching out his long legs, resigning himself to hear more bad news.

"Tate will." Luke gestured at the sheriff with his fork.

Tate sat his coffee cup down and leaned forward. "The sheriff in Grand Junction returned my call this afternoon. He found Drew Ellis."

"Great!" Jack said, relieved.

"Not great," Tate countered, "Ellis is dead—murdered.

"How?—When?" Jack barked out the questions.

"By a single bullet fired pointblank to the head. The corner's best guess is that he was killed sometime Friday evening."

Jack had planned to present his theory that Ellis was the mastermind behind the robbery and murders to Luke, now that theory had literally been shot down. "Where was he found?"

"In a seedy hotel, just off the railroad tracks— According to the hotel manager, Ellis had never been there before. Another thing—no one, so far, has admitted to hearing the shot."

"That's probably because of the hotel's close proximity to the railroad yard," Luke said.

"There was a do not disturb sign on the door," Tate continued. "And Friday night, the manager found an envelope with Ellis's name and room number on it under the door to his office. It contained money to pay for an additional night. So, the body wasn't discovered until this morning, when Ellis was supposed to have checked out."

Jack's stomach was in freefall. The hangman's noose was in his hand. The answer to one more question could put it around Kedra's neck. He cleared his throat and asked, "Did anyone see someone go into, or come out of, Ellis's room on Friday night?"

"That is the one small glimmer of light the Grand Junction sheriff has, Tate said. "He questioned the other occupants of the hotel. Most of them are drunks and derelicts. The one in the room next door, Joe Dobbins, swears he was woken up by a crashing sound in Ellis's room, around eight-thirty on Friday night. He said he heard something hit the wall between the rooms, followed by the sound of bottles or glasses falling over. That fits with the description of the crime scene. Ellis fell into the wall, crashed down on a table containing glasses and a couple of bottles of whiskey, before he hit the floor. There were glasses and bottles lying around Ellis's body."

"Then the sheriff believes he's telling the truth?"

"He does. When Dobbins heard the door to the room open, he peeked out the window. He says he saw a woman coming out of Ellis's room."

Jack's whole body tensed as though preparing to take a punch he couldn't avoid. "Can he describe her?"

"He didn't see her face. She was turned away from him, wearing a dark colored dress. But he described her as being tall and slender. Her hair was black, and, he swears, she was wearing something white, and I quote, 'like feathers in her hair'."

Jack sagged back against his chair. He forced the words out, slipping the noose over Kedra's head. "Miss Moore was in Grand Junction Friday night."

"What?!" Luke exploded. "How do you know she was in Grand Junction Friday night?"

"She told me last night, over dinner."

Resigning himself to the truth, Jack rehearsed everything Kedra had told him about her trip to Grand Junction.

Tate looked like he'd aged five years. "I guess there's no doubt now. Miss Moore did commit the robbery, and she killed four men to cover up her crime." He shook his head, "I still can't believe it."

"Believe it!" Luke snapped. "After what I found out about her father, I'd say she's just a chip off the old block."

"What did you learn about Eli Moore?" Jack asked

"It took three deputies, working around the clock for the past week, to come up with the information, but it was worth it." Luke wiped his mustache. "Eli Moore was born Elijah Moorland. His family lived up in the Dakotas during the gold rush years. They were farmers, but Elijah wasn't satisfied with that life. He ran off with a miner's daughter by the name of Eulalie O'Shea."

"O'Shea!" Jack exclaimed. *Effie never mentioned Isaac's mother's maiden name.*

"That's right. Do you know that name?"

"I do, but it can wait. Go on."

"My deputies tracked Moorland to the vicinity of Cheyenne Station in September of 1878, where the last big treasure coach out of Deadwood was held up. The gang that robbed it got away with 300,000 dollars."

"Wow!" Tate exclaimed.

"Yeah— Most of the money was recovered, but not all of it."

"You think Eli Moore, or rather Elijah Moorland was in the gang that robbed that coach and got away."

"Can't prove it, but a young man fitting his description was part of the gang. He was never caught. After the robbery, Moorland disappeared. We couldn't find any trace of him until we began looking into his wife's family. He turned up in New Orleans, where his wife's family was originally from, calling himself Elisha Lander."

"How do you know, Elijah Moorland and Elisha Lander are the same person?" Tate asked.

"His wife's name was Eulalie, and Lander fit the description of Elijah Moorland. The *Landers* lived in New Orleans for nearly four years. They had a son, who they named Isaac, about a year before Mrs. Lander met with a suspicious accident and died. Nothing was ever proven, but Mrs. Lander's sister, Ursula Warren, went on the record as saying she was sure Elisha Lander had killed her sister."

"From what Effie told me, that same sister was the one Eli sent Isaac to live with after his wife died, because he didn't feel he could take care of a baby," Jack said.

"It was more than that. According to my deputies, Lander didn't want the baby. One of the wet nurses overheard him cursing his late wife and wondering if he could tolerate living with a son that looked exactly like his mother."

"That surprises me," Jack said. "Effie Blue, the housekeeper on the Moore's ranch, told me Eli was anxious to get Isaac back from his sister-in-law and did it as soon as he got the ranch going."

"Maybe he had a change of heart," Tate suggested.

Luke frowned. "Or, what the nurse said was misinterpreted. He might have wanted to keep his son, but couldn't. Lander was flat broke when he left New Orleans in 1882. It seems Mrs. Lander had very expensive tastes. The domestic help said the Landers used to have terrible fights over the money Mrs. Lander spent."

"No wonder he doesn't talk about his first wife. It sounds like love turned to hate over money," Jack mused. "Where did Eli go after he left New Orleans?"

"We lost him for a few years, but he finally turned up in Wyoming, still using the name Elisha Lander. He was working on the Sweet Grass Ranch; a big spread about five miles west of Douglas. According to the only ranch hand the deputies could find, who had worked on the ranch during the time Elisha Lander was there, Lander was determined to prove he had what it took to be the ramrod for the ranch. He got his chance to shine when another big ranch near them, the River Rock Ranch, started encroaching on the Sweet Grasses' range. Lander suggested they evict the River Rock's cattle from the range the Sweet Grass Ranch considered their territory. A range war started."

The hair on the back of Jack's neck stood on end. Suppressed memories, pushed against the barrier he'd erected to keep them out of his mind. "Are you saying Eli, or rather Elisha, started that range war?"

"Don't know—I only know what the ranch hand told us, that the idea was put into the owner's head by Elisha Lander. The ranch hand my deputies talked to, an old geezer, wouldn't tell them about the range war, except there was some kind of tragedy that stopped the war. At that point Elisha Lander disappeared."

Jack's heart was pounding against his sternum. He knew what had stopped that range war, but it wasn't relevant to his present investigation, at least he didn't think it was. He decided to keep it to himself. There was no point in dredging up horrors that had nothing to do with the emerald robbery and the murders of two U.S. Marshals.

Instead he said, "I know the rest of it. According to Effie, Eli's wife, a Nahtow Indian, was badly injured in a carriage accident about the same time the range war started. She gave birth to Kedra and died that same day. Effie, who lost her first husband in that range war, delivered a stillborn baby the day Kedra was born. The doctor asked her to be Kedra's wet nurse." Jack frowned. "Effie didn't tell me Eli went by a different name in Wyoming."

"She probably didn't know him as Elisha Lander. My deputies believe he left Wyoming calling himself Eli Moore," Luke explained.

Jack was silent, processing all the information he'd just learned. Then he asked, "Has Moore been in trouble with the law since he came to Colorado?"

"An old timer, who said he was in the saloon in Leadville when Moore won the High Peak Ranch in a poker game, told my deputies Moore won the ranch by cheating, but it couldn't be proven."

"Elijah Moorland, alias Elisha Lander, alias Eli Moore, has led quite a charmed life. If all your information is correct, he's not only gotten away with grand larceny, but murder too," Jack said slowly. "That makes me wonder if he had a role in the emerald robbery. Was he the brains behind it, and how far would he go to protect himself?"

"What do you mean?" Tate asked.

"Would he frame his own daughter for the crimes he committed?"

"Jack, that's a pretty far reach. I agree he might be the brains behind it, and that would make him just as guilty, but nothing we know, so far, says he had anything to do with the crime."

"No, everything we know *absolutely* points to Kedra Moore," Jack agreed, bitterly. "In fact, everything I've learned in the last few days labels her a thief and a murderer. What bothers me is that there's almost *too much* evidence against her. I can't help feeling she's being set up as the scape goat—whether or not she was involved in the theft and murders."

"What else have you found?" Luke asked.

"For one, she's a crack shot. She can move and shoot with amazing speed. I watched her pull a rifle, turn and fire, bringing down an elk at a hundred yards with a head shot in less than five seconds."

"That's good shooting," Luke said.

"She also told me she'd do anything to save the ranch, which by the way is in severe financial trouble."

Jack went over everything he knew about the ranch's growing debts before he told them about his search of the house.

"When I searched Miss Moore's room, I found the special edition of the Avalanche inside a chemistry book. The page it was inserted in was about Chloral Hydrate."

"Knock out drops?" Tate asked.

"Yes. I believe Drew Ellis put them into the coffee he brought into the express car while Harry was gone."

"If that's true, it could account for what happened to Will," Luke growled.

"If he only drank—say half a cup of coffee. He might not have been fully knocked out, just groggy enough to lie down on the bed."

"So, when Kedra came out of hiding and Harry opened the safe, Marshal Forbes surprised them," Tate put in.

"That would account for the head wound Will had," Jack said grimly.

"And if Miss Moore thought he was dead, that would explain how she was able to shoot Harry without Will shooting her," Luke speculated.

"Will must have only been stunned for a few moments, but it was long enough for Kedra to shoot Harry, before Will attacked her."

"I can't imagine where he found the strength." Tate shook his head.

"Must have been pure will power," Jack said.

There was a moment of reverent silence for Will's bravery.

Luke broke the silence, "Did you find anything else?"

"I found a Webley Bull Dog revolver in a hidden compartment in her desk." Jack pulled it from his pocket and laid it on the table. "Four of the cartridges have been fired. Then there's this"—he pulled the letter from Morgan O'Shea out of his pocket and tossed it to Luke—"Read this and you'll get a wallop of surprise."

Luke opened the flap, pulled out the content, and demanded, "What is Harry's picture doing in this letter?"

"Look at the signature at the bottom of the letter."

Tate leaned over Luke's shoulder as he found the signature.

"O'Shea?" Luke asked in surprise, looking up at Jack.

"Read the lines I've underlined."

Luke's eyes widened. "Are you're telling me Harry is Morgan O'Shea?"

Jack told him about Kedra's reaction to Harry's picture in the paper.

"Then Kedra Moore must be the woman Harry met on the day of the robbery," Tate exclaimed.

"It also means Harry Walsh was in on the robbery," Luke said with cold conviction.

"The contradiction is—I'm almost certain Kedra didn't know who Harry was until after he was killed." Jack told them what Kedra had said about recently being deceived by a man.

"I don't get it," Tate said.

"I'm not sure I do either," Luke put in. "If Harry was this Morgan O'Shea—and he and Kedra planned the robbery—she must have known who he was."

"Then, why did she kill him?" Tate asked.

Jack leaned forward. "I'm not sure she did. Ellis could have killed Will, Harry, and Ito."

"But now Ellis is dead too. So did Kedra kill him because he killed Harry?" Tate wondered.

"The thing that keeps bothering me is all the carefully placed evidence leading us directly to Miss Moore. The only thing I haven't found so far is a single emerald. If she felt safe leaving the murder weapon in the hidden compartment in her desk, then why not the emeralds? For that matter, if she intended to kill Ellis to eliminate everyone who was involved in the crime, why didn't she do it on the train? By his own admission, Ellis banged on the door of the express car before he pulled the emergency stop cord. If Kedra wanted to kill everyone else who was involved, she could have easily opened the door just enough to shoot Ellis and still have made her get away. So why did she wait? She's the one who had the emeralds. All that was left was the getaway."

Tate shook his head. "I'm getting more confused by the minute."

"And I'm starting to see the light," Jack said. "I believe Kedra Moore is being systematically framed for this crime." The words rang true in his heart as he said them, and he found the first glimmer of hope. "I think when we find out more about Morgan O'Shea, and who he associated with, we'll find out who's behind this crime. Think about it. The name O'Shea is tied to Isaac. We need to know if there is a connection between Harry and Isaac. Somehow I don't think the name Morgan O'Shea is just a coincidence."

Luke nodded solemnly. "I'll admit that other people in Miss Moore's family may be connected to the crime, but I still believe Miss

Moore was involved, because I can't just discount the evidence against her. I agree, that there's more to this crime than we know—yet." He threw Jack a pained looked. "I think we both knew that either Will or Harry had to be in on it. Ortiz was too paranoid to talk about the emeralds to anyone. The information about the emeralds had to have come from Will or Harry."

"Maybe it's time to bring Miss Moore in and find out just what she knows," Tate said.

"That's what I think," Luke said.

"I want a few more days. I feel like I'm getting close. Kedra is beginning to trust me. She wouldn't have told me about Morgan O'Shea if she didn't. My feeling is, she wasn't involved in the crime, but she knows something—something she's afraid to come forward with."

"Do you think she's being threatened?" Tate asked.

"Or she may be protecting her father and brother," Luke muttered.

"Either way, I intend to find out. If I can get her to tell me, then I might be able to recover the emeralds before whoever stole them finds out she's told me. I'm afraid if we don't recover them before we bring Miss Moore in, we never will."

How are you going to get her to confide in you, without telling her who you are?" Tate asked.

"Our date last night told me she needs someone to talk to. If I can get her alone, in the right circumstances, I think I can coax her into telling me what she knows."

"I don't like it. The longer we wait to make an arrest, the more likely it is that the emeralds will disappear," Luke countered.

"If she won't tell me anything in the next couple of days, I'll call you. I want both of you to come out and arrest her. I'm going to stay undercover and watch her father's and brother's reactions. I believe one of them is our real culprit."

"Other than the name O'Shea, why do you think her brother may be involved?" Luke asked.

Jack outlined what Effie had told him about Isaac's feelings toward Kedra. The things he'd done to her in the past and the mean spirited trick he'd talked Trent into playing on her.

"He's definitely capable of framing Kedra," Jack said with absolute certainty.

"Jack, right now we don't have any evidence that Miss Moore's father or brother were involved in the crime. You didn't find anything in their rooms when you searched the house, did you?" Luke asked.

"No, I didn't," Jack admitted. He'd thought the women's clothes in Isaac's closet were odd. Now he understood them. The initials E.O. on the handkerchief stood for Eulalie O'Shea, Isaac's mother. *Those clothes are probably all he has left of his mother, just like the totem and jewelry Kedra has is all that's left of her mother.*

"We have solid proof against Miss Moore," Luke continued, holding Jack's eyes. "It may not all make sense right now, but the sheer weight of it is compelling." Luke's face, hardened. "I warned you not to be fooled by a pretty face, Jack. I can tell you don't want to believe Kedra Moore is guilty—Tate doesn't either. But if you can't produce any evidence to the contrary by the time we come out to arrest her . . . say no later than Wednesday morning, it will be because she *is* the one who committed the robbery and murders, and we have all the proof we need to convict her, whether or not you find the emeralds."

26

Isaac unlocked and opened his bedroom door. A wave of hot, stagnant air hit him. It was one of the disadvantages of always keeping his room locked. He crossed the dark room and opened the window. He couldn't turn on the light and open the window without inviting an invasion of moths and other night insects.

Kedra had assured him the screens for the upstairs windows would arrive before the hot summer months set in. He grimaced, *So much for Kedra's promises.*

Thrusting his upper body out the window, he breathed in the crisp night air, letting it flow over his heat flushed skin.

A dark shadow moved across the yard toward the house. It vanished before Isaac could identify it.

Reluctantly, he pulled his head back into the stuffy room and crossed to the door. He opened it wide, hoping to draw the air from the window into the room. Normally, he kept his door locked when he was in his room, and he always locked it when he left.

The errand he had to do would only take him away from the room for a few moments. He reasoned that his short absence, couple with the fact that no one else was upstairs, made it safe for him to leave his bedroom door open.

He lowered the dropdown attic steps, climbed into the attic, and retrieved his suitcase.

Back in his room, he shut and locked the door, switched on the light, and deposited his suitcase on the bed as he crossed the room to the window. The room was still uncomfortably hot. He inhaled another breath of cool air, stated to shut the window, and then decided to just pull the heavy shade down, hoping to discourage the bugs, while still allowing the refreshing night air to waft into the room.

For the next ten minutes, he pulled clothes from his closet and drawers, packing them neatly in the suitcase. When the majority of his packing was done, he walked around the bed and moved aside a small lamp table. Dropping to his knees, he pulled back the edge of the carpet. His fingers moved over the floorboards and stopped. He inserted a pocketknife between two boards and lifted away a section of the floor.

He put his hand into the hole in the floor and drew out a thick stack of twenty-dollar bills. He tucked some of them into the inside breast pocket of his jacket, before replacing the stack of bills in the hole. His hand stopped to caress a beaded leather pouch. Then abruptly, as though compelled by a force beyond his control, he lifted the large pouch out of the hole. He opened the neck of the bag and poured part of the contents into his hand, rolling the green gems around in his palm. He sighed, and forced himself to pour them back into the pouch.

A hard knock sounded on the door.

Isaac started at the unexpected interruption. The hand funneling the gems into the pouch jerked. Some of the gems fell onto the floorboards and rolled into the hole in the floor. Others rolled under the bed.

"Mr. Isaac, I have your clean shirts and collars, and I'd like to empty your trash," Effie called.

"Just a minute!" Isaac shouted irritably. Stuffing the rest of the emeralds back into the bag, he shoved it into the hole, and then quickly replaced the floorboards, the rug, and the table.

Letting Effie into the room, he growled, "I only want these two shirts and three extra collars. Put the others in the closet, get the trash, and be quick about it."

"You could be a little more courteous, seeing as how it's Sunday, and I went out of my way to get these shirts washed and pressed for your trip," Effie snapped.

"You're only doing a job you get paid for," Isaac retorted.

Effie sniffed and said, "If you'll leave your door unlocked, I'll clean your room tomorrow, while you're gone."

"No! I don't want you in here. Just put the other shirts in the closet, collect the trash, and get out."

Effie opened the closet door and started to hang up the shirts.

"Not there," Isaac growled, going over to the closet.

After the shirts were arranged as Isaac wanted, Effie took the trashcan and headed for the open door. Isaac followed, intending to close and lock it behind her.

Effie suddenly shrieked, "How did you get in here? Get away from that door, you no good varmint."

Isaac grinned, spotting the source of Effie's outburst. That ring-tailed varmint was one more reason why Isaac always kept his window closed and his door locked.

Effie rushed toward Scoundrel.

The wily raccoon was standing on his hind legs trying to twist Kedra's doorknob. He managed to open Kedra's door just as Effie swung her foot at him. The raccoon deftly dodged Effie's foot and shot into Kedra's bedroom.

Isaac laughed as Effie rushed after him. Before he closed his door, Isaac heard Effie yell, "You may have escaped this time, but I'll make a coon skin cap out of you yet!"

Still laughing, Isaac shut and locked his door, aware he was running behind schedule. He had to make the last train to Aspen.

The Sunday night train mostly took miners, who'd spent the weekend in Glenwood, back to the mines in Carbondale and Aspen. If he didn't hurry, he wouldn't make that train. A glance at the clock told him the train was already at the station. It would leave in forty minutes.

Again he opened the hiding place in the floor, took out the items he'd recently purchased—expensive gifts for Goldie Yates. Her invitation to visit, while she stayed with her aunt in Aspen, saved him the cost of going to Denver, where Goldie lived.

After tucking the gifts in his suitcase, he packed the shirts and collars Effie had brought, and then carefully arranged the new blue stripped waistcoat on top of the shirts. Satisfied, he closed and locked the suitcase.

For a moment he considered searching for the gems that had rolled under the bed. *No time,* he decided. *The emeralds won't go anywhere. I'll find them when I return. Right now I have to make that train. My future depends on it.* After again closing and concealing the hiding place, he shut the window.

The clock on the dresser chimed the half hour.

He pulled the key from his pocket, grabbed his suitcase, went out the door, and locked it.

Buck had his horse standing ready. He swung himself into the saddle, cursing Kedra under his breath for taking the buggy to her church meeting and telling him she wouldn't be home in time for him to take it, while Buck lashed his suitcase to his saddle.

"I'll leave the horse at the train station. Kedra said she'd go pick him up and stable him at Voorhees before she comes home—so no one needs to come pick me up when I return," he told Buck and kicked the horse's flanks hard.

It was late when Kedra pulled into the ranch. Buck met her when she stopped Molly in front of the barn.

She lifted a questioning brow.

"Jack's not back yet," Buck said, helping her out of the buggy.

"He was going to visit the Bowles' ranch after lunch," Kedra said carelessly. "He may still there."

She'd been glad Jack had gone to the Duke's for lunch. By the time church was over, she was tired of all the knowing and enquiring looks everyone was casting at her and Jack.

At lunch, she'd told Sarah and Jacob, "It was only a date of convenience—on both our parts. No one else asked me to the dance," she confessed, humiliating herself. "And it would have been embarrassing to go by myself. He told me he wanted to be introduced to people, that's why he asked me to go with him."

"Did you introduce him to a lot of people?" Sarah asked lightly.

"Well, no—"

She told them about Isaac's trick and how she and Jack had gotten even with him and Trent.

"So, the tender looks I saw you two exchanging on the dance floor, were strictly for the benefit of Isaac and Trent?" Jacob asked.

"That's right. Now can we change the subject?"

Thankfully, the Powells let the subject go, but as Kedra got ready for bed, her mind relived the evening with Jack. She could have introduced him to any number of people, except he didn't ask her to, and she hadn't thought of it.

She put herself back into the last dance they'd shared on the lawn of the Hotel Colorado, reliving it. The whole thing was so romantic, with the orchestra playing in the distance and the stars and moon overhead. Jack's embrace was so gentle, almost as though he was afraid to hold her too tight.

"No!" She came out of the memory on a jarring thought. Her fingers stopped braiding her hair.

When her mind quit spinning, she relived the dance again, this time allowing herself to see and feel the reluctance in his embrace. *He was uncomfortable, just as he was on the drive home. He wasn't being honest with me when he said he enjoyed the evening with me. He was being polite!* She was certain of it. *I made a fool of myself with him—again. I took his kindness, and yes, his pity, over the trick Isaac played on me for something more. He was just trying to make up for Isaac's horrid behavior by being especially charming.*

Her face burned. Placing her cool hands on her cheeks, she got up from the dressing table and climbed into bed. *From the moment we met, I knew it would be a mistake to get involved with Jack Garrison.* A little sob worked its way up her throat. She turned her face into her pillow before she let it out. *At least I won't have to endure the shame of seeing him for much longer. He'll be gone by the end of the week, along with all the other ranch hands.*

That thought made her cry in earnest. Not just because Jack would leave, and she couldn't deny she would miss him, but also because she knew her father meant to sell, not only the cattle, but the ranch too.

He hadn't said so, but there was no doubt in her mind that he still meant to sell the High Peak Ranch. There was nothing she could do to save the ranch, and losing it was the worst thing she could imagine.

Aba Nahtow—1798: I am chief of the Nahtow and keeper of the library. As the children of Lehi are pushed westward, off their native lands, the Nahtow have gone with them. The government of The United States is confining the Indians—the whites have displaced by their coming—to places they call "reserved lands". Many tribes have been forced to settle on these reserved lands. We travel among the tribes, in these reserves, that we may learn their genealogies and histories. But like our brothers, we find the lands, the white men have delegated to the Indians, less than desirable and hard to live upon.

27

MONDAY, JUNE 22, 1908

No one was in the dining room when Jack entered, hungry for breakfast. The table wasn't even set. The smell of hot muffins and bacon pulled him toward the kitchen. He could hear Effie in there scurrying around, muttering to herself.

"Can I help?" he asked, looking at her heat flushed face.

"Yes! Get the muffins out of the oven and put them into that bowl over there," Effie said, brushing back a tentacle of hair that had escaped her bun, and nodding at a large mixing bowl.

Jack grabbed a pair of hot pads and opened the big oven door. He pulled out four pans of blueberry muffins, and set them on the large butcher-block table behind him. After retrieving the bowl, he juggled the hot muffins out of their muffin tins, stacking them in the bowl.

"Where are all the Moores this morning?" he asked.

"Isaac left on the train last night for Aspen, before you got home. Kedra took her father into town early this morning to catch the train for Carbondale." Effie paused. "I hope you don't mind eating with the crew in the mess hall today."

"Not a bit, but won't Miss Moore be back before lunch?"

"I doubt it. After she drops her father off at the station, she has to see that the canvas floors are swept, rolled up, and stored. The band stands have to be dismantled, and then she has a meeting with Ed Wallace and the Strawberry Day committee to review how the event went and what they could do better next year."

"Will she be back by dinner?"

Effie smiled in that "you miss her, don't you" kind of way and said, "She told me not to expect her."

Jack's hopes to talk with Kedra plummeted. *Maybe I should go into town and see if I can help with the Strawberry Day clean up.* Except, even if he went and helped, he knew she wouldn't have time to talk with him privately. And what he needed to learn from her demanded privacy—and time.

Effie's hands went to her hips. Almost as though she'd been reading his mind, she said, "You might as well put going after Kedra out of your mind. I need you here today to help me. Since Kedra is gone, you'll have to deliver the men's lunches. Now get those muffins out to the table, and then get back in here to help me with the bacon."

"Yes, ma'am," Jack said and picked up the large bowl of muffins.

He knew when to argue and when it was pointless to try. With a sinking feeling, he went into the ranch hands' mess hall and put the muffins on the table, trying to figure out when he could talk to Kedra.

"I should be back by about ten o'clock tonight, if everything goes well," Eli said, giving Kedra a hug. "Don't come get me. I'll just stay in town for the night. You can fetch me in the morning, when I call."

"All right," Kedra said, kissing his cheek.

The whistle on the Midland Train to Carbondale and Aspen blew a long blast. Eli hurried along the platform. He turned and waved at Kedra, before he climbed into the train.

She returned his wave; then quickly turned toward the long day of work ahead of her. Strawberry Day was always held on Saturday and went well into the night. That meant the cleanup had to wait until Monday. Sunday was a community day of rest, well except for the saloons, but even they were being pressured by the churches in town to observe the Sabbath day.

Kedra was grateful she had enough to do in town today to keep her away from the ranch—and Jack. Already, this morning, she'd had to push their evening together out of her mind multiple times. Turning her mind firmly to her assigned clean up tasks, she drove the buggy down Cooper Street.

In the early afternoon, the regularly scheduled D&RGW passenger train from Salt Lake City pulled into the Glenwood Springs station. The usual hustle and bustle of arriving and departing passengers ensued. In the midst of the commotion, a very tall Indian got out of the livestock car.

He towered over the people, eliciting stares and whispered comments as he walked along the platform. This was such a common occurrence in the big brave's life that he thought nothing of it.

In a pair of elk skin moccasins, with a bedroll and ditty bag over his shoulder, he walked up the grassy slope of the train station in buckskin pants, a cotton shirt, and a bead worked leather vest. His long black hair was braided at the temples, which were beginning to show some gray. The two braids were pulled back and held in place with a silver ornament. From it dangled two white feathers and a row of tiger-eye stone beads.

His association with the white man had taught him to keep his weapons out of sight. The gasp of a woman assured him, he was intimidating enough without displaying the knife and ax he carried.

He reached the street and looked around. A wide-eyed mother stopped short, obviously reluctant to cross his path. She clutched her two small sons as though he would steal them from her.

He looked down on her with bright gold eyes, and said in better English than the woman had probably ever heard or spoken, "Forgive me, ma'am. I do not mean to terrify you or your children. However, I can help neither my race nor my size." He smiled warmly, something he'd learn to do when he attended Harvard University. There was something about his smile that usually pacified the whites.

"My brother," a voice called from down the street.

The big brave winked at the woman's two sons. He could tell they were more intrigued by him than terrified. Turning away, he lifted a hand in greeting and strode toward John Gray Wolf.

Aba Nahtow—1820: I am old now. In my days I have seen the decline of my people, the Nahtow. Once we were five thousand strong, now we number less than three hundred and our numbers dwindle daily.

The white men have enticed my people and my children. Because their minds are bright, they have sought learning among the whites and found jobs in the government agency that deals with the Indians. Many of the Nahtow now live among the whites and say the mission of the Nahtow is over, but this is not true. The prophecies of our father, Nahtow, are not all fulfilled. Still, there are fewer of my people who desire to fulfill the mission with which we were entrusted. They have lost their honor and now seek the things of the white man's world and its honors.

Mark Nahtow—1829: There are barely two hundred that still wear the Nahtow totem. Most of them are of the royal line and the spirit of our mission is still strong in their hearts. The rest of the Nahtow have drifted away into the tribes of the land and the world of the white man. We are too few now to do more than keep our own genealogy and that of the Delaware nation among whom we have chosen to live—as least for a time.

It has been five years since the Nahtow gathered on the Footstool of God and it is in my heart to go and see if any of my scattered brethren will come for our pow-wow. I have pages to put into the book of Nahtow and many genealogies from the Cherokee, Chickasaw, Choctaw, Creek, Seminole, and Natchez Indians to place in the library. Moreover, I long to see my brothers, the Ute Indians. Long have the Utes lived in the place called Colorado, near the traditional home of the Nahtow.

Kedra started for home, just as twilight settled in. The odd feeling, which had come over her during the afternoon, again crawled over her. She slowed Molly and listened, but heard nothing. It wasn't in her nature to be spooked by the darkness or by being alone. Still, she couldn't shake the feeling she was being watched—followed. As a precaution she took the rifle from under the buggy's seat and laid it across her lap.

When the gate to the ranch came into view, she realized how tense she was and rolled her shoulders. The ride home had seemed unusually long. Now the lights of the house and the cabins welcomed her with the assurance that everything was all right.

The tension in her shoulders returned when Jack came out of the house as she pulled Molly up in front of the barn.

He stepped to Molly's head and held her still, while she got out of the buggy.

"You've certainly put in a long day. Effie told me about the Strawberry Day cleanup."

Taking the opening he'd just provided, she said wearily, "Yes, it's been a *very* long day, and I'm worn out." She smiled at him sweetly. "Would you mind, very much, taking care of Molly for me? All I've been able to think about for the last hour is a hot bath and a soft bed."

"I'd be happy to take care of Molly."

"Thank you."

Jack smiled, and said invitingly, "I was hoping we could spend some time together this evening."

The warmth of his voice made a little demon of hope raise its ugly head. She ruthlessly squashed it. *I've made a big enough fool of myself with you Mr. Garrison. I don't intend to continue that folly.*

"I wouldn't be good company tonight. I'm too tired, and . . . it's a bit awkward being alone with you in the house overnight."

"Kedra, if you don't want me in the house while your father and brother are gone, I'll go bunk in with Buck."

It was on her tongue to tell him to do just that, when the eerie feeling of being watched again shivered along her arms. It was so unnerving; she nearly offered to let Jack sleep in her father's bedroom.

"Jack, I'm not worried about your being in the house. I trust you. Now, if you'll excuse me, I'll say goodnight."

"Sleep well," he called as she walked away.

Sinking into a hot bath, Kedra let go of all the tension Strawberry Day had built up inside of her. The responsibilities she'd undertaken for the music and dances had weighed heavily on her. Now that it was successfully over, the things she'd kept locked in the back of her mind escaped their prison and pushed their way forward. They wound around her in ever tightening bands.

What should I do? If I come forward now, what will that U.S. Marshal think? How can I explain why I didn't come forward right away? I can't tell him what I suspect. I can't do that to Papa.

She stayed in the bathtub wrestling with her dilemma until the water was noticeably cool. Before she got too chilled, she got out, dried off, put on a warm flannel nightgown and a heavy robe.

As she tied the belt on her robe, something moved across the floor beyond the door.

She froze. The relaxation infused by the hot water vanished in an instant. The eerie sensation she'd been troubled by all afternoon loomed over her.

The house was never locked. Anyone could come in at any time.

"Jack, is that you?" she whispered through the door.

A series of rattling taps answered her.

Her heart pounded in her ears. Frantically, she looked around the bathroom for something she could use as a weapon.

The medicine cabinet!

Opening the cabinet, she reached for the heaviest object in it, a tin of talcum powder.

A loud crash in the hall made her jump. She inadvertently knocked the tin of talcum powder from the shelf, fumbled to keep it from falling, and managed to catch it before it crashed into the sink. With fear rattled nerves, she twisted the lid of the talcum powder tin to open the holes in the top.

As frightened as she was, she wasn't about to let someone invade her home without putting up a fight. Quietly stepping to the bathroom door, she reached for the doorknob. Fear pulsed through her fingers. She paused, thinking of a few more weapons she could use.

On an inhaled breath, she twisted the handle, threw open the door, and let out an ear splitting shriek. At the same time she flipped on the light in the hall, squeezed the talcum, moving her arm in a wide arch, and managed to hit the intruder in the face with the powder—who was momentarily blinded by the sudden flood of light.

28

Jack pulled off his boots and dropped them next to the bed, disappointed Kedra hadn't wanted to spend even a few minutes with him. Last night she'd been so friendly, so warm. Tonight she wouldn't even consider his invitation to just talk for a little while.

Will I ever understand women?

He was unbuttoning his shirt when something crashed upstairs.

Kedra!

Bolting through the bedroom door, he ran toward the stairs that led up to the Moore's private living area.

Kedra shrieked.

He took the stairs three at a time and raced across the Moore's dark sitting room.

The light in the hall was on. The umbrella stand had been tipped over. Umbrellas and white powder covered the pine floorboards of the hall.

From inside Kedra's dark room, he heard her exclaim, "Let go, you ornery sneak thief!"

Jack burst into the room, fumbling for the light switch. His fingers found it. He flipped it, leaped forward, and skidded to a stop.

Kedra was on the floor wrestling with Swindler. Her nightgown was up around her knees, her robe was askew, and both she and Swindler were dusted with white powder.

In the instant it took Jack to take in the scene, he thought he saw Kedra close her hand around something shiny and green. She released her hold on Swindler and he immediately escaped out her open window.

"I'm sorry if I woke you," she said, slipping her closed hand into the pocket of her robe and getting to her feet. She straightened her robe and pushed back her long loose hair.

He hadn't seen her hair loose before. It was magnificent, falling around her like a shining veil.

"You screamed," was all he could say.

"I thought Swindler was an intruder." She sat down in the chair under the window and leaned back as though needing the support. "I've had the strangest feeling of being watched or followed all day. I was in the bathroom when I heard a noise in the hall and then the crash of the umbrella stand. I'm afraid my imagination got the better of me. Shrieking was one of the few things I could think of to do."

He looked down at the tin of Talcum powder.

She laughed shakily. "That, was one of the other things I did. I got him square in the face."

"I'm glad it was only Swindler. What was he up too?"

"His usual stunts—although it's been sometime since I caught him coming through my window."

"What did he try to make off with this time?" Jack asked, trying to be curious without being too probing.

She looked away from him. "I don't know."

It was a lie and he knew it instantly.

"Everything is all right now. Thanks for coming to my rescue."

He recognized her thanks as a dismissal. His lips tightened and he was about to turn away when he became aware that there was something small and hard under his foot. It felt like a rock. A sudden notion made him slide his foot over the rock, until it sat between the pad of his foot and his toes.

"I'll say goodnight then." He took a shuffling step back tightening his toes around the rock. "I'm glad you're all right."

"Would you please switch off the light in hall before you go down?"

"Sure."

Pivoting on his foot, he managed to turn and go out the door with the rock still under his foot.

He closed the door behind him and stood absolutely still. All along his heart had believed in her innocence. But if he was right about what was under his foot, then there was no doubt about her guilt.

Lifting his foot, he bent down and picked up the emerald. His fingers curled around it into a tight fist. He raised his fist, eyed the wall, paused, and then dropped his fist.

She has the emeralds. He said the words over and over in his head as he went down the stairs, trying to make his heart accept it.

Back in his bedroom, he examined the emerald closely. He had a written description of all the stolen gems. This was one of the bigger ones, cut in the classic emerald style. The color was deep and rich. It sparkled in the overhead light and doused every remnant of compassion in his heart.

Quietly going into Eli's office, Jack called the desk in the Hotel Colorado, asked for room 317, and waited for the operator to put him through.

Luke's sleepy voice said, "Hello."

"Luke . . . Kedra has the emeralds."

"Jack! Are you sure?"

"I'm sitting here looking at one I found in her bedroom tonight."

"Are you bringing her in?"

"No. I want you and Tate to do that, first thing tomorrow morning. I'm going to stay here, undercover, and wait for Eli. I want to see what he'll tell me before he knows I'm a U.S. Marshal."

"All right, but keep a close eye on Miss Moore. We don't want her escaping with the emeralds tonight."

"Don't worry, she's not going anywhere."

Jack hung up the phone. *If she suspects I saw the emeralds, then Luke's right, she might try to make a break for it before morning.*

Returning to his room, Jack put his boots on, buttoned up his shirt, turned out the light, and sat in a big easy chair with his gun in his lap. He wouldn't have any trouble staying awake. His heart was in too much pain to sleep. He leaned back in the chair and put in order all the evidence he had against Miss Kedra Moore.

Isaac was still cursing Goldie's Aunt Selma when the train pulled into Carbondale. *The old witch!*

She'd had him investigated, but hadn't let on about it when he first arrived. Throughout the day, Aunt Selma had warmed to him. She'd even played croquet on the lawn with him and Goldie, laughing when he gently teased her.

A picture of interested, innocent inquiry, she'd asked all the familiar questions: Where had he gone to college, what was his degree in, where was he working, what were his ambitions, who was his family, what did his father do, where was their ranch? Those were always the questions families of wealthy girls asked, and Goldie was a very wealthy girl—her father's only heir.

She was a plain little thing, but to Isaac she was solid gold. He'd worked her like the gold mine that had made her father rich. She'd fallen for him in a matter of days, but he had been careful not to rush the idea of marriage. Instead he'd been patiently courting her for months. It had cost him a bundle too.

Then the most wonderful thing happened. Her father died, and she'd inherited everything.

He'd done all the right things during her bereavement, being kind and understanding, supportive, letting her take time to grieve her father. Her invitation to come to Aspen and meet her aunt had made Isaac hope her period of mourning was over. He was especially hopeful when she told him that her aunt was looking forward to meeting him.

The way Aunt Selma treated him, at first, made him believe she genuinely like him. He'd told her the same lies he always used to secure his inclusion in the society of the wealthy. But this time he'd embellished the lies. Goldie had explained to him that Aunt Selma's approval was vital to any future they could have. Her sanction was stipulated in Goldie's father's will. Her aunt had to approve of the man Goldie married, or the inheritance would go to some distant cousins.

How could I have known the old crone would have me investigated? Goldie's father hadn't investigated him. In fact, he knew the old man had liked him. It made him believe Goldie's aunt would like him too.

She'd certainly been cordial all the way through lunch, this afternoon. After lunch, he and Goldie went for a walk. When they returned, Aunt Selma was in the parlor with a man she introduced as Alex Maxwell, a private investigator.

Mr. Maxwell laid out the information he had on Isaac like a prosecutor. He'd barely graduated from college. He'd never been gainfully employed. His father had won the broken down ranch he lived on in a card game. He didn't even have a bank account, and his father's bank account was virtually empty.

Isaac couldn't deny any of it. The private investigator had documented everything.

Goldie told him to leave and never try to see her again.

He looked out the window of the train while he waited for the people going to Glenwood Springs to board.

His father walked along the platform.

What's he doing in Carbondale?

Isaac watched him board the train two cars down, and relaxed. Even if his father had boarded the train in this car, he wouldn't have recognized Isaac. Once Goldie shunned him, he knew there wasn't any other choice but to go with his alternative plan. He'd boarded the train in Aspen in a persona he often employed when he didn't want anyone to identify him.

He'd decided it would be best if he just disappeared in Aspen. Then any search for him would start and fail there. In the guise of Eyes O'Shea, not even his own father would recognize him. He settled back in his seat as the train left the Carbondale station. It would be in Glenwood in a couple of hours.

His father's presence could present a problem, if he'd arranged to have Kedra come pick him up. *I've got to get out to the ranch and into my room, collect all my things and get out without being seen, before he and Kedra get there. With any luck, he'll just stay in town for the night.*

Counting on that luck, he pulled a coat around his shoulders, and leaned his head against the seat's cushioned back. With his face turned to the window, he let the sway of the train put him to sleep.

The train's whistle woke Eyes O'Shea. He opened his remarkable blue eyes and sat up as the train pulled into the Glenwood station.

The other people in his compartment collected their things and left. Eyes peered out the window and saw Eli walk toward the station. Eyes gathered his things and quickly followed.

Eli left the station, crossed the street, and entered a saloon.

Good! Eyes knew his father wouldn't just have one drink and leave. He wasn't capable of that discipline. It was one of the reasons his father didn't keep liquor at the ranch. Especially after the drunk he went on, which gave Isaac the upper hand.

Eyes O'Shea hurried down Cooper Street to the livery stable. His own horse was there, but in his current persona he couldn't ask for it. Instead he rented a small buggy and left town as quickly as possible. As soon as the town lights faded, he stopped the buggy, changed into more appropriate clothes for what he had to do, unhitched the slow buggy and rode the horse bare back, pushing it hard.

His years at college hadn't all been wasted. He was a fair shot, good at fencing, an elegant dancer, and an excellent horseman. As he rode he planned out how he would get into the house unseen and unheard. The presence of Jack Garrison, which he thought was highly suspicious, complicated things, but with luck everyone would be asleep.

I'll tie this worthless plug up about thirty yards from the ranch and walk in. If I go through the back door and up the stairs, I won't have to go by Garrison's room.

29

Kedra put her hand into the pocket of her robe and drew out three large emeralds. They were incredibly beautiful. She stared down at them until her vision blurred. Her mind reviewed the pictures of the emeralds in the special edition of the Avalanche, trying to understand what these stolen gems were doing in her house—in her hand. *How did Swindler get them? And why did he only have these few? Where are the other ones?*

She immediately dismissed her father. If he had robbed that train, then he wouldn't be in Carbondale trying to sell the herd to pay off his debts. *Besides, Papa wouldn't do something that terrible.* But she didn't doubt Isaac was capable of committing the crime. She'd endured enough of Isaac's viciousness over the years to be sure. She even knew where he'd hide the gems—*if he's the one who robbed that train and killed those U.S. Marshals.*

An unwanted memory, from long ago, surfaced. On the day of her fifth birthday she'd begged Effie to braid her hair. Effie always curled her long hair into ringlets with a curling iron, or put it into a ponytail. She said Kedra would look too much like an Indian if she wore her hair in a braid.

"But I am an Indian," Kedra said. "And it's my birthday. Please!"

Effie gave in and braided her hair down her back in one long rope.

The first person she wanted to show her braid to was her father. Feeling the swish of it as she moved her head, she ran into her father's office. His praise made her happy and proud. He told her she looked like a princess, an Indian princess—his princess.

Delighted with his praise, and wanting more admiration, she ran up the stairs to find Isaac. He was always in his room, something she didn't understand. Without knocking, she burst through his door.

He was on his knees with his hand inside the floor.

As soon as he saw her, he jumped to his feet, flew at her, pulled her into the room, and slammed the door.

He leaned against the door, his blue eyes cold and hard. "Don't ever open my door and come in my room again, without my permission!" His nose pressed against hers. His face, contorted with anger. "And if you ever tell anyone about my hiding place—I'll kill you!" He pulled a knife from his pocket and grabbed her by her long braid. "Do you understand me?"

Terrified by the knife he pressed to her cheek, all she could do was gulp down breaths.

He jerked her braid hard.

She started to cry.

"Shut up or I'll hurt you."

She cried harder.

"Have it your way."

He began to saw through her braid.

"I—I . . . won't tell, I promise . . . I'll never . . . tell," she said through sobbing breaths.

He finished cutting off her long braid. Threw it on the floor and stomped on it. "I'll kill you just like I have your hair. Remember that, you stupid little savage."

What remained of her hair fell around her face. "I'll . . . remember, I won't tell—I won't!" she sobbed.

He opened the door a crack. "Get out," he growled, shoving her through the door and slamming it after her.

Her father found her in her room an hour later, still crying. She didn't tell him, but somehow he just knew it was Isaac who had cut off her braid. She admitted that Isaac had been mad when she came into his room without knocking.

To date, she had never told anyone about Isaac's hiding place. She had also never gone into Isaac's room again. *Not that I ever wanted to. Besides, his room is always locked. So how did Swindler get in there and take the gems?* She stared down at the emeralds. *If the rest of the emeralds are in Isaac's room—in his hiding place—I have to get in there.* The thought made her stomach churn, but didn't detour her determination.

Bedroom door locks were fairly simple mechanisms. Going to her dressing table, she opened the middle drawer. On rare occasions, when she put her hair up, she used a variety of hairpins.

Armed with different kinds of hairpins, she decided to practice on her own door first. Opening it, she switched on the hall light, and engaged the lock. From the locked side she began to experiment.

Five minutes later, the door lock slid back. She practiced until she could unlock the door quickly. Crossing the hall to Isaac's door, she confidently inserted a hairpin into the lock. A moment later, she heard a click and twisted the doorknob.

The room smelled of Isaac—the soap he used. Quickly crossing to the window, she pulled down the shade and closed the heavy blue velvet curtains, before turning on the light.

Memory led her, unerringly, to Isaac's hiding place. She moved the small table that now stood over the place, and pulled back the rug. It took a few moments, and the aid of her hairpin, to locate and lift away the section of the floor that covered the hiding place.

Inside the hole there was a lidless metal box. A stack of twenty-dollar bills immediately caught her eye. *There must be hundreds of dollars here . . . certainly more than enough to pay off the ranch hands and Dr. Pell's bill.*

Knowing Isaac was unemployed, she decided, *he either stole the money, or blackmailed Papa into giving it to him.* Without a pang of conscience she took the money from the box.

Next, she took out a black velvet case. Inside she found the pearl necklace with matching earrings, which the newspaper said had also been stolen in the train robbery. Additionally, the case contained a stunning diamond ring. She set them next to the money and reached into the box again. This time she took out a heavy leather pouch. Opening the pouch's neck, she poured some of the contents into her hand. Emeralds, magnificent, sparking emeralds filled her hand. She stared at them, sick with horror. Her hand trembled as she quickly funneled them back into the bag and set it aside.

In the bottom of the metal box she found her braid, on the end hung two white feathers. *Why would he keep my braid? For that matter, why would he put a make shift totem on it?*

She gulped down fear, again reliving that horrible day and what Isaac had done. The memory made her breath come in gasps, just as it had on the day he'd cut that braid off. It was the only thing she sometimes regretted about the way her mind worked. Not only could she remember everything, she could actually relive it, with all her feelings and senses.

Dropping the braid next to the pouch, she ran her hand over the bottom of the metal box. Her fingers found five more emeralds. They joined the others in the leather pouch.

For several moments her mind raced. She knew what she had to do. *But if I turn in the emeralds, my association with Morgan—Harry—is sure to come out. They might even think I'm responsible for the crime. How can I prove I wasn't involved?*

She put her braid, the black velvet case, and the money back in the box; replaced the floor, the rug, and the table. *I'll tell Sheriff Hadlock about Isaac's hiding place. If I leave the pearls and money here, then hopefully he'll believe Isaac is responsible.*

Isaac hadn't told anyone when he would return. It might be as soon as tomorrow. The thought made her inhale sharply and glance at the door. *I've got to gets the emeralds to Sheriff Hadlock—tonight!*

Back in her bedroom, she dressed quickly, her mind going over the kinds of questions Sheriff Hadlock would ask her. She decided she'd better bring the letters from Morgan. It would be easier to explain her connection with Harry Walsh if she had the letters.

As soon as she picked them up, she knew the last one was missing. She sorted through the letters, but it was gone. Fingers of panic clutched at her. *Who could have taken it and why?* Her mind read over the missing letter. She saw how incriminating it might sound. If the sheriff didn't know about Harry being Morgan, it might be better not to tell him. She was about to put the other letters back in her desk, when another thought struck her.

All day she'd had the feeling of being watched. Now she had no choice but to go into town, alone and in the dark, but not without protection. She opened the hidden compartment in the drawer.

Her Bull Dog revolver was gone. She stared at the empty drawer, thoroughly alarmed. *I don't have time to worry about this now.* She quickly replaced the drawer's false bottom, and put the letters back in. *I can't go into town unprotected. I'll go get a gun from Papa's room.*

No lights shone in any of the cabin windows, when Isaac reached the ranch. *Good. The Blues and all the ignorant cowboys are asleep.*

The light came on in Jack's room just as Isaac approached the house. Kedra's light was on too. *Did he just go into his room? It's after eleven. What are Kedra and the saddle tramp doing up?*

The upstairs hall light went on. Isaac could see its glow through the bathroom window. *Is she meeting Garrison?* The most obvious place would be in the upstairs sitting room. He waited but the light didn't go on. *Where are they?* After the way they looked at each other at the dance, he was sure they were together. *I'll bet they're in the sitting room, enjoying each other in the dark.* That created a considerable problem. *How do I get into my room without being seen?*

If he was right, there might be one way. He couldn't go through his own window, because he always closed and locked it before he left, but Kedra's was almost always open.

He went into the barn and got the ladder. With the stealth he'd used so many times to carry out his nefarious deeds, he leaned the ladder against the house and climbed. When he reached the top he peeked cautiously into Kedra's bedroom.

Astonishment almost brought him through the window. The pouch of emeralds was lying on Kedra's bed. He couldn't be mistaken. The pouch had been his mother's, a gift from his Mi'kmaq grandmother.

Kedra was at her desk. If he came through the window now, she would cry out, and Garrison would be sure to come.

He waited.

She looks scared, and she should be. I laid everything out so neatly to hang her for the train robbery and murders. His eyes narrowed. He hated her, oh how he hated her. Somehow, she'd found out about the emeralds. He didn't waste time trying to figure out how. She'd ruined his plan. Now he simply had to get the emeralds, kill her as quickly and quietly as possible, and get out of there.

Maybe I can make it look like Garrison killed her. He was about to put his hand on the windowsill when Kedra suddenly left the room.

Sitting in the darkness hadn't helped Jack resolve the conflict in his heart. He snapped on the light, still trying to explain away Kedra's possession of the emeralds. He paced the floor. *Why can't I just accept it? She's guilty!*

He threw his door open and trooped up the stairs. He didn't care if Kedra was asleep. He'd drag her out of bed if he had to, but one way or another, he was going to get the truth out of her.

She came out of her father's bedroom as he crossed the dark sitting room. There was a gun in her hand.

"Drop it," he growled out of the darkness.

She whirled towards him.

He stepped into the light of the hall. His gun pointed directly at her.

"What are you doing?" She gasped, dropping the gun to the floor, her gold eyes wide with fright.

"I'm a United States Marshal, *darlin',* and I'm putting you under arrest for robbery and murder."

"What?! You can't possibly believe—"

"I know you have the emeralds. I saw them in your hand. I even got one out of your bedroom under my foot. It's over, Kedra."

"I didn't steal them. You have to believe me!"

"I've got enough evidence on you to hang you three times over, so why should I believe you?"

Kedra's mind reeled. Nothing he said made sense. "What evidence? How could you have any evidence against me?" She felt the color drain from her face. "It was you! You took my letter and the gun."

"That's right. I know all about you and Harry, a.k.a. Morgan O'Shea."

"How dare you go through my private letters!"

"I have a warrant to search this house. I found the special edition of the Avalanche stuck in your chemistry book in the page with instruction on using Chloral Hydrate too. Neat trick, using that to subdue Marshal Forbes, so Harry could open the safe for you." He took a step toward her. "What I want to know is why you killed

Harry? Were you just using him until you got your hands on the emeralds?"

"Stop this insanity, and listen to me!" Kedra shouted at him. "I didn't kill anyone. I didn't steal anything. It was Isaac."

"If it was Isaac, then why did I find your pendant in Will's fist?"

"You found my pendant—"

"In William Forbes' cold, dead hand!"

"No!" She was trembling so hard she was afraid she would collapse right at his feet.

"You were seen leaving the train too. A boy saw your totem attached to your braid."

"That's not possible! I was in Glenwood when the train left!"

"Did anyone see you?"

"No, but, Jack, how can you believe I'd do something so monstrous?"

His green eyes were as hard and dark as the emeralds. There was nothing but condemnation in them.

"I want the emeralds—right now."

"How do I know you aren't Isaac's accomplice? I only have your word for it that you're a U.S. Marshal. Show me your badge and your warrant—then I'll give you the emeralds."

He pulled a badge and a paper from inside his shirt.

She looked at the badge and took the paper from him. It was a genuine warrant, signed by a local judge.

"The emeralds are in my room," she said meekly

"Let's go."

Emotion clogged her throat. She fought it down. Again she'd been deceived by a man she felt drawn to. No, that wasn't quite true. She felt more than just drawn to Jack Garrison.

They walked into her room. She raised her hand to point at the pouch on the bed.

It was gone.

30

Tuesday, June 23, 1908

Kedra ran over to the bed and dropped to her knees. *Maybe they rolled off the bed.* She swept her arm under the bed, and felt nothing. She got up and looked through the pillows on the bed—nothing. Panic took hold of her as the truth dawned on her.

She faced Jack.

"Where are they?" he asked, his voice as cold as an icehouse.

She swallowed. *He isn't going to believe me,* but she said it anyway. "I've been out of the room for several minutes."

"So?"

"The window is open."

"I can see that."

"Swindler must have come in and taken them."

Jack took hold of her arm and leaned down. "Stop stalling, Kedra. *Where are they?*"

"I'm telling the truth. I took a few of them from Swindler's paw, just before you found me wrestling with him. You saw him escape. He must have just been waiting outside the window for another chance."

Disbelief stared at her from Jack's eyes. "Where did he get them in the first place?"

"From a hiding place in Isaac's room."

"Isaac always keeps his door locked. How did Swindler get in?"

"I don't know, but when I thought about it, I knew they must have come from the hiding place in Isaac's room. So I went in and—"

"How did *you* get in to Isaac's locked room?"

I . . . uh . . . picked the lock."

"Quite a clever girl, aren't you? There doesn't seem to be any limit to your criminal skills."

Kedra bristled. "I don't have time to defend myself against your ridiculous accusations, but for your information, the reason I'm dressed is because I intended to take the emeralds to Sheriff Hadlock—right now."

"Oh really?"

"Yes! I don't know when Isaac will get back, but I think it will be"—she glanced at the clock. It was just after midnight—"today. I wanted the emeralds safely in the sheriff's hands before Isaac returned."

His grip on her arm slackened, and he surprised her when he said, "I want to believe you, but all the evidence I have says I can't. There isn't a shred of evidence against your brother."

She let her eyes plead her case and watched his soften. "Believe me, Jack. I have proof it was Isaac that stole them. But right now, if we don't find Swindler before he stashes those emeralds in a place I don't know about, we won't ever find them."

"Does he have a nest—besides the one up in the barn loft?"

"Yes. I followed him once to an old mineshaft. After he left I went in and found it. I saw him come out of that mineshaft just the other day— when I was tracking the elk."

"How far is it?"

"About half a mile from here." She reached for the handles on the top drawer of her dresser.

Jack's gun came up. "What are you doing?"

"I'm just getting a flashlight. We'll need it for the mineshaft." She pulled out a flashlight with a transverse switch, to keep the light on. "We can check the barn before we head for the den."

"Let's go," Jack said, taking her arm.

Swindler's nest in the barn was littered with small objects from around the ranch. There were bottle caps, nails and screws, string, wire, a few buttons, and even a kitchen spoon, but no emeralds.

Jack was mentally kicking himself as they left the barn under a half-moon with the stars skidded in and out of the rapidly gathering clouds. He should have taken possession of the emeralds as soon as he saw the one under his foot, but he'd wanted to keep his cover intact. Now if the emeralds couldn't be found, it would be his fault.

The wind picked up as Kedra led him up the slope behind the barn.

"If you're leading me on a wild goose chase, it won't do you any good," Jack said as they entered a deep ravine.

The ravine was steep sided and heavily timbered by pinion pines and sagebrush.

As much as Jack wanted to believe her, he kept his guard up. *She might be leading me into a trap.*

"I'm not leading you down a false trail, but I can't guarantee we'll find the emeralds in Swindler's nest. The night is his favorite time to hunt and roam. He might not go directly back to his nest. If he gets interested in chasing something, he might just stash the emeralds somewhere, intending to come back for them later."

"For your sake, I hope not. If we can find them, and you come in with me willingly, it might help your case. But it's going to be nearly impossible for you to refute the evidence I have against you."

"There are some other things in Isaac's hiding place that I think will help prove my innocence."

"Where is this hiding place, and what else does it contain? I searched Isaac's room thoroughly and didn't find it."

She described the hiding place under the floorboards, and listed the contents, including her braid with the fake totem on it.

Jack questioned her closely. The weight on his heart began to lift. If she was telling the truth, the things in Isaac's hiding place might prove she wasn't involved in the robbery, particularly the diamond ring.

If she saw the pearls too, then— "Why didn't you take everything out of the hole?"

"I thought about it, decided Sheriff Hadlock might suspect me of the robbery and the murders, even though I was turning over the emeralds. However, if I could tell him where to find the pearls—"

"Then Isaac would have some explaining to do." *But, what if she planted those things in Isaac's room to throw me off, after I saw the emeralds in her hand?* Jack didn't like the possibility, but had to consider it. *She's smart enough to have implicated Isaac, just in case I caught her sneaking out during the night.* His hand tightened on the grip of his gun. *If you're not careful Marshal Garrison, she might make a fool out of you, yet.*

Kedra slowed, peering up the side of the ravine that was steadily evolving into a narrow canyon. "Up there."

He followed Kedra's pointed finger, but didn't see the opening to a mine. "Where is it?"

"See that faint track, follow it up to the cluster of bushes. It's in there," Kedra said.

Jack put a hand on her arm. "I don't want to, but if I have to, I'll do whatever is required to retrieve the emeralds from Swindler. I want you to understand that."

"It won't come to that. Just let me handle it."

"All right, I'll only step in if things start looking ugly," he said, following closely behind Kedra, his senses attuned to his surroundings, still looking for a trap.

They pushed through the bushes, covering the mouth of the mine and stopped. Jack turned on the flashlight. Kedra put a finger to her lips and ducked into the mine.

The opening to the mineshaft was low and narrow, forcing Kedra and Jack to go single file. The claustrophobia Jack suffered from gripped him as he doubled over and followed Kedra. She dropped to her knees and crawled along the uneven floor of the mine. Jack dropped to his knees, put his gun in his pocket, and held the flashlight high as he followed close on Kedra's heels.

By the dim beam of the flashlight, they crawled into the shaft for about twenty feet. The mineshaft abruptly ended in a large pile of rock.

"It probably caved-in and the miner gave up," Kedra said, as Jack swept the light over the rocky blockage. "That happened frequently up here. This plateau is covered with old mines and caves, most of them don't go in very far before you run into a cave-in."

"I don't see any nest."

"It's there."

Jack followed her finger with the light and saw a breach in the rocks. It was about a foot wide.

"May I have the flashlight?"

Jack handed it to her. She crawled over and poked the light into the breach.

"What's in there?"

"Swindler's nest, but he isn't here. Wait—I think I see something." Kedra flattened out onto her stomach and reached her arm inside.

Jack leaned over her. "Give me back the flashlight, I'll hold it so you can see what you're doing and use both hands."

She returned the flashlight. He leaned on his elbow, directing the beam over her shoulder and into the nest.

After a few moments she said, as she started to roll onto her side, "The pouch isn't— *Lookout!"*

Out of the corner of his eye, Jack saw the blur of a blackjack flying toward his head. He dropped the flashlight, jerking sideways. The edge of the blackjack caught him behind his right ear hard enough to knock his hat off his head. He fell forward on top of Kedra, the crown of his head bashing against the wall of the mine.

Just before he blacked out, he heard Kedra scream.

31

Isaac backed out of the cave, giddy with triumph. Those first years of his life had been spent in the home of his aunt, with his Mi'kmaq grandmother as his nanny. She taught him about the Mi'kmaq, taught him to be proud of that heritage—and he was. For years he practiced moving soundlessly over all the different kinds of terrain on the ranch. He'd practiced leaving the house unheard and unseen, even in the daytime when there were people coming and going. In his heart, he was a good Mi'kmaq brave, cunning and bold—ruthless against his enemies, something he'd just proven.

He knew Kedra and Jack weren't dead, but he didn't want them dead. From his pocket, he pulled out a matchbook and lit the bushes in front of the mine on fire. All the way down and into the ravine he lit the bushes and trees as he went, until all his matches were gone.

Kedra should come to in time to appreciate the death I've planned for her. Even if they both come to, and manage to drag themselves out of the cave, they'll be too groggy to get out of the ravine. The wind is in my favor. It will blow the fire through the ravine and up the sides. There will be no escape. If they stay in the mine, the smoke will kill them. If they leave, they'll be burnt to death.

Killing Kedra this way wasn't what he wanted, but it would still devastate his father and accomplish his goal. *The old man will live out his days wondering if Kedra committed the robbery and what became of her.* Isaac smiled broadly. He'd been on the ladder outside Kedra's window long enough to learn that Jack was a U.S. Marshal. *It will be delicious to make the law think Jack Garrison turned traitor to his badge and ran off with Kedra and the emeralds, never to be found.* He laughed out loud. *And I know just how to make the cops believe that, while getting myself off the hook too.*

He hurried back to the ranch. The fire was sure to wake someone. Already he could hear its ferocity grow as he ran. Unless the wind suddenly changed, the ranch was in no danger. Not that he cared, he just needed enough time to retrieve what he'd left in the hiding place, gather his belongings, and craft an incriminating journal entry. *I'll put it in Kedra's desk, with her letters from Morgan O'Shea.*

Isaac nearly gaged on the name. *How could Harry betray me like that, after all we dreamed of and planned?* Isaac's lip curled. Harry's betrayal had sealed his fate. The bitter taste killing his cousin left in Isaac's mouth was one he knew would stay there for a long time. But he also tasted a delicious satisfaction too.

Harry was two years old when Isaac came to live with his Aunt Ursula's family. He'd worshiped Harry. They had seven wonderful years together before Harry's father died. His mother remarried just a few months later. Harry's new stepfather, Clyde Warren, didn't like him or Isaac. He beat them both. When Eli decided he wanted his son back, Clyde Warren was happy to send him.

By then, both boys had been well indoctrinated by their Mi'kmaq grandmother and Irish grandfather. Their O'Shea grandparents were the only people who had truly loved them. They taught them to think of themselves as special—better than anyone else. Their Mi'kmaq grandmother had been a princess in her tribe. Their Irish grandfather was of the nobility. That meant people owed them honor and respect. Life owed them wealth and ease.

They made a pact to secretly take their grandparents' name and be Morgan and Eyes O'Shea. When they grew up, they would claim their rights to wealth and privilege. They made a blood pact to get even for how life had treated them as children. The emerald robbery was the key to firmly establishing themselves in the society they were born to and the wealth they deserved.

Kedra came to, coughing and choking. Her head was on fire. Her battered arms felt like dead weights as she tried to lift them. The pain made her wonder if they were broken.

Jack still lay unconscious on top of her, making it even harder to breathe. She tried to shift him, but her arms were too weak and painful to be of any use. There wasn't any way to roll over, pinned as she was between Jack and the wall of the mine. She reached out a trembling hand, touching Jack's face.

His forehead was warm.

He's alive!

"Jack," she choked on the smoke billowing into the mineshaft, stroking his face, hoping to rouse him. "Jack, wake up."

He groaned and moved his head, slightly.

Suddenly a figure loomed over them.

Kedra shrieked, throwing her arms over her face.

Seconds went by.

Nothing happened.

Kedra peeked out through her raised arms.

It was hard to see the man through the smoky light of the flashlight, which had rolled over against the opposite wall. His mouth and nose were covered by a bandana. As he leaned over, Kedra gasped. He had gold eyes.

"Do not fear, my daughter, I have come to help you."

"Who are you," Kedra choked.

"That can wait. There isn't much time."

He wrapped his long arms around Jack's shoulders and pulled him off Kedra, leaning him back against the opposite wall.

Jack groaned, "What . . . happened?"

"Isaac—that's what happened!" Kedra croaked out.

"We must leave here quickly before the smoke overcomes us," the Indian urged.

Kedra sat up, hugging her wounded arms to her. The Indian helped her to her knees. She leaned over gingerly bracing her arms on her thighs.

Jack took the kneeling Indian's out stretched hand. He rose to his knees too. He swayed dangerously. The Indian wrapped an arm around his body.

"Can you crawl on your own?" he asked Kedra.

"I'll try."

"Let's go. The fire is spreading fast. When we reach the mouth of the mine we must go up and get out of this ravine. The wind will blow the fire along the bottom. It will climb the sides but not as quickly."

The wind was blowing hard when they reached the mouth of the mine. Just as the Indian had predicted, the fire was racing along the bottom of the ravine, hissing and crackling, climbing up the sides.

"Use the tree branches to pull yourself up," the Indian said to Kedra.

"I don't know if I can, Isaac battered my arms."

"Help her," Jack choked, grabbing hold of a sturdy tree branch. "I can manage."

The Indian gave him a doubtful look, but stepped away from him and took hold of Kedra.

They began to climb.

Jack stayed by the tree. His fingers probed the wound on top of his head, and then the one behind his ear, they came away bloody.

The moment before Isaac hit him with the blackjack came back to him. He heard Kedra scream a warning. *She didn't know he was behind us. It wasn't a trap she laid for me.*

His head was swimming, but at least Kedra's warning had kept him from taking the full force of the blackjack. He looked up at Kedra and the Indian who seemed to be almost carrying Kedra up the slope.

It was obvious Kedra had been hurt by Isaac too. But what did it mean? *Was Isaac simply trying to rid himself of the last accomplice in the robbery scheme?* Or did it mean what he hoped, that Kedra was completely innocent.

The heat from the fire grew. Pinecones crackled and popped as they burst into flames and exploded. The fire was blazing a path up the ravine's slope. Jack pushed off the branch he was clinging to and took a step. Everything swirled around him. He fell forward and caught himself before he slid down the hill. *The only way I'm going to make it up this slope is to crawl.*

On hands and knees he scrambled and clawed his way up. The smoke got worse. He covered his mouth and nose with his bandana. The help it rendered was minimal. He couldn't see Kedra and the Indian any longer. *Good they made it to the top.*

The fire was licking at his boots. He had to go faster, but his head was too fuzzy. It wouldn't quit spinning. *Just another few feet and I'll rest,* he told himself.

Then, through the smoke, he saw the Indian coming down the slope. He pulled Jack to his feet, put Jack's arm over his shoulder, and wrapped his other arm around Jack's waist.

"Come," he said, pulling Jack upward.

Somewhere in his swimming head, Jack noticed the Indian was almost as tall as he was. The brave was strong too. Gritting his teeth, Jack forced his legs to move. Step by step they climbed.

Kedra was lying on the ground when they reached the top. The blood on her face sent Jack's heart racing.

"Kedra, are you all right?" he gasped out.

She looked up at him and tried to smile, "I'm at least as all right as you appear to be."

Over their heads the stars had disappeared. The moon was gone too. A deafening crack of thunder made Jack moan and Kedra cry out. Both clutched their heads.

The sky opened up and poured down on them.

"We must find shelter quickly. Where should we go?" the brave asked Kedra, helping her to her feet.

Kedra pointed east. "There's a cave—not too far from here."

With the Indian in between Kedra and Jack, supporting both of them, they started off.

It seemed to Jack as though they walked for miles before Kedra stopped.

"It's up there." She pointed toward a rocky incline.

"Take Kedra up first. I don't think we can do it altogether," Jack said, sitting down on a fallen tree trunk.

The Indian didn't waste words. He nodded and propelled Kedra up the incline.

Jack peered through the dark rain, watching the brave's white feathers as he pulled Kedra up the incline. They stopped and disappeared near a large outcrop of rock. A moment later the Indian reappeared, coming back down the slope.

Jack struggled to his feet, grateful for the Indian's supporting arm. The rain was helping to keep him conscious, but he was still dizzy.

As the Indian looped Jack's arm across his shoulder, he suddenly took hold of Jack's left thumb. His eyes widened.

"Jack Garrison! Long have I wondered what became of you."

Maybe it was the dizziness, but Jack could have sworn the Indian had just said his name. He tried to focus on the Indian's face, but he was too dizzy and the rain was too heavy.

"Do I know you?" Jack asked as the Indian pulled him the last few feet to the mouth of the cave.

"We will talk when we have a good fire going," the brave said. He sat Jack down next to Kedra and went back out into the rain.

"Do you know that Indian?" Jack asked.

"No. I've never seen him before."

"He knows my name."

"What? How could he know your name?"

"I don't know."

"He has gold eyes—like mine. I saw them in the light of the flashlight, when he found us," Kedra said. "And he called me, 'daughter'. I don't know why he would do that, except he also wears the totem of the Nahtow."

"He's Nahtow, and you don't know him?"

"No."

The pain in Kedra's voice made Jack reach out through the darkness, He found her hand and she surprised him by letting him take it. "Whoever he is, I'm just thankful he found us."

She leaned into his shoulder.

He felt the sob she tried to swallow as she said, "So am I!"

He released her hand and wrapped her in his arms, finding immediate comfort in holding her. "What did Isaac do to you?"

She laid her head on his shoulder. "He tried to bash me in the head with the blackjack he used on you. I couldn't move with you on top of me, so I used my arms to protect my head."

"I'm sorry."

"It wasn't your fault. When I couldn't hold my arms up anymore he hit me in the head. I blacked out, but I don't think it was for long."

"I don't understand why he didn't kill us."

"I think the fire or the smoke was meant to do that. He wanted us to suffer. He only wounded us enough to keep us from being able to escape the mine."

"Leaving us in that mineshaft would keep anyone from finding us too."

Kedra shivered, pressing her face into his shoulder. "I've always been afraid that Isaac would kill me—someday."

"You don't act like you're afraid of him."

"I gave into my fear of him just once. After that, Effie taught me to stand up to him. She said if I let him intimidate me, then I'd always live in fear."

"Why does he hate you?"

"Effie says it's because Papa loved my mother more than his mother."

"But they both died so long ago, so why would that matter? You are, after all, his sister."

"Yes, but papa kept me when I was born, after my mother died. He gave Isaac to his aunt when his mother died. I don't think he has ever forgiven Papa, or me, for that."

32

Kedra heard the Indian coming up the incline to the cave before he stepped into it. She strained her eyes to see him, but the darkness in the cave was too deep. The sound of wood falling reverberated through the darkness.

"Give me just a minute and I'll have a fire going," the Indian said.

A light flared to life in the darkness. Jack shielded his eyes. Kedra turned her face into Jack's shoulder. The light hurt her head and she could tell by the way Jack winced, it hurt him too.

"Indians sure aren't what they used to be," Jack said.

Kedra blinked at the Indian. In his hand he held a match safe.

The Indian lit a stick and handed it to Jack, with a grin.

"Sometimes rubbing two sticks together takes too long, especially when the sticks are wet." His face became grave. "I've got to get you two warmed up, fast."

"You don't talk like any Indian I've ever met," Jack said.

"But you have met me, Jack Garrison—a long time ago."

The Indian arranged the dry tinder he'd found beneath a fallen tree, and laid out the wood he'd brought in. He took a match from the match safe and lit the fire, blowing gently on the small flames that licked the wood. In a few minutes the fire was burning brightly.

Shivering with cold, Kedra and Jack moved in close to the warmth of the blaze.

"Now let's have a look at your heads," the brave said.

He poured water from a water bag onto a handkerchief, gently washed the wound on the side of Kedra's head, and examined it.

"Not large or deep," he said. "But I'm sure it is painful. The bleeding has stopped too." He bound a bandana from his knapsack around her head. "Let's look at your arms."

They were heavily bruised from her wrists to her upper arms. He gently probed her bones.

"They aren't broken," he said in a relieved voice. He handed her a pair of buckskin clothes. "Go get out of your wet clothes."

"What about Jack?" Kedra asked.

"I'd give the clothes to him, but he's too big for them. I have blankets he can wrap up in," he said pulling a blanket from his knapsack.

When Kedra returned, Jack's head was also wearing a bandana bandage. He was lying on his side, his arm under his head, wrapped from shoulders to knees in blankets. She noticed his eyes were closed, and his clothes were laid out near the fire.

She looked at the Indian, "How is he?"

Jack's eyes opened, but it was the Indian that answered.

"He sustained more severe head wounds than you did. I believe he has a concussion and should see a surgeon. The wound on the top of his head isn't too bad, but the one behind his ear is deep and still bleeding."

"However, I will survive," Jack said.

"So you can still arrest me?"

Jack grimaced, painfully.

The Indian asked, "Arrest you for what?"

"Do you want to explain it to him Marshal Garrison, or should I?"

"I liked it better when you called me Jack," Marshal Garrison said. He shifted his head. "I don't know how long I'm going to be able to stay awake, and I'd like to know who rescued us and how he knows me."

"I'd like to know that too," Kedra said, turning her gold eyes on the Indian.

He met her eyes with his own equally gold ones. "I am Zedekiah Long-Sight, my friends call me Zed. I am your uncle, Kedra."

"All day I've felt as if someone was watching me. Was it you?"

"Yes. I have been watching you since I got into town today."

"If you really are my uncle, why haven't I known about you? Where have you been all these years?"

"You haven't known about me, because I did not know about you, until a week ago."

"How did you find out about me?"

Zed explained about the visit of his old friend John Gray Wolf of the Utes to Glenwood and seeing her totem. "He knew that totem and wondered why you wore it, for he knew of only one Nahtow."

"You?"

"Yes. He thought, perhaps, you wore the totem only as an ornament. However, when he asked about you, he found you called yourself a Nahtow Indian. He wired me and I came to see if it was true. I have believed since before you were born that I was the last of our people. The last Nahtow to know and understand who our people were and what they were charged to do by our first parents. I believed that when I died the Nahtow would be no more. I believed your mother died before you were born, because after the massacre, I could find no trace of her."

Jack gasped, "The massacre! That's how you know me! That's why the word Nahtow sounds so familiar to me."

"Yes, Jack Garrison, we were together when those we loved were killed." He turned to Kedra, "As soon as I looked into your eyes and heard your name I knew you were Nahtow, the daughter of my brother."

"No. My mother was Nahtow. My father is a white man."

"The man who calls himself your father—is not your father."

Kedra stared at Zed. "You are mistaken!"

"Tell me, Kedra, what is your earliest memory?"

"Why do you want to know?"

"Because if you are truly Nahtow, you will be able to remember everything you see and hear, touch and taste, feel and experience. How far back can you reach?"

Kedra looked away. For years she'd been told the thing she believed was a memory was only a dream or her imagination. But she had never been able to let go of the feeling that it was a memory. *Will he believe me?*

Zed began to rummage through his large knapsack.

"I—I remember the day I was born," Kedra finally said.

"The day you were born!" Jack exclaimed.

Zedekiah glanced at Jack. "Many of the Nahtow can remember the day of their birth." He asked Kedra, "What do you remember about that day?"

She silently let the memory come to her. "A tired looking man handed me to a woman with a cap on. She bathed me and wrapped me in a gray blanket. She laid me in the arms of me a woman who was lying in a bed."

"What did the woman in the bed look like?"

"She had hair the color of honey and eyes like blue crystals. Her face was beautiful, but very tired, and she was in pain."

"Did she speak to you?"

Kedra hesitated, and then whispered, "Yes."

"What did she say to you?"

"She said . . . 'You are Kedra Long-Sight. You are a Nahtow princess'. Then she pulled the totem, I now wear, from her hair and put it on my blanket. She looked up, but I couldn't see the person she addressed. She said, 'Promise me you will mail my letter, and if you don't get any reply, then promise me, you will tell her who she is. Promise me you will take care of her. Love her, and if there are any of the Nahtow left, you will find them.' The person she spoke to was Eli Moore. I know his voice. He promised to do as she asked. Then she said, 'give her my letter and the pages of the book. Allow her to wear her tribe's totem, if she desires too. Give her the necklace and earrings of her people when she is old enough to appreciate them. Tell her they hold the knowledge of her people back to her first parents.'"

Tears were running down Kedra's face by the time she finished. She wiped them on the sleeve of the buckskin shirt.

Zed placed a worn photograph in her hand. "Is this the woman?"

Kedra sucked in a sharp breath. The woman in the photograph was obviously expecting a child. She stood next to a tall Indian. He looked very much like Zedekiah. In his hair was Kedra's totem.

Kedra studied the woman's face. "She is the woman that spoke to me, and she—she looks like me."

"No, Kedra, you look like her, because she is your mother and the brave beside her is your father, Seth Long-Sight, the last chief of the Nahtow."

Anger and bitterness took hold of Kedra, squeezing out all her finer feelings for the man she'd thought of as her father, until she couldn't see or feel his love and the devoted care he'd always given her. The world she'd known and felt secure in died.

Lies!

The fire glowed in Zed's eyes—her eyes.

The words sobbed out, "He"—she couldn't call him father, not now—"didn't tell me. He has lied to me all of my life. He told me my mother was a Nahtow Indian, the last surviving member of her people." She gripped her uncle's hand. "Why was Eli Moore with my mother when I was born?" She looked down at the picture of the beautiful woman and the tall, handsome brave. "Where was my father?"

"I know where he was," Jack said softly, his face pale and drawn in the light of the fire.

"Then you remember how we met and what happened?" Zed asked.

"The memories are coming back to me," Jack admitted, somberly. "I taught myself to suppress them until I thought they no longer remained in my mind."

"What do your memories have to do with where my father was when I was born?" Kedra asked Jack.

Jack exchanged a look with Zed.

"What—what is it?" Kedra asked.

Zed put more wood on the fire. Outside the rain fell. The scent of wet earth and pinion pines drifted into the cave. In the distance the rumble of thunder could still be heard.

"It's time she knew the truth, and I need to quit running from it too," Jack said to Zed.

"Then begin this story, Jack Garrison. Tell her about coming to America and your trip across the country."

Jack slowly sat up, holding the blankets tightly around his body. He said, "My parents joined the church in Ireland, before I was born. Their families disowned them. They saved for years to make the trip to America. In the spring of 1885, they finally had enough money to pay for passage to New Orleans. I remember how excited they were. We were going to Zion."

Kedra interrupted, "Uncle Zed probably doesn't know about the Mormon church."

Zed smiled at her, "But I do. You see I am a member of the church—as were your parents."

"What?"

"That is a large part of this story," Zed said, and began relating his people's conversion from the book of Nahtow.

Shem Nahtow—1831: White missionaries have come from Ohio and a great meeting has been called among the Delaware to hear the preaching of these men. I have been asked to interpret for the white men. They carry with them a book they say contains a history of our people. I am most anxious to see this book.

Chief Anderson, the Grand Sachem of the ten nations of the Delaware, has reluctantly agreed to meet with the white missionaries, something he has been opposed to doing with other missionaries.

As the white preacher, Oliver Cowdery, spoke my heart began to burn within me. He knew the name of our first father and Mormon, our last great prophet warrior. The book he read to us from was translated by a prophet from plates of gold.

I gathered all the Nahtow to listen to Oliver Cowdery. He and his companions, Frederick G. Williams and Parley P. Pratt, spent several days with the Delaware, who received their teachings with great interest and joy. Because I, and my people, can read, write, and speak in the white man's tongue, Mr. Cowdery gave us a copy of the Book of Mormon.

After only a few days, the Indian agents and other sectarian missionaries caused the Mormon missionaries to be driven out of Indian Territory.

In the days following the visit of Oliver Cowdery, I read the Book of Mormon and now hold it in my mind. My heart ponders it continually. I am determined to go to Kirtland, Ohio and meet the prophet of God. Many of my people wish to be baptized into the kingdom of God. We need those who hold the authority to perform this scared ordinance. I desire more knowledge and understanding of my people's place in the church. I desire to counsel with Brother Joseph, as the prophet is called, on the mission of the Nahtow.

Shem Nahtow—June, 1831: I have eaten in the house of the prophet of God. I have been baptized and ordained under his hand–that I might have power to baptize my people and confirm upon them the gift of the spirit. Brother Joseph has instructed me to continue the Nahtow's mission. He has told me there will come a day when all the records we have kept will be presented before the Lord and many will rejoice in that day as heirs of salvation.

Shem Nahtow—August, 1838: I came east to Far West to see the prophet. The great Sioux nation, dwelling in the territory of Dakota, sent messengers to me to come, that the Nahtow might learn and record their genealogy. The spirit whispered to me that I should take my people there. Brother Joseph confirmed my impression. He blessed me and commissioned the mission of the Nahtow to the Sioux Nation.

"In this same year, I took my people north, off the white man's reserved lands. My son Sakowin was born in the Dakota Territory, where we now sit at the campfires of the Lakota Sioux.

After Zed finished account of the Nahtow's conversion, he nodded at Jack to continue.

"When we arrived in New Orleans, we didn't have enough money to keep going west. My father was a blacksmith and found work in New Orleans. He worked for a year until we finally had enough money to continue our trek. We took a riverboat to Fort Madison in Iowa. There we met a small group of saints who were also trying to reach Zion. We joined their wagon train and started west in April."

"How old were you?"

"I was four, almost five." Jack's face lit for a moment. "It was a grand adventure, riding in the wagon, chasing prairie dogs and rabbits, camping out at night, listening to the wolves howl and the stories of the other people in our wagon train."

"How many wagons were in your train?"

Jack looked at Zed.

"There were six," Zed said.

"How do you know?" Kedra asked Zed.

"Be patient and you will learn," he replied.

"We followed the Mormon trail. Our wagons traveled from fifteen to twenty miles a day, depending on the weather, trail conditions, and the wagons. We made it to Ft. Laramie by the beginning of June and stopped there for a few days to get supplies."

"What?" Kedra asked when Jack smiled ruefully at Zed.

"I was excited because we were now in real Indian country, and I had never seen an Indian. It was my greatest wish to see an Indian before we got to Zion."

"His wish was granted five days later." Zed grinned, and Kedra could almost visualize the scene as Jack described it.

"We were nearing Douglas, Wyoming, when we met a band of Indians. They were the most beautiful people I'd ever seen. All of them had spectacular gold eyes and long black hair. They were tall and majestic, dignified and well spoken. Their clothes were finely made and all of them wore two white feathers, held in their hair by different kinds of silver clasps. They weren't at all what I expected Indians to be like. And the biggest surprise was—they were all Mormons heading for Zion too."

Kedra gaped at Jack and then at Zed. "Are you saying you met on the Mormon trail heading for Salt Lake City?"

"We did," Zed confirmed. "But things did not go well for our small company."

33

Kedra studied her uncle's face as he stared into the fire with evident grief. A curious dread crept along her spine. What he was about to tell her was bad, so bad his hands had curled into fists. She considered stopping him, but she had to know the whole truth about herself and her parents.

"I have not allowed myself to touch these memories for many years. Doing so now is very painful for me." He held Kedra's eyes and then moved on to Jack. "It will be difficult for both of you to hear what I will tell you. Perhaps more difficult for you, Jack Garrison, because it will bring back memories you have suppressed."

"There comes a time, when everyone has to face their demons," Jack said tightly. "I have run from these demons for too long. Perhaps if I face them—I can finally lay them to rest."

Zed nodded and smiled faintly. "Your wagon train met the Nahtow just east of Douglas, Wyoming, on the south side of the North Platte River. The Nahtow had been living in South Dakota."

Sakowin Nahtow—1864: In this year, I have been blessed with a son, who I have named Seth. The Nahtow now number only fifty-eight souls and I fear unless we can again grow as a people, my son will be the last chief of the Nahtow. It will be his responsibility to decide what the Nahtow should do with all the records we have stored in the Nahtow library.

Sakowin Nahtow—1877: I have taken my people from among the Sioux, who continue to fight the white men. We have found a safe place to settle–for a time–in the mountains the white men call the Black Hills.

"Did my parents meet in South Dakota?" Kedra asked.

"Yes. Your mother's parents had a farm. It was in an area the government had opened up to white settlers—in violation of their treaty with the Sioux Indians. The broken treaty stirred up the Sioux. There were many skirmishes between the Sioux and the white men. My father, Sakowin, tried to reason with the Sioux, but the Sioux would not hear him. He died just before Seth met your mother, Caroline Barlow."

"Would Sakowin have approved of my parent's marriage?"

"Yes. You see, Seth's heart had never been given to one of our own people. My father worried he would not marry, but when he met Caroline Barlow, my mother, Oleah, told me it was as though they had been waiting to find one another all their lives. Our mother was very happy for Seth."

"Were you glad too?"

"Yes, but I didn't meet Carrie, as she was called, until after she and Seth were married. I was in the east, finishing my college education."

Sakowin Nahtow—1883: I have let my son, Zedekiah, go to the school, Harvard, in the east. Zedekiah has a great thirst for knowledge. He wrote to the governor of the school and told him of our ancestor John Nahtow, who attended the school in 1650. The governor has invited Zedekiah to come and study the wisdom of the white man. Zedekiah married his cousin, Yarley three years ago when he was just fifteen. Together, with their son, they have gone east. I have received news that they have been well received and have settled in a dwelling place on the grounds of the school. I believe it is wise for Zedekiah to learn from the white man. Not many more years will pass before we will need to adapt to the white man's ways if we are to continue to live as a free people on the land. Zedekiah's understanding of the white man's laws will help us fit into their world.

"You went to college?" Kedra asked.

"Yes, but that is not important now. What I want you to know is that the love was strong between your parents. However, Carrie couldn't tell her parents about Seth, because her father hated the Sioux and thought all Indians were alike. After they had secretly courted for a few months, Carrie ran away with Seth. They were married by our tribal law and later, when Carrie's pregnancy began to show, by a justice of the peace in Hill City."

Kedra looked at the photograph of her parents. "Is that when this picture was taken?"

"Yes. By then, I had returned from the east and the Nahtow were moving south. Seth had begun to have dreams. In them he saw a beautiful building—a temple. His heart yearned for the blessings given there. With so few of us left, Seth wanted us to go and do the work for our families. In his dream, I think he saw the end of the Nahtow. He spoke to me of his fears, but also said that even if we were lost as a people our bloodline and gift would continue, for he had seen it."

"How many Nahtow were there when you met Jack's wagon train?"

"There were just fifteen who still wore the Nahtow totem. Only five of them were children."

"Daeden!" Jack exclaimed. "He was your son. I remember him. We played together."

Kedra watched her uncle as joy and then sorrow touched his face.

Zed pointed at Jack's thumb. "And you became blood brothers."

"Yes!" Jack held up his thumb, displaying a scar. "Is this how you knew who I was?"

"That, your red hair, and your height told me." Zed put more wood on the fire. "You are the image of your father, although you are a few inches taller. Your father, Connor, was my height."

"You and my cousin became blood brothers when you were only four years old?" Kedra asked, astonished.

"It was Jack and Daeden that brought the Garrison's wagon train and the Nahtow together. They both wandered off and found each other. When Connor Garrison and I discovered our children playing with each other, we began to talk. Once we knew we were headed for the same place, both the Garrison's wagon company and the Nahtow agreed we should travel together."

"Everyone in the wagon train was fascinated by the Nahtow. They were such regal people, so friendly, so—Mormon," Jack said.

"We camped just outside of Douglas. Our white brothers went into town and bought supplies, while the Nahtow hunted game. We left Douglas two days later, well supplied for our journey to Zion."

Kedra smiled picturing the wagon train made up of both white men and Indians, who shared the bond of church membership and the same dreams and goals.

"We went a day's journey and camped in the trees close to the river just west of a place called Deer Creek Station. There was good grass for our horses and the three cows the wagon train had brought with them. We set up camp for the night."

"That's when Daeden and I decided to become blood brothers."

"Jack's mother, Fiona, and my wife, Yarley, thought the two of them were too young."

Jack said to Kedra, "They thought we would cry when it came time to cut our thumbs and mix our blood."

"Connor and I told them we would let them become blood brothers when they were eight years old," Zed said.

"But Daeden and I didn't want to wait. Daeden took a small knife from his mother's things. We hid in the bushes and cut our thumbs." Jack smiled broadly. We wouldn't let each other cry, even though it really hurt. We pressed our thumbs together and vowed to always be Nahtow-Irish. He gave me a tiger-eye bead. I gave him the penny I had to buy candy when we got to Casper."

Kedra smiled. "How did your mothers take your new kinship?"

"We both got a good scolding, but by then all we wanted was to have our mothers make our thumbs stop bleeding. We'd done too good a job of cutting them," Jack said, grinning at his scared thumb.

"Connor and I told them they wouldn't be allowed to hunt with us in the morning. Their thumbs would be too sore to handle a bow or a knife." Zed's expression was pained. "Over the years, that decision is the one that haunts me the most. If I had let Daeden come with me that morning, he and Yarley would still be alive."

"What happened?"

Jack and Zed exchanged a tragic look.

"Just before dawn, Jack's father and I went out to hunt. He wanted to learn how the Nahtow hunt," Zed said. "We bagged two rabbits and a small deer. We were on our way back when we heard the sound of gunfire. It was coming from the camp. We dropped the meat and ran."

"I woke up to the sound of gunfire. At first I thought it was Dad and Zed. I poked my head out from under the wagon, where Daeden and I were sleeping, next to my brother, Jared." Jack swallowed and held his head. "I heard the sound of cattle, lots of them. The ground began to tremble. It woke the camp. The adults rushed into the center of the camp. They were all yelling at once, trying to decide what to do. The sound of cattle and gunfire seemed to surround our camp. Someone yelled, 'the river is our only escape'. In the next moment, the stampede was on top of us." Jack ran a shaky hand over his eyes. "Daeden and I stayed under the wagon, with Jared. When there was a small break in the stampede, Daeden darted out from under the wagon. He ran toward the wagon his mother had rolled under, trying to reach her. As he ran, men on horses burst into the camp, firing their guns, driving more cattle through the camp. Daeden fell and—and . . ."

"He was shot by a horseman and trampled by the cattle," Zed said, his face blank.

Kedra reached her bruised and aching arms out to the two men on either side of her and took hold of their hands, her own trembling.

Jack turned to Kedra. "I crawled out from under the wagon, trying to reach Daeden. I don't know where your father came from, but he scooped me up and ran with your mother toward the river."

"What about your mother?" Kedra asked Jack.

Jack drew several shallow, rapid breaths. "I saw her jump out of the wagon box and push Jared back underneath it, just before a man on a horse . . . shot her. She fell into the stampeding cattle." Jack stared into the fire. "I didn't see what else happened in the camp after that, but a masked rider rode after your parents and me. He fired his gun. Your father began to fall." Jack's hand tightened on hers. "He dropped me. Your mother picked me up and put me in a tree. 'Climb up high,' she said and turned back to your father. She had almost reached him when—when the man on the horse fired again. She fell and began to crawl toward your father, just as she reached his side, the man on the horse stepped down. He put a gun to the back of her head. She turned and looked up at him. He dropped the gun and said her name. As he bent over, she pulled off his mask, gasped, and said, 'Elisha, why?'"

Kedra was shuddering. Jack's grip on her hand was almost painful, but far less painful than what he was saying. Tears were running down his face and hers.

His grip slackened. "Kedra, I had Eli Moore investigated. He told her what Luke Laramore had found out. "Elisha Lander was the name Eli Moore was using when he worked as a ranch hand in Wyoming for the Sweet Grass Ranch."

"You're saying my mother knew Eli Moore as Elisha Lander, and—he killed my father?!"

Jack rubbed a hand across his face. "That is a question you will have to ask Eli. The man your mother called Elisha said he had to get her away before anyone could stop him. She argued with him, throwing herself on the body of your father. Elisha tore her away from him. She pleaded to take your father's totem, a large pouch that hung on his hip, and a gold chain from around his neck. He allowed her to take the items. Then he put her on his horse and they rode east along the river."

"The gold chain your mother took from your father's body belonged to our father Nahtow. On it hangs a unique and precious jade pendant." Zed said.

"I have, or rather had, that pendant. I still have Nahtow's gold chain and the earrings that go with the pendant." Kedra turned to Jack. "The pendant is now in Jack's, or should I say, the law's hands." She turned back to Zed. "The pendant and earrings fit together to form a map—my mother whispered that to me."

"The map leads to the Nahtow library, containing all the records we have compiled for over a thousand years," Zed said to Jack.

Sakowin Nahtow—1884: It is in my heart to return to the Footstool of God and settle what is left of my people there. I will take Seth and we will go to see the library. I will put my pages into the book of Nahtow and I will teach Seth how to make more pages of the gold ore that the people of this land find so precious. Its worth to me is only in its power to preserve our history and genealogy. While Seth and I are near the Great Altar we will decide where the remnant of our people will end their days. Our small numbers are not a threat to the white man. It is my hope that we may be able to buy land for our people to settle on in the remote area where the library resides.

"Do you know where to find the Library?" Kedra asked Zed.

"No. I have only seen the earrings, which your mother always wore," Zed said. "My brother wore the pendant under his shirt, as all our chiefs had before him for ten generations. Only the chief of the Nahtow knew where the record chamber was. He kept the pendant hidden, although the tribe was aware he wore it. The heavy gold chain it hung from could be seen around his neck. It was a badge of his authority, his right to rule the Nahtow. Your Grandfather took Seth to the chamber after he'd seen sixteen summers. When they returned, my father no longer worn the pendant under his shirt, Seth did."

Kedra quickly drew the pendant and earring map in the dirt, connecting the earrings to the pendent by the double and single dots of gold at the edges. "Do you know where the library is now?"

Zed stared at the map. "Yes."

"I'd like to know, if you'll read the symbols to me, and tell me what they mean."

"The earrings are landmarks that sit south of library." Zed pointed to the one on the left. "The long flat line that tapers off at the top of the earring is a flat top mountain called the Great Altar—that is what the symbol under it says. It sits southwest of the library. The earring on the right depicts a mountain the Nahtow call the Footstool of God. It sits southeast of the library." Zed paused staring at the pendant.

"And the library?" Kedra prompted.

"The entrance to the library sits over the side of a narrow land bridge." Zed pointed to the two parallel lines and the small box below it. "The symbol at the top of the pendant says: The path of honor that leads to knowledge."

"Have you seen this land bridge?" Kedra asked.

"Once—at the last gathering of the Nahtow on the Footstool of God, but I did not know it led to the library. When I found your father, after the massacre, the pendant was gone. I assumed one of the marauders took it from him. I thought the Library's location was lost forever."

"So you didn't see what happened in the camp?" Kedra asked, bringing the subject back to the massacre.

"When Connor Garrison and I reached the camp, the marauders were beginning to retreat. They were still shooting their guns, trying to move the cattle out of the camp. When we saw them and what they had done, Connor began to shoot at them. He hit one of them, although the man managed to stay on his horse and ride off."

Kedra gasped, "Effie's first husband."

"I'm afraid so," Jack said.

"I drew my bow and shot at them too. Jared Garrison came out from under the wagon, screaming his mother was dead. Connor started to run to him, he was cut down by one of the riders as they rode out of our camp."

"How—how many died?" Kedra asked in a hushed tone.

"Most of the Nahtow were trampled by the cattle as they ran from the camp. I found a few of them in the bushes. They had been shot. My wife, Yarley, was the only one that survived. She was close enough to one of the wagons, when the cattle burst into our camp, to roll under it. She screamed for Daeden to stay where he was, but she later told me he must have thought she was calling for him to come to her." Tears rolled down Zed's face. "She saw him dart out from under the wagon. Before she could do anything, a man on horseback shot Daeden and then the cattle stampeded through the camp. She couldn't bear the sight. She worked her way into a hollow log, inside a tight group of trees behind the wagon. That's where I found her."

"What about the members of the wagon train?"

"A young couple, Hyrum and Jenny Creamer, were the only other survivors, besides my brother and me," Jack said. "The Creamers survived because they were up river fishing, when the marauders came. They heard the commotion and hid until it died down."

"Of the thirty-nine people in our camp, only six of us survived," Zed said; his eyes haunted with the memory. "When the Creamers came back to camp they decided to leave as quickly as they could. They were afraid the marauders would return. They urged us to come with them. Yarley refused to leave, until after we buried our son. The Creamers were too afraid to stay, while I dug Daeden's grave. They took Jack and Jared and told us they would go back to Deer Creek Station and bring back help. After they left, I dug graves for my brother, Jack's parents, and Daeden. Yarley and I searched for Carrie, but found no trace of her. We left the site of the massacre before the Creamers returned—if they did return."

"They did," Jack said. "A number of people from Deer Creek came with us. They buried the rest of the dead. Most of them attributed the massacre to a range war, which had started just a couple of days before we arrived. There were two big ranches near Deer Creek, the Sweet Grass Ranch and the River Rock Ranch. Everyone agreed what had happened was probably a tragic mistake. They speculated that the cowboys, from one of the ranches, saw the smoke from our fires, heard our cows, and thought we were from the rival ranch, trying to horn in on land they thought was theirs. They started the stampede and once they rode into our camp and realized they'd just attacked a group of pioneers, they tried to cover it up by killing everyone."

"Did the people from Deer Creek Station search for my mother?"

"I told them what had happened to your mother, and the name she said when she saw the face of the man who killed your father," Jack said. "The town's people said they would send to Douglas for the sheriff to look into what had happened and search for your mother."

"And did they?"

"I don't know. The Creamers were anxious to leave. The people from Deer Creek gave them all the money they found on the bodies of those in the wagon train and all the supplies their wagon could carry. They took my brother and me, and went to Casper. We stayed there for a week, until another wagon train came through. We joined that wagon train and went on to Utah. The Creamers settled in Huntsville. They took Jared and me in. I lived with them until I was twelve, then I struck out on my own."

"What did you and Aunt Yarley do, Uncle Zed?"

Zed stared into the fire. "At first, Yarley wouldn't leave the area where Daeden was buried. We camped out, staying away from the white man's settlements and ranches. Daily, Yarley and I visited Daeden's grave. It was the only place Yarley wanted to be. Her memory of that terrible day and seeing our son die began to consume her. She couldn't stop it from playing over and over in her mind. I finally convinced her to leave, but before we did, I went into Deer Creek Station and asked if anything had been learned about your mother. I was told the sheriff from Douglas had called off the search two days after the massacre. Yarley and I went on to Utah and were sealed in the Logan temple and had Daeden sealed to us."

Kedra smiled. "That's wonderful."

Zed returned her smile, but it faded quickly. "I wanted to have your parents sealed together too, but I didn't know if Carrie was dead or alive."

"It's all right," Kedra said squeezing his hand, "their work can be done now, and I can be sealed to them, too."

Zed nodded and continued, "After that, Yarley got better for a while, but she couldn't bury the terrible memories of that day deep enough to keep them away. She became very ill in her mind and died a year after the massacre."

A heavy silence fell over them. Outside the rain had stopped. The darkness was giving way to a silver dawn. The clean smell of rain washed earth blew into the cave, over the top of the dying fire.

There were so many more questions Kedra wanted to ask, so many more answers she needed, but the grief on Zed's and Jack's faces wouldn't let her ask them, at least not now.

Zed finally roused himself and put the last of the wood he'd gathered on the fire. "It will be light soon."

"We have to get back to the ranch," Jack said. "I'm sorry, Kedra, but after I found the emerald in your room, I called Marshal Laramore. He and Sheriff Hadlock are coming out to the ranch this morning to arrest you."

"For what," Zed asked sharply.

Kedra stood up and picked up her dried clothes. "I'm going to change while you explain to my uncle why you are arresting me."

34

The hoof beats of riders galloping away and Buck issuing orders to the ranch hands, reached Kedra before she, Jack and Zed got to the end of the trail behind the barn. Kedra spotted Effie and Josiah, huddled together with Buck as soon as she came into the yard.

"What's going on?" Kedra called.

"Kedra!" Effie screeched, "Where have you been?"

"We've been searching everywhere for you and Jack," Josiah said.

"Who's your friend," Buck asked, sizing up Zedekiah.

Before Kedra could answer, Effie pointed at the bandages around Kedra's and Jack's heads and cried, "What happened to you two?"

"Bushwhacked," Jack spat, disgustedly.

"By Isaac," Kedra added.

Jack clamped a hand on Zed's shoulder. "Zed, here, saved our lives."

"Isaac has had a busy night," Effie said bitterly. She took hold of Kedra's hand. "Come with me. Isaac shot your father two hours ago, and Dr. Robinson doesn't think he'll live."

Kedra felt the impact of the news as though she was the one who'd been shot. Bitterness lost its grip. She acknowledged that although Eli Moore had lied to her all of her life, he had taken care of her, even loved her. The anger she felt toward him dimmed. It was impossible to go from loving him as a father to hating him for what he'd done to her real father. A man she'd never known. Still, it would take time to forgive Eli and she couldn't call him Papa anymore. She had a picture of her real father now and she could see, not only her mother in herself, but her father too. *Zed can help me know and love him.*

Lifting her throbbing arms to massage her hammering head was almost more than she could physically do. She needed to lie down, but more than that she needed answers. If Eli Moore died, she would never get all the answers to the questions bombarding her. As heartless as it might be, she intended to get the answers she needed, before he died.

She came back to what Effie was saying.

"That's why we've been searching high and low for you. Eli has been asking for you," Effie said, tugging on Kedra to come with her.

Kedra broke away from her. "Uncle Zed, will you come with me?"

"If it is what you want," he said.

Effie gave her an incredulous look and then stared up at Zed. Her eyes widened. "Well I'll be."

"Maybe it would be a good idea for the law to come along too," Kedra said to Jack.

"Your pa told us not to call the sheriff," Buck said.

"I thought we should, anyway," Effie declared.

"No need, Jack is a U.S. Marshal and his posse will be here shortly," Kedra said, eliciting astonished expressions from her father's employees.

"Well what do you know . . ." Josiah muttered.

Effie overcame her astonishment and said, "Come along then. I don't know how much time Eli has left."

"Tell me what happened," Jack said to Josiah, putting on his Marshal's demeanor, as they went into the house.

Kedra listened, but only with part of her mind. Most of it wondered what to say to the man who had deceived her for twenty odd years. *How can I comfort him and at the same time accuse him? If he really is dying, maybe he'll want to tell me the truth.*

The thought of Eli dying brought genuine sorrow. The good times they'd shared, all he'd done for her, given her, touched her with compassion, and she realized Eli Moore had changed his life for her. *That's why Isaac hates me! He knows I'm not his sister and that Eli loved my mother and me more than he ever loved Isaac and his mother, but why?* For a moment she was overcome with pity for Isaac. *Is that what has made him into such a monster?* It was one more sin to lay at Eli Moore's feet, but she wouldn't be the one to do it.

"A gunshot woke me up," Josiah explained, limping along beside Jack. "Not that I was really asleep, the gout doesn't let me sleep too well, you know."

Jack nodded. "What did you do when you heard the shot?"

"I roused Effie, told her I heard a gunshot, and it sounded like it came from the house. She told me it was thunder, said I was just a silly old man and told me to go back to sleep. But a minute later, Buck knocked on our door."

"I heard the shot too," Buck put in. "I looked out and saw the light on in Mr. Moore's office. That surprised me, because Mr. Moore told me he was going to stay in town for night when he got back."

"Buck and I went over to the house," Josiah continued. "We knocked on the office door, no one answered us, but we heard moaning inside."

"We found Mr. Moore on the floor behind his desk, shot in the belly," Buck said grimly.

"Did you see Isaac?" Jack asked.

"I caught a glimpse of him scurrying like a rat into the trees," Effie said.

"You say that as though he was on foot," Kedra said.

"He was, and I thought that was strange."

"Did anyone go after him?" Jack asked.

"I'm afraid not," Buck said. "We were too busy taking care of Mr. Moore to think about anything else. I got some of the boys to help me put Mr. Moore in his bed, while Effie called the doc."

"Dr. Robinson got here an hour ago." Effie shook her head. "He said its remarkable Eli is still alive, but told us not to expect him to survive." She put her arm around Kedra. "It's best you know the worse before you go in to see him, child."

They reached the stairs and Josiah struggled to go up them. Jack reached out his hand to help.

"Appears to me, I'm in better shape than you are," Josiah muttered.

When they reached Eli's room, Zed asked, "Are you sure you wouldn't like to speak to Eli Moore alone for a few minutes, Kedra?"

She hesitated, and then shook her head. "No, I want you and Jack to come in too. You can stay near the door, until I need you."

Flanked by her two towering pillars of strength, Kedra knocked on Eli's door. Dr. Robinson answered it and stepped out into the hall, closing the door behind him.

"Miss Moore, I'm glad you're here." Dr. Robinson looked at her with concern. "It appears you also need my services."

"We do," she said, gesturing at Jack. "But we can wait. How is my— he doing?"

"He's getting weaker, but holding on by the strength of his will. He told me he wasn't going to die until he talked with you."

"Isn't there anything you can do for him?"

"I'm afraid not. At this point, surgery to remove the bullet would only kill him faster. Now, you better go in."

Zed's arm came around her. She leaned into him feeling the need for his comfort and looked up at Jack.

Jack gave her hand a reassuring squeeze. She nodded, and Jack opened the door.

Isaac, again dressed as Eyes O'Shea, bought a ticket for Denver. It wasn't what he wanted to do. Going to Denver was a dangerous move, but necessity was forcing his hand. He'd spent too much money on Goldie Yates, a gamble that would now never pay off.

Keeping his eyes lowered beneath the wide brim of his hat, he favored the ticket agent with a mournful expression, which went admirably with his black mourning outfit, something he often wore while traveling as Eyes O'Shea. The outfit discouraged people from approaching him. He noticed the agent's interested look, but polite manners kept the man silent. Eyes put the ticket into the bag he carried and found an empty bench in the station.

With his face largely hidden by his hat, he had little fear of being recognized. It was one of the things he'd learned about people. Most of them only saw what they were expecting to see.

Dressed in mourning garb, with his hair and face disguised, it was virtually impossible for anyone, even those who knew him, to recognize him. Only his eyes had the power to give him away, which was why he kept them lowered and shielded beneath the brim of a hat.

His sorrowful demeanor belied the rage burning in his belly. He'd spent so much money on Goldie Yates that he now needed more money to finance his trip to Argentina and his life for the next year. The Emeralds were so unique that he didn't dare sell them too soon. Even in South America it might not be safe to do it in less than a year. He had to come up with enough money to see himself through until it was safe to sell the gems, and he didn't intend to live like a pauper during that time.

It was crucial to make the right connections when he got to Buenos Aires, in order to secure the future he deserved, but he couldn't do that without sufficient financial resources. The money he'd left in the hiding place wasn't enough.

Under his breath, he cursed his father, wondering why the old man had come home just before dawn, instead of checking into a hotel in town.

His father had surprised him while he was going through the office, looking for money. It left Isaac without a choice. He knew he would have to kill Eli. He couldn't afford to let anyone on the ranch see him. He wanted them all to believe he was still in Aspen. That he had disappeared in Aspen.

Eli's unexpected arrival had thwarted his carefully laid plans to make his father suffer. Kedra too had thwarted his plans. She'd cheated him of seeing her hang and watching his father's anguish, but she hadn't given him a choice either. His thin lips disappeared into a hard line.

Killing Eli hadn't held any gratification. It had simply been a necessity. He did, however, let himself enjoy the shock on his father's face when he shot him. Anger immediately followed. He hadn't come away with any more money. The gunshot made it impossible for him to stay and continue to look. Even as he climbed out a window, on the other side of the house from the cabins, he heard boots and voices entering the house.

Denver was now his only hope. Isaac had friends and connections there with people who only knew and did business with him as Eyes O'Shea.

As Eyes, I'll sell the pearls. They should net me sufficient funds to allow me to keep the diamond ring. I'll have to chance going to Drew's hideout too. He probably has money squirreled away somewhere in the place, unless the cops have already found the hideout and taken everything, but that isn't likely.

He'd killed Ellis on Friday night, and it was only Tuesday morning now. *If I'm lucky, they won't find Drew's hideout in Denver until after I can search it. The cops probably haven't even connected Drew's death with the emerald robbery. When they do, they'll believe Kedra killed him too. What luck—seeing Kedra in the Grand Junction station that night.*

He looked up at the clock on the wall of the station. There was still an hour before the train arrived. Sitting in the station made him feel exposed. Still, it would be better not to walk around town. The fewer people he came in contact with the safer he'd be.

He spotted a newspaper stand and bought a paper. Settling down in the least visible corner of the station, he held the paper in front of his face, knowing it was going to be a long, tense hour.

Kedra trembled as she approached the bed where Eli Moore lay mortally wounded. In the dim glow of a bedside lamp, it seemed as though he'd aged ten years since she'd dropped him off at the train station. He looked so helpless, something she'd never imagined he could be, and deathly still.

For a moment, she wondered if his trip to Carbondale had been successful. Had he convinced Oran Kerr to buy the cattle? It suddenly seemed so trivial.

She hesitated, glancing back at Zed, standing by the door, and then at Jack. He was standing at the foot of the bed. She drew on their strength, before taking the final steps to the side of the bed.

Eli's eyes were closed. He was ghostly pale, and his breathing was labored.

Hesitantly, she covered his hand with hers. The effect astonished her. All the years of loving him as her father came back to her. Compassion filled her, and sorrow encompassed her for this man who had made choices in his life that had brought him to this deathbed.

He opened his eyes and grasped her hand. "Kedra," he whispered. "I was afraid you wouldn't come."

"I wouldn't want to be anywhere else."

She brushed her fingers through his thinning gray hair, searching for the courage to ask the questions she needed answers to.

His brow furrowed. "What happened to your head?"

"Isaac," she said, wincing as his hand squeezed hers painfully.

"I tried so hard to make it up to him—for the years I left him with his aunt. Nothing I did made any difference. He hated it here, hated me, hated you, because I loved you more than him, and he felt it."

Kedra took a breath and said, "And because you loved my mother, more than you loved his mother, despite the fact my mother was never your wife and you aren't my father."

He gasped and choked, coughing and struggling to breathe. "How—how did you . . . find out?"

Kedra gestured to Zed. He stepped out of the darkness and into the light of the lamp, his arms folded across his broad chest.

"This is Zedekiah Long-Sight, my uncle."

Kedra shrank back from the intensity of the hate that radiated from Eli toward Zed. His whole body tensed with it, as though he might suddenly spring up from the bed and attack Zed. It drained away from him as suddenly as it came, leaving him with an expression of heartrending remorse.

"Zed kept Isaac from killing Jack and me tonight," Kedra continued. "He and Jack were both there at the massacre. They told me what happened. Jack was the boy my mother put into the tree. He was the boy my father was holding in his arms, when you shot him. Jack saw you shoot my mother too—recognize her and take her away."

Tears rolled down Eli's face, into his mustache and onto the pillow beneath his head. "I'm so sorry. I hoped you'd never find out. It was what Isaac was blackmailing me with." His eyes beseeched her. "Don't hate me, Kedra. I tried to be the best father I could to you."

"I know—I know you love me, and you did your best by me, but there are questions I must have answers to." She brushed away a tear. "Did you send the letter my mother asked you to send?"

His astonishment was acute. "How do you know about the letter?"

"I am Nahtow. I remember my birth. You tried to make me believe that what was a memory was just a dream. I know now it was real."

His eyes closed, and Kedra's heart jumped. His breathing was so shallow it was almost undetectable.

"No," he finally said. "I didn't send the letter your mother wrote to your grandmother Barlow. You were all I had left of Carrie. I couldn't let anyone take you from me."

"How did you know my mother?"

Eli moaned. His whole body convulsed.

"Kedra, he hasn't got much time left," Jack said, quietly.

"Jack," Eli rasped out. "Take care of her—promise me!"

"I will, Eli—on my honor," Jack replied solemnly.

Kedra shot Jack a sardonic look.

Eli closed his eyes and let out a breath. It seemed as though minutes crept by before he drew in another one. His eyes fluttered open, looking intently into Kedra's eyes. "I love you, Kedra. Everything you want to know . . . is locked in the safe downstairs."

She ran a gentle hand down the side of his face, acknowledging his love.

A hard fit of coughing shook him. Blood seeped from his lips as he recovered. "I wouldn't open the safe for Isaac when he demanded to search it for money. That's why he shot me. I couldn't let him . . . rob you . . . of the truth. The combination is fifty-seven . . . four . . . elev . . ." The breath wheezed out of him. His hand went slack around Kedra's.

"No!" Kedra cried. She bent down and brushed his brow with a kiss. "I know you spent your life making up for the wrongs you did by loving and raising me. I can't find it in my heart to hate you. Be at peace, Eli Moore."

Jack stepped to the side of the bed and closed Eli's eyes. He took Kedra's hand from Eli's and pulled the bed sheet up over his face.

35

Kedra turned to Zed, weeping and shaking. He folded her into his arms.

Jack experienced a sharp dig of envy. It was natural for Kedra to seek comfort from her uncle, but he wished she also needed his comfort. It was an absurd wish. He was her enemy, sworn by honor and duty to bring her to justice. *That's all she'll ever see me as now.*

His head hammered mercilessly and he was beginning to feel sick to his stomach. He knew he should sit down before he fell down. *Kedra needs to as well. She looks so tired, so desolate. I can't imagine how she must feel right now. Her life has changed in an instant. Nothing she believed or knew about herself or her family was true. Worse, she's facing a hangman's noose, unless I can prove she's innocent.*

A commotion beyond the door sent Jack striding across the room. He went through the door, closed it behind him, and leaned against it, needing the support. Effie, Josiah, Buck, and Dr. Robinson were all arguing with Marshal Laramore and Sheriff Hadlock.

"Jack!" Luke exclaimed. "I'm going to arrest all these people if they don't quit interfering with the law."

Tate eyed him with alarm. "What the devil happened to you?"

"Bushwhacked—but that can wait. I want to talk to you two in Eli's office, privately, for a few minutes." He motioned for Luke and Tate to go and turned to Dr. Robinson, a competent looking middle-aged man with spectacles. "Eli is dead. Please get Kedra to bed and examine her head and arms." He turned to Effie. "Make her something to eat and you two"—he pointed at Buck and Josiah—"keep this ranch running until things can be sorted out."

Dr. Robinson took hold of the doorknob, and said to Effie, "Make Miss Moore some warm broth and bring her some bread." As he opened the door, he said to Jack, "I'll see you as soon as I finish with Miss Moore."

Jack nodded. "I'll be in Mr. Moore's office. The rest of you—get going." He turned on his heels, and by sheer willpower made it down stairs to Eli's office.

"What's going on?" Luke asked as soon as Jack opened the door.

Jack collapsed into a chair, holding his head. "Give me a minute."

He took several deep breaths and leaned his head against the chair's padded back, trying to make the room stop spinning. As briefly as he could, he filled Luke and Tate in on what had happened.

When he finished, Tate reached for the phone. "I'll call my deputy, Quinn Rawlins, and have him round up some help and start the search for Isaac Moore in town."

"Have someone go to Voorhees Livery Stable. Find out when, or if, Isaac picked up his horse. Effie said he left here on foot, but I'll bet he didn't go far on foot. I think he just didn't want to be heard approaching the house, so he left the horse in the trees beyond the fence line. Have Effie show you where he disappeared and see if you can track him."

"I'll get on it right after I call Quinn."

"I'll go upstairs and see if I can find anything in Isaac Moore's hiding place," Luke said. He stood up and paused. "You know we still have to arrest Miss Moore, Jack."

"I know, but we aren't going to do it today. She's in no physical condition to be put in jail right now. Why don't you go to town, grab your gear, and put up here for a day or two. I'll let her know she isn't allowed to leave the premises without our permission. As soon as the doctor says she's all right, we'll take her in."

"Fair enough," Luke said and left the room.

Tate hung up the phone. "Quinn will have men searching the town for Isaac in the next few minutes. He'll call me back about Isaac's horse. I'm going to deputize some of the ranch hands and have them help me search the ranch for Isaac's trail, in case Isaac is hiding out somewhere on the property. They know this plateau better than any of my men."

"Good," Jack said, rubbing his forehead. "Keep me informed."

"Right," Tate replied, going out the door.

Effie and Dr. Robinson came into the office as Jack struggled to his feet. "I'm all yours, Doc."

Dr. Robinson grasped Jack's arm. "I want you in bed, right now."

Effie took hold of his other arm. "It looks to me as though you're going to need more tending than Kedra, and it will be easier on me if you are both on the same floor. Kedra suggested you stay in Isaac's room. That is if you can make it back upstairs."

Dr. Robinson and Effie got Jack up the stairs and to the bedroom. Effie left him at the door and went to check on Kedra, while Luke gave the doctor a hand. Between them they got Jack onto the bed.

"There's nothing in the compartment under the floor," Luke said, setting the bedside table back in place.

Jack groaned. "I was afraid of that."

"I'll go through the office—see if Eli knew what Isaac was up to."

"If he knew anything it will be in the wall safe, behind the picture on the east wall."

"Do you know the combination?"

"Yes, but I want to wait until tomorrow. Right now Miss Moore and I aren't in any condition to go through it, and we both need to be there when it's opened."

Luke started to protest.

Jack raised an exhausted hand. "Luke, please, it can wait. Right now would you bring my gear up from the guest room? It seems I've been reassigned for the time being."

"Would you also call Mr. Schwarz, the town mortician?" Dr. Robinson asked. "He's listed in the phone directory. Have him come out for Mr. Moore, please."

"I'll take care of it," Luke said.

Thirty minutes later, Jack had five stitches behind his ear

Dr. Robinson gave him a mild dose of morphine and watched him take it. "I'll be back out tomorrow to look at you and Miss Moore. Until then, you are to stay in bed." He paused as he packed up his medical bag. "In my opinion, you need to stay in bed and rest for the next three or four days."

Jack nodded, although he had no intention of staying in bed for four days. "How is Miss Moore?"

"She, like you, has been given a little morphine for pain and is resting comfortably. Her uncle is watching over her."

"Good," Jack murmured groggily and let the morphine take him away.

The room was dim with evening shadows when Jack woke. For several moments he wondered where he was and why his head felt so awful. Movement, from across the room, made him lift his head. He moaned, dropping his bandaged head back on the pillow.

"Do you think you could eat something?" Zedekiah asked.

"How long have I been out?"

"Over eight hours."

"Kedra?"

"I was with her when she woke up, about thirty minutes ago. She has already eaten and is asleep again."

"Good." Jack massaged his temples. The sleep had done him good. His head ached with a dull throbbing pain, but at least it was bearable. "Did she take more morphine? I'd like her to sleep through the night—she needs it."

"As do you." Zed walked over to the bed and helped Jack sit up, putting pillows behind his back and head. "I want you to try to eat.

Then I have been instructed by the doctor to give you another dose of the morphine."

Jack shielded his eyes from the light when Zed turned on the lamp next to the bed. He brought over a tray and set it on Jack's lap.

The room swam.

Zed frowned at him. "I brought up a bucket, just in case the food doesn't sit well."

"I'm not sure I want to eat."

"You need to drink some water, even if you don't eat."

Zed lifted a cup to Jack's lips. Jack took a tentative sip. The water tasted good and soothed his dry throat. He took the cup from Zed and slowly drank it down.

"What's been going on while I've been out?" he asked setting the empty cup on the tray.

"The body of Eli Moore has been taken to the morgue. Effie Blue has cleaned up Eli's room and Kedra asked me to sleep there. Marshal Laramore has taken up residence in your old room and has made an exhaustive search of the house and barn. He has taken into evidence letters from Kedra's room, along with a page from a journal he found with the letters. The page was torn out of a journal written in by Isaac Moore, which he found in this room. Isaac claims he knew Kedra committed the robbery and murders, although he didn't say how. He said, you were succumbing to Kedra's charms and he was afraid you and she would run off with the emeralds. He also feared Kedra knew what he suspected and would kill him."

Jack snorted, and then groaned. The page had obviously been planted after he'd searched the house. Everything on the page was a lie, except for him succumbing to Kedra's charm, and he was painfully aware of that truth. "What else is going on?"

"I went back to the mine shaft and retrieved your hat." Zed pointed to the dresser where he'd put it.

"Thanks, I'm very fond of that hat. What else is happening?"

"Half the ranch hands are still out searching the plateau for Isaac Moore, because Sheriff Hadlock received word from his deputy that no one has seen any sign of Isaac in town. He hasn't even been to the stable to get his horse. It's still there, and, according to the proprietor, it's been there since Sunday night when Kedra brought it in after Isaac went to Aspen."

"Then how did he get out here and get away after he shot Eli? He's not the sort to go for an extended hike." Jack huffed out a breath and made a face at the broth on his tray.

Zed pulled up a chair beside the bed and sat down.

"What else is on your mind, Zed?"

"I've been talking with Marshal Laramore. He is convinced Kedra committed the emerald robbery and murders. I want to know if you believe that too." He held up a hand to forestall Jack's answer. "I'll admit the evidence is very condemning. He says you intend to arrest Kedra as soon as she is able to get up."

"I don't believe Kedra committed the robbery and murders—anymore. Not since Isaac attacked us. But I don't have a choice about arresting her. If I don't, Marshal Laramore will. I believe Isaac set Kedra up." Jack's jaw tightened. "He did a darn good job of it too." Jack set the tray aside. "Somewhere out there, there has to be proof, not only of Isaac's guilt, but of Kedra's innocence. It won't help just to prove Isaac committed the crime, that won't save Kedra, there's too much circumstantial evidence against her. She'll simply go from being the mastermind to being an accomplice. I have to find conclusive proof that she didn't have anything to do with it."

"*We* have to find that proof. I have just found the only living member of my family, the only other Nahtow. I can't lose her, Jack. I won't lose her. I don't care what I have to do. I won't let her die for a crime she didn't commit."

"Then we are agreed, because I won't let it happen either."

"Where do we start?"

"She told me she was still in town when the train left on the day of the robbery. There must be someone who saw her. Put an ad in the Avalanche. Ask if anyone saw her that day." He pointed to his pants, lying at the foot of the bed. "There's money in my pockets."

"I have sufficient funds to meet my needs and to do what Kedra needs. What else?"

Jack sat forward. "Talk to Kedra. At this point, I doubt she'll talk to me. She's bound to think of me as the enemy, and I don't blame her. But if I'm going to prove she's innocent, I need to know everything she can tell me about Isaac: His habits, his haunts, anything odd he does, people he associates with, friends here and in other places. You know the kind of mind she has. You'll know the kinds of questions to ask to jog her memory—pull out things she knows, but hasn't considered." Jack paused, trying to think and finding it harder and harder to do. Finally he said, "I don't believe Sheriff Hadlock or his men are going to find Isaac. He has too much of a head start. If I'm going to find him, I've got to know how he thinks—find the right trail, the right bait."

"I will do as you wish. We must find him, Jack Garrison."

Jack sagged back against the pillows. "At the moment, finding Isaac looks like Kedra's only hope."

36

Wednesday, June 24, 1908

Eyes O'Shea slipped by the front desk in the Garden Arms Boardinghouse without waking the night clerk. The sleazy flophouse sat at the edge of Denver's old Chinese Hop Alley district. It boarded on the bawdy red-light district and was a place now frequented by only the lowest forms of humanity. The Garden Arms had a single virtue. No one ever asked questions. As long as the rent was paid and the police weren't call in, the landlord never saw or heard anything.

Isaac knew coming to Drew's room was a big risk. Coming as Eyes O'Shea minimized the risk. If any of the bums or thugs that lived here approached him, they would be in for a surprise. His disguised made him look helpless, but if it came to defending himself the element of surprise was on his side. He'd taken fencing and boxing in college. He'd learned to use the tools of the street gangs. His hand slipped into his coat pocket, grasping the handle of his blackjack as he noiselessly climbed the stairs.

He wanted to avoid being seen. Eyes always attracted attention. He didn't want anyone to describe him coming or going from Drew's room. It was only a matter of time before the police found Drew's hideout. Once they did they would ask about visitors.

Eyes stopped in the shadow of the stair landing, listening to footsteps on the stairs above him. The sound moved away from him. He cautiously resumed climbing to the third floor, still seething with anger and wallowing in bitterness. *Right now I should be on my way to marrying wealth and position, not scrounging for money in Drew's sleazy digs.* At least he'd had the foresight to take the key off Drew when he killed him. He'd done it to keep the law from easily finding Drew's hideout. *Now if only Drew has a money stash. I have to come up with enough cash to live on for the next year.*

Only when he'd secured sufficient funds could he go to San Francisco. When he got there, he'd assume one of his new identities and buy a boat ticket to Argentina. Once he made the right connections in Buenos Aries, he'd sell the emeralds, and go to

Europe. There, he'd marry into the nobility. He would finally have the life he deserved.

If Drew's stash is small, I'll have to risk hocking the pearls to increase the size of my purse. That was something he hoped to avoid.

Opening the door to the third floor hall, Eyes peeked out. The night was the time most of the occupants of the Garden Arms were out, pursuing their nefarious deeds. Nothing moved in the dim light of the hall. Eyes traded the blackjack for the key to Drew's room and hurried toward it. He pushed the key into the lock, turned it, and opened the door in one clean movement.

A sound from down the hall made him dash into the dark room and shut the door. Footsteps stomped by the door. Eyes fumbled for the light switch. The inadequate light from a single bulb glowed overhead, leaving deep shadows around the edges of the room.

Instinctively, Eyes locked the door before looking around. He noticed the raised gold wallpaper was peeling around a window with a torn shade, which was drawn down. Beneath it, the wooden windowsill was marred by cigarette burns. The room smelled of body odor, cigarettes, and more exotic drugs.

Drew would have hated it, but it was a necessary precaution before the robbery for him to move to an undisclosed location. If he was suspected of being involved, Isaac advised him to make it as hard as possible for the police to find him. Eyes admitted Drew had chosen well. However, he didn't see any place that looked promising as a money stash. The room contained nothing more than a bed, a small table and a single chair, with a row of drawers built into the wall next to a narrow closet.

Eye's searched the bed, turning over the mattress, looking for tears in the mattress cover where money could be concealed.

"Nothing," he grumbled under his breath.

The same results met his inspection of the underside of the table and chair. He moved on to the drawers dumping them out, searching through the contents. Finding nothing, he examined the undersides of the drawers and the spaces they had occupied. Irritated he pulled Drew's belongings out of the closet and rifled through them. He was about to admit defeat when one last idea came to him.

It was too dark to see inside the closet, which was undoubtedly alive with things he'd rather not run into, but he was desperate. Running his hand along the inside wall of the closet and then up over the doorframe, he was rewarded by the feel of an envelope taped to the wall. He pulled it out and opened it.

His immediate elation dwindled. There was only a couple hundred dollars in the envelope. *I'll have to sell the pearls. I'll do it as Eyes. That should be safer.* He thought about who he could get to fence them for him. It wouldn't be wise to use the same fence he went to as Isaac. No, he needed someone new, someone reliable. *At least I know where to look.* Stuffing the money in his pocket, he crossed the room, and stood next to the door, listening for sounds in the hall. Cracking the door open he peered out—the hall was empty.

He made it down the stairs and was almost across the lobby, when the desk clerk suddenly awoke on a loud snore and looked his way. He quickly turned his face away. *At least the clerk doesn't know what room I went to visit.*

Leaving the hotel, he stepped onto a streetcar headed east toward Curtis Street. He paid his five cents, found a seat, and rode out of the seedy neighborhood. When the streetcar reached Curtis Street, he got off in front of an exclusive saloon, walked around to the back, and went up a private set of stairs to the third floor landing. Using his passkey, he unlocked the door and entered a hall, dimly lit by wall lamps. He moved the base of a wall lamp. A wooden panel sprang open. Inside, a narrow set of stairs led to an attic room.

He climbed the stairs to his hideout, planning his next move. *With luck I can sell the pearls for a good price. Added to what I already have, and Drew's money, I should have enough to see me comfortably through a year's exile in Argentina within a couple of days. That's as long as I dare take. Hopefully the law will think I'm dead, after they read that journal entry and can't find me. Still, the sooner I leave here, the better.*

Jack woke with a start. The heavy blue velvet curtains at the window were still pulled shut, making it impossible for him to know if it was night or day. Something moved in the darkness next to him. His hand shot out in a defensive reaction and grabbed an arm.

"Ah!" Kedra cried.

Jack let go of her arm. "I'm sorry, I couldn't see you and my immediate instinct was to protect myself. Did I hurt you?"

"Well you probably added to the bruises Isaac gave me."

"Forgive me. I didn't mean to."

Kedra's voice moved away from him. "I know." She pushed back the heavy drapes.

Jack shaded his eyes, blinking while they adjusted to the light. "What time is it?"

"It just after eleven—you've been asleep for over twelve hours."

Actually, Jack hadn't slept for nearly that long. He'd put off taking the morphine so he could think, a hard prospect with his head threatening to explode. Still, he'd persisted, going over everything from the moment he arrived in Glenwood Springs to the present, but this time looking at the crime with Harry as part of it and Isaac as the mastermind—the one who committed it. He'd reviewed everything he knew about Isaac, which wasn't much, and everything he knew about Harry. What Luke had always said about Harry had suddenly popped into his head. It grew into a nagging notion, one he wanted to pursue.

Kedra sat down in the chair next to the bed. Her head was no longer wrapped in a bandage, and Jack could see the bruising that feathered out beyond the hairline of her right temple.

She leaned forward in the straight back chair. "Jack, Zed told me you don't believe I committed the emerald robbery and murders."

He dropped his head back against the pillow. "That's right, but unless we can find proof of your innocence, the Justice Department will prosecute you."

"If you believe I didn't do it, then why prosecute me?!"

"All the evidence I have says you did, and . . . I'm sorry, but I'll have to testify about the evidence I have against you."

"Then what hope do I have?"

"I'm duty and honor bound to bring the person who killed two U.S. Marshals to justice. After what Isaac did to us, I'm convinced he committed that crime. I won't rest until I can prove it."

"He tried to kill us! Isn't that proof enough?"

"I'm afraid not. It could be argued that you were both in on the crime, and he simply tried to eliminate the last accomplice, so he could keep the emeralds for himself."

"Oh!" Kedra straightened in the chair. "It was Isaac who took the emeralds out of my room—not Swindler. Wasn't it?"

"I'm afraid so, and by now he's long gone with the emeralds, the pearls, the diamond ring, and the money."

"Leaving me to hang for his crimes!" she said bitterly.

Jack sat up and reached for her hand. "I won't let you hang. I'll find Isaac and make him talk."

"Except, he hates me so much that I'm afraid if you do find him he'll proclaim I was in on the plot all along."

It felt as though she'd read his mind, because that was Jack's fear too. The hate that had plotted out this crime to frame Kedra was a fiend Jack had never encountered. Jack was sure Isaac would rather see Kedra hang than tell the truth, even in exchange for his own life.

The realization hit him forcefully. Finding Isaac wasn't going to help him prove Kedra's innocence. *What I have to find is some kind of solid proof of her innocence, but where can I find it.* He tried to think, but his mind was still muddled.

Kedra's stood up. "I didn't come in here to talk about Isaac. Marshal Laramore won't let me open the safe until you can come downstairs. I hate to ask it of you, but if Zed came and helped you, could you make it downstairs?"

"Send Zed up to help me get out of this bed and into my clothes. We'll meet you in the office in ten minutes."

Kedra sat in a chair near the wall safe, waiting for Zed to bring Jack down, aware of Marshal Laramore's condemning eyes. *I'll have to get used to that look from people. The law says I'm innocent until proven guilty, but most people will believe I'm guilty until proven innocent. I'm glad my trial won't be here.*

Marshal Laramore had just told her that because she'd killed two federal agents, she would be tried in the federal court in Denver.

At least I won't have to endure the suspicion and condemnation from people here in Glenwood Springs.

The door opened, Jack ducked through it. Zed had a steadying hand under his elbow. They stopped next to the wall safe, which Kedra had already uncovered.

"Open the safe, Kedra," Jack said, leaning against the wall. "I'll remove the contents piece by piece and recite what I have found." Jack looked at Marshal Laramore. "Are you agreeable to that, Luke?"

Marshal Laramore nodded.

Kedra opened the safe and sat down. Zed sat next to her.

Jack addressed Marshal Laramore, "As I told you last night, there are things in this safe that have nothing to do with the emerald robbery or murders. They are the sole property of Kedra Long-Sight, known as Kedra Moore. These are things that have been unlawfully kept from her. It is my intention to turn them over to her. If you have any objections, please make it known when I remove the article."

Again Marshal Laramore nodded and Jack proceeded.

He removed a large envelope and read the listed contents aloud, "This envelope contains the deed to the ranch, the contracts to cut timber in the White River National Forest, bills of purchase and sale for cattle, contracts with the hired hands, and a certificate of marriage."

Kedra handed the envelope to Marshal Laramore without looking at the contents.

Luke opened the envelope and pulled out a sheet of paper. He asked her, "Did you know Eli Moore's wife's last name was O'Shea?"

"N-no," Kedra stammered. "Eli never spoke to me of his marriage to Isaac's mother."

"So you were unaware that Harry Walsh or as you knew him, Morgan O'Shea and Isaac were cousins?" Luke asked.

"Cousins?!" Kedra exclaimed.

"Harry's mother, Ursula Walsh was Isaac's mother's sister. The one Isaac went to live with."

"You didn't tell me last night that you'd made that connection," Jack said accusingly, to Luke.

"I got the information this morning. Harry's and Isaac's O'Shea grandparents came back from the gold fields in South Dakota broke. Ursula and her family took them in. They became the driving influence in the lives of their grandsons, according to Ursula Walsh Warren."

"Neither of them ever said anything to me about it. I didn't even know they knew each other," Kedra said.

The betrayal Kedra felt at the hands of Eli and Morgan burned inside her. *Eli lied to me. Isaac lied to me. Morgan lied to me. Even Jack lied to me.* All of them made her feel so used, so ignorant, so foolish. She reached out her hand. Zed took it. He was all she had to rely on. The comfort of his touch calmed her, reassured her, and grounded her in her identity. Zedekiah Long-Sight was who he said he was, and she had no doubt of his love and loyalty.

The next item Jack removed was Eli Moore's will. Kedra took it from him, but didn't open it. She handed it to Marshal Laramore without comment.

Luke took it with a puzzled expression. "Don't you want to know what is in your father's will?" he asked removing it from the envelope and quickly scanning the document.

"Eli Moore was not my father. All I want from him is what my mother left in his keeping for me, which he failed to give me, and the information he promised me was in the safe concerning his association with my mother."

"But, other than a couple of small bequests, he has left you everything his owns, including this ranch."

Kedra already knew the contents of the will. Eli had told her, just a few days ago, that Isaac had gotten all he was going to get from him. The ranch, or the profits from its sale, would be her inheritance. It was an inheritance she no longer wanted. Still, she knew what she would do with it. If all went as she planned, the matter would be settled today—without the interference of the U.S. Marshals.

She gestured for Jack to continue.

He removed a large leather bound volume with a clasp holding it closed. Tooled into the leather was the word, Diary.

Undoing the brass clasp, Jack opened the volume. "The first entry is dated, October 17, 1877. It details—"

"Could you jump forward and see if there is an entry about how he met my mother?" Kedra interrupted. She didn't want to hear all the details of Eli Moore's life right now.

Jack flipped through more pages and stopped. He silently read for a minute, and then said, "In December of 1884 Eli was back in South Dakota still going by the name of Elisha Lander. He tried gold mining, but the gold mines were pretty well played out by then or had been taken over by large mining operations. It seems he was down to his last penny when he met Grayson Barlow, your grandfather. Elisha went to work for him on his farm. He fell in love with your mother the moment he met her. She was seventeen. He says, 'She is the most beautiful, innocent creature I have ever met. She is everything kind, gentle, and good. I could start over, be a good man, settle down and farm. If she would consent to marry me, I'd be the happiest man alive. I wouldn't need wealth or prominence. She would be the greatest treasure I could ever have.'"

Kedra blinked back tears. The grief of never having known her mother grew inside her as Jack continued to scan the diary's pages.

He stopped. "Listen to this. It's dated March of 1885. 'I thought I was making progress with Carrie. Her parents are all for my suit. I thought Carrie was too, but things have changed in the last few weeks. She will hardly talk to me and avoids me whenever she can. I have noticed a kind of glow about her. The kind of glow a woman has when she's in love. I'm not the only one who has noticed it. Mr. Barlow mentioned it to me yesterday. He thinks it's because she's in love with me. I wish that were true, but it isn't. There is someone else. I know it. Carrie has been sneaking away from the farm. She disappears and returns with some sorry excuse when she's questioned about where she's been.'"

Jack ran his finger down the page. "'I followed Carrie this afternoon. She met an Indian down by the creek. He isn't Sioux. I have never seen an Indian like him. He is very tall, and muscular. He speaks perfect English. I watched him with Carrie for an hour. There is no doubt in my mind that she is in love with that savage. I'm going to tell her father about the Indian. I can't let her throw herself away on some savage she's having romantic delusions about.'"

Kedra sat forward. "Skip ahead, please. I want to hear what Eli has to say about the massacre and what happened to my mother."

Jack's finger skimmed the pages as he turned them. He paused and recounted, "When your mother ran off with your father, Elisha chased after her with the idea that he could bring her to her senses. He quit searching for her when the trail led into the heart of Sioux territory." Jack looked at Kedra. "He was devastated by your mother's choice and left South Dakota."

Again his finger skimmed over the pages of the diary before he reported, "When he got to Wyoming, he went to work on the Sweet Grass Ranch. He was working his way up to foreman when the trouble with the River Rock Ranch started. Jack's eyes shifted to Zed. "He says the 'show of strength' was his suggestion. The Sweet Grass Ranch wasn't as big as the River Rock Ranch was. If they were going to increase their herd they needed more grazing land. He thought it would only take a single decisive incident to make the River Rock Ranch stay off the territory the Sweet Grass Ranch wanted. His boss bought the idea and put him in charge of securing the range land the ranch needed."

"That means he's responsible for everyone who died in that massacre," Kedra said bitterly.

"He saw the smoke from our fires and the lowing of our cattle, the night before the massacre, and thought it was the River Rock Ranch trying to establish a hold in that area."

"Where did he take my mother?"

Jack's finger ran down the page, and then the next. "To a doctor in Douglas. Eli's bullet left a deep gash in her side. After the doctor patched her up, she demanded to go back and find out what had happened to the rest of the company. Eli promised to take her after she recovered. A couple of days later, she insisted she was well enough to travel. Your mother was running a fever by the time they reached Deer Creek Station. Her wound was inflamed, and Eli was sure she had an infection. He wanted to take her back to Douglas, but she wouldn't go until she saw the massacre site and your father's grave. Her grief was so great that she tried to make Eli leave her there. When she was too weak to fight him anymore, he brought her back to Douglas. By then the infection was too far along. She went in to labor the day after they returned to Douglas." Jack paused. "The doctor told Eli, she used all the strength she had left to deliver you. Eli says she knew she was dying, but was absolutely joyful about your birth." Jack looked down at the diary and quoted, 'Seth and I will live in our daughter. The Nahtow will live in our daughter.' Then she made Eli promise her the things you remember."

Kedra wept in Zed's arms. In a moment of despair she wished she had been allowed to go with her parents in death. They would be together—a family. The longing grew and deepened as she thought about what her future now held. *Maybe I'll be with my parents sooner than I think.* It was morbid, but curiously comforting, thought.

Zed stroked her hair and held her tenderly. Guilt rose up in her. *How can I wish to leave Zed? I'm all he has. Life has been so unfair to both of us, but we have found each other now.* The love that radiated from his gold eyes was a beacon of hope and strength. She smiled tremulously through her tears up at him. *I do still have a family and I'm going to fight for that future.*

"I'm sure you will want to read the entire account," Jack said closing the diary. "For the moment, we need to keep this diary. From the little I've read, I can see it contains information that might help us close some cases we believe Eli Moore, or rather Elijah Mooreland, or Elisha Lander, was involved in," Jack said, handing the diary to Marshal Laramore.

"I hope it will also give you some insights on Isaac and where he might be," Kedra said.

"So do I," Jack said, reaching into a side section of the safe and drawing out two sealed envelopes. The wax seals were old, but unbroken. He handed both letters to Kedra.

"These are the letters Eli told me about," she explained to Marshal Laramore, who eyed them curiously.

She held them up so he could see they were beginning to yellow with age and the seals were old fashioned. "As you can see, one is addressed to me. The other is addressed to my grandmother. My uncle and I will read these privately," she said, setting the letters in her lap.

The only other thing in the safe was wrapped in leather. Jack took it out and carefully removed the leather wrapping from the rectangular object.

Zedekiah was on his feet as soon as he saw the thin gold pages. "Pages from the Book of Nahtow, my brother's writings!" he exclaimed, reaching for them. "I thought one of the marauders took them from my brother's body. Long have I mourned their loss."

He reverently turned the three gold pages over in his hands, handing them one by one to Kedra. "These pages will tell you of your father and mother, your father's position as chief of the Nahtow, and his dreams that sent us on our way to Zion."

Kedra's fingers ran over the strange characters, neatly inscribed in the gold. "My father's words," she whispered, hugging the pages to her heart. "You must teach me to read them, Zed."

Zed smiled broadly. "Not only will I teach you to read them, but you will also write in the book of Nahtow. You are the hope of our people, our future. That is what your name means in Nahtow. It is why your parents decided to give it to you before you were born."

"What if I'd been a boy?"

"Then you would have been Kedran—the male equivalent."

Kedra stood up, still hugging the gold pages and her letters. "Will you excuse us? I'm sure there are things you and Marshal Laramore want to discuss, as do my uncle and I," she said to Jack.

"Before you go there are a couple of things we need to discuss with you," Luke said.

"What?"

Luke addressed Jack. "After you called me Monday night, about coming out to arrest Miss Moore, I wired the Department of Justice, outlined the evidence, and told them we were going to make the arrest this morning. They called me just before we came here to tell me Miss Moore's arraignment is set for next Monday in Denver."

Jack shot him a furious look.

"Rather anxious, aren't you, Marshal Laramore," Kedra said tightly.

"She's not leaving here until her fath—Eli Moore has been laid to rest," Jack snapped.

"I had Effie make arrangements to take care of that tomorrow," Kedra said softly. "Will I be allowed to attend the graveside service?"

"You will," Jack said, glaring at Luke."

"Will you, or will Marshal Laramore be my . . . escort?"

"I will," Jack said firmly.

"Anything else?"

"Yes. Do you have a recent picture of Isaac?" Luke asked.

Kedra thought about it for a moment. Isaac had avoided having his picture taken in the last few years. Then it came to her. "There is a picture of Isaac as an adult at his college graduation."

"Where would we find it? I didn't see a graduation picture when I searched the house."

"Neither did I," Luke said.

"I'm not surprised. My father didn't display it, because Isaac would have destroyed it."

"Why would he do that?" Luke asked.

"Several years ago, Eli caught Isaac destroying all the pictures he and I were in together. I, unwittingly, ended up in Isaac's graduation picture."

"Do you know where he kept that picture?" Jack asked.

"I suggest you look in the diary," Kedra said, walking toward the door. She paused on the threshold. "Are we done?"

"Yes," Luke said, already searching through the diary.

As Kedra and Zed left the room, Effie came hurrying toward them. "Oran Kerr is in the front parlor. He's here to finish the deal he and Eli made to buy the cattle." She paused. "I didn't tell him Eli is dead. How do you want to handle this?"

37

"**Zed, would you mind waiting upstairs** in the sitting room for me?" Kedra asked, handing him the gold pages and the two letters. "I shouldn't be very long."

"Take your time. It will give me the chance to read my brothers pages."

"Thank you." She turned from Zed to Effie. "Please go find Buck and have him come to the parlor."

Effie bobbed her head and hurried off.

Kedra glanced at herself in the hallstand mirror, inspecting her appearance before she went into the parlor. She didn't look her best. Her face was pale and the bruise on her temple was bright and ugly. *At least my long sleeves cover my bruised arms.* She consoled herself, entering the parlor.

A beefy man with a full beard was sitting on the edge of the settee, his Stetson on his knee. He looked as out of place in that room as a walrus would have been. Kedra's lips twitched. A walrus was a good comparison for Oran Kerr.

He stood as soon as she entered the room. His brows came together as he looked her over. "Miss Moore?"

"Yes." Kedra walked toward him with an outstretched hand. "And you are Mr. Kerr."

He took the hand she offered with a smile. "That's right."

"Please, sit down, Mr. Kerr." She gestured at the settee and sat in a chair across from it.

"I came to finish my deal with your father."

"I know, and I'm sorry to tell you, but . . . he was killed early Tuesday morning." As succinctly as she could, she told him about Eli's death, although she didn't tell him who the intruder was that killed him.

"I'm so sorry for your loss. I won't intrude on you any longer." Mr. Kerr started to stand.

"Please, Mr. Kerr. I know about the deal my father hoped to make with you. As Eli's heir, I'd like to conclude that deal," she said and started to describe the ranch's financial troubles.

Mr. Kerr interrupted. "I know. Eli told me that was why he had to sell the herd." He hesitated, turning his hat over in his hands, thoughtfully. "I haven't inspected the herd yet, and I would need proof you have the authority to sell them to me."

A knock sounded on the door. Buck poked his head in. "You wanted to see me, Miss Moore?"

"Yes, Buck. Will you take Mr. Kerr to see the herd?" She stood up and Mr. Kerr followed suit. "I'll have Eli's will ready for your inspection when you get back."

Kedra followed the men out of the room and went to find Effie. She was in the kitchen finishing up preparations for lunch. Her married daughter Dora was helping her.

"Thank you for coming to help," Kedra said, giving Dora a hug.

"I'm glad to do it, and sorry for your loss."

She smiled at the blond haired, blue-eyed young woman whose pregnancy was beginning to show, and said to Effie, "Would you go get Josiah and meet me in the parlor? I need to talk with both of you."

"But I have to get lunch on."

"I'll take care of it, Mama," Dora said.

"All right then." Effie untied her apron and went with Kedra.

They parted ways in the hall.

Kedra went to the office, knocked on the door, and entered without waiting for an answer.

The Marshals were both staring at a picture.

"I see you've found it," she said, stopping in front of the desk.

"We have," Luke confirmed.

"Would you mind helping me for a few minutes?" she asked Jack.

"Not at all, what do you need?"

"If you'd bring Eli's will into the parlor, I'll explain."

Luke started to rise from his chair.

"I only require Marshall Garrison's help," she said firmly.

Luke sat back down.

"I won't keep him long," she said, instinctively taking Jack's arm when he got up and swayed slightly.

He smiled down at her, seeming grateful for her supporting arm.

"Where's the will?" he asked Luke.

Marshal Laramore shuffled through the papers on the desk and handed him the envelope with the will.

When they were settled in the parlor on the settee, she read over the will. It was a simple document. Eli had left everything he possessed to her, with the exception of two bequests. Twenty-five dollars was to be given to Buck Gilbert and fifty dollars to the Blues. She read it without comment and handed it to Jack.

After he read it, she asked, "It means I can do what I want with the ranch and everything on it, isn't that right?"

"Yes." He paused. "Is there any money to pay the bequests Eli made to Buck and the Blues?"

"No, but if things go as I hope, there will be shortly."

"How?"

She explained about Oran Kerr and the deal her father wanted to make with him. "He's here right now—down looking at the herd with Buck. What I want to know is can I go through with the deal my father made."

"Did they have a signed agreement?"

"I don't know, but I need to put this deal through today. I want to pay the bequests Eli made to Buck and the Blues. The ranch hands also need to be paid off, and then let go. Selling the herd is the only way I can do those things. You can see that, can't you?"

"I'm not a legal expert in this kind of a matter. You should probably have a lawyer look the will over; just to be sure you can proceed with what you want to do."

Kedra favored him with rueful expression. "I guess I better find a criminal one as well as an estate one—hadn't I?"

His green eyes darkened. "Yes, Miss Long-Sight, you'd better," he said earnestly."

She shook off fear's momentary grip. "I didn't ask Mr. Kerr if there was a written agreement. If there is, could I make the deal?"

"If there is, and it's dated before your father's death, then I believe so. Still, it would be best to check with a lawyer. Is there a lawyer in the telephone directory?"

"I know there are a couple of lawyers in Glenwood. I assume they're in the directory, although I haven't dealt with either one."

Jack stood up, I'll go make a couple of telephone calls and see what a lawyer will tell a U.S. Marshal."

"Thank you."

The Blues came in as Jack went out.

"What do you need us to do, Miss Kedra?" Josiah asked.

"Sit down for a minute," she replied, gathering her thoughts.

Effie and Josiah sat on the settee and waited silently.

Kedra reached for their hands. They were as much her family as Eli had been. She loved them dearly and had watched them struggle over the years with hard work and low pay. There were times when she wondered why they stayed on. Now they would have a choice.

"I'm sure you know what I've been accused of doing," she began, putting up a restraining hand when Josiah started in on how insane the whole thing was. "I know, but there is so much you don't know. The truth is; I've been so brilliantly set up by Isaac that it's going to take a miracle to convince a jury I'm not guilty."

"What you need is a good lawyer!" Effie said.

"What I need is to settle things before I'm taken to Denver." She paused and held their eyes. "Eli left me the ranch. I don't want it."

Protests immediately came from the Blues.

"Listen to me. After all I've learned in the last thirty-six hours, I have to tell you, I don't want to stay here anymore—even if I'm found innocent and they don't hang me. I'm not coming back."

Tears rolled down Effie's face. "You can't mean that, Kedra."

"But I do. I'm going to go live with my uncle. If my grandmother is still alive, I'm going to find her. I want to know my family, my real family. So, as soon as a lawyer tells me I have the right, I'm signing the ranch over to you two."

Again she was interrupted by protests.

"You can do what you want with it. Keep it. Sell it. Burn it down. I don't care. It's yours to do with as you please. Next, I'm going to take whatever deal Mr. Kerr will give me for the herd. I intend to pay off the hands and let them go. If you want to keep them you'll have to talk with them. I'll be leaving here with the marshals as soon as Eli is laid to rest. I'm not going to take much with me. If they don't hang me, I'll send for my personal belongings." She leaned across the space that separated her from the Blues, put her arms around them and hugged them tight. "This is what I want. I hope you will respect it," she said to her weeping friends.

They nodded their heads, unable to say anything.

Jack came back into the room.

Effie looked up at him accusingly, "She's not guilty," she said hotly. "And if you think so, then you aren't the man I thought you were, Jack Garrison!"

"I know she's not," Jack sat down in a chair across from the Blues.

Josiah scowled at him. "It was Isaac that done it. Why aren't you out looking for him?"

"The hunt for Isaac is already underway." He leaned forward. "I promise you, I'm going to do everything I can to find proof of Kedra's innocence. I won't let her pay for Isaac's crimes."

"Then why arrest her?" Effie demanded.

He explained Luke's call to the Justice Department and the resulting arraignment date. "Now that the legal wheels are turning, I can't stop them."

The sound of the front door opening turned their heads toward it.

"That will be Buck and Mr. Kerr," Kedra said. "I want all of you to stay, but please don't say anything about my arrest."

Kedra made the introductions. She deliberately omitted Jack's position as a U.S. Marshal, introducing him, instead, as an expert cattleman. By saying that, she hoped to ensure Mr. Kerr would offer her a fair price for the herd.

She showed Mr. Kerr the will.

Jack made him aware of the possible legal issues and what he'd learned from Mr. Charles W. Darrow, a local lawyer.

Mr. Kerr listened politely. When Jack finished he said to Kedra, "The legal technicalities don't apply in this case." He pulled a sheet of paper from his pocket. "Eli gave me this bill of sale after we agreed on a price. As you can see, it's signed and dated. That should take care of the legalities." He took a check from inside his coat and showed it to Kedra. "I'll keep this check and write another one, made out to you, if you are agreeable to the price your father and I settled on."

"The price is more than fair," Jack said to her.

An enormous burden was instantly lifted from Kedra's shoulders. Her throat closed and she blinked rapidly. "I'm agreeable."

The check was big enough to pay off all Eli's debts and bequests. There wouldn't be much money left for her, but she hadn't expected there to be. Over the years her father's habits had caused her to put away a little money each month for unexpected needs. It wasn't a sizable bankroll, but it was at least enough to retain a criminal defense lawyer, once she got to Denver.

"Good, then I want you to endorse this bill of sale your father gave me," Mr. Kerr said.

Kedra signed the bill of sale.

Mr. Kerr wrote out a check in her name.

"There's one other thing I need to talk with you about." He looked sympathetically at Kedra. "Eli also told me the ranch had to be sold, but that you don't have a buyer yet. I wonder if you would hold off selling the ranch until after I sell the herd this fall. I want to leave the herd here for the rest of the summer. Buck has agreed to be in charge of the herd and the few ranch hands I'll retain to work the herd." He turned to the Blues, "I'll also pay you to stay on and do the cooking and general upkeep."

"Actually, Mr. Kerr, the ranch now belongs to Josiah and Effie Blue." Kedra stood up. She was anxious to read the letter her mother had written to her. "You will need to discuss all of this with them."

Kedra and Jack left them to do just that.

Jack stopped Kedra, once they were alone in the hall. "That was a very generous thing you just did, giving the ranch to the Blues. Are you sure about it?"

"Absolutely," she said and went up the stairs.

Jack sat down across the desk from Marshal Laramore. He eyed a thick roast beef sandwich, feeling hungry. *That must mean I'm on the mend.* His head still ached, but the dizziness was finally gone. Before he could take a bite of the sandwich, the office door opened. Sheriff Hadlock strolled in.

"Glad you're feeling better," Tate said, taking a seat.

In his direct way, Luke said, "You know the fact that Isaac and Harry were cousins doesn't help Miss Moore. It makes it harder to believe she didn't know Morgan O'Shea was really Harry Walsh."

Jack nodded. It was one more thing a jury would have a hard time buying. "Have you found Drew Ellis's residence in Denver?" he asked biting into the sandwich.

Luke shook his head. "He moved out of his apartment a few days before the robbery and didn't leave a forwarding address. I'm afraid it's going to take a little time to track his residence down."

"Make it a priority. Wire your deputy and have him get on it right away. I have a feeling Drew Ellis, even dead, can tell us a lot more about what really happened in that express car."

"I'll go into town now and do that, along with getting our train tickets to Denver. How soon do you want to leave?"

"Not until Saturday morning," Jack said firmly.

"Why?"

"After Eli Moore is laid to rest tomorrow, Miss Long-Sight has an appointment in town with Mr. Darrow, a lawyer, to see to the details of Eli's will and settle things here on the ranch. She can't leave without making provisions for the people who work and live here. Mr. Darrow will make up the legal documents as quickly as he can, but he said not to expect them before Friday afternoon."

"Then I'll book our train for Friday Night. That will allow Miss Moore to arrive in Denver in time to find a lawyer and meet with him before the arraignment."

Jack struggled to suppress the anger he felt toward Luke for calling the Justice Department before an arrest was made. This was, after all, his case. Luke had stepped over an ethical line in doing it. *He probably thinks I'm the one that's stepped over an ethical line with Kedra.*

His anger must have been apparent, because Luke said defensively, "Her lawyer can get the trial delayed if he needs too." He stood up. "I'll head for town now and get everything done."

"Don't buy a train ticket for me. I may not be accompanying you."

"Why not?"

"There are things I need to follow up with here, before I leave."

"If you'd rather go with Miss Moore on Friday night, I can follow up on anything you want," Tate offered.

"Thanks, but I've got a hunch I want to work on personally."

"Care to elaborate?" Luke asked.

"Not just yet," Jack said and gave his sandwich his full attention.

38

Kedra sat next to Zed on the big dusky-red Victorian sofa in the upstairs sitting room. The letters from her mother lay unopened in her lap. With rapt attention, she listened to her uncle read her father's words from the gold pages, he'd meant to place in the book of Nahtow.

Seth Nahtow—December, 1885: The Nahtow now number only twenty-five. Many have been lost in the quest for knowledge and have gone to seek it, never to return. Others have sought lives among the tribes of our brothers and are lost to our knowledge. Whether their children possess the gift of our first parents, I know not, but none returned to the Footstool of God at the appointed time to fulfill the mission given us by our first parents. My father and I waited many days, but no one came. I mourn that the names of their children are lost to us.

The Nahtow are now too few to continue the mission we were given by our first parents. I have prayed over the matter. And I know that with the restoration of the gospel of our Lord, the mission given to our first parents, to seek and keep the names of the people of this land in remembrance, as our honor has compelled us to do, is at an end. I also know there is yet a great work to be done by the Nahtow.

The gift is strong in me and in my brother, Zedekiah. It is strong in Zedekiah's Wife, Yarley, and his son, Daeden. In Daeden I have hope for the next mission of our people, for his blood is pure.

I have mixed my strength with that of a white woman, whom I love, more than my gift. Whether our child will inherit the gift, I know not. In my heart I pray my child will inherit the gift and participate in the work that is yet to be done.

The records must be translated into English, before they can be presented to the prophet of the Lord. Only then can the work for my people and many of Lehi's children, which have wandered in darkness for too many generations, be done. I know this because of the dream which was sent to me.

In it I saw a great and glorious building, sitting on a hill, the temple of our God. I saw my father and grandfather and great-grandfathers back through the generations lined up at the door of the temple, but they could not enter. Their names were unknown. My father looked at me and said, "The time is at hand; take the remnant of our people and go join with the saints of the Most High God. After you have received the blessings of the temple, go to the sacred place where our records are kept, translate them and bring them to the house of God. Do the work that will set us, and the children of Lehi, free."

I have determined in my heart to seek the blessings of the temple. Even now my people are preparing to leave our home in the Black Hills of Dakota. It has been a place of safety for us for many years. Now the wars between the Sioux and the white men threaten our peace, growing ever closer. I do not wish the remnant of this people to be caught up in this continuing conflict.

My fear that the Nahtow will disappear from the earth and the memory of men has troubled me. Long have I prayed over this matter. I have been given the assurance that in me, my people will survive and the knowledge of the Nahtow will continue. This is a comfort I cling to with all my heart.

Seth Nahtow—1886: We have met a group of Mormon pioneers on their way to Zion. They have welcomed us warmly, and we have decided to travel with them. Tomorrow we will start our journey together. The excitement in the camp is high. Our children and the white children are already fast friends. It makes me believe our brethren in the church will welcome us, when we arrive in Utah.

After Zedekiah finished, she asked him to read it again, this time pointing at the characters as he read. Her perfect recall eagerly ingested each one.

She pointed to where the writing ended. "There is more room to write. You must write more about the Garrison's pioneer company and deciding to travel with them to Zion—and . . . the massacre."

Zed's eyes filled with pain. "Yes," he agreed. "Over the years I have known I must write it, but I didn't know where the Book of Nahtow was, or Seth's pages. I have mourned that our people came to their end in such a tragic way. Now I can write it, knowing it is not the end of the Nahtow. You are the future of your people, the last known strand connecting us back to our first parents. The gift of the Nahtow is strong in you. You must go to the Library. Deposit your father's pages. I will help you make more pages, pages you will write on and tell about the regrowth of our people, our honor, and our future. You will be the translator and custodian of all the records the Nahtow have kept."

Kedra ran her hand over the letters in her lap. "Uncle Zed, the probability that I will be found innocent of killing those U.S. Marshals is very small. There's just too much evidence against me, and I have no alibi." She looked into Zed's gentle eyes. "If I was on the jury that heard this case and listened to all the evidence, I would vote to convict the person the evidence pointed to, wouldn't you?"

Zed folded her into his arms. "Jack believes in your innocence. He will do everything he can to prove you had nothing to do with the robbery and murders."

"Except he's the one who found most of the evidence against me, and that means he has no choice but to testify against me." She pulled back. "I don't want you to get your hopes up, but I do want you to stay with me. I don't know anything about being put on trial"—she trembled—"and I have to admit I'm . . . terrified."

"You must not let fear overtake you. There are things you can still do to help us find proof of your innocence."

"What?"

"I want you to remember everything and anything you can recall about Isaac: His characteristics, habits, idiosyncrasies, experiences you had with him. Reach back in your mind and see him from the day he came to live here, look for patterns of behavior, moods, and what triggered them. Jack hopes something you remember will help him find Isaac. Jack is determined to find him and bring him to justice."

"I don't know that finding Isaac will help me, but he does need to at least pay for Eli Moore's murder. But first, I'd like to read my mother's letter. I don't intend to read the one to my grandmother, unless she can't be found."

"Would you like to read your letter privately?"

Kedra hesitated and then nodded. "I'll read it in my room and then lie down for a while." She kissed Zed's cheek and stood. "Tell Jack to come see me in a couple of hours. I'll tell him then, whatever I've pulled out of my mind about Isaac."

Sitting in the big chair beneath the window with the sun shining in, Kedra broke the wax seal on the letter her mother had written to her, and carefully unfolded the heavy paper. Before she started to read, she let the memory of her mother come back to her. She was being cradled in her mother's arms. Her mother's breath was warm on her cheeks. Her mother leaned down and kissed her forehead, murmuring her love. Wiping her eyes, Kedra began to read.

My Darling Kedra,

I feared I wouldn't have the strength to bring you into the world and it was my final desire to do so. Your arrival has brought me overwhelming joy and abiding peace. Your father, Seth Long-Sight, is waiting for me, and I can't stay much longer. The thought of leaving you breaks my heart, but I can feel myself slipping away.

I have made the man, Elisha Lander, who caused your father's death and mine, promise to find your grandmother and give you to her. The massacre that killed your father may have also killed all that remained of the Nahtow. I have made Elisha Lander promise me he will find out if any of them lived through that terrible ordeal.

Kedra, you are a Nahtow princess. Your father was the chief of his people—small though they were. Because I am a white woman, you are only half Nahtow, yet I hope you will inherit the gift of your father. I'm leaving you everything that is of worth to the Nahtow. Seek your heritage, for it is glorious; one grounded in duty and service to the native people of this land—the children of Lehi.

What I want you to know more than anything else is that your parents love you. Our greatest desire was to go to the temple and be sealed together as a family. We are members of the Church of Jesus Christ of Latter-day Saints, often called Mormons. Seek out this heritage too, my daughter. It is the only path to everlasting happiness. The work of our people is grounded in it.

That which I have left you will lead you to the knowledge of your people—if you are truly Nahtow, for I have whispered the secret the jewelry contains into your ears. When you read this, you will remember how to use what I have given you.

It is my hope that a few of our people have survived and you will find them. They can teach you all you need to know to be true to your heritage. However, you are a child of dual heritage. My own people came to this country as pilgrims on the Mayflower. They were adventurers, seekers of truth and freedom. Learn of them too, my daughter.

If your grandmother is still alive, I have given instructions to Elisha to take you to her. She too is an adventurous soul. She will understand you. I have written to her about you. Her name is Martha Barlow. Your grandfather was killed in an Indian raid soon after I ran away with your father. I do not know if she is still living on the farm outside Deadwood in the Dakotas.

She came from a well-to-do family in Philadelphia, but like me, she had an adventurous spirit and when she met your grandfather, Grayson Barlow, a young man whose desire was to open up new territory and brave the wilds of this new country, she went with him.

I don't know what she did after he died. But if she isn't to be found in Deadwood, look for her in Philadelphia. Her family name was Howland.

Kedra, remember who you are. Be true to your heritage and your blood. Search out the truth, and live by it. You are our hope to be together eternally. Know that your parents loved you, even before you were born.

I know you will make us proud. Always remember—you are the hope of many generations of Nahtow and all the work they have done since Mormon gave to Nahtow and Elan their charge. Honor that charge, and complete the mission of the Nahtow.

With abiding love,
Your mother,
Caroline Barlow Long-Sight

Kedra felt the encircling love of her parents as she finished the letter. Their spirits filled her with warmth and strength and a determination to fight for her life. Her mother's words were now part of her. They would always live in her mind and in her heart. She understood her mother's ability to feel great joy while being brokenhearted. It was exactly how she felt.

Her fingers ran over the sealed letter to her grandmother. It contained her introduction to her mother's family. *I have more family out there—somewhere.* She found herself praying that her grandmother was still live. *I'm not alone in the world. I belong to two families. If only I could meet my grandmother, as I have Uncle Zed.*

The threat hanging over her pressed down, robbing her of her newfound hope. She wondered if she would ever have the opportunity to meet her grandmother and give her this letter. *If helping Jack find Isaac will enable me to accomplish that, then I'll do my best to think of something he can use.*

She lay down on her bed, rubbing her throbbing head, searching her mind.

More than an hour slipped by before a soft knock on her door brought her out of her memories.

"Whose there?" she asked sitting up.

"Jack— I thought if you were feeling up to it, we could talk for a few minutes."

She opened the door and stepped out. They went into the sitting room and sat down in a pair of companion chairs. Jack moved his to face her. Concern weighed heavy on his brow.

"I'm sorry to disturb you, but I need your help."

"Zed told me what you wanted me to do and I've been thinking about it for the last hour."

"Have you come up with anything that might be useful?"

"I guess you'll have to be the judge of that, but I have thought of several things."

Jack sat forward. For a moment she thought he was going to take her hand. He abruptly stopped himself.

"What can you tell me?" he asked in a gruff tone.

She realized his gruffness wasn't directed toward her, but himself. He was reminding himself of who he was and what his duty required. She needed to remember who he was too. He was first and foremost a U.S. Marshal, honor bound to do his duty. His testimony could hang her, but she had no doubt about his unwillingness to do it. *At least I'll have the small satisfaction of knowing he'll be haunted forever if I hang.*

"I don't know how helpful what I've remembered will be, but it's all I can think of."

Jack opened a small notebook, his pencil poised and ready.

"Isaac has always been fascinated with the theater. He loved acting in school plays and community pageants. When he was a child he used to pretend to be different people. Eli bought him costumes and he would practice using different voices for his characters. He was good at imitating voices and doing original ones too. His favorite place is an opera house. He is always at the one here in town. If anyone knows Isaac, it will be the choirgirls. He even went out for a while with the opera's star, Ada Reese."

"Was the girl, we saw him with at the dance, from the opera?"

"I haven't attended the opera for a while, but it's a fair bet she is—either that or she's a new bordello girl."

"Are opera and bordello girls his usual fare?"

"As far back as I can remember—they are."

"What about the girl he went to see in Aspen?"

"She's the only girl he's ever been serious about, and that has to do with his superiority complex. You see, Isaac feels he's better than everyone else is, and he deserves to live like the high and mighty. To him, Miss Goldie Yates was a ticket to that life. She is an heiress of vast wealth."

"I see. Did he court high society when he went to college?"

She shrugged. "Probably— I do remember he came home one Christmas, bragging about his friend Freddy Garland, whose father made a fortune in the Leadville silver and gold strikes. He invested the money and is now one of the wealthiest men in Colorado. As I recall, Isaac bragged about staying in the Garland's mansion, so they must have been fairly good friends."

"Does Freddy live in Denver?"

"Yes, in the swanky Capitol Hill district."

Jack jotted that down in his notebook, and asked, "Do you know his father's name?"

"Morton."

"Anything else?"

"Isaac always attends the theater when he's in Denver. I'm sure he knows quite a number of people in Denver's theatrical community. He used to say if he couldn't make a fortune, then he would go into acting, because he enjoyed that life and those people. Oh, and he likes to frequent saloons too."

"How do you know that?"

"I overheard Eli ranting at him about the bills." She tisked. "Isaac could sure make Eli's temper rise."

"I think that's the effect Isaac has on most people—me included."

"Is that because he got the better of you?" Kedra teased. "Don't feel too bad. Isaac is as light and fast on his feet as Swindler is."

Jack grimaced. "I hate being caught by the bad guys with my gun holstered—so to speak. But that wasn't what made me take an immediate dislike to him."

"What did?"

"The way he shoved you aside when he came out of the office, the day I came out here to meet Eli."

"Did he? I didn't even notice. I guess I'm just used to how he treats me."

"You should never have had to put up with him." Jack closed his notebook and stood up. "Thank you for your insights."

"I hope something I told you will help you find Isaac. He's a dangerous man, one who won't stop hurting other people to get what he wants."

"I agree." He stepped away and stopped. "I meant to tell you. Sarah Powell called while you were resting. She heard about what happened to Eli. That news is all over town. She's concerned about you and wants to come out to see you. I told her you were resting and would call her back."

"Does she—along with the rest of Glenwood—know I'm about to be arrested too?"

"No, that information is only known to Sheriff Hadlock, Marshal Laramore, and me, well, except for Zed, Effie, Josiah, and Buck. I've talked with all of them and they aren't going to say anything about it. You have the right to bury Eli without everyone in town knowing your business. No one else will know about your arrest until after you leave Glenwood Springs."

"Thank you, Marshal, I appreciate that."

"I liked it better when you called me Jack."

A poignant sorrow built inside her. "I think it's better if we both keep in mind that you are a U.S. Marshal with a duty to do, and I'm the suspect you're arresting for several brutal murders."

She looked away from the pain in his eyes.

"I can appreciate why you would feel that way, Miss Long-Sight."

39

Thursday, June 25, 1908

Kedra knew laying Eli Moore to rest would linger in her mind and haunt her. Her grief for him was genuine, but not in the way everyone assumed. She grieved for what he'd done to her parents—and to her, while acknowledging how hard he'd worked to be a good father to her, and he had been a good father. Still, he'd robbed her of the opportunity to grow up knowing her real family—of being with them, a part of them. She knew she would have to forgive him for that, and she would—with time.

If it hadn't been for Jack deftly fending off the curious inquires of several well-meaning people, she wasn't sure she would have made it through the brief graveside service for Eli. At her request, Zed didn't attend. He was just one more thing she didn't want to explain to the town's people, many of whom came out to pay their respects at the Linwood Cemetery where Eli was buried.

After the service, Kedra went to Sarah's home to rest and have lunch, before she was scheduled to meet with the lawyer who had agreed to take charge of Eli's will. She intended to ask him if he could recommend a good criminal lawyer in Denver.

Jack declined Sarah's invitation to stay for lunch. He wanted to look into his hunch, which had been growing stronger, as soon as possible. *Besides,* he reasoned, *if Kedra wants to confide in Sarah, she won't do it with me around. I owe her that opportunity.*

Stepping out the door of the Powell's house, Jack spotted Marshal Laramore across the street, determinedly keeping an eye on Kedra. He knew trying to dissuade Luke would be pointless. If Luke wanted to stand around in the hot sun, that was his business. Still, he walked over to him and warned him not to intrude on Kedra.

As he rode Soldier toward the opera house, Jack found himself praying that Kedra *would* confide in Sarah. *She is Kedra's closest friend, and right now, Kedra needs the understanding and support of a woman she trusts.*

Their last conversation made it clear she wasn't going to confide in him. *And why should she? I'm the enemy—unjustly persecuting her. But I'm not going to let things stay that way.*

Soldier plodded down the street. The people of Glenwood went about their business. The sun shone cheerfully down and the air was alive with the sounds of everyday life. Jack, usually attuned to everything going on around him, didn't take notice of any of it. His mind was turned firmly inward.

He faced the truth squarely, something he'd deliberately refused to do for most of his life. Just as he'd faced his feelings for Kedra Long-Sight and the tragedy in his past; he knew it was time to face his real demons.

Feelings of deep loss and the fear of loving people, who might be taken from him, as his parents and Daeden had been, tormented him. Then the horror of being unable to do anything to save the people he loved—of watching them die—racked him. Those same demons were growing inside him again. His duty demanded he hand the woman, he now admitted he was in love with, over to be tried and hung.

It had only been two weeks since he'd met Kedra, and yet his heart was absolutely certain of what he felt and wanted. That last dance on Strawberry Day, and the ride home, had made him believe she felt something for him. His duty required him to use that *something* to try and extract information from her.

The horror of his predicament grew on him. His head wounds started to pound as his internal conflict grew. He couldn't—wouldn't betray his badge or President Roosevelt's trust for Kedra. And he wouldn't let her hang for crimes he was now sure Isaac had committed.

He pulled up in front of the opera house and tied Soldier to the hitching post. *Isaac's habits and tastes might be the key to tracking him down. They will at least help me get a better picture of Isaac and what he's capable of doing—whether or not my hunch pays off.*

The front door to the opera house was locked. Jack went around to the back, found the stage door, and went in.

A bouncer shouted at him, "You can't come in here."

Jack produced his badge and let the burly bouncer take a close look. He towered over the bouncer, and said in a soft, steely voice, "I'm investigating a murder. Take me to your boss—right now."

For the next hour, Jack interviewed every girl in the opera production, including the opera's star, Ada Reese. He finished the interviews with Lillian Lee, Isaac's most recent love interest.

"When did you meet Isaac Moore?"

Miss Lee's rouged lips pouted in thought. She twirled a finger around a bright copper curl and looked at Jack with a coy but unmistakable invitation. "Well now, let me think." She tapped her pursed lips, and posed prettily.

She was very young, and Jack pitied her for the life path she'd chosen. He couldn't see it bringing her anything but unhappiness. Her obvious artifice told Jack that she was still fairly innocent. She hadn't mastered a more seasoned woman's charms in the art of flirtation.

He deliberately glowered at her.

Her china blue eyes widened with offense. Her face became that of a pouting child. "It was the day that extra edition came out about the emerald robbery and murders. I remember because all the girls were reading about it when Isaac's flowers came with an invitation to dinner after the show."

"Did you know who he was before the invitation came?"

"No. His note said he would be sitting down front, and I would recognize him by the blue columbine he would be wearing in his lapel. The note said if I wanted to accept his invitation I should meet him at the stage door after the show."

"I assume you met him."

Her back straightened defensively. "Why shouldn't I have accepted his invitation? He is a very handsome gentleman, and he treated me like a lady."

"Did you take him to your residence?"

"I don't think that is any of your business!"

Jack leaned toward her. "It may interest you to know, Miss Lee, that Isaac Moore is wanted for the murder of his father, among other things. He is a very dangerous man. You might want to keep that in mind before you invite the next man you barely know to your lodgings. Not only that, if Isaac thinks he's welcome in your home, he just might show up there hoping you'll hide him from the law." Jack leaned in even closer. "That would be a very dangerous, even deadly, thing to do."

Miss Lee's jaw dropped. She swallowed and pressed a frightened hand to her heart. "I—I had no idea . . . and he won't come back to my place. Not after I caught him stealing my best scarf, after he brought me home from the Strawberry Day dance."

"Tell me about that."

She shrugged. "I invited him in and went to get us a couple of drinks. When I found I was out of whiskey, I went back into the living room to ask if beer would be okay. I caught him tucking my scarf into his coat pocket. He tried to tell me he just wanted a memento to remind himself of me while he was gone on business to Aspen. But I didn't fall for that line. The girls in the chorus had already warned me about him. They told me he liked to take—well, souvenirs from them."

"The other choir girls told me he *stole* collars, gloves, stockings, and even jewelry, from them."

"I should have listened to them, and I might have, except he's so dreamy that I just couldn't resist."

"Was the night of the Strawberry Dance the last time you saw Isaac Moore?" he asked.

"Yes. I told him to leave and not come back. I mean, that scarf cost me almost a week's salary. If I hadn't come back into the room when I did, he would have taken it—the louse."

With growing optimism, Jack left the opera house and rode over to Voorhees Livery stable. *I believe my hunch is going to pay off. Now if only someone at Voorhees stable can confirm what I believe—I may be on Isaac's trail before sundown.*

Old Mr. Voorhees spoke with a heavy Dutch accent. He was bent and wiry from years of hard labor. As soon as Jack met him, he knew the man was a horseman and loved what he did. He practically danced around Soldier and wanted to know all about him. Jack satisfied Mr. Voorhees curiosity, before he brought the conversation around to what he was interested in knowing.

He showed Mr. Voorhees his badge. "I'm interested in who your customers were late Monday night and early Tuesday morning. Did anyone unusual come in?"

"Sure did, came in real late on Monday night."

"Who was it, and what did he want?"

Jack left the livery stable, elated with the information Mr. Voorhees had given him. He went over to the sheriff's office and found Tate at his desk.

"Can I use your phone?" he asked, before Tate could even say hello.

Tate waved a hand at the instrument on his desk. "Help yourself. I'll go get a cup of coffee."

The sheriff came back into the office just after Jack finished talking with Effie.

"I need a good artist," Jack said, grinning broadly.

"What for?"

"Just humor me, Tate. Do you know someone who can draw faces?"

"Like the kind on a wanted poster?"

"Yes, like that."

Tate reached for his hat. "Let's go."

They went to the home of Debra Gordon. Jack was surprised when Debra turned out to be a fourteen-year-old girl. She was short and plump, with huge brown eyes and a cheerful countenance.

Jack handed Debra Isaac's graduation picture, and the girl set to work, drawing an enlargement of Isaac's face.

"I've seen him before—around town," she said as she put the finishing touches on the drawing. "He's very . . . pretty."

"Pretty?" Tate asked.

"Yes, he'd make a beautiful girl."

"Debra, could you draw me a picture of Isaac as a girl, wearing a wide brimmed hat with a veil pulled down over his eyes?" Jack asked.

"Sure."

Jack held his breath as Debra drew, watching her progress over her shoulder. She was an exceptional artist.

The puzzled expression on the sheriff's face, when Jack made his request, grew into comprehension. "Well I'll be—" Tate caught himself before the colorful expletive came out of his mouth. "How did you—"

"I'll explain later," Jack said, taking the pictures of Isaac as a man and a woman from Debra. "Right now I have to get to the train station. I'll meet you back at your office in about hour." Jack handed Debra five dollars and tapped Isaac's graduation picture, which was still on Debra's desk. "How long would it take you to make two more copies of this man, as both a man and a woman, and get them over to Sheriff Hadlock's office?"

Debra took the money with effusive thanks. "I could probably have them there in about an hour. Would that be all right?"

"That will be just fine," Jack said, putting his copies of Isaac, as a man and a woman, in his pocket.

He went to the depot and found the ticket agent that was on duty Tuesday morning. The young man looked at Jack's badge with alarm.

"I've never met a U.S. Marshal before," he said, staring up at Jack with the apprehension Jack had seen so many times before.

Why is it that honest folks suddenly feel threatened when a lawman shows them his badge? Marshal Garrison quickly put the anxious agent at ease by stating his business.

"I want to know if you sold a ticket to this woman, early Tuesday morning." Jack showed the agent the picture of Isaac as a woman.

Recognition leaped into the agent's brown eyes. "I should say I did! You don't forget a woman who's that beautiful."

"Where did she want to go?"

"She bought a ticket to Denver—on the morning train."

"Did you see her board the train?"

"Yes. She's a hard woman to miss, being as tall as she is and dressed all in black as she was. It made me think she was in mourning, but I didn't want to ask. She kept her eyes down and it seemed to me she wanted privacy. After she purchased the ticket, she bought a newspaper and sort of hid behind it until the train came."

He has a two-day lead on me. "When does the next train to Denver leave?"

"At six o'clock this evening."

"I need a ticket on that train and the use of a phone."

After buying a ticket to Denver and calling the ranch to arrange for Zed to bring his belongings to town, Jack went to find Kedra. He knew when she was scheduled to meet with Mr. Charles Darrow, attorney at law, and where his office was located. Her buggy was tied up in front of the lawyer's office when he arrived. He found Luke sitting in it.

"You are nothing short of tenacious, Luke, but Miss Long-Sight isn't going to skip out on us."

"She's gotten to you, Jack, and you aren't thinking clearly."

"It's precisely because I've gotten to know her that I'm sure she isn't going to run. She wants her name cleared, and you are going to help her do that."

"What?"

"As of now, you are going to turn over every rock and question every citizen in this town, and on the High Peak Ranch, until you know where Isaac Moore was and what he was doing every minute during the day of the robbery. You have until the train leaves on Friday night to account for his whereabouts at the time of the robbery. Get Tate to help you if you need to, but find proof of where he was."

"I've already told you it won't help the girl."

"You can't be sure of that until you can prove where Isaac was when the robbery and murders were committed." Jack pulled out the drawing of Isaac as a woman. "And don't just ask about Isaac Moore, ask about the woman Isaac can turn into whenever he likes. That's how he left Glenwood on the train to Denver Tuesday morning."

Luke didn't hold back his expletive as he studied the picture. "How did you come up with this?"

"You were the first person to put the notion into my head when you said Harry was pretty enough to be a woman. The notion grew when I searched Isaac's room and found a dress and a woman's veiled hat in the back of his closet. Then, when we learned Harry and Isaac were cousins, I got to comparing them in my head. They're both pretty enough to be women. I called Effie. She told me the woman's clothes in Isaac's closet are gone."

"Well I'll be a—"

"The only thing you've got time to *be* is a good detective. I suggest you start by seeing if anyone saw Isaac, in either of his personas, near the boat dock the night before the robbery. Then talk to the women in the local bordellos. Kedra told me Isaac has a taste for them. I've already talked to the opera girls. He wasn't with any of them on the day of the robbery. They also told me Isaac used to steal things from them, girly things."

"Don't you want to follow all this up with me?"

"I don't have time. He—or rather she—has a two-day lead. I'm headed for Denver on the evening train." Jack put a hand on Luke's shoulder. "I'll meet you at Tate's office in half an hour. He'll have this same set of drawings for you by then. Don't let me down, Luke. I believe we're finally on the right track." Jack paused and thought for a moment. "Find out if Isaac took the train to Grand Junction as a woman the day Ellis was murdered. And one more thing—you do know Zed will be coming to Denver with Miss Long-Sight. If you do anything on that trip to offend his niece, I've given him permission to scalp you."

"But I don't have any hair left," Luke said rubbing his bald head.

"I was talking about your upper lip, and he won't be using a straight razor either."

Luke held up surrendering hands. "I don't know why you believe in this girl's innocence, when everything we've got says otherwise, but I'm a man of the law and I'll go with the letter of it, which says, innocent until proven—in a court of law—guilty."

"Thanks. Now get going. You're running short on time."

40

Kedra came out of Mr. Darrow's law office into the glare of the afternoon sun and shaded her eyes, something the narrow brim of her hat failed to do. She spotted Jack standing beside her buggy, talking with Zedekiah. Her uncle handed Jack a large satchel.

"What's going on?" she asked, walking up to the men.

Jack gave her a rueful smile. "You're going to be rid of me for a couple of days."

"Rid of you?"

"I have a number of things to tell you, which we can't discuss on the street. Let's go over to Sheriff Hadlock's office, and I'll explain."

She drew back. "Am I being put under arrest?"

"No, but I have a meeting scheduled with Marshal Laramore there, which concerns you."

Zed took hold of her hand. "It's all right. Jack has invited me to come too."

"Okay," Kedra said, letting Zed help her into the buggy.

She tried to ignore the stares and whispered comments as she walked into the sheriff's office with Jack and Zed. What she overheard relieved her anxiety. Everyone thought she was there about Eli's death. No one appeared to know Jack was a U.S. Marshal, who was about to arrest her for the most dastardly crime ever committed in Glenwood.

Marshal Laramore was waiting for them with Sheriff Hadlock, in the sheriff's private office, when they entered. Both stood until she was seated before again taking their seats.

"There are several things I think you should know, Miss Long-Sight," Jack began.

"Just a minute," she said, looking pained. "I'd rather you didn't refer to me as Miss Long-Sight. If I hang, it will be as Kedra Moore, and if, by some miracle, I don't hang—then I'll be able to start my life over clean as Kedra Long-Sight."

Jack stared straight at Luke. "Is that understood?"

Luke nodded, curtly.

Kedra pulled the totem from her hatband and started to hand it to Zed with an apology.

Jack interrupted her. "I'm afraid I'll need to take your totem."

"As evidence, no doubt," she said putting it in his hand. She held Jack's eyes before she released the totem. "I want your word you will give everything that's mine to Zedekiah after the . . . trial. I made my own will when I was with Mr. Darrow. The pendant and totem will belong to him."

"You have my oath," he said solemnly.

She released the totem. He put it in his pocket, sat down on the edge of the sheriff's desk, and outlined what he'd learned during the course of the day.

Kedra listened with stunned fascination. She gasped when he handed her the picture of Isaac as a woman, and stammered, "With my braid pinned to the back of his head. He would look just like me from the back, wouldn't he?"

"Yes, and I believe that's what young Mr. Gentry saw when Isaac came out from under the train," Jack said.

"What braid?" Luke asked.

Kedra recounted Isaac's reaction to her entering his bedroom uninvited when she was five-year-old; then finding her braid with a fake totem attached to it in his hiding place, along with the pearls and diamond ring.

"We only have *your word* that Isaac has your braid," Luke said.

"Yes, but you can ask Effie about the day Isaac cut it off. At the time he said he'd burned it, but Effie said it didn't smell like burnt hair in his room, when she and Eli went up to confront him."

"Finding that braid is one of the things I hope to do," Jack said, glaring at Luke.

"If he's smart, he's probably gotten rid of it by now," Tate said, frowning.

"He hasn't," Zed said with conviction. Kedra had told him everything about Isaac and his Irish-Mi'kmaq heritage. "It's a trophy. Cutting it off was probably his first attack on a person he deemed an enemy. It was, in a way, a scalping."

"I hope you're right, Zed," Jack said. "If I can capture him with it in his possession it will be a step toward proving Kedra's innocence.

A small cuckoo clock on the wall chimed five.

"I'm taking the six o'clock train to Denver. Isaac has a two-day start on me. I don't even know if he'll still be in Denver when I get there."

Luke muttered, "I'm surprised he went to Denver. That's not what I'd do if I was running."

"Except he isn't running—he's just hiding. He doesn't know he was seen leaving the ranch or that Eli was still alive and named him as the shooter. At the moment, he thinks planting that page from his journal in Miss Moore's desk will make everyone believe he's missing because Kedra and I killed him."

"That will give you an advantage," Luke exclaimed.

"Not for long— Eli said Isaac wanted money. My bet is he thinks he can get it in Denver. The train agent confirmed he, or rather she, was on the train. It would be a good place to fence the diamond ring and pearls, so it isn't surprising that he's gone to Denver. I'm sure he has the right contacts there. Fencing the jewelry may take some time. I hope it will hold him there until I can draw him out," Jack said.

"How are you going to do that?" Tate asked.

Jack said to Kedra, "He believes you're dead. I want you to go to Denver, voluntarily, with Marshal Laramore." He turned to Tate. "As soon as Luke and Kedra leave town, I want you to announce her forthcoming arrest for the robbery and murders." Jack shifted his gaze back to Luke. "As soon as I get to Denver, I'll have the Department of Justice announce the same thing. They'll make sure it goes out over the wires and gets into every paper in the country."

Luke scratched his head. "I thought you believed she was innocent. Now you want to publicize her guilt?"

"What I want is for Isaac to see she's alive and going to be tried for the crimes he committed. If I'm right, the desire to see her humiliated and convicted in a public trial will be a pull he can't resist."

"So you're using me as bait to lure Isaac in," Kedra said flatly.

"That's right. Isaac's hatred will only be satisfied when he's killed you, or watched the state do it. He framed you brilliantly, but his flair for theatrics, and his underlying fear, has also caused him to make mistakes. He should have killed us outright, instead of trying to let a fire finish us off, and he should have made sure Eli was dead before he ran. Fear robs him of his reason, just as it did after he killed Will and Harry. He was so rattled that when he got to the boat he cut the line instead of untying it. I wouldn't have been able to figure out how he got away if he'd simply untied the line. I've also been thinking over what you told me about Isaac wanting you to suffer. If that's true, he won't be able to resist watching you suffer up close, especially if he thinks he can do it safely—posing as a woman."

Luke smacked his knee and grinned. "I like it!"

"I don't," Zed said, his arm encircling Kedra's shoulders. "Once Kedra is arrested, the courts will proceed with her prosecution. The evidence is strong against her. You'll be putting her in the jaws of the lion, without having enough proof to draw her out before it's too late."

"She already has a court date on Monday, so she's going to be arrested anyway," Luke said.

"Miss Moore, I want you to come to the courthouse and give yourself up Monday morning, just before you're arraigned. You won't be put under arrest until then." Jack's gaze shifted to Luke. "Is that understood?"

Luke gaped at him, but nodded. "I suppose it will look better if she gives herself up voluntarily."

"I hope I can track Isaac down before you're arraigned, Miss Moore. If I can't, and he's already left Denver, then I'm betting the news of your arrest will draw him back to your trial," Jack said.

"Wait a minute. As soon as he knows Kedra's alive, he'll also know we're looking for him because of his attack on both of you. I think it's more likely he'll just cut and run," Luke said.

"No." Jack smiled grimly. "Once he knows he's going to get the full measure of victory he's wanted for so many years, he'll come."

Luke's forehead puckered. "You may be right," he conceded.

"I am right, that's why he didn't just kill Kedra when he had the chance in the mineshaft. There wouldn't have been any satisfaction in that. He didn't kill us because he wanted us to suffer, to suffocate in that mine or be burned to death in the fire."

Tate blew out a low whistle. "You two were lucky that Zedekiah, and a good storm, came along."

"Down right blessed," Jack agreed. He slid off the desk and sat down in the chair next to Kedra. "The Justice Department is anxious to prosecute this case, because Will and Harry were U.S. Marshals. They'll be using a special prosecutor, and it's unlikely you'll be allowed bail."

"Will I be allowed to have visitors?"

"Yes, but the time they'll have with you will be limited."

"They will also keep you in isolation," Luke said flatly.

"I don't mind that, if they let me have things to read."

"I'll make sure of it," Jack promised.

He touched her arm. She flinched away from him and watched regret cloud his eyes.

"I know several very good criminal attorneys," he said.

"Thank you, but Mr. Darrow gave me the name of his mentor, Mr. TJ Farnsworth. I intend to send him a wire as soon as we're done here."

Luke straightened in his chair. "I know him. He's a big-time defense attorney. He's gotten more than his share of criminals off the hook. You'll be in excellent hands with him, Miss Moore."

Kedra's lips quirked up. "I find your recommendation of my choice of attorney particularly comforting, Marshal Laramore. Now if he'll only take my case."

"Don't worry about that. Thomas Jefferson Farnsworth is always looking for those cases that generate national press, and yours is going to generate more than Farnsworth has had in some time," Luke said gruffly.

"You almost give me hope," Kedra murmured.

"I want to give you more than hope, Miss L—Moore," Jack said earnestly. I'm going to find Isaac and proof of your innocence. There will be time between your arraignment and your trial. I'll use that time to do everything in my power to get the charges dismissed."

Kedra sputtered out a chuckle. "You're the one who found the proof against me, and now you want me to trust you to get me off? That's asking a little too much of me, Marshal Garrison." She held up a hand before he could speak—again in her mind hearing the sarcastic endearment he'd use when he'd pointed a gun at her and accused her of the crime. "I'm grateful you believe in my innocence, and I have no doubt you will do your best to prove it. But, I also know your testimony is the key to my conviction and execution. I've learned enough about you to know your honor will bind you to your duty," she said looking away from that unalterable truth in his deep green eyes.

Jack stood up, addressing Luke and Tate. "Show the picture of Isaac as a woman around town. See if anyone has seen her, particularly on the day of the robbery, but don't attach Isaac's name to her. I don't want the press to tip our hand about this just yet, so don't hand out the picture to anyone. Do everything you can to tie Isaac to the train robbery and find out where he was that day. Now, I have a train to catch." Jack picked up his satchel. "What time will you and the Long-Sights be arriving in Denver, Luke?"

"Our train will be there Saturday morning at about seven."

"I should tell you, Marshal Laramore, that my friend Sarah Powell will also be coming with us," Kedra said. "I told her everything this afternoon"—her eyes moved between Jack and Zed—"she wants to come support me."

Zed squeezed her shoulder with approval.

Jack gave her a relieved smile. "I'm glad. I was hoping you would tell her. You need everyone you can get in your corner. I hope I'll have something good to tell you when I see you on Saturday morning." He shook Sheriff Hadlock's hand. "I'll see you at the trial."

Jack had warned Tate and Effie to expect to be subpoenaed for the trial.

"It's been a real pleasure meeting you, Jack. Let me know if there is anything I can do for you before I get to Denver," Tate said.

41

Denver—Friday, June 26, 1908

Jack yawned as he got off the train. In the cramped confines of a sleeping car, he'd managed to get some sleep. His head felt better for the rest, and he found the fog in his mind had cleared.

After securing a room at the Winsor Manor, a small hotel near the courthouse, he stabled Soldier, found a phone, and woke up Luke Laramore's deputy marshal, Darrius Jones.

"Have you made any progress on finding Drew Ellis's residence?" he asked, once he'd introduced himself.

"Catching up with railroad workers, who are always out of town on the job, is hard work, but I got a break last night. I finally got to talk with Abe Stout, one of Ellis's long time co-workers. It seems a few days before the robbery, Ellis told Stout he had to move out of his apartment building because it was being rewired. He gave Stout an emergency telephone number and told him to ask for room 301, in case the railroad needed him in a hurry. I called the number late last night and got a place called the Garden Arms Boardinghouse."

"Do you have an address?"

Jones recited the address and asked, "Do you want me to come with you? It's a rough neighborhood."

"No, but why don't you meet me at the courthouse in say . . . an hour. You can tell me everything you've learned about Ellis then. In the meantime, get word to the Justice Department of Miss Kedra Moore's impending arrival on Saturday. Make sure the local press knows she'll be arraigned on Monday and send the notice out on the national news wire."

"Will do," Darrius said cheerfully.

Jack left his hotel and hopped on a streetcar. He got off half a block from the Garden Arms Boardinghouse. His badge won him the immediate attention of Lester Trout, the Garden Arms owner. Under the threat of having his building raided by the police, Trout agreed to escort Jack up to room 301.

One look at the torn up room told Jack that Isaac had already been here. The condition of the room made it unlikely there was anything of worth left to find. Still, Jack dismissed the owner, deciding to poke around anyway.

The dim light from the overhead bulb was insufficient to light the room. Jack went to the tall window, pulled down on the roller blind, and let it go. It raised a couple of inches and stopped. Jack tried again, but the blind wouldn't roll up. He examined both ends of the roller. His fingers brushed the back of the blind and stopped on something bulky that was taped there.

He pulled an envelope free and opened it. Inside he found an address book. *It must be important or Ellis wouldn't have hidden it, and I'll bet Isaac didn't find this because it was dark outside when he came and searched the room.*

Jack slipped the small book into his pocket and continued to poke around for another fifteen minutes without finding anything else of interest.

Before he left the Garden Arms, Jack had Trout round up his night clerk. He showed the wary clerk the picture of Isaac as a woman. The clerk admitted to seeing the woman leave the building, sometime after two in the morning on Wednesday the 24th. Satisfied he'd learn all he could, Jack warned Lester Trout not to let anyone into Ellis's room unless it was cleared with the U.S. Marshal's office.

Back on a streetcar, he flipped through Drew Ellis's address book. There were only a dozen names, most with just local phone numbers listed, but a few were long distance ones. Only two names jumped out at him. There was a telephone number for a drugstore near the Garden Arms. *Now we're getting somewhere.* A few pages later he found a listing for Dolores ~~Ellis~~ Scott. He glanced at the Casper, Wyoming address wondering if she was a sister or an ex-wife. It seemed reasonable, since the Ellis part of her name had been crossed out. *At least there's a telephone number so I'll know soon enough.*

Jack met Luke's suave deputy at the U.S. Marshal's offices on the second floor of the federal courthouse. He thought Jones's pencil thin mustache and polished manners made him appear more like a society swell than a Deputy Marshal. That impression soon faded as Jones told Jack everything Luke had wired ahead for Jones to look into.

"I called the marshal's office in San Francisco and had Burt Rohmer go through Harry Walsh's apartment. There was only one thing of interest. Burt found a telegram on the floor when he opened the door. It came from Glenwood Springs and was dated June 6th."

"What did it say?"

"Read it for yourself." Darrius took an envelope from his pocket and handed it to Jack. "It came this morning."

Jack pulled the wire from the envelope.

Darling,
Don't worry. My plan is foolproof. We'll be rich!
Love Kedra.

"Harry must have left for the train station before this telegram arrived." Darrius said.

The train carrying Will, Harry, Ito, and Señor Ortiz's emeralds had left San Francisco at dawn on June sixth. Jack stopped his fingers from crumpling up the telegram. *It's a lie. If Kedra was in on the robbery, she would have known when the train left San Francisco. This message is another plant by Isaac to make Kedra look guilty—and it will.*

Returning the telegram to Darrius, he said, "File it with the evidence."

He explained what he needed in terms of information and manpower to hunt for Isaac. The deputy assured Jack he would find out if Isaac had hocked the stolen pearls.

Thirty minutes later, Jack left Darrius dialing the first number in Ellis's telephone book, confident the deputy would be able to glean anything of worth from the book's listings and, in particular, make contact with Dolores Ellis Scott.

Armed with the addresses Darrius had dug up, Jack again hopped on a streetcar, heading first for Morton Garland's posh mansion in the north Capitol Hill district. He walked the final block to the Garland's magnificent red stone mansion with its wrap around porch, asymmetrical façade, and three-story polygonal tower.

He strode up the granite steps and boldly knocked on the front door. An elderly man, dressed in the livery of a servant, answered the door. Jack produced his badge and requested to see Mr. Freddy Garland.

He was ushered into a small waiting room, off the large foyer, and took a seat on a blue baroque settee. A Victorian grandfather clock ticked off five minutes before the door opened.

Mr. Fredrick Garland stepped into the room in an elegant morning suit and stared at Jack as he drew the smoke of a cigarette into his lungs through a long cigarette holder. Jack stared back at this tulip of fashion and kept his face carefully blank. *He sure is a dandy.*

"I understand you're a U.S. Marshal," Freddy said, extinguishing his cigarette in a crystal ashtray and gliding into a seat across from Jack.

His air of elegant nonchalance was spoiled by the nervousness Jack detected in his voice.

"You are correct, Mr. Garland. I have been told you were friends with Isaac Moore during your school days."

Freddy appeared to consider the statement, before he said, "We were friends, though not particularly close ones."

"But close enough to have invited him to stay here as a guest on more than one occasion."

Freddy, shifted in his chair, brushing a bit of wayward ash from his sleeve. "What is it you want to know, Marshal?"

"When was the last time you saw Isaac Moore?"

Freddy frowned. His teeth pulled on his lower lip. "I believe it was at our college graduation."

"Then you haven't kept in contact with him?"

"Our friendship faded during our last year of college." Freddy leaned forward. "Frankly, he just couldn't afford to run with my crowd and I got tired of financing him."

"Did he borrow money from you?"

"Borrow?" Freddie laughed. "He wheedled, cajoled, persuaded, and on rare occasions begged, but he never borrowed money. Once the money was in his possession, it wasn't going to be returned."

"How did you feel about that?"

"I didn't mind it too much at first. Isaac was a very entertaining fellow. He also had the ability to attract the prettiest women."

"So your relationship was mutually beneficial?"

"You could say that."

Jack considered Freddie more closely. Despite the young man's money and social grace, he was in fact a very plain, and even shy, young man. Isaac would have been very useful to him socially.

"Where did you and Isaac go to find the prettiest women?"

"He liked going to the opera houses to see the musicals and plays. They were filled with beautiful girls and he knew just how to get their attention—along with everyone else's too. He had quite a flare for acting. I found him to be very amusing when he was pretending to be one of the characters he'd invented." Freddie's eyes laughed with memories. "He would often go out on the town as one of his characters. It was always such a lark to go with him and watch people's reactions to his antics."

"Was there a favorite opera house he frequented?"

"Well . . . yes. But it wasn't—or rather it *isn't*—exactly an opera house, not in the true sense."

"What *is it*, then?"

"A rather wonderful saloon called the Golden Garter. Not only is it a superb saloon, but a high-stakes gambling hall, with a top-notch theater, and a very exclusive bordello. It also holds other delights—if you know what I mean."

"Did, or does, Isaac have friends there?"

"Ton's—the owner is a particular friend of his. She even let him take part in the weekend reviews she put on while we were in school. I have to give Isaac credit; he could play any part and do it with style."

"Where is this saloon?"

"On Cutis Street—in the fourteen hundred block."

"Who owns it?"

Freddie's finely manicured fingers reach inside his jacket and drew out a gold cigarette case. "Bessie Louder." After selecting a cigarette, he tapped the end on the table next to his chair. "I've answered your questions to the best of my ability, Marshal. Now, perhaps you will answer one of mine. Why are you interested in Isaac Moore? What has he done?"

"Isaac's father was murdered early Tuesday morning. A page from Isaac's journal was found suggesting he might also be a victim of murder. He hasn't been seen since before his father's death," Jack replied, bending the truth just a bit in case Isaac contacted Freddie.

"Oh my! I'm sorry to hear that, but I can't say I'm surprised about Eyes. He always did live on the edge."

"Eyes?"

"That's what most of his friends, during our school years, called him, because he has such devastating eyes."

"Just how did he live on the edge?"

"Gambling, spending beyond his means, associating with rather shady characters, and always over playing his hand with the women."

Jack stood up. He had what he'd come for and wanted to escape before Freddie lit the cigarette, which was now inserted into the cigarette holder.

"If you should hear from Isaac please call the U.S. Marshal's office." He handed Freddie a card with the number and saw himself out.

Riding a streetcar in a southwestern direction, Jack got off at Curtis Street, in front of the Golden Garter Saloon and read the notice on the door. The Saloon opened at noon. *That will give me plenty of time to set up a stake out for tonight.*

In Jack's experience, those hiding from the law slept during the day and were most active at night.

His last stop was two blocks from the Garden Arms. The Corner Chemist was a busy store. Jack waited for several minutes before the druggist gave him his attention. Once he saw Jack's badge he immediately became guarded.

"I run an honest, upstanding business—no backroom dealing here," the balding man with round spectacles insisted.

"I'm sure you do," Jack said, hoping to smooth the druggist's ruffled feathers. "All I want to know is if you sold any Chloral Hydrate during the first week of June."

"I'll have to check my books, if you don't mind waiting."

Jack nodded and the druggist hurried into the back room. He came back a minute later with an open receipt book.

"I remember now," he said tapping the entry. "He was a new customer—kind of nervous too."

"Do you remember what he looked like?"

"He had short blond hair and a thin mustache, was of average height and weight, and in his late twenties or early thirties—not a man you'd take any particular notice of."

"What date did he buy the Chloral Hydrate?"

The druggist's finger ran across the page. "On June 5th."

Three days before the robbery. "I'm going to send a deputy over here with a picture of the man we believe bought the Chloral Hydrate and take a deposition from you. The Chloral Hydrate you sold may have been used in a murder."

"Oh my! Am I in trouble?"

"No, but I'll need your deposition on the sale of the Chloral Hydrate and your identification or description of the man you sold it to."

Heading back to the courthouse for an appointment with Turner Scrogin, the special prosecutor the Justice Department intended to use, Jack yawned and struggled to keep his eyes open. His head was beginning to throb and he needed more sleep. It was essential that he be clear headed when his men staked out the Golden Garter Saloon. *If I don't find Isaac in the next couple of days, I may have to see what I can get out of Bessie Louder. But before I do, I better check in with the police.*

Years ago, he'd made it a policy to always go into a saloon with an ace up his sleeve—not to mention a gun.

Turner Scrogin was a hard faced, beady-eyed, no nonsense kind of man. Jack got the impression he'd go into a fight with everything he had and never throw in the towel no matter how badly he was being beaten. It didn't bode well for Kedra's chances.

"My congratulations, Marshal, you've put together a rock solid case for me."

"Have I?" Jack asked, sourly.

Scrogin raised an eyebrow. "Do you have doubts?"

"No. I'm certain Kedra Moore *didn't* kill anyone or steal Señor Ortiz's emeralds. Matter of fact I'd stake my life on it."

Disbelief grew on the prosecutor's face. "But you're the one who gathered all the evidence—it's iron clad. How can you possibly believe Miss Moore is innocent?"

"Miss Moore was very cleverly set up by her brother, who bushwhacked Miss Moore and me and then murdered his father early Tuesday morning. I intend to make that clear at the trial, sir."

"Are you planning to meet with Mr. Farnsworth—Miss Moore's attorney—and tell him this?"

"I am. I have an appointment with him this afternoon."

"Am I to understand that you are planning to undermine my case, Marshal Garrison?" Scrogin said, shocked.

"I intend to tell the whole truth, Mr. Scrogin, and leave it to the jury to decide. Now do you have any questions for me?"

Mr. Scrogin grilled Jack for thirty minutes before he sat back in his chair with a satisfied smirk on his lips. "I'm grateful you're an honest man, Marshal. I have no doubt the evidence you've found will be sufficient to convict Miss Moore."

Jack abruptly stood up. "When do you think the trial will start?"

"Because of my busy schedule, the Justice Department will push for the soonest possible date."

"Have you talked with Miss Moore's attorney?"

"Mr. Farnsworth contacted me as soon as Miss Moore retained him. I'm sure the court will grant him ample time to prepare. He has been informed of all the evidence in the case—with the exception of the telegram found in Harry Walsh's apartment and the druggist's record of the Chloral Hydrate purchase, which you just went over with me. Since you're meeting with Farnsworth this afternoon, I'll let you fill him in on the latest evidence."

Jack ran down the second floor hall of the courthouse to use the Justice Department's private wire service. He sent off identical wires to the U.S. Marshals' offices in Rapid City, South Dakota and Philadelphia, Pennsylvania, He arrived back in the marshals' office just before Darrius walked in, grinning.

"It's all set," Darrius said. "I've briefed the men for the stakeout and I got in touch with Free Dealin' Dan. If anyone knows who's fencing stolen goods it's Dan. He owes me a favor and will be happy to find out if someone has hocked the jewelry you're looking for. If not, he'll keep his eyes and ears open. He always knows about the big deals that go down in this town."

"Thanks, Darrius." Jack clapped the deputy's shoulder, nearly knocking him over. "If I wasn't going to turn in my badge after this job is over, I'd try to lure you away from Luke to be my deputy."

Darrius's thin mustache quivered. "Thank you for that vote of confidence, but I don't think I'd like picking myself up off the floor every time you approved of my work."

Jack fell into bed at three-thirty in the morning. His head was throbbing and his gut was churning from spending so many hours in a smoke filled theater. Because Isaac knew him, he hadn't gone into the saloon. Instead he'd waited in the lobby of a theater next door to the Golden Garter Saloon, while Darrius and his men watched for Isaac. Every hour they'd brought him a report, but Isaac never showed. At least not that any of Darrius's men could detect.

It was what Jack had feared would happen, after talking to Freddy Garland. Isaac had more personas than just the female one he used to escape Glenwood. Identifying Isaac in a dimly lit saloon, with nothing more than his disturbing eyes to give him away, was going to be nearly impossible, but Jack had to keep trying.

As he drifted off to sleep, he reflected that instead of having good news to tell Kedra when she arrived in a few hours, he would only be able to greet her with bad news. Even so, he couldn't deny that he was anxious to see her.

42

Saturday, June 27, 1908

Kedra left the sleeping car feeling restless in the confined space. When she reached the coach car she found Zed there, staring out the window into the early morning darkness. He opened his arms when he saw her. She settled into them and they'd sat for the last two hours, before the train reached Denver, in peaceful silence.

Her future was too frightening to contemplate, and she refused to let her mind speculate. Her past held nothing but deception, and she couldn't afford to let her mind wallow in bitterness. The only solace she could find was in this moment—in the arms of her uncle. Their strength reassured her while the steady rhythm of his heart infused her own with comfort. She let her mind rest in the calm of her uncle's spirit, fortifying her own soul for whatever was to come.

The blowing of the train whistle announced their arrival in Denver. At that moment, Sarah entered the car and sat down beside her, taking hold of her hand. The gesture relayed all Sarah's love and concern. Kedra gave her a tremulous smile.

As the train came to a stop, Kedra looked out at the crowd of people milling around on the platform and spotted Jack. He towered over everyone. Seeing him unaccountably warmed her heart, and then appalled her. *He's the man who is personally putting a noose around your neck—stupid!* Even knowing Jack would hold to his code of honor and do his duty, the sweet ache of seeing him persisted.

"Are you ready?" Marshal Laramore asked, coming into the car. Kedra turned away from the window. *Ready? To be arraigned, tried, and most likely hung for a crime I didn't commit—what an absurd question.* "Yes," she said softly.

"I have to warn you, the platform is crawling with reporters." Marshal Laramore nodded at the window. "That's why Jack is here. He's brought reinforcements. We'll get you out of the station as quickly as we can."

"Thank you."

"But first we'll wait until the train clears out and the station is less congested."

The wait seemed interminable.

Finally Marshal Laramore stood up. "I've arranged for a porter to collect your bags. They will be delivered to your hotel. Now, I'll go out first, Miss Moore and Mrs. Powell will follow. Mr. Long-Sight will bring up the rear. Let's go."

The little parade walked single file out of the coach car and down the steps of the train. Jack was standing by the stairs and reached for Kedra's hand as she came down. His grip conveyed warmth, tenderness, but mostly compassion. Her eyes flew to his and those green eyes made her want to cry. His stark concern—no fear— for her was jarring.

Voices suddenly started to shout at her. Questions and accusations flew at her from all sides. Cameramen yelled for her attention. Before any of them could line up a shot, she found herself surrounded by heavily built men. With Jack in front of her and Zed at her back, they walked out of the station.

The doors of a car opened. Jack handed her inside. He allowed Zed and Sarah to enter the car too, before he shut the doors. Jack's wall of men blocked the reporters as the car drove off.

Kedra looked out the car's back window, watching Jack swing onto Soldier's back. The men he led also mounted horses. With Jack in the lead, the posse followed them.

Jack is the perfect picture of a U.S. Marshal.

"Miss Moore," a man said, drawing her attention into the car. "I'm Thomas Jefferson Farnsworth—my friends call me Tom."

He extended his hand. Kedra took it, looking into the face of the man she was about to entrust her life to.

His hair was thick and silver. His eyebrows bushy and his goatee pointed. Deep blue eyes searched hers with penetrating scrutiny. A slow smile grew on his face.

Tom Farnsworth was a man of considerable presence, although he didn't appear to be a very big man. Kedra felt that if he entered a room, no matter the size, he would fill it up—somehow.

The confidence he radiated ignited an ember of hope inside her. She held on to it, even as she held on to Mr. Farnsworth's hand.

"Thank you for taking my case, Tom, and call me Kedra."

"Not at all, Kedra—I know you may feel your situation is dire and I wouldn't disagree, still, after the chat I had with Marshal Garrison yesterday, I believe there is room for hope."

"What did he tell you?"

Tom patted her hand. "After I've settled you into the Adams Hotel, where I booked rooms for you and your friends, we'll go to my office and talk. I think you'll find the Adams is a comfortable and reasonably priced hotel. It is also close to the courthouse, which will make it convenient for your friends."

Kedra introduced Zed and Sarah and explained that they would be coming with her to the meeting.

"Whatever makes you feel comfortable is fine with me. There is one thing I think I should say to all of you. I know you all have kind feelings for Marshal Garrison, and I'll admit he does want to help prove your innocence, Kedra. However, I believe it will be in your best interest not to speak with him unless I'm present. He is after all, one of the most damaging witnesses the prosecution has against you. It would be wise for all of you to keep that in mind."

Eyes ate brunch in Bessie Louder's boudoir; only half listening to her recite the gossip from the previous evening. He'd been out all night, and his mind was fuzzy with fatigue. He finally had the name of a fence he thought he could trust to sell the pearls, but he was running out of time to negotiate and complete the deal.

Staying in Denver was pushing his luck. Eyes, and many of his other personas, were too well known in this town. Fortunately, Bessie had helped him contrive a new female persona, which he was currently using, exclusively.

As he ate eggs and toast, he considered going to San Francisco and trying to sell the jewelry there, but he had no connections there, and the security of having ample funds at his disposal to ensure his comfort made him hesitate. *I'll give it a couple more nights.*

Bessie tapped his arm with her fan, which she was already using. The night hadn't cooled off much, and the morning was already heating up.

"There were some unusual men in the saloon last night."

"Oh," he murmured, without interest.

"Yes. They didn't seem to know each other, and yet, they all ate hardily, drank sparingly, and seemed to always be moving around the rooms."

Isaac's put down his fork. "Cops?"

"Maybe, but none of my bouncers recognized any of them."

"Competition, just looking you over?"

"Could be they were private detectives—looking for someone." She stared into Isaac's pale eyes, fanning the plunging neckline of her negligee. "I haven't asked what brought you here, my pet, and I don't intend to. Your business is your own. However, you should know I can't risk being raided right now. My opium parlor is just getting off the ground and I won't want anything to keep it from becoming the success I'm sure it will be—if you understand me."

Being Bessie's special pet had been a boon to Isaac. As her pet, he was given privileges even paying customers weren't allowed. The sanctuary of Bessie's house was especially important to him, and he was careful not to involve the Golden Garter in his intrigues. It was one of the reasons he'd developed his multiple personas. He always came and went from this sanctuary in differing disguises, never as Isaac Moore. It protected both him and Bessie. That trust was one of the few things he held sacred.

He cupped her face in his hands and kissed her painted lips. "You have nothing to worry about from me. If things go the way I hope, I'll be gone in a couple of days, my dear."

"I'll be sorry to see you leave, Eyes."

A knock on the door was followed by the entrance of a scantily clad young woman. She kissed Bessie's cheek, handed her the morning paper, smiled seductively at Isaac, and sauntered out.

Isaac watched the girl leave regretfully. "I shall miss this home, but when I have achieved all I hope to, I'll return to you."

"Even if you don't achieve everything you hope to, come back to see me, my dearest pet."

"I will," Isaac promised as his eyes fell on the newspaper. He snatched it up and read the headlines.

WOMAN TO BE ARRAIGNED FOR MURDERS OF U.S. MARSHALS!

Kedra is still alive and going to be put on trial after all! The news of her pending prosecution sent a delicious surge of pleasure through him, followed by a large dose of fear. He wanted to know the details, wanted to gloat over this triumph in private, and consider how much danger Kedra's arrest put him in.

"Dear"—he caressed Bessie's cheek—"I'm dead with fatigue. Would you mind if I retired to my room and took the newspaper with me? There are some ads I need to look at before I go out tonight."

Bessie pushed back a stray lock of his hair. "Come to see me before you leave this evening," she said, kissing him.

Eyes left Bessie's luxurious apartment on the third floor, walked to the far end of the hall and moved the wall lamp. The panel sprung open. He flicked on an inside light switch and closed the panel behind him, feeling the trapped heat of the enclosed space and knowing his room wouldn't be any better. Still it was a safe sanctuary and that was the most important thing right now.

Once sequestered in his hidden room, he removed his velvet smoking jacket, spread the newspaper out on a table, and read about the forthcoming arrest and arraignment of Kedra Moore.

So Marshal Garrison is also still alive and going to be the prosecution's star witness. He was only pretending to be interested in Kedra until he could get enough evidence on her to arrest her. How humiliating for poor Kedra. He laughed uproariously.

The known details of Kedra's crime were rehearsed, with the admission that Señor Ortiz's emeralds, with the exception of one, had yet to be recovered. *The rest of the emeralds, unfortunately, will never be recovered by Señor Ortiz. They are his gift to me, enabling me to live the life I was born to live.*

He read the vow of the special prosecutor with a sense of smug satisfaction: "I have more than enough evidence to convict Miss Moore of the murders of Marshal William Forbes, Marshal Harry Walsh, Haru Ito, and Drew Ellis. I will bring down the hand of justice upon her. She will hang for her heinous crimes as a warning to all others who would threaten the rule of law in this country."

In a side note to the article, the murder of Eli Moore was mentioned along with the fact that Isaac Moore was missing and being sought in connection with an assault on Marshal Garrison and Miss Moore. Marshal Garrison was quoted as saying, "Our search for Isaac Moore hasn't turned up anything. I'm afraid he may have been caught and killed in a lightening started fire on the Moore's ranch early Tuesday morning. He is known to have been in the vicinity of the fire and hasn't been seen since—either on the ranch or in Glenwood Springs. The U.S. Marshal's office is looking for his remains in the fire burned area of the ranch, but it's going to take some time. There are several old mines in the area. He might have taken shelter in one and subsequently found himself overcome by smoke and suffocated."

A gale of laughter shook Eyes. *They think the fire was started by lightning, and they're looking for my remains! It couldn't be more perfect. I'll be safe here—at least until they decide I wasn't killed in the fire and widen the search for me. It means I can afford to stay and enjoy my victory over Kedra.*

He longed to attend the trial and watch her suffer, but knew that would be far too dangerous. *However, I suspect the crowd at her hanging will be enormous. Not even Marshal Garrison will be able to pick me out in that sea of humanity—especially not as a white haired, spectacled old man.* His jaw hardened. *I will give myself the ultimate satisfaction of watching my dear sister hang, before I leave the country.*

His eyes fell on a small drawing beneath the headlines. A tirade of profanity poured from his mouth as he stared at the pearl necklace and earrings. A reporter had been contacted by a Mrs. Eunice Capshaw. She accused Miss Moore of also stealing her custom-made pearl necklace and earrings, during the emerald robbery.

Eyes shoved the newspaper away. The pearls had just become too hot to hock, especially as Denver was Mrs. Capshaw's home. *I won't be able to hock them in San Francisco either.* The article had named a famous jeweler in San Francisco as having made the set of pearls for Mrs. Capshaw. They were valued at five thousand dollars. Isaac knew he would only have gotten half that amount when he fenced them. It wasn't enough to live in the style that befitted the man he intended to become in Buenos Aires.

I won't be able to sell them until I'm out of the country. Now all I have left is the diamond ring.

Set in white gold, Asscher cut diamond was a stunningly designed ring. A jeweler in Aspen had appraised it at eight thousand dollars. The ring had been meant for Goldie, an engagement ring. *I should have killed Goldie's old biddy of an aunt before I left Aspen.* He choked down his disappointment. There was no point in thinking about it now.

He'd taken the ring in the train robbery near Eagle. In his mind, he'd always seen the ring as the one he would give the heiress he married. It made just the right statement. He hated the idea of fencing it, knowing he would only get half its value. *But I don't have a choice.* He huffed out a disgusted breath. *At least it will bring me enough to live on comfortable for the next year.*

Isaac lay back on his bed and closed his eyes, trying to think of a more lucrative solution. *If I could hock the ring myself, I could get more for it. But who would have the money to buy it from me—with no questions asked?*

43

MONDAY, JUNE 29, 1908

Kedra walked up the stairs to the courthouse with Mr. Farnsworth at her side. They were surrounded by five bodyguards from the U.S. Marshal's office, with Jack in the lead. It astounded her that there were so many people anxious to look at her. What didn't surprise her were the catcalls and condemnation shouted at her.

Jack's host of guards stayed with her until she and Mr. Farnsworth were inside the courtroom. They fell away as Mr. Farnsworth led her up the aisle and they took seats behind the balustrade, to await the Judge's summons.

The room was utterly quiet, except for the voice of the man Mr. Farnsworth told her was the District Attorney. Kedra listened as the DA went over the charges and what the state wanted in the arraignment of the man before the court. The defendant and his lawyer stood. He entered a plea. His attorney asked for bail. It was set, and the judge banged down his gavel. He shuffled the papers in front of him and called for the people verses Kedra Moore.

With a queasy stomach, Kedra followed Mr. Farnsworth to the defendant's side of the balustrade, watching a hard looking man take the place of the District Attorney.

A tide of whispers arose behind Kedra. She stiffened, realizing the courtroom had filled with people during the first defendant's arraignment. Her heart rate picked up and she was thankful none of the curiosity seekers could see her face. Mr. Farnsworth gave her a reassuring wink.

The judge, a rotund man, smiled warmly and greeted Mr. Farnsworth and the special prosecutor by their first names. He told Mr. Scrogin to proceed with the charges.

"Your Honor, Miss Moore is being charged with the following crimes: The premeditated murders of U.S. Marshal William Forbes, U.S. Marshal Harry Walsh, the wanted smuggler, Haru Ito, Drew Ellis, a dining car steward on the D&RGW Railroad, and grand larceny."

"Miss Moore, how do you plead?" the judge asked.

Kedra lifted her chin and said in a strong voice, "Not guilty."

The judge instructed the plea to be entered into the court record and addressed Mr. Farnsworth, "As you know, Mr. Scrogin, is the special prosecutor appointed by the federal government in this case. Because of his busy schedule, he has requested the earliest possible court date. Therefore, the trial of Miss Kedra Moore will begin at 9 a.m. on Wednesday the first of July, unless you can show cause for a delay."

A murmur ran through the courtroom. The judge tapped his gavel. The room stilled, but Kedra's heart refused to obey the judge's call for quiet. It felt as though it was beating loud enough for the whole courtroom to hear.

She gripped Mr. Farnsworth's arm.

He shot her a cocky grin. "The defense has no objection."

No objection? Kedra thought she would hyperventilate on the spot. She'd spent two grueling days with Mr. Farnsworth. But despite his legal prowess, and Sarah's and Zed's insightful questions and suggestions, which Mr. Farnsworth said were immensely helpful in seeing the scope of Kedra's situation and how to approach it, she felt far from prepared.

Her fingers squeezed his arm.

He patted her hand. "Now to the matter of bail, Your Honor. I would like to point out to the court that Miss Moore, of her own free will, gave herself up. I do not believe she is a flight risk. Her desire is to have her name cleared."

"Your Honor," Mr. Scrogin objected. "It is the request of the Department of Justice that Miss Moore be held without bail because of the brutal nature of her multiple crimes."

The judge sat back in his chair and stared at Kedra. She met his eyes resolutely, hoping she looked as innocent as she was.

"The court appreciates Miss Moore's gesture in turning herself in, however the shear violence of the crimes, of which she is accused, is such that I must agree with Mr. Scrogin. Therefore the defendant, Miss Kedra Moore, will be held without bail."

The judge's gavel came down with a bang.

"Marshal Garrison, please take the defendant into custody."

Kedra stood there shocked and humiliated. It was all so cold, so absolute. She flinched when Jack touched her arm, looking pleadingly at Mr. Farnsworth.

"It will be all right, Kedra. I'm sure Marshal Garrison will take excellent care of you, and I'll come to see you in a little while." Mr. Farnsworth squeezed her hand, which still clung to his arm. "Trust me, child, I know what I'm doing."

Her hand fell away from Mr. Farnsworth's arm. She turned to search for Zed and Sarah in the packed courtroom. They were standing right behind her, on the other side of the balustrade.

Zed leaned over the railing, hugged her tightly and whispered in her ear, "Hold on to the blessing the Lord gave you under my hand. Have faith my daughter."

She nodded mutely, and Sarah took a turn hugging and reassuring her, before Jack led her out of the courtroom, through a side door.

"I'll take you through the booking process and then to the cell I had prepared for you," Jack said gently.

The next ten minutes were a blur, as she was photographed and fingerprinted. Part of her mind was intrigued by the developing science of fingerprinting that was being done in more and more states.

When the fingerprinting was finished, Jack handed her a cloth and allowed her to wipe the ink off her fingers. Again taking hold of her elbow, he led her down a narrow set of stairs, into the basement. He stopped at the bottom of the stairs.

"Miss Moore—Kedra, I hoped to have Isaac in custody before you were arraigned. I have men watching the haunt's Freddy Garland told me were Isaac's favorites, but so far, he hasn't been seen in either of the personas I've heard about. The truth is, Freddy Garland told me Isaac can transform himself into any number of characters, and that will make finding him very difficult. The one thing I do know is that he hasn't tried to fence the stolen jewelry yet. My office has a good informant in that trade. He hasn't heard anything, yet."

Discouragement swirled around her like a cold wind. "Then Isaac may not still be in Denver."

"Call it a gut feeling, but I believe he's here. And with today's announcement of your arrest, I think he'll stay to see the outcome of your trial." His finger gently lifted her chin, forcing her to look at him. "I won't stop hunting him. You have my word."

She backed up and looked away from the growing desperation she saw in his eyes, unable to bear his fears as well as her own.

"I'm so sorry you are being put through this ordeal. Please, forgive me for my part in it," he pleaded.

"It isn't your fault, and I don't blame you for doing your duty."

It was all she could manage to say without dissolving into tears. She blinked hard and looked down at her ink stained fingers.

Jack again took her elbow and led her down a dim hallway to an armed guard who stood in front of a locked door. They waited silently while the guard unlocked and opened the door.

The room they entered held banks of open bar cells on either side of a narrow corridor. As soon as they entered the corridor, the prisoners began to howl crude invitations. As Jack sped her through the gauntlet of cells, the prisoners' relentless assault tore away her dignity, pulling her down into the mire of their minds.

By the time Jack dragged her through another door, into an enclosed room, she was gasping for air as though she was drowning.

Jack pushed her down onto a chair, filled a glass with water from a pitcher on a nearby desk, and handed it to her.

She couldn't keep the glass from shaking as she put it to her lips and slowly sipped the water. A glance at Jack told her how distraught he was, how angry.

He dropped to one knee beside her chair, his arm running along the back. "Just take your time."

"Isn't there another way into my cell, besides going through that—that sewer?"

"No, and I'm ashamed to have put you through that ordeal. It's one more offence to add to all the others I've committed against you."

"Please, Marshal, can you just put me in my cell?"

He took the glass from her as she stood up and considered the three closed doors across the room. Unlike the open barred cells, these cells had solid doors on them, with a movable panel which allowed someone on the outside of the cell to look in. *At least I'll be allowed a little privacy.*

Jack retrieved a set of keys, hanging on a peg behind a desk in the corner of the room, and unlocked the cell on the left.

Kedra walked straight into it without a word. It was small, not more than six feet wide and seven feet long. It held a narrow cot, a small sink, and a toilet. A vaguely sour smell infected the cell. There was no window to open for air, and the overhead light was inadequate to dispel the cell's inherent gloom.

"I hate leaving you in here."

She reluctantly faced Jack. He stood hunched over in the doorway of the cell, seeming unable or unwilling to shut the door.

"The jail matron will give you toiletries as you need them. During your trial, Sarah can bring you the clothes you want to wear or the matron will give you a change of clothes, whichever you prefer."

The cell walls seemed to press in around her. She needed him to leave before her emotions got the better of her. "Thank you," she said dismissively, turning her back on him.

"Kedra—"

"Please, just go."

The door closed.

She listened to the key turn in the lock. Spinning around she looked at the door. On this side she saw that the moveable panel covered a wire mesh. Once she knew the panel was closed she sat down on the edge of the hard cot.

"Happy Birthday," she whispered, wrapped her arms around herself, and cried.

Jack stood outside the cell, staring at the door, berating himself and, for the first time since putting on a badge, hating his job. He said the words he'd wanted to say to her before she dismissed him. "You have my word, Kedra. I won't let you hang—no matter what I have to do!" *Including breaking the law myself,* he vowed.

He sat down in a chair unwilling to leave Kedra alone in this terrible place. She was the only prisoner in isolation and soon the matron would come to see to her needs. He wanted to wait until the matron arrived and make sure she understood how he expected Kedra to be treated.

His desire to unlock the cell and just sit with her, until the matron came, tugged at his heart. But she had wanted him to leave, and he had to respect her wishes.

Then he heard it.

A muffled sob reached him through the closed door of her cell, and then another.

He dashed across the room and opened the cell.

She jumped to her feet, turning away.

He ducked through the doorway, and wrapped her in his arms. She turned, and he thought she would push him away. Instead her head dropped onto his chest, and her hands clutched the front of his shirt.

"I overheard Zed say he gave you a blessing. Believe in that blessing," he whispered, resting his cheek against her hair. "And believe me when I tell you, you *are* going to walk out of here a free woman. No matter what I have to do, I'll see to that."

She abruptly pushed away from him, wiping her eyes with the palms of her hands. "I don't want you to do anything for me but tell the truth. The rest I'll leave in the hands of the Lord."

"The Lord often works through the hands of men, and I intend to work for you until you're free again."

Her hypnotic eyes held his. "I believe you—Jack, and I'm . . . going to be all right now."

Again, Jack locked the cell door, but this time feeling as though he'd won a victory. She'd said his name as if he was a friend, and let him hold her, if only for a moment.

That little victory felt so good, he smiled.

44

WEDNESDAY, JULY 1, 1908

The noise coming from the courtroom put knots in Kedra's stomach.

Jack stopped her as they reached the side door to the courtroom. "Just look straight ahead or down at your hands. Don't look at the crowd, and don't listen to them. The bailiff will call the court to order as soon as you reach the defense counsel's table." He took hold of her arm. "Are you ready?"

On a silent prayer, she nodded.

Refusing to look down at her hands as though she was guilty or ashamed, she held her head high and stared at the opposite wall as they entered the courtroom.

There was no need for the bailiff to bring the room to order. As soon as she stepped through the door, a heavy silence descended. Out of the corner of her eyes, she caught sight of Zed. Sarah was sitting next to him. She turned her head, slightly, and focused on Zed and Sarah. Both gave her reassuring smiles. Holding on to those smiles for courage, she allowed Jack to guide her to her place beside Mr. Farnsworth.

"Excellent entrance," Mr. Farnsworth said, as she sat down. "You looked just like a persecuted heroine." He chuckled. "Half the people in the courtroom—mainly the men—are already on your side."

"That's nice, but what I *need* is for the jury to be on my side."

"All rise," the bailiff called.

Everyone in the room rose as the Honorable Clifton Bunker took the bench. He was a tall man, though stooped and too thin. Thick glasses obscured his eyes and his face gave nothing away.

"You may be seated," the bailiff said, once the judge was in his chair and shuffling the papers in front of him.

Without looking up, Judge Bunker asked, "Mr. Scrogin is the prosecution ready in the case of the people verses Kedra Moore?"

"It is," Mr. Scrogin confirmed.

"Mr. Farnsworth, I see you've had little time to prepare." Judge Bunker looked down at Mr. Farnsworth. "Is the defense ready?"

"Yes, Your Honor."

"Very well, we will proceed with opening arguments."

Mr. Farnsworth had prepared Kedra to hear what the prosecutor would say about her. However, as she listened to him refer to her as a brazen, immoral temptress, whose cold, calculating ruthlessness had taken the lives of four men; she found her fingernails digging into the palms of her hands. By the time he was finish destroying her character, she was seething.

Tom must have sensed how she felt, because he took hold of her fisted hand and whispered in her ear, "Do not allow your feelings to be seen on your face. Right now Mr. Scrogin is not only preparing the jury to look at you in a certain way, but he's judging your ability to hold up under a fierce barrage of accusations—if you elect to take the stand."

Fighting humiliation, Kedra directed her perfect memory to recited verses from the scriptures dealing with loving ones enemies and how she was expected to treat those who persecuted her. It was an exhausting exercise and she was grateful when Mr. Scrogin finally yielded the floor to Mr. Farnsworth.

The first words out of Mr. Farnsworth's mouth revealed why he was such a dynamic lawyer. He was a spellbinder. It wasn't so much what he said, but how he said it. The intonation of his voice, his body language, his expressive face, his direct eye contact with the individual members of the jury, captivated the courtroom.

He described Kedra as an intelligent young woman, active in her community, faithful in her church, loved by numerous friends, and who, because her brother hated her, had been fiendishly framed by him. He emphasized that it was her brother, Isaac Moore, who had committed the crimes she was accused of, and proclaimed that the police were searching for him in connection with his brutal attempt on her life and that of Marshal Garrison.

"Thank you," Kedra whispered as Mr. Farnsworth sat down.

The hard condemning looks from the jury had faded. In their place she saw confusion and doubt. It was all she could hope for at this point.

"You may call your first witness, Mr. Scrogin," Judge Bunker said.

Frank Sullivan, the conductor on the train, was the first witness. He wiped his brow as he expressed his shock and dismay when he opened the door to the express car and found everyone in it was dead, and the safe was open and empty.

Then Frankie Gentry was brought into the courtroom, holding his mother's hand. He looked scared and was very reluctant to let go of his mother when he was called to the stand.

Judge Bunker patiently explained that all Frankie was being asked to do was to tell what he saw, what he knew to be true.

The boy sat straight and tall in the witness chair, after he was sworn in. Kedra could barely see him over the solid balustrade surrounding the witness box.

All Mr. Scrogin harshness disappeared as he asked Frankie to tell what he'd seen.

Frankie described the press of people trying to see out the windows on the landside of the train, and then said, "When I couldn't see out, on account of all the grownups blocking the windows, I went back to my seat. I was looking out the window, when all of a sudden, I saw an Indian come out from under the train."

"How did you know you were looking at an Indian?" Mr. Scrogin asked.

"I saw a long black braid."

"Was there anything on the braid?"

"Yes, sir. At the bottom of the braid, there were two white feathers. They were spinning in the breeze."

Mr. Scrogin held up Kedra's totem. "Did it look like this?"

"Yeah, that's it!"

Kedra's totem was entered into evidence, and Mr. Farnsworth was allowed to cross-examine.

"Frankie, have you seen many Indians, other than in books or magazines?"

"Only one, sir."

"Who?"

"Her." He pointed to Kedra.

"Then you had already seen this totem before you saw the Indian come out from under the train—is that right?"

"Yes, I've seen her wear those feathers on her braid lots of times. Everyone in town knows she's proud of being an Indian."

"When you saw the Indian come out from under the train, did you tell anyone?"

"I told my ma. She told me not to tell tales."

"Have you ever made up a story about seeing an Indian, before you saw the one come out from under the train?"

"Well . . . yes."

"Is that why your mother didn't believe you?"

Frankie frowned. "I suppose so."

"Have you ever pretended to be an Indian, Frankie?"

"Lots of times."

"What things do you use to make yourself into an Indian?"

"Feathers."

"What do you do with the feathers?"

"I tie two of them together and put them on my hat."

"Is that because Miss Moore wears her feathers like that?"

"Yes."

"That's very interesting. Have any of your friends done that too?"

"Yeah, and once my friend, Jimmy, and I, cut the tail of his horse off and made two braids. We attached feathers to the braids, pinned them to our hats, pulled our hats down over our faces so no one would recognize us, and scared some girls, real good."

"Frankie, did you see the face of the Indian that crawled out from under the train?"

"No. It was hidden under a hat."

"Then how do you know it was Miss Moore and not someone just pretending to be an Indian, the way you and Jimmy did?"

"Well—" Frankie paused and frowned. "I guess it could have been someone else just pretending to be an Indian."

"Thank you, Frankie. I have no more questions."

Frankie was followed by Sheriff Tate Hadlock who took the stand as the first official investigator on the scene. Kedra was shivering by the time he finished describing the scene in detail. The newspapers hadn't been given an exact description of how everyone in the car was killed, except to say they'd been shot. This was the first time the public was allowed to hear the details.

Mr. Farnsworth did not cross-examine.

The faces of the jury told Kedra how horrified they were. She didn't have to feign her own horror, blinking back tears of grief.

The court recessed for lunch.

When the court reconvened, Jack took the stand looking cool and relaxed. It was immediately apparent that he was a reluctant witness.

Kedra smiled beneath her hand. *Mr. Scrogin is going to have to pull every bit of Jack's testimony out of him.*

Jack spent a grueling hour on the stand, as Mr. Scrogin pried out the facts. The chemistry book, she'd borrowed from Sarah, was opened to the page where she'd inserted the newspaper about the murders. Mr. Scrogin made Jack read the entry in the book on Chloral Hydrate and prompted him to explain why the entry was important. It brought Drew Ellis into the picture and Jack testified that Ellis had purchased Chloral Hydrate three days before the robbery. An affidavit from the druggist was entered into evidence, along with the page from Harry's notebook, containing Ellis's initials and the timetable for the train run between Grand Junction and Denver for June 8th.

Mr. Scrogin held up Kedra's Jade pendant. Jack described finding the pendant in William Forbes' dead hand. Mr. Scrogin asked who owned the pendant. Jack reluctantly said Kedra had told him the pendant was hers; admitting she'd worn it the day before the crime.

As it was entered into evidence, Kedra gave thanks that it wasn't really lost. *No matter what happens here, the pendant and earrings will be returned to Zed. They belonged to the Nahtow. They're part of the Nahtow heritage, and even if there isn't anyone left to pass them on to, at least Zed can place them in the Nahtow library.*

Her mind returned to the trial as Mr. Scrogin pulled her relationship with Morgan O'Shea out of Jack. He said she knew Marshal Harry Walsh as Morgan O'Shea. She'd admitted meeting him when the train stopped in Glenwood on the day of the robbery. He'd found a friendship feather in Harry's pocket, which she'd also later admitted giving him.

The friendship feather was entered into evidence and the letters Morgan O'Shea had written to her were produced.

Mr. Scrogin made Jack read part of the last letter Morgan had written to her. As Kedra listened, her heart raced. *It sounds as though Harry and I were conspiring together.* The faces of the Jury told her they thought so too. That letter, along with all the others Morgan had written to her, was entered into evidence.

Then the prosecution produced a telegram sent to Harry from Glenwood Springs, signed with her name, in which she expressed her confidence in the plan she'd constructed to make them rich. It confirmed Harry's complicity.

She watched Mr. Farnsworth make notes on his pad as Mr. Scrogin drew out of Jack the fact that she was a deadeye shot. The prosecution produced the Bull Dog revolver, found concealed in her desk. Jack confirmed four shots had been fired from the gun, which was the right caliber and number of bullets fired and found in the express car and bodies of the victims. The gun was entered into evidence.

Lastly the emerald Jack found in her room was entered into evidence. Jack's jaw barely moved as he told about finding the emerald on her bedroom floor, and confirmed the rest of the emeralds were still missing, along with the pearls belonging to Mrs. Capshaw.

Kedra's throat constricted as she realized how many things had been entered into evidence against her.

Mr. Scrogin asked Jack if Kedra had said she'd do anything to save her father's financially troubled ranch. Jack admitted that she had. Scrogin cut him off when he tried to explain what she'd meant.

Again Mr. Farnsworth chose not to cross-examine at that time and Jack left the witness stand. His eyes sought hers, pleading for her forgiveness. Those pained green eyes were the only indication of how he felt. Kedra found them surprisingly comforting.

Her comfort was short lived.

After the gruff sheriff from Grand Junction described the murder of Drew Ellis, Marshal Garrison was called back to the stand.

He explained more fully Ellis's alleged involvement in the robbery, and testified that Miss Moore was in Grand Junction on the night Drew Ellis was murdered, which she, herself, had told him. The express car workers had also confirmed it.

Lastly, Joe Dobbins, the drunk who saw a woman leaving Ellis's room wearing two white feathers in her hair, just after hearing something crash against the wall of the room, testified.

Again Mr. Farnsworth waved cross-examination until a later time.

On that finishing touch, Mr. Scrogin declared to the court, in a triumphant voice, that the prosecution rested its case.

The jury's stony stares told her they no longer doubted her guilt.

"As the hour is growing late, the court will adjourn until tomorrow morning at nine o'clock. At that time, the defense will present its case." Judge Bunker banged down the gavel.

The people were directed to rise as the judge left the bench, and the court was adjourned.

Kedra shut out the hum of voices as the people left the courtroom and sat back down, letting her mind replay all the evidence against her. She was disconcerted by Mr. Farnsworth's lack of cross-examination, even though he'd explained he had the right to recall the witnesses and when he did, they would all become defense witnesses.

She couldn't imagine how. *Except, he did throw doubt on Frankie's testimony, and very cleverly too. He may be able to do that with the other witnesses, but wouldn't it have been better not to have let the jury leave today with the solid prejudice in their minds that I'm guilty. I know that's what they all think, and, if I was on the jury, I'd think the same thing. It's an open and shut case—except, it isn't.*

Jack intercepted the matron, who headed toward Kedra. "Why don't you go and have dinner. I'll take charge of Miss Moore for a while."

"That's fine with me," the matron said, holding out a set of handcuffs to Jack. "I'm hungry."

Jack held up a hand. "Those won't be necessary."

The heavyset woman looked Jack up and down. "I don't suppose they are for a mountain like you."

Jack strode over to the defendant's table where Mr. Farnsworth and Kedra had their heads together, talking quietly.

"Just a few more moments, Marshal," Mr. Farnsworth said, putting a hand on Kedra's shoulder to keep her from standing.

Take your time," Jack said.

"Kedra, I know you're concerned about what the jury is thinking after all the evidence the prosecution presented today and my lack of cross-examination, Farnsworth said. "However, in this case, where we have had so little time to prepare, I needed to simply listen and digest everything the witnesses said." He held up his note pad, displaying several pages of notes. "After I have had some dinner, I'll come back, and we will discuss how we are going to proceed tomorrow," he said, patting Kedra's hand reassuringly.

"I have no choice but to trust your judgment, Tom, and I do trust you. I was impressed by the doubt you created in the jury's mind over Frankie Gentry's testimony." She paused. "Why did you decide to cross-examine him and not the others?"

"Being a witness in a murder trial is difficult, even for an adult. I didn't want young Mr. Gentry to have to return tomorrow. Besides, once Mr. Scrogin finished questioning him, and Frankie knew he'd done well, he relaxed. That allowed me to get him to share his fascination with Indians, bring out the fact that a simple piece of costuming was really all he saw, and anyone could impersonate you by wearing a braid and a totem that looked like yours, especially since everyone in Glenwood is familiar with it."

"If you can do that tomorrow, with some of the other evidence against me, I might have a chance," Kedra said pensively.

"Go have dinner. Then I'll show you how good a chance you have."

She stood up and Jack immediately took hold of her arm. Protocol dictated he handcuff her, but no one challenged him when he simply led Kedra away.

Holding onto her, even if it was just her arm, comforted him.

There were so many things he wanted to tell her, but expressing his feelings had never come easily to him. As they silently went down the stairs and walked to the door leading to the gauntlet of cells, he tried to organize his thoughts. When they entered, he felt her cringe as the shouts and lewd suggestions assaulted her.

Once they were safely in the room of solitary cells, he let go of her arm. She walked straight over to her cell and stopped, keeping her back to him.

"Kedra, I want—"

"Marshal!"

Her sharp tone was a direct reminder of their positions, one she obviously wasn't going to put aside or let him forget.

"Miss Moore," he began again. "Will you please just turn around for a moment and let me say something?"

She turned, keeping her eyes hidden under her long black lashes.

"I know how bad things looked for you today."

Her eyes suddenly came up, blazing gold fire. "No, you don't! It's impossible for you to know how I feel. You aren't the one being slandered and accused of horrible crimes. You aren't the one fighting for your life." Her laugh came out like a sob. "You're the one who found most of the evidence against me, the one who fell for Isaac's plot and put me in this position." She pressed a finger into his chest "If I remember correctly, and I always do, you're the one who assured me, if I gave myself up, you would prove my innocence. Well, *tomorrow's* the day I've got to do that, and what have you found that can help me?"

Jack had faced off with gunslingers, gangsters, thugs, and murders with calm assurance. But he found this magnificent little savage to be the most daunting person he'd ever faced. He couldn't remember the last time he felt so inadequate. She robbed him of his confidence, tied his tongue, and made him feel like the most inept man alive.

"I—I can't tell you how sorry I am that I've failed you." His jaw became a hard line. "But I haven't given up. I've got men looking for Isaac—in all his personas. I've sent wires and made telephone calls asking for information that I hope will discredit some of the evidence against you. I should have the answers tonight. Tomorrow when I testify it will be *for* you, not against you. Everything I've learned about Isaac should be enough to create reasonable doubt."

"Except you don't have any evidence against Isaac, not like you do against me. Unless you can produce some, everything you say will only be conjecture, and Mr. Scrogin will shoot you down like a varmint."

He reached for her shoulders.

She backed away until she stood against the door. "Mr. Farnsworth told me not to talk to you. Now, please, let me go into my cell."

Her distrust and despair ached through Jack. Yesterday she'd let him hold her, comfort her, but that was before he'd taken the stand and condemned her with every word he spoke.

He dropped his head, letting his hat hide his face as he took the cell key from his pocket, his own despair too close to the surface to hide. Freeing Kedra and earning her respect—no love—was all he wanted. Now he knew she was beyond his reach. Nothing would keep him from freeing her, not even his oath as a U.S. Marshal. But after what he'd done to her today, he knew she could never love him.

He slid the key into the cell's lock.

Her hand stopped him from turning it.

He let go of the key and grasped her hand, searching her hypnotic eyes. They were filled with tears.

"I'm sorry, Jack, I don't blame you for doing your duty today. It's just that I'm just so scared right now, and the memories of this day are already tormenting me. Forgive me for taking my fears out on you."

She let him pull her into his arms, her tears falling onto the front of his shirt.

Hope teased him unmercifully.

"Can't you lock the memories away somewhere in your mind and never look at them again?"

"Zed says it's possible, but it takes time and practice—something I don't have." Her hands turned into fists. "After today, and everything that was said about me, I don't think I'll ever be the same. Even if I'm found not guilty, there will still be people who believe I committed the robbery and murders. Those whispered suspicions may always follow me, and I'll have to live with them."

"I know," Jack said sadly. "That's why you were wise to use the name Moore. Once you're free, you can leave that name behind you, start new as Kedra Long-Sight."

"Yes, but will I ever be able to go back to Glenwood Springs? I love it there, and now it's spoiled for me." She sniffed and wiped her eyes. "If I'm set free, I will go with Zed—if he'll let me."

"I'm sure he will. He loves you and wants to keep you near him."

"I've wondered for years if I could live as an Indian. I've worn my totem with pride, but I know nothing of how the Indians really live. I've lived my whole life in the white man's world. Now I can't go back to that world. But can I learn to truly be a Nahtow Indian? How will Zed feel if I can't? What will I do if I can't? I feel so lost right now, so helpless—so desperately afraid."

Kedra looked up at him, her eyes pools of liquid gold—astonishment filled them. She reached up and brushed a tear from his face. "Why are you crying?"

He caught her hand and pressed it against his heart. "Forgive me. I didn't want to believe you were guilty, but the evidence just kept piling up. Then, when I found the emerald in your room, I thought—well, you know what I thought. Now you're paying for my blindness and I'm afraid of the cost and what it will do to you, whether or not you're found guilty. He paused, his hand tightening around hers. "We both need hope, comfort, and direction." He searched the depths of her eyes and asked, "Will you pray with me?"

Her face crumpled. She hiccupped on a little sob, but managed to whisper, "Yes."

They went into her cell, closed the door, and knelt in the cramped space beside her cot. Jack poured out his heart to the Lord until the spirit of peace filled the tiny cell, stilling their fears.

45

Eyes, stylishly outfitted as a red headed woman, with the delicate veil of a fashionable hat covering his eyes, sat in a crowded teashop near the courthouse, listening to the excited chatter of those who had just come from Kedra's trial.

He found it necessary to frequently employ his napkin to hide the smiles that sprang to his lips. All around him condemnation was poured down on Kedra's head. With unequaled delight, he realized his carefully designed plan was going to succeed. Everyone, without exception, was completely convinced of Kedra's guilt.

It was the final triumph in a day that had gone his way at every turn. He'd asked Bessie to help him dress for this part, purposely wearing the diamond ring from the Eagle robbery on his pinky finger.

Bessie was drooling over it in no time.

Over the course of the hour it took to transform himself into a woman, Bessie continually gazed at the ring, questioning him about it. He told her it had been left to him by his grandmother, and although he hated to part with it, his financial situation made it necessary, which was why he was going out as a woman. He felt a woman could get more for the ring by enlisting male sympathy for her plight. On a pitiful sigh, he told Bessie the ring would go to the highest bidder.

Bessie asked, in an off-handed way, what he wanted for it. He set the price higher than he knew he could get if he hocked it. She expressed surprise over the price, but said, with a pout, that she understood why he needed to sell the ring for the best price he could get.

Just before he left, she broke down and offered him more than he'd hoped to get. It wasn't the price he'd quoted her, but it was close.

With cunning insight he told her if he couldn't find a buyer that would pay the price he was asking, then he would consider her offer.

His ploy paid off. Rather than risk losing the ring to another buyer, she agreed to pay his price.

The money was now safely stashed in the hiding place he'd created in his Attic room, as were the emeralds, the pearls, and the two passports he'd had forged, one for Miss Eileen Adair, the other for Professor Thaddeus Drake.

As he sipped his tea, the table next to him was vacated, cleared, and reoccupied by a pair of attractive women. They placed their order and then, as he expected, began to discuss the trial.

"You have to admit, Jenny, Mr. Farnsworth did a brilliant job of discrediting the boy's testimony."

"I do admit it. I will also concede he gave a brilliant opening argument. He had everyone eating out of his hand when he redirected guilt to Isaac Moore. What I don't understand was his lack of cross-examination."

"All I have to say to that is, the prosecution had better be on guard tomorrow when Mr. Farnsworth takes over. I don't know what his strategy is, but if he can cast as much doubt on some of the other witnesses' testimonies, as he did with the boy, and show some proof Isaac Moore committed the crimes, I believe Miss Moore has an even chance of walking away from this with her life."

"If that dreamy marshal has anything to say about it, I believe she will. I've never seen a more reluctant witness. You could see he was dying to tell more than Mr. Scrogin would allow him to."

"If you want my opinion, that *gorgeous* titan is in love with Kedra Moore. Why else would he be so reluctant to testify against her. Mark my words, Meg, he'll be back on the stand tomorrow, and we will get to hear a whole new version of this crime."

"I can hardly wait," Jenny said, picking up a scone.

The women's conversation doused Isaac's euphoric mood. *So Farnsworth discredited one witness and is going to try and implicate me—impossible. He won't be able to produce even a shred of evidence.*

He paid for his tea and left, walking quickly to a nearby newsstand. The extra edition of the Rocky Mountain News, containing all the highlights from the trial of the infamous Kedra Moore, was already on the stand. He bought a paper and caught a streetcar.

During the five-minute ride to his destination, he read a legal expert's opinion of the trial. Isaac's spirits were somewhat revived as the legal expert praised the prosecutions solid case against Kedra Moore. However, he, like the two women in the teashop, was also impressed with Mr. Farnsworth's legal prowess and warned the readers that a conviction was far from certain.

Posing as a fashionable lady, Isaac couldn't express the feelings that swelled his chest. He settled for thoroughly cursing Mr. Farnsworth in his mind.

For a moment, in the teashop, when he was certain his victory was sure, he'd considered leaving Denver, something he was growing anxious to do, especially now that he had the money he needed. He wanted to get on with his new life, put Isaac Moore behind him. But he couldn't quite bring himself to leave until he'd tasted the full measure of his victory over Kedra. He'd worked too hard on this plan to deny himself the final pleasure of being present at her execution. Still staying would be risky. With Mr. Farnsworth accusing him of setting Kedra up, and the law still looking for him, he'd have to be very careful.

An ugly notion surfaced. *What if everything Garrison said to the press about me was only to lull me into a false sense of security? What if Marshal Garrison is keeping the search for me quiet?* Eyes's teeth tugged on his lip as he thought it over. *That's it! He believes I'm in Denver and doesn't want to scare me off.*

The unusual men, Bessie had mentioned observing in the saloon the other night, were obviously looking for him. Isaac beat down his fear and chuckled softly. *Kedra is his bait, but that fool of a marshal will never catch me.*

He left the streetcar and walked half a block to a Chinese laundry. Woo Fong, the owner of the place, was a slave driver to those who worked in his very prosperous laundry business, which provided the front for his more lucrative business, something only a select few of his employees knew about.

Eyes walked through the front door and gave the woman at the counter a ticket.

She examined it and said in an apologetic voice, "There has been a small problem with your order, if you will please come with me, Mr. Fong will take care of you."

She took him through a side door and out into an enclosed garage with five laundry trucks. He paid the woman and she directed him into one of the trucks. He climbed into one of the large, empty laundry bins. She tagged the bin, and covered him with a sheet, followed by clean towels and sheets. After listening to more bins being loaded into the truck, the doors were shut and Isaac settled in for the ride to the Golden Garter Saloon.

Being transported in and out of the Golden Garter in a laundry bin had been one of Isaac's more brilliant ideas. Bessie had a long list of high ranking and prominent men that didn't want their association with the Golden Garter known. Years ago, when Eyes had approached Bessie with this very discreet solution to her problem, she had praised his ingenuity, and it had cemented their friendship.

Woo Fong was well paid for his services and besides being discreet, he was no fool. When Eyes initially questioned Fong, Fong told him that he knew better than to kill the goose that would continually lay golden eggs. When Eyes presented Fong to Bessie, she made it very clear that if he tried to blackmail any of her well-known clients, he wouldn't live to see their downfall.

Jack leaned back in his chair and rubbed the tender place behind his ear, trying to keep desperation from taking hold again. The long hours he'd spent sending wires, making telephone calls, and receiving updates from his men in the field had been fruitless.

Western Union couldn't tell him who sent the wire to Harry Walsh using Kedra's name.

No one had seen Isaac or his female counter part come or go from Grand Junction on the day Drew Ellis was murdered. There was some comfort in knowing Isaac's whereabouts were unknown on that Friday and Tate and Luke had been unable to account for him on the day of the robbery too. *The guy seems to be able to transform himself into a ghost whenever he wants.*

The men staking out Isaac's known haunts had nothing to report. It heightened Jack growing fear that Isaac had left Denver. Everything seemed to point in that direction.

Even Darrius Jones's fence, Free Dealin' Dan, hadn't heard as much as a whisper about anyone trying to hock a set of custom made pearls or a diamond ring of the description Jack had given him. But the thing that bothered him the most was the lack of response to his numerous calls and wires to Dolores Ellis Scott. Thoughts of her kept nagging at him and he wanted to put them to rest.

He glanced at the clock through tired eyes. It was two o'clock in the morning. *There's nothing more I can do tonight.* He called his hotel and told the night clerk he would be staying at the courthouse—if anyone should asked for him before morning. After writing a quick note and posting it on the door, he went down to the jail in the basement, had the matron unlock the cell next to Kedra's, told her to wake him up in the morning, no later than seven, and shut himself in.

The bed was narrow and far too short, but just laying his throbbing head down eased the pain. Being so close to Kedra, brought him an odd sort of comfort. In a way, sharing her confinement made her burden more fully his.

He put his hand on the wall that separated them and whispered as though she could hear him, "I'm here, and—I promise you—everything will be all right."

46

Thursday, July 2, 1908

Effie Blue, wearing her best Sunday dress, looked wide-eyed and nervous when she took the stand. Kedra smiled at her, encouragingly. Still, when Mr. Farnsworth addressed her, she stiffened.

"Mrs. Blue, yesterday Marshal Garrison testified to seeing Miss Moore take, what he thought might be, a few of the stolen emeralds from Swindler in her bedroom on Monday night, June 22nd. You also saw Swindler in the house on Sunday night, June 21st, didn't you?"

"I most certainly did!"

"Will you tell the court about that?"

"I brought clean shirts to Isaac's room that evening, before he left for Aspen. When I knocked on his door, he yelled at me to wait. I heard indistinguishable sounds in the room, and it was a full minute before he opened the door. When he finally did, he was very agitated. As I stepped into the room, I noticed the window was open. He'd pulled the window shade down and it was moving in the breeze. It caught my attention, because it was very unusual for Isaac to open his window."

"How long were you in Isaac's room?" Mr. Farnsworth asked.

"Not more than five minutes."

"What happened when you left the room?"

"I saw Swindler—that nasty ring tail thief—trying to open Miss Moore's bedroom door. He was standing on his hind legs as brazen as could be, twisting the knob."

"What did you do?"

"Why I rushed across the hall ready to give him a good hard kick, but he managed to open Miss Moore's door and escape out her window before I could."

Did you see how he came into the house?"

"No, but he couldn't have come into the hall through the sitting room. The door to the hall was closed when I came to give Mr. Isaac his shirts. I opened it, went through it, closed it behind me, and turned on the hall light. Swindler wasn't in the hall at that time."

"Could he have come in through Miss Moore's window, or her father's window?"

"No. All the doors in the hallway were closed when I knocked on Isaac's door. They were also all closed when I came back out of his room. The only door that was opened into the hall was Isaac's."

"Is there any other way he could have gotten into the hall, beside through one of the upstairs windows?"

"No, sir—he must have come in through Isaac's window and been under his bed when I came in. Isaac told me to put some shirts in the closet, but then got upset when I did. He came over to the closet to show me how he wanted the shirt hung up. Our attention was on the closet for at least a minute. I left right after that and that's when I saw Swindler trying to open Miss Moore's door."

"Was there anything in his paws?"

"No, but just before I went back into the hall I heard something, like the ping of pebbles dropping."

"Thank you Mrs. Blue. Your witness, Mr. Scrogin."

Mr. Scrogin pursed his lips as he slowly appraised Effie.

She stared right back at him.

Kedra hid a smile. Effie might feel nervous about testifying in front of all these people, but she would never permit a mere man to intimidate her.

"Mrs. Blue, did you actually see Swindler in Isaac Moore's room?"

"No, my back was turned away from the door while Isaac and I were arranging his closet."

"So you didn't see Swindler exit Isaac Moore's room."

"Well, no—"

"In fact you didn't see anything in his paws either, because as you testified, he had to use both paws to open Miss Moore's, door, isn't that right?"

"Yes, but I heard—"

"That's all Mrs. Blue."

Effie left the stand frowning.

Mr. Farnsworth called Jack to the stand. The difference in Jack's demeanor was evident to everyone. He enthusiastically answered the questions Mr. Farnsworth put to him, and the attorney let him explain to his heart's content.

He's certainly making up for what Mr. Scrogin wouldn't allow him to say yesterday, Kedra glanced at the jury, *and he's definitely making them think.*

The way he looked right at the jury as he answered Mr. Farnsworth's questions was very effective. He explained what Kedra meant when she'd said she'd do anything to save the ranch by outlining the plan she'd shared with him to stop the logging, downsize the crew, sell most the cattle, and go to work as a school teacher to earn the money to rebuild the ranch's financial base, which Isaac Moore had been draining for the last few years by blackmailing his father. This, too, he'd heard from Eli Moore's mouth before he died.

Mr. Farnsworth had him describe his initial meeting with Kedra, and Swindler's antics, allowing the jury to see a pattern of behavior for the raccoon. Jack then recounted the commotion in the upstairs hallway on the night he found the emerald in Kedra's room. The racket had sent him running up the stairs. He gave his eyewitness account of Kedra's wrestle with the raccoon and seeing her remove something green and shiny from the raccoon's paw, before Swindler escaped out her open bedroom window. He concluded that was how one of the emeralds ended up on her floor.

Most impressive to Kedra was the responsibility he took for not immediately confronting her about the emerald he'd found. He admitted that was a poor decision on his part and one that could have changed the outcome of this trial. When asked how, he responded that if he'd been with Kedra when she opened Isaac's room, and the secret hiding place in his floor, he could have proven her innocence by the content in the hiding place.

The prosecution shot this part of his testimony down, in cross-examination, by making him admit he didn't know conclusively where Swindler had originally gotten the emeralds, and he only had Kedra's word for what was in Isaac's hiding place. However, Mr. Scrogin couldn't refute Isaac's brutal attack on Jack and Kedra or the lack of any proof that Kedra knew, or had ever met, Drew Ellis.

Jack brought out that everyone in the house had access to the jewelry box key, inside the bible in Kedra's nightstand, and therefore, the pendant. There was also no way of knowing if the gun in her desk drawer had been used in the robbery, even though it was the right caliber. He testified that the telegraph office had no record showing Miss Moore had sent the incriminating wire to Harry Walsh. But they had found a receipt, showing Isaac Moore had sent a wire at that time.

Kedra gave Jack a prim little smile as he left the stand.

Mr. Farnsworth had Effie return to the stand. "Isn't it true that you saw Isaac Moore very early in the morning on June 23rd running away from the house—just after Eli Moore was shot?"

Kedra cringed. *No! He knows Jack wants to keep who killed Eli out of the press. As soon as Isaac learns the law knows he's alive and he killed Eli, he's sure to run.*

"Yes, sir, I did."

Jack returned to the stand and Farnsworth asked, "Before Eli Moore died, did he confirm, within your hearing, that Isaac shot him?"

"He did."

Mr. Farnsworth recalled Joe Dobbins, the drunk who saw a woman leaving Drew Ellis's room the night he was murdered.

"The police testified that you'd been drinking heavily, before you saw the woman out your window. "Weren't you in fact, drunk?"

"No, tipsy, but not drunk."

Farnsworth glared at the shaggy haired, rumpled derelict and asked, "If you were tipsy, how can you be sure what you saw was a woman or that the ornament in her hair was white feathers?"

"I'm certain about what I saw," Dobbins said mulishly.

"Then with the courts permission, I'd like you to look at the backs of five women and choose the one that most resembles what you saw."

Mr. Scrogin objected and was over ruled.

Five veiled women entered the courtroom. They turned their backs to the witness stand.

Dr. Dobbins chewed his lip, squinting at the different white objects in the women's hair. Finally, he a pointed a finger and said, "That one there. She's tall enough, and those feathers look just like what I saw."

Mr. Farnsworth tapped the woman's shoulder. "Would you please turn around and unveil your face."

The courtroom gasped. The person Mr. Dobbins chose was a man.

Jack returned to the stand.

"How did Isaac manage to escape after he killed his father?"

Jack showed the picture of Isaac Moore as a woman and testified to the number of people who had identified seeing Isaac disguised as one.

"Don't you also have proof that Isaac left Glenwood Springs, the morning he killed his father, dressed as a woman?"

"Yes," Jack said, producing the ticket agent's affidavit.

"Then, Isaac's journal entry, found in Kedra's room is a lie, isn't it?"

"Yes."

Lastly, Jack testified about Isaac's character, and his record of petty theft, producing several affidavits from the opera girls as proof.

When the court adjourned for lunch, Kedra was feeling flutters of hope.

"Mr. Farnsworth has blown apart my hunt for Isaac," Jack said with a shrug, as he escorted her back to her cell. "However, I told him if he needed to use Eli's death to solidify reasonable doubt in the minds of the jury, to do it."

"I'm sorry he did, and I'm not sure it worked. Some of their faces were still hard, almost angry."

"But more of them looked uncertain, and that's good—very good."

"Mr. Farnsworth did a great job of discrediting some of the evidence, didn't he?"

"He did." Jack stopped before they got to the guarded door of the jail. "All he has to do is create doubt in the minds of a couple of jurors. If he can reinforce the doubts some of them are already harboring this afternoon, then the jury will go into deliberations divided and that will give you a real chance of being acquitted."

They stood in silence as a man came out of the jail.

Kedra waited until the man started up the stairs before she said, "Thank you, for helping Mr. Farnsworth create that doubt. I—I'm truly grateful for your support."

Jack held up his scarred thumb. "I'm a blood brother to the Nahtow. I don't intend to stand by and let one of the only two remaining Nahtow be executed for crimes she didn't commit. I owe it to Daeden to do all I can to help you." Grief and loss twisted Jack's face. "It may seem strange to you, but from the moment Daeden and I met, there was an instant bond between us. I felt like I'd always know him, always loved him, and he and I were meant to be brothers."

"I wish I could have known him and my aunt Yarley and . . . my father," Kedra said in a wavering voice. "The letter from my mother, and remembering her from the day I was born, has helped me to know her—a little."

"Getting to know Zed will help you know your father. They are very much alike."

Kedra could almost see the memories coming back to him. "Yes," she agreed thinking of the words her father had written in the book of Nahtow. Her father had possessed the same kind of faith she saw in Zed, and from what he'd told her about her parents, her father had the same deep abiding love for her mother as Zed had for Yarley. It was a love she knew her father had for her too, even before she was born.

That love sustained her as she walked through the gauntlet of cells to her own cell.

"If you'd like, I'll send out for something to eat and stay with you," Jack offered.

"That's very kind of you. However, Mr. Farnsworth is coming with my lunch in a few minutes. We're going to spend the next hour going over what we plan to do when court reconvenes."

He nodded and closed her into the cell.

She waited, listening for the key to turn in the lock. It did, and she dropped to her knees. There was a vital decision she had to make, before Mr. Farnsworth arrived.

47

Exclamations of surprise erupted throughout the courtroom as Mr. Farnsworth called the next witness for the defense.

Judge Bunker's gavel pounded down. He called for silence as Kedra stood before the bailiff and swore to tell the truth, the whole truth, and nothing but the truth.

She cleared her throat, stated her name for the record, and took the stand. Looking out over the courtroom for the first time, she noticed Jack's concerned expression. Sarah looked concerned too, but Zed's expression radiated confidence. It reinforced the underlying peace she felt, which she hoped would empower her to answers the questions put to her boldly and honestly.

A quick glance at Mr. Scrogin told her he was delighted she'd decided to take the stand. It would give him the opportunity to cross-examine her. This could turn out to be the best, or the very worst, decision she would ever make, but she felt she had no choice. There were things she knew that no one else knew, things that couldn't be brought out because they would only be classified as hearsay unless they came directly from her.

She calmly listened to Mr. Farnsworth's first question.

"You and Isaac don't have the same mother. Is that correct?"

"Yes."

"But you do share the bond of Indian blood, do you not?"

"Yes. However, I'm Nahtow, and Isaac is Mi'kmaq.

"Describe Isaac for the court."

"Isaac is slightly taller than I am and very slender. He has black hair, olive skin, high cheek bones, and unusual large pale blue eyes."

"So other than your eye color, you and Isaac resemble one another because of your Indian heritage."

"We do, and from the back, when my hair is pulled up under a hat, we are indistinguishable."

"Are you saying you have been mistaken for one another?"

"Yes, we have."

"Tell the court about that."

Kedra sat forward and look directly at the jury. "A year ago, when Isaac wanted to go hunting with his friends, he borrowed my buckskin pants and jacket. He was in the barn, saddling a horse when our foreman, Buck Gilbert, came in, saw him from the back, and started talking to him, thinking it was me. I walked in just as Isaac turned and angrily corrected Buck. Buck and I had a good laugh over the incident."

"Is that the only time?"

"No. We were both invited to a costume party. We arrived separately, dressed as identical Harlequins. When we realized we were both wearing the same costume, our friends made a game of trying to guess who was who. They were wrong half of the time."

"Yesterday you heard Frankie Gentry say he saw someone with a long black braid with two white feathers on the end, come out from under the train after it stopped. Was it your braid and totem he saw?"

"I believe it was my braid he saw—"

A rippled gasped ran through the courtroom.

Judge Bunker tapped his gavel. "Quiet!" He turned to Kedra. "Please continue, Miss Moore."

"However, the totem he saw wasn't mine."

Mr. Farnsworth stood by the jury box. "How is that possible?"

Kedra related Isaac's attack on her when she was five and her belief Isaac kept the braid as a trophy, a common practice among Indians when they scalped an enemy. She described finding the braid in the hiding place in Isaac's room and went on to describe the white feathers attached to the braid.

"What was different about the white feathers on the braid Isaac had and your totem?"

"My totem is held in my hair by a silver clasp, shaped like a feather. It also holds a strand of tiger-eye beads—the color of all the Nahtow's eyes. Those two things weren't mentioned in the descriptions Frankie Gentry and Mr. Dobbins gave. But their descriptions do match the feather totem I found attached to my braid in Isaac's hiding place."

"There is something more unusual about the Nahtow Indians than just their gold eyes, isn't there Miss Moore?"

"Yes. All true Nahtow Indians have photographic memories, some better than others. Some actually relive things in their minds."

"I'd like you to demonstrate your memory for the court."

Mr. Scrogin was on his feet. "I object, Your Honor. Miss Moore's Nahtow heritage and memory have no bearing on this case."

"With the courts indulgence, I intend to show how very relevant Miss Moore's memory is to this case," Mr. Farnsworth said.

"Objection over ruled. You may proceed with your demonstration and questions, Mr. Farnsworth," Judge Bunker said.

Mr. Farnsworth picked up two copies of the King James Bible and handed one to Mr. Scrogin and the other to the judge.

"Mr. Scrogin, will you please select a chapter in the Bible for Miss Moore to quote?"

Mr. Scrogin scowled, but flipped open the Bible. "Have her recite the 59th Psalm."

"Wait a moment while I locate the page," Judge Bunker said.

"It's on page 750," Kedra said.

"Judge Bunker's eyes widened as he turned to that page. He motioned for her to begin.

"Deliver me from mine enemies, O my God: defend me from them that rise up against me. Deliver me from the workers of iniquity and save me from bloody men. For, lo, they lie in wait for my soul: the mighty are gathered against me; not for my transgression, nor for my sin, O Lord. They run and prepare themselves without my fault; awake to help me and—"

"I believe that will be quite sufficient, Miss Moore," Judge Bunker said.

Kedra didn't allow the smile she felt to show. Mr. Scrogin couldn't have chosen a more appropriate chapter. She'd recited it with all the feeling of a prayer and now everyone in the courtroom, with the exception of Zed, was either wide-eyed or dropped jawed.

Jack grinned broadly and winked at her.

"Now, Miss Moore, tell the court about the last time you wore the jade pendant."

"I wore it to church on June 7th, with a white shirtwaist blouse and a dark green skirt. I also wore the pendant's matching earrings. When I returned home that evening, I took off the pendant and the earrings and locked them in my jewelry box."

"When did you discover the pendant was missing?"

"The following Sunday, when I went to put it on."

"Do you wear the pendant during the week—around the ranch?"

"Never, it is very special to me. It came to me from my mother and I take great care of it. I was devastated when I found it was gone, as Marshal Garrison can attest."

Mr. Farnsworth stroked his goatee. "Tell the court about your relationship with Morgan O'Shea."

Kedra explained her collision with Morgan at the train station and the soda they shared that day. She related the lie he'd told her about become a traveling salesman for a men's wear company because he hadn't had opportunity for higher education and liked to travel.

"What was the length of your association with Harry Walsh, who you knew as Morgan O'Shea, and how many times did you see him?"

"He wrote me every week for six months. I wrote to him twice a month and sent the letters to his home in San Francisco, because he told me he was only home a couple of times a month. We only saw each other on three occasions: The time we met, about three months into our association, and the day of his death."

"What was the nature of your relationship?"

"For my part, I thought of Morgan as a friend—only a friend. I enjoyed hearing about the places Morgan went. He was a good descriptive writer and often described the cities he visited, sharing something interesting or unique about them. From time to time he sent me small trinkets, representative of the city he was working in."

"How did Morgan feel?"

"If the court will permit me, I'll answer that by quoting from the letter postmarked April 9th of this year."

She waited until Judge Bunker was given the correct letter and then quoted, "Seeing you again was wonderful. I can't get you out of my mind. I hope you enjoyed our visit as much as I did. It was far too short and as we parted, I longed to kiss you. That has become a daily longing. I want more than just letters between us. Is that possible my darling, Kedra? I'll be home in five days and hope to hear your answer then. With deep and growing affection, Morgan."

"How did you feel about Morgan's growing affection for you?"

"It was at that point, I knew our relationship would have to end. When I came into town on June 8th, I came dressed in clothes that would be unfamiliar to those who knew me. I wore my hair up under a floppy hat and left my totem at home. I didn't know how Morgan would react, and I didn't want anyone to recognize me if things got ugly."

"Did they?"

"No. I gave Morgan the friendship feather I'd made for him, hoping for his understanding. It was the first and only gift I gave him. I told him I had enjoyed our letter conversations, but I didn't have romantic feelings for him and wouldn't consider deepening a relationship with someone not of my faith."

"How did he react to that?"

"He tried to talk me out of it, but then the train whistle blew the ten minute warning, and he couldn't stay any longer. He said he would continue to write to me. I told him not to. He told me that even if I didn't answer his letters he would still write to me, and hurried away."

"Who knew about the letters you exchanged with Morgan O'Shea?"

"Only my friend, Sarah Powell. She warned me not to believe everything Morgan said; as I only had his word for it that he was who he said he was." Kedra shook her head. "She was right about him."

"Why didn't your father or brother know about Morgan?"

"He wrote to me as he traveled, and because he posted his letters in many different places, he never put a return address on any of them. As far as my family knew, the letters were just more answers to the many inquires I sent out for information on new products and inventions, which I was looking into using on the ranch."

Mr. Farnsworth picked up several of the letters and showed the lack of a return address to Judge Bunker and Mr. Scrogin.

"At times, I felt a bit dishonest about keeping my friendship with Morgan a secret, but having a secret friend was fun . . . intriguing."

"Let's go back to what you did after Morgan ran for the train."

"I got back in the buggy and waited."

"Why?"

"I wanted to wait until the train left and the crowd dispersed."

"How long was it before the train left?"

"Under ten minutes."

"Did you leave town as soon as it pulled out?"

"No. I waited for the traffic around the station to disperse."

"Did you see anyone you knew?"

"No, but then I wasn't looking out of the buggy. I didn't want to be seen. I hid under my hat and just read the newspaper until the noise around the station died down."

"When did you learn that Morgan O'Shea was in fact Harry Walsh?"

"Not until a week later. Isaac brought home a copy of the extra edition of the Avalanche, dealing with the robbery and murders." I saw Morgan's picture in the paper. Under his picture it said, 'Marshal Harry Walsh.'"

"How did you feel about that?"

"Betrayed—the paper said he had a fiancée, so I knew he had just been toying with me. I was glad I hadn't let the relationship go beyond friendship, but I was also horrified that he'd been killed."

"Why did you cut Harry Walsh's picture out of the newspaper and put it in the last letter you got from Morgan?"

"Because I realized the letters were from a man I didn't know. I intended to put Marshal Walsh's picture in with the letters and burn them—to sort of cauterize the wound he'd inflicted on me."

"When did you learn Harry was Isaac's cousin?"

"The day after Isaac attacked Marshal Garrison and me. Marshal Laramore told me."

"Why didn't you come forward when you knew Marshal Laramore was looking for the woman who was with Harry Walsh just before the robbery?"

"After I read all the details of the robbery and murders in the Avalanche, as far as they were known, I was afraid to come forward."

"Why?"

Kedra dropped her head for a moment, this was going to be the most damaging part of her testimony, but she hoped if she told the truth it would help the jury see her as being totally honest. She sat up tall and looked straight at the jury.

"Because I did plan the train robbery, and I thought either Eli or Isaac had committed the robbery and murders."

The courtroom exploded.

48

Judge Bunker banged down his gavel, threatening to clear the courtroom. When silence was again established, he told Mr. Farnsworth to continue.

"Miss Moore, will you please tell the court how you came to plan a train robbery?"

"I have a friend, Donna Parlee, who teaches piano lessons. I've taken lessons from her for years. She comes from Toronto, Canada, but her family is English. They subscribe to the Strand Magazine, which is printed in London. After her family reads the magazine they send it on to her. The Strand runs Mr. Conan Doyle's stories about Sherlock Holmes. After Donna reads the magazines, she lets me have them. I love the Sherlock Holmes mysteries and thought about trying to write a mystery myself. So, when a national writing contest was announced in the Avalanche in January of 1902, sponsored by a New York publisher, I decided to write a mystery involving a train robbery and submit it."

"Did you read your story to anyone?"

"I read it to Eli and Isaac Moore."

"What did they think of it?"

"Eli thought it was very good, but Isaac told me it was stupid. He said my plan for the train robbery wouldn't work."

"Did that discourage you?"

"Not at all, I was used to Isaac's disapproval of everything I did. I put it in an envelope and set it in the outgoing mail bin in Eli's office."

"Who took the outgoing mail into town?"

"At that time, Isaac did."

"Did you ever hear anything from the contest?"

"No, and I just assumed they didn't like my story. I knew they weren't going to return it, because that was in the rules."

"Are you aware that there was another very similar robbery, to the Glenwood Springs one, committed in June of 1902 near Eagle?"

"Not until a few days ago. You see, I graduated from High School that year, just before I turned sixteen. Sarah and Jacob Powell took me on a cross-country road trip as a gift. I was gone that entire summer and knew nothing of the robbery, nor did I hear anything about it when I returned."

"Who told you about the Eagle robbery?"

"Marshal Garrison."

"Miss Moore, the one point that hasn't been cleared up in the Glenwood or the Eagle robberies is how the thief got into the express cars. Would you please tell the court how the thief got in and out of the express car in your story?"

Kedra nearly laughed as the entire courtroom leaned forward. She wondered if she paused long enough how many of them would pass out from holding their breath. Even Jack seemed to be sitting on the edge of his seat.

"In my story the robbery happened at night, and that made it easy. When the train stopped at a rural station, which only had lights on the platform side of the station, the thief simply came out of some heavy bushes on the dark side of the train and slid underneath it. He came up through the toilet in the express car, while the marshal was out of the car. When the train was moving again, his partner, the deputy, said a particular line. That told him everyone's attention had been drawn away from the toilet stall so he could come out. After he locked up the officers and robbed the safe, he fired off two shots to tell the dining car steward—his other accomplice—that he was ready to get off the train. The steward then pulled the emergency stop cord and the robber left the way he'd come. In my story, the robber wore a flour sack over his head, keeping his identity hidden, eliminating the need to kill anyone."

"Then there wasn't any Chloral Hydrate involved in your story?"

"No, there wasn't. The fact that I put the extra edition of the Avalanche into the chemistry book on the page containing the entry for Chloral Hydrate was pure coincidence. And I have no idea how the bandit got into the express car in the crowded Glenwood station."

"Your Honor, I would like to enter into evidence a copy of Miss Moore's story, rewritten from her perfect memory."

The bailiff accepted the story and labeled it. The Judge extended his hand and the bailiff put the story into it.

Mr. Farnsworth faced the jury. "Miss Moore, why would your brother want to frame you for these crimes?"

"Isaac Moore is not my brother."

"Are you saying Eli Moore wasn't your father?"

"Yes."

"When did you learn Eli Moore wasn't your father?"

"The morning he died."

"Did he confess this to you?"

"Yes. Eli also told me Isaac hated me because he knew I wasn't his sister, and he knew Eli loved me more than him."

"Now, let's turn to the emerald Marshal Garrison found on the floor of your bedroom. Tell us how that happened."

Kedra recounted what happened, admitted to lying to Marshal Garrison when he asked her what Swindler had been after, and to slipping the emeralds she'd taken from Swindler into the pocket of her robe, hoping Marshal Garrison hadn't seen them.

"As soon as I saw the emeralds, I knew they'd come from the train robbery. I also felt sure I'd find the rest of them in the hiding place in Isaac's bedroom."

She recounted opening the hiding place, going through what it contained, her decision to take the emeralds to the sheriff and leave the other things in the hiding place, and why. She explained her need for a gun because of the eerie sensation of being watched all day and her surprise when she found her gun was missing, something she kept in the locked desk drawer to keep it out of Swindler's hands, and then going to get a gun from Eli's room.

"I was flabbergasted when Marshal Garrison came out of the dark sitting room with his gun drawn, told me to drop mine and accused me of the emerald theft and the murders of four men."

"Miss Moore, did you ever see or meet Drew Ellis?"

"No. The first time I even heard a description of him was in this courtroom."

Miss Moore, did you commit the emerald robbery and kill Marshal William Forbes, Marshal Harry Walsh, Haru Ito, and Drew Ellis?"

Kedra lifted her chin and slowly looked each juror in the eyes. "No, I did not commit any of the crimes for which I am charged."

Mr. Farnsworth smiled. "Your witness, Mr. Scrogin."

Mr. Scrogin rose slowly to his feet, his thumbs tucked into the pockets of his vest. His cold smile sent a chill down Kedra's arms.

"You certainly seem to have an answer for every question, Miss Moore. Tell me, why you didn't know Morgan O'Shea was Isaac's cousin? After all, they do bear a certain resemblance to one another and you must have known Isaac's mother's maiden name."

"Neither Isaac nor Eli spoke of Isaac's mother to me—ever. I was completely unaware of her maiden name or the connection between the man I knew as Morgan O'Shea and Isaac."

"If your relationship with Morgan O'Shea was as innocent as you say, why did you feel the need to keep it a secret?"

"Keeping the relationship secret appealed to my sense of drama. Besides, I knew if my family found out they would pester me about it, and I just wanted to enjoy it for what it was—an innocent pen pal relationship. One I didn't expect to last."

"Marshal Garrison testified that Isaac kept his door locked at all times, which was common knowledge on the ranch. However, you want this court to believe that your raccoon, Swindler, somehow got into Isaac's locked room, took a few of the emeralds out of a secret hiding place in the floor, and ran off with them, without Isaac's knowledge. How is that possible?"

"I believe Mrs. Blue covered that, sir."

"Mrs. Blue testified that there wasn't anything in Swindlers paws, and it required both his hands to open your door, didn't she?"

"Yes, but he did drop the emeralds he had in an umbrella in the hall tree, because one was pulled out and torn apart when I found him in the hall with the emeralds."

"We only have your word for that, Miss Moore."

"But Mrs. Blue—"

"Didn't see Swindler in Isaac's room, nor did she see him put some of the emeralds in an umbrella in the hall tree. Isn't that true?"

"Yes," Kedra admitted, softly.

"Isn't it also a fact that we only have your word for what was in the hiding place in Isaac's room?"

"Yes."

"When did Marshal Garrison tell you about the diamond ring taken in the Eagle robbery?"

Kedra's eyes blazed for just a moment. He was trying to trick her into saying something that would contradict her testimony. She looked straight into his cold eyes and said, "Marshal Garrison didn't tell me about the diamond ring. I found it in Isaac's hiding place and told Marshal Garrison about it. That's when he told me about the Eagle robbery. I had no idea where the ring had come from. For all I knew it belonged to Mrs. Capshaw as it was in a case with her pearls."

"Again we only have your word for what was in Isaac's hiding place, but by your own admission you knew about the diamond ring, before it was public knowledge."

Kedra lips pressed together. She'd fallen into Mr. Scrogin's trap. He'd cleverly twisted the facts to cast doubt on her veracity.

Mr. Scrogin leaned against the witness box. "Why would Isaac take the pendant from your jewelry box and leave the matching earrings?"

"Because the pendant, along with my braid, and a pair of white feathers was all the evidence Isaac needed to make it look as though I committed the robbery and murders."

"You want this court to believe Isaac Moore framed you for his crimes—that you are his scapegoat. But setting you up as the scapegoat with the *overwhelming* amount of evidence we have against you would have taken time and very careful planning, wouldn't it?"

"Objection, calls for a conclusion on the part of the witness," Mr. Farnsworth said.

"Sustained," Judge Bunker said.

"You testified that your relationship with Morgan O'Shea, which ties you to Harry Walsh and these crimes, started six months before the robbery, isn't that true?" Mr. Scrogin continued.

"Yes."

"Then doesn't it logically follow that the plot against you started six months ago?"

"Objection," Mr. Farnsworth said. "Again the question calls for a conclusion on the part of the witness."

"Sustained," Judge Bunker said.

Mr. Scrogin glared at her. "The Justice Department didn't inform Marshal Forbes or Marshal Walsh that the emeralds would be under their protection until the day before they left San Francisco. Please tell the court how Marshal Walsh and Isaac Moore could have planned and executed such a convincing frame job in just three days?"

Kedra's heart dropped into her stomach. She and Mr. Farnsworth hadn't thought about or discussed the limited time Harry and Isaac had to plan the crime and convincingly frame her for it. The length of her relationship with Morgan made it seem more likely that she'd been in cahoots with Harry, and or Isaac, and they were just waiting for the right cargo before they put her plan into action, the telegram reinforced that too.

Mr. Scrogin's smug expression told her he'd score a hit.

Mr. Farnsworth was on his feet. "Objection, the question calls for speculation on the part of the witness."

"Sustained," Judge Bunker said.

"I have one last question, Miss Moore," Mr. Scrogin said. "It has been evident to this court that Marshal Garrison has been more than reluctant to testify against you, even though he was the one who uncovered most of the evidence of your crimes. I'd like you to tell the court, what your personal relationship is with Marshal Garrison."

The question took Kedra completely by surprise. She felt the blood rush into her cheeks. Her eyes flew to Mr. Farnsworth. *Surely he'll object to this question!* But he didn't.

What could she say—that they were friends, except she wasn't sure that was true. There was definitely something between them, but what? She didn't know how Jack felt about her—not really. And since the day they met, she'd resisted and denied having feelings for him.

She didn't dare look at Jack, while her mind frantically searched for a truthful answer. What he'd said to her during the lunch recess came to her rescue. It was as close to the truth as she dared let herself come.

"Marshal Garrison was my cousin Daeden's blood brother, as such, he feels a deep attachment to my family, but he made it very clear to me that he would do his duty as a U.S. Marshal, regardless of his relationship with my family—and he has."

Mr. Scrogin scowled at her for a moment and then addressed Judge Bunker. "I have no more questions."

Mr. Farnsworth, do you have any more witnesses?"

"No, Your Honor, the defense rests."

"The court will take a fifteen minutes recess and then hear closing arguments," Judge Bunker said, bringing down his gavel with a bang.

The closing arguments were much like the opening ones, except Mr. Scrogin meticulously went over every piece of evidence against Kedra. He pointed out that the overwhelming amount of evidence should conclusively prove Miss Moore's guilt.

Mr. Farnsworth did a masterful job of poking holes in the evidence and pointing out that there was so much doubt about the so-called evidence that in all good conscience they couldn't convict her.

Studying the faces of the jurors as the prosecution and defense presented their arguments, Kedra found it impossible to tell how they felt.

After the closing arguments, Judge Bunker instructed the jury. He then dismissed them to deliberate and come to a verdict.

Kedra flinched when the gavel came down, dismissing the court. The trial was over, and the unbearable waiting had begun. Her life was now in the hands of twelve men. They would decide whether she was guilty or not guilty, whether she lived or died.

49

Eyes waited for the court to adjourn in a fashionable little bistro, a block from the courthouse. Like the day before, fifteen minutes after the court adjourned, the bistro was filled to capacity. As Isaac listened, again dressed as a fashionable redheaded lady, he found himself hiding his disquiet behind a coffee cup.

The bistro resonated with discussions concerning the trial. Isaac listened to arguments both for and against convicting Kedra Moore. It was apparent after only a few minutes that the room was almost evenly divided as to her guilt or innocence.

Isaac pulled his delicate veil lower over his troubled eyes and frowned into his coffee cup. *How can anyone doubt her guilt? The evidence is so overwhelming, so conclusive—I made sure of that.*

When he tired of listening to the ongoing arguments, he paid his bill and left, again going to pick up the extra edition of the Rocky Mountain News. He first read the legal expert's opinion of the trial and found little to encourage him. It was the opinion of the legal expert that the case could go either way.

He turned to the full account of the trial and skimmed the content until he came upon the mention of the Eagle robbery and the thief of a unique diamond ring, which the paper described in detail. A jab of alarm pierced him. His alarm grew when he read that Eli had lived long enough to name him as his killer.

Isaac's fingers curled into the newspaper, wanting to tear it apart, but that would be unladylike. These new revelations held a deadly threat. They would force his hand, and he hated being forced.

The laundry basket ride, back to the Golden Garter, gave him time to think. By the time he arrived, he knew what he had to do.

He laughed out loud. *Maybe it's all for the best.*

Jack and Zed sat in the back of a dimly lit restaurant, famous for its western barbeque, eating dinner and discussing the trial, trying to buoy each other up, while Sarah had dinner with Kedra, in her cell.

"I can't lose her, Jack. Kedra is all that is left of my family, my people. All the others were lost long ago. She has the gift possessed by our first parents, and her gift is very great. She has a mission to perform for her people. I won't live long enough to do everything that needs to be done."

"She's not going to hang," Jack said quietly.

"You don't know that."

"Yes I do, because I won't let it happen."

"What are you saying?"

"That if she's found guilty, I intend to get her out of the country. I won't let her die for something I know she didn't do. What I need to know is—will you help me?"

Jack watched Zed's stunned expression turn into allegiance.

"Yes, I will help you. Tell me what you want me to do."

Pushing aside his half eaten dinner of pork ribs and fried potatoes, Jack began to outline his scheme. He'd only gotten through the escape from the jail when a man and a woman approached the table.

"Marshal!" A hardy man in a bowler hat clapped Jack on the back. "How do you think the jury will vote?"

"I don't know," Jack said, glowering at the man and his decorative companion.

The woman was past her prime, but with the artifice of makeup, and an expensive gown and jewelry, she was quite a sight.

"Forgive the interruption, Marshal. I'm Bessie Louder and this is Herbert Toone. I told Herbert not to disturb you, but he simply wouldn't listen to me." She extended her hand to Jack. The light of the candle caught the gleam of a diamond ring on her hand.

Jack took her hand and pressed it to his lips, taking a long look at the ring. "I never mind being interrupted by a lovely lady." He paused, keeping hold of her hand. "Your name seems familiar to me, but I can't quite place it."

"You must be from out of town if you don't know Miss Bessie Louder. She owns the best saloon in Denver," Toone exclaimed.

"I'm the proprietress of the Golden Garter Saloon. You ought to pay me a visit sometime, Marshal. I promise I'll show you a *very* good time," Bessie said, suggestively.

"I believe I'll do that," Jack replied, releasing her hand and smiling.

Bessie tapped her companion's arm with her fan. "I think we've taken enough of Marshal Garrison's time, Herbert."

Jack apologized to Zed after they left. The pair hadn't even acknowledged Zed's presence.

Zed waved his apology aside. "I've become quite accustomed to being invisible in the white man's world." He laughed. "Either that, or I'm too visible and largely frowned upon. However, I have a very thick hide. The white man's opinion of me hasn't bothered me for many years."

"I guess my hide isn't as thick, because it bothers me." Jack leaned in and whispered, "Did you see the ring Bessie Louder was wearing?"

"Yes, quite spectacular, as diamonds go."

"Not just spectacular, but very unique." Jack laid his napkin on the table. "We may not have to break Kedra out of jail after all. That ring is the one that was stolen in the Eagle robbery." He looked across the room at Bessie Louder. "Miss Louder ought to be here for the next hour. That will give me the time I need to get a warrant for the Golden Garter." He looked at Zed thoughtfully. "How would you like to be a Deputy U.S. Marshal for a few hours?"

Over a dozen Deputy Marshals listened to Jack's final instructions.

"Once Zed and I go in, don't let anyone else into the saloon. You can let people out, only after you've searched them—thoroughly. All of you have the pictures of Isaac Moore. Make sure you check for wigs, fake mustaches, and the like. He's an expert at disguise. This search is to find Isaac Moore. I want it to be done as cleanly and as quietly as possible. It will be easier to get Miss Louder's cooperation if we conduct this search discreetly. Any questions?" Jack looked around the room. "All right, you all know your assignments so let's get going."

Jack's men were all in place by the time Herbert Toone's carriage pulled up in front of the saloon.

Zed hung back as Jack approached it.

"Miss Louder, I need to have a word with you," Jack said quietly, wearing his badge prominently on the front of his jacket.

"What's this?" Herbert exclaimed.

"This doesn't concern you," Jack said, keeping his voice low.

"What's this about?" Bessie asked.

"I have a warrant to search your saloon. I would prefer to execute it quietly—unless you insist on making this into a spectacle."

"A search warrant?!" Herbert bellowed.

"Hush, Herbert, do you want the whole street to hear? What cause do you have to search my saloon, Marshal?"

"You are in possession of stolen merchandise. Only the man I'm searching for could have passed that merchandise to you. Now will you come with me quietly or shall I call in my deputies?"

"You're making a big mistake, Marshal, I have connections—"

"I know all about your city and state connections, Miss Louder. However, I'm a United States Marshal. All your connections don't mean a thing to me. I represent the United States Government, and, in the matter I'm currently engaged in, I personally represent the President of the United States."

Bessie swallowed and allowed Jack to help her out of the carriage. She glanced over her shoulder at Herbert Toone. "Call my attorney Herbert, immediately!"

Jack nodded at Zed and they escorted Bessie into the saloon.

"Indians aren't welcome in my place," Bessie said tightly.

"He's a Deputy U.S. Marshal and where I go, he goes," Jack said taking hold of Bessie's arm. "Now we can play this two ways. I can call in my deputies, and we will systematically tear your saloon apart. Or we can go into your office, you can inspect the warrant, and I'll tell you what I'm looking for. It's up to you, but no one is going to be allowed into your saloon until I give the word. Those going out will be thoroughly search. So what's it going to be, Miss Louder?"

"We'll go quietly to my office. Please smile so my patrons don't become alarmed."

Bessie greeted people as they crossed the saloon and answered a question for one of her employees, before finally taking Jack and Zed through a door at the back of the saloon.

Bessie Louder's office oozed with red brocaded femininity.

She sat down behind her desk. "All right what's this all about?"

Jack showed her the warrant, giving him the right to search her saloon. "The ring you're wearing is stolen property, Miss Louder. It was taken in a train robbery six years ago. Unless you can prove you didn't know the ring was stolen, I can charge you with receiving stolen goods." Jack held out his hand.

The lines on Bessie's aging face became more prominent as she pulled the ring from her finger and dropped into his hand. "I swear I didn't know it was stolen."

"Where did you get it?"

"I bought it from a friend. He told me it was his grandmother's and he needed to sell it because of his financial situation."

"Who is this friend?"

Bessie pressed her lips together and stared at Jack.

"Are you willing to go to jail for this man?"

"No," she said through her teeth. "His name is . . . Eyes."

"Is he currently staying here?"

She hesitated, seeming to make up her mind, and then said, "Yes."

Jack stood up. "Take us to his room."

"He may not be in. He usually goes out at night."

"Then we'll wait for him." Jack gestured to the door.

Bessie threw him a murderous look and got up.

She took them up a back staircase to the third floor and down the hall. Stopping in front of a wall lamp, she moved the lamp slightly to the right. A spring-loaded wall panel opened.

"You go in first, Miss Louder, and don't do anything to give us away. Is that understood?"

"Yes," she said, switching on the light and starting up the stairs.

Jack drew his gun and followed, with Zed close on his heels.

When they reached the attic room, Bessie knocked. "Eyes, are you in?" she asked sweetly. "I'd like to talk with you."

There was no answer.

Jack reached around her and tried the door. It was locked. "Do you have the key, Miss Louder?"

Bessie pulled a ring of keys from the pocket of her dress and unlocked the door.

"Where is the light switch?" Jack asked.

"On the left side of the door."

Jack let his gun lead the way, turning on the light as he entered. The room was small, well furnished, and vacant.

"He's gone!" Bessie exclaimed. "All his things are gone."

"Zed, go downstairs and get Luke and Darrius. I want this room searched." Jack turned to Bessie. "You are going to tell me everything you know about Eyes."

Bessie fanned her flushed face. "Do you mind if we talk in my apartment? It's so hot up here. It's just down the hall and will be so much more comfortable."

"As soon as Zed returns, we will." Jack pulled out the pictures of Isaac. Is this the man you know as Eyes?"

"Yes," Bessie sighed on a resigned breath.

"Do you know his real name?"

"No. I have only ever known him as Eyes O'Shea."

"When did you first meet him?"

"Seven years ago. He was looking for a job in my theater company. He was very good at playing any part." She gestured to the pictures of Isaac. "As you can see he could stand in for either men or women, but he didn't have much time—he was in school. I hired him to be a stand in on weeknights, if he was needed, and to be in the shows on the weekend."

"Have you helped him financially?"

She shrugged. "From time to time, but nothing substantial."

"How long has he been here?"

"He got here about ten days ago."

Jack nodded and asked, "Why did he come here?"

"I never pry into Eyes's business. Over the last few years, he's just shown up randomly. He stays with me for a while and then leaves. I rarely know what he's up to, and I don't care. He amuses me and that's all I care about."

Zed came back into the room with Luke and Darrius.

"Do a good job, and don't forget to look for secret places in the walls, floor, ceiling, and down the stairway."

"Will do," Luke said as Jack took Bessie out of the room.

"Where else might Eyes stay, if he wasn't going to stay with you?" Jack asked as they walked down the hall. He stopped as he caught a whiff of an unusual odor. *So that's what Freddy meant by other delights. She's running an opium den up here.* That information he would pass along to the Justice Department.

Bessie winced and hurried down the hallway. He caught up with her as she opened the door to her apartment. Like her office, the place was dripping with femininity, elegantly done in pink and lavender.

"I don't know where Eyes would stay, if not with me," she said, answering the question Jack asked before he got distracted in the hall.

"Tell me about the different characters he likes to transform himself into—particularly the ones he's been since he arrived here."

"He's only portrayed one character since he got here—a woman."

"Describe this woman?"

"I gave him a red wig and let him alter some of my old clothes."

"I've had this place watched for the last week, Miss Louder, and my men haven't seen Eyes. How is he coming and going from here?"

Bessie again hesitated.

"You do know that harboring a wanted criminal is a felony, don't you?" Jack asked, sternly.

Bessie leaned back into the cushions of her baroque sofa and said through her teeth, "In a laundry basket."

Jack calculated the possibilities of that mode of transportation, into and out of this establishment, and decided to also pass this piece of information on to the Justice Department.

"Miss Louder, the women I have interviewed, who have had any kind of association with Eyes, whose real name is Isaac Moore—"

Bessie gasped. "Not the man that is wanted for the murder of his father and is said to have taken the stolen emeralds from his sister?"

"That's right, and all the women he has associated with tell me he has stolen things from them. Has he stolen anything from you?"

"No—never!"

"Are you sure? Was he here when you left for dinner?"

"He was. He told me he would see me tonight, after I got back."

"You know now that was a lie. I think you should look through your belongings, particularly your jewelry."

Bessie got up and went to her safe. "Everything I have of worth I keep in here. Eyes doesn't know the combination to this safe."

"Has he ever been in this room when you opened it?"

Yes, but—"

"Check it for me, please."

Bessie opened the safe, and whirled around, "My best jewelry is gone! Why that no good—and to think I treated him like a—"

"What else might he have taken? Look through your closet, your accessories, your wigs, and makeup."

Ten minutes later, Bessie was fuming as she described the items that were missing from her closet and bathroom.

"You've been very helpful, Miss Louder. I may have other questions for you later. Right now, you're going to go downstairs and announce that the saloon is closing for the night. Tomorrow, you will be allowed to open again without any interference from the Justice Department."

"What am I supposed to tell my patrons?"

"Tell them the U.S. Marshal's office received a tip that a fugitive came in here and you have agreed to help us find him. Cooperating with the law will keep your reputation in tact as a reputable establishment. My men will check everyone as they exit, so there will be no need for them to enter until the saloon is empty. Then we will search the place from basement to attic—in case Isaac is hiding somewhere in the saloon."

"All right." She paused. "Are you going to charge me with receiving stolen goods and harboring a felon?"

Jack thought about it for a moment, weighing all the charges he could bring against her, and said, "As long as you willingly cooperate with me, I'll consider you an innocent victim in Isaac Moore's game. That means, if you hear from him you are to contact me immediately." He handed her his card. "Is that understood? If I find you have helped him, or warned him, after tonight, I'll arrest you."

Isaac was well connected to an unsavory underground grapevine. He knew, just after Marshal Garrison left the Golden Garter, about the raid. He laughed hardily, reclining in a comfortable chair, secure in his hotel room. There was nothing Bessie could tell the marshal that could hurt him. She didn't know about Professor Drake, the persona he was now playing. He sighed, *but I'll never be able to go to Bessie again, not that I care to. She was becoming much too possessive. She has served her purpose. Hopefully, the jury will come back with their verdict tomorrow. I'm sure the special prosecutor will push for a speedy execution and I will leave in the next few days.* His brows drew together, thoughtfully. *I suppose it wouldn't be wise to go out. I'll let the management know I have a cold and take my meals here in my room.* Isaac lifted a glass of brandy and toasted himself. "You are, without peer," he said and downed the brandy.

50

Friday, July 3, 1908

Kedra tensed when she heard the key turn in the lock of her cell. It was too early for visitors, which could only mean one thing. She sent a prayer heavenward as the door opened.

Jack ducked into the cell. "The jury has just come in."

Kedra stood up, her heart pounding. "I didn't think they would come to a decision so soon."

"They deliberated for a long time last night and again very early this morning. That's a good sign," Jack said encouragingly. He handed her the dress Sarah sent her. "No matter what happens, everything is going to be all right, you have my word on that," he whispered.

She wanted to ask him what he meant, but the jail matron walked toward them, bringing soap and a fresh towel.

Jack gave her fifteen minutes to change from her prison garb into her dress and fix her hair, before he led her out of her cell. She looked back at it, wondering if she would be back to spend the last days of her life in that dank cell or if she would never have to see it again.

Similar thoughts afflicted her as she walked through the gauntlet of cells, trying to block out the ugly suggestions of the inmates.

Judge Bunker and the jury were in place when Jack escorted her into the packed courtroom. She looked at the expressionless faces of the jury, trying not to let them see her fear.

Mr. Farnsworth stood.

She took her place at his side.

Judge Bunker asked, "Mr. Foreman has the jury reached a verdict?"

The foreman, a professional looking man in a neat sack suit, responded, "We have, Your Honor."

The bailiff took the jury's decision from the foreman and handed it to the judge. He looked at it and then at the foreman. "You will please tell the court your—"

The door to the courtroom burst open. Darrius Jones and Tate Hadlock, accompanied by two women and a man, rushed in.

"Wait, Your Honor! We have witnesses with new testimony for this court," Darrius Jones announced.

Judge Bunker banged down his gavel, peering over the rims of his spectacles at Darrius. "You are out of order, Deputy Jones."

"I beg the courts pardon, but these witnesses must be heard before a verdict is rendered, if justice is to be done."

A swell of voices ran through the courtroom.

Judge Bunker's gavel banged down. "Quiet! Or I will have this courtroom cleared."

Kedra couldn't take her eyes off the lovely woman with chestnut hair and soft brown eyes, standing directly behind Tate Hadlock. Donna Parlee had been in Canada for more than two weeks.

The other two people were strangers to Kedra. The woman was an attractive, petite blond, the man who held her hand was husky and dark headed.

"Do you know about these witnesses, Mr. Farnsworth?"

"No, Your Honor."

Kedra pulled on his sleeve and whispered into his ear.

"Miss Moore tells me, one of the young women, Miss Donna Parlee, is her piano teacher."

"Who are the others?"

"Your Honor, I'm Dolores *Ellis* Scott. Drew Ellis's sister. A Marshal Garrison has left numerous telegrams at my home in Casper, Wyoming, which I only opened forty-eight hours ago. I have vital information for this court."

"As do I," Donna Parlee said.

"Your Honor," Mr. Scrogin protested, "you can't just let these people come in here and disrupt—"

"I'll decide what I will or will not allow in my courtroom, Mr. Scrogin." The judge looked at the new witnesses coldly. "Why are you only coming forward now?"

"I've been out of the country since the morning after the robbery and murders, Your Honor," Donna said. "I didn't learn Kedra—Miss Moore had been charged with these crimes until I got back in the states thirty-six hours ago."

"The same is true for me, Your Honor," Mrs. Scott said. "I have been on an extended honeymoon—"Mrs. Scott blushed prettily—"and only arrived home two days ago, myself. I knew nothing of Drew's murder or about his involvement with these crimes until I opened a letter he sent me."

Kedra began to tremble, she forced herself to take slow breaths in through her nose and blow them out through her lips. The dizzying sensation of hope was almost painful.

Judge Bunker sat back in his chair, letting the silence in the courtroom draw out. He leaned forward after a minute and said,

"This is a court where we seek for justice. Therefore, I will permit these new witnesses to testify. Miss Parlee, you will please come forward and be sworn in."

Kedra took her seat, at Judge Bunker's direction. Her fingers gripped the edge of the table in an effort to steady her nerves.

Donna was sworn in and took the stand.

"Miss Parlee, before you testify before this court I will remind you that you will be subjected to cross-examination by both counsels. Now, you may tell this court what you know, pertaining to this case," Judge Bunker said.

"On the day of the robbery, I went to the Glenwood Springs train station to purchase a ticket to Toronto Canada. I had just received word of my grandmother's death and my family was anxious for me to come. I purchased my ticket and left the station about five minutes *after* the train pulled out. As I was walking toward the bridge, I saw the Moore's buggy. I raised my hand to wave, just as Kedra started Molly off—Molly is the buggy horse the Moores always use. I kept waving but Kedra didn't see me. She seemed preoccupied and I wondered why, but didn't get a chance to talk with her before I left for Canada the next morning."

"Mr. Scrogin, would you care to question this witness?"

"I would, Your Honor." Mr. Scrogin came forward. "Miss Parlee, tell me what was Miss Moore wearing?"

Donna laughed. "She was dressed very unusually, for her. She was wearing a very large straw hat, which flopped down over her face, a white blouse, and a pale yellow skirt."

"If the hat was down over her face, how did you know it was her?"

"At first I thought it might be Effie Blue, but then the wind caught her hat just as she came abreast of me, blowing it back for just a moment. I saw her face very clearly. She looked distressed."

Mr. Scrogin pressed his lips together for a moment. "I have no more questions."

Mr. Farnsworth, is there anything you would like to ask this witness?"

"No, Your Honor, I have no questions."

Kedra's throat closed with emotion as Donna smiled at her. She pulled a handkerchief from her pocket and dabbed her eyes, returning Donna's smile.

"You may leave the stand, Miss Parlee," Judge Bunker said, beckoning to Mrs. Scott. "Please come forward and take the stand, Mrs. Scott."

The judge gave Mrs. Scott the same instructions after she was sworn in. She looked out over the courtroom and said in a small voice, "I hardly know where to begin."

"Just take your time, Mrs. Scott," Judge Bunker said soothingly.

She nodded and said, "My husband, Jimmy, and I got home from our honeymoon to Jamaica two days ago. We had a ton of mail waiting for us, because we'd been gone for almost a month. I didn't know what to make of all the telegrams from Marshal Garrison, until I came to the letter from Drew." She pulled the letter from her purse and asked, "Your Honor, may I read some of his letter?"

"Please do, Mrs. Scott."

She looked at the letter for a moment and then began to read.

"I have done something bad, really bad. I'm in trouble up to my neck and I'm afraid for my life. I'm the only one left who knows what happened and how. If I die, I don't want Isaac Moore, known as Eyes O'Shea, to get away with it. I have sent you a key to a safety deposit box in Denver. If anything happens to me, go open the box. Take the contents to the U.S. Marshals in Denver. I'm going to leave the country as soon as I can arrange it. I hope that will satisfy Eyes and he'll let me live. I wrote to him and told him I didn't want to meet him in Grand Junction, as we planned after the robbery, and I didn't want any of the emeralds he was supposed to give me for my part in the crime.

"I hope he'll let me go. If he shows up, I'm afraid he'll kill me, just as he did the two marshals and their prisoner. I don't know why he killed them. That wasn't part of the plan. Something must have gone wrong, but that doesn't explain why he killed Harry, his own cousin.

"Eyes is a demon—a man without a soul. I regret the day I met him and became involved in his schemes. It was just that I didn't want to spend the rest of my life as a railroad worker. With the money he promised me, I was going to open that bookstore I always told you I wanted. After our first successful robbery near Eagle, I was sure it would happen. Isaac told me to be patient, he said the Eagle robbery was just a dress rehearsal, and we would have to wait until a really big prize was being transported before we robbed the train again.

"Six years went by before he again contacted me. The rest of the story is written in my journal, which you'll find in the safety deposit box. There is also a story written by Eyes's sister. It was what Eyes based the robbery on. I've also put a diamond pin from the Eagle robbery and a telegram from Eyes, telling me to purchase Chloral Hydrate and how to use it, in the safety deposit box.

"I'm sorry, Dolores, for everything I've done. If I could undo it I would, but if I can keep Eyes from committing any other crimes then that's at least something."

Mrs. Scott looked at Kedra with teary eyes. "I'm so sorry you have been put through this terrible ordeal, Miss Moore. If only Jimmy and I had gotten home sooner." She pulled several items from her large bag and handed them to Judge Bunker. "Here is the journal, the letter, the telegram, and the diamond pin from the Eagle robbery, Your Honor."

Judge Bunker took several minutes to look the items over, before he gave them to the bailiff to enter into evidence and addressed the prosecutor. "Considering what we have just heard, Mr. Scrogin, what would you like to do?"

Mr. Scrogin stood. "I would like time to examine this new evidence. If it turns out to be genuine, then I will move to dismiss the charges against Miss Moore."

Mr. Farnsworth was on his feet. "Your Honor, can there be any doubt about Miss Moore's innocence, after the testimonies of these two totally unrelated witnesses?"

"I agree with you, Mr. Farnsworth. I can see no reason to hold Miss Moore any longer." For the first time he smiled at Kedra. "Miss Moore, you are free to go. However, I know Mr. Scrogin will want to examine all of Mr. Ellis's evidence, and I would ask you not to leave Denver until you hear from my office." The judge's gavel came down. "This case is dismissed."

Zed leaped over the banister and pulled Kedra into his arms. Tears ran down their faces as they held each other. "I have prayed so hard, and my prayers have been answered," he said.

Kedra couldn't say anything through her tears, but she grasped the hand Sarah extended to her.

Jack rushed over to them. "Kedra, Zed, come with me, before the reporters swarm you"—he touched Sarah's arm—"you too." Above the commotion in the courtroom he shouted, "Darrius! Tate! Bring Miss Parlee and the Scotts." Then he roared, "Deputies!" Several Deputy Marshals closed in around Kedra and her friends.

They went out a side door into a hall, which the public wasn't allowed to use.

A bailiff followed them.

After the bailiff closed the door, he said, "Mrs. Scott, Judge Bunker would like to know where he can reach you, should he have any questions."

Mr. Scott furnished the bailiff with the information.

Kedra embraced Mrs. Scott. "I will be forever grateful your brother wrote that letter to you. I know it must have been very painful for you to tell everyone what he did. Thank you for coming forward."

Mrs. Scott wiped her eyes. "Our brothers made terrible choices in their lives, but at least you won't have to pay for them. I hope the law can catch up with your brother soon so no one else will get hurt."

"So do I!" Kedra exclaimed squeezing Mrs. Scott tightly. She released her and turned to Donna. "And thank heaven you came home in time too! I didn't see you that day, but I'm so grateful you saw me after the train left." She kissed Donna's cheek and wiped a tear from it. "I want to know how you got here in time."

"There are a great many things I think we would all like to know," Mr. Farnsworth said. "What do you say we all go out to eat and celebrate? It will be my treat."

"That would be very nice, I could use a good meal and to eat it sitting in a room as a free woman." Kedra smiled at her friends. "What do you say? Shall we go have lunch on Mr. Farnsworth?"

"By all means," Sarah laughed.

Zed nodded.

Kedra turned to the Scotts. "Would you come too?" She hesitated. "I almost hate to ask, but did you read your brother's journal?"

"I did, and it will answer many of the questions I'm sure you have."

Mrs. Scott consulted her husband; they agreed to come along.

"Wherever you go, you'll be mobbed by reporters," Jack warned.

"You just let me take care of that," Mr. Farnsworth said. "I have connections with a very exclusive restaurant. I'll go call for a private room. What time shall we say?"

"I'd like to go check back into the hotel and wash the smell of the jail off," Kedra said.

"All right—shall I make the reservation for one o'clock? We can all meet in front of the Cotillion Room, on Colorado Boulevard, then. How many should I make the reservation for?"

Kedra turned to Jack, "You will come, won't you?"

"I'm sorry—I can't. Isaac *is* in Denver. I almost had him last night, but he left the Golden Garter before my posse got there. He will probably run as soon as the news of your acquittal is out. I've got to stop him. I have to go check in with the deputies staking out the train station and the roadblocks on main roads out of Denver. I'm going to be working all night."

"Will you come to see me tomorrow?"

Jack's green eyes went as soft as a summer meadow. "Absolutely."

Kedra was already euphoric with victory, but Jack's eyes made her feel like she was floating.

"Are you ready to face the reporters?" Jack asked. "They're going to swarm you as soon as you step out of the courthouse."

"Let them. I feel like crowing." Kedra grinned at her friends. "Are you all brave enough to come with me?"

"Give me just a minute to arrange our luncheon reservation, and I'll lead the charge," Mr. Farnsworth said.

Kedra stood next to Mr. Farnsworth and as the reporters bombarded them with questions. She gave the photographers her best smiles. At one point, she noticed the foreman of the jury come out of the courthouse. A reporter immediately intercepted him. Kedra tuned out the questions being directed at her to listen to what the foreman had to say.

"Tell me, Mr. Foreman, what was the jury's verdict?"

The foreman made eye contact with Kedra, before answering the reporter. "Let's just say the jury is very grateful Miss Parlee and Mrs. Scott testified *before* our verdict was read."

"Then she would have been found guilty. What tipped the balance for the jury?"

"We couldn't get around the emerald in her room and couldn't buy the story about the raccoon taking them from a secret hiding place in the floor of a locked room.

Kedra felt the shiver run from her head to her toes.

Zed's arm came around her. "Are you all right?"

"Yes, by the providence of heaven, I am."

51

Isaac opened the door to his hotel room and let room service bring in his lunch, welcoming the interruption. He'd been working all morning to perfect Professor Thaddeus Drake's character.

"I brought you the extra edition of the newspaper. It just came out, Professor," the maid said, uncovering the roast beef sandwich and fruit plate he'd order. "Can I get you anything else?"

"No thank you," Isaac croaked, as though he had a cold. "This will be fine, thank you." He tipped the Chinese girl and shut the door behind her.

There could only be one reason for an extra edition of the Rocky Mountain news today. *The verdict must be in!*

He snatched up the newspaper, and let out a stream of profanity. "No!" He dropped onto the sofa, his lunch forgotten as he read the news. *I should have taken my time killing Drew. Now the dragnet for me will go nationwide. I've got to get out of here, now! That bulldog of a marshal will have every way out of this town staked out in no time.*

Throwing the paper to the floor, he jumped to his feet and went to get his suitcases.

Over lunch, Kedra quizzed Donna. "How did you find out I was on trial? Don't tell me the news reached all the way to Toronto."

Donna reached over and squeezed her hand. "It didn't. In fact I was in Chicago before I read about it in the newspaper. I put in a call to Tate, but couldn't reach him at home, so I called his office. They told me he was in Denver, testifying at your trial. I got the number to his hotel, but couldn't get a hold of him until last night—when my train stopped in Kansas City. Even then I wasn't able to reach him until just before my train left Kansas City. There was barely enough time to tell him when my train was due to arrive in Denver."

"I was elated when she told me she'd seen you the day of the robbery—*after* the train left," Tate said, his arm wrapped possessively around Donna's shoulder. He frowned comically at Kedra. "I should be upset with you. You ruined my proposal."

"What? Are you two finally going to get married?"

Tate beamed and Donna glowed. "Yes," they said in unison.

"Well then, we must make a toast to these two heroes," Mr. Farnsworth said, raising his glass, as Kedra hugged her friends.

After the toast, Kedra turned to Dolores Scott. "Would you mind answering a few questions for me?"

"Ask away."

"I think we would all like to know how Isaac got into the express car in Glenwood without being seen."

Dolores set aside her fork. "It was amazingly simple. Drew said there was a general resemblance between Isaac and Harry. They both had black hair, were nearly the same height, and equally as slender—that's what made it easy. After Marshal Forbes and the deputies who were to exercise Haru Ito left, and the mail carriers finished their job, Harry left the car too, leaving the door unlocked. A minute later, Isaac, dressed exactly like Harry, entered the car from the riverbank side of the tracks. If people saw him, I'm sure they simply thought it was Harry. As soon as Isaac was in the express car, he shed Harry's look- a-like clothes, putting them in Harry's suitcase. Underneath them, he was wearing buckskin clothes. When Harry came back into the car a few minutes later, Isaac was hiding under the bed."

"Ingenious," Mr. Farnsworth murmured.

"Yes. If anyone saw either one of them, or both of them, they would have just thought Harry had gone out twice," Kedra said.

"Did Isaac use the boat to escape the scene as Jack surmised?" Tate asked.

"Yes. He took it the night before. Loaded it on a wagon and took it up river."

"How did he mange that?" Donna asked.

'The boat is only a small canoe. He could have easily loaded it into a wagon, which I'll bet he got from Voorhees' stable," Tate said.

Kedra stared thoughtfully into her water glass. "But how did he set me up to take the fall for this crime so fast? As Mr. Scrogin pointed out, even Harry didn't know about the emeralds until the day before they left San Francisco."

"According to Drew, even though Harry only had a day's notice, his wire to Isaac gave Isaac three days to prepare before the train arrived. When Isaac got in touch with Drew about taking part in the robbery, he told Drew he'd been planning this heist, as he called it, for six years. He assured Drew he had everything planned out and had even arranged for a fall guy to take the blame, if things went wrong. I think that was what made Drew especially nervous. He thought the fall guy would turn out to be him," Dolores said.

Kedra gazed down at her plate, her appetite waning. "Isaac came much too close to hanging me as his scapegoat. If he escapes Jack with the emeralds, he'll have won what he wanted most—wealth.

And you can bet he'll do something like this again when he needs more money."

"Jack is getting very close now," Zed said. "We nearly caught Isaac last night, I'm sure of that. I'm also sure Jack will find him, even if he has to hunt him down outside this country."

"I hope it won't come to that. You know he wants to quit being a marshal, but he won't turn in his badge until he catches Isaac." Kedra's eyes swept over the company. "He gave President Roosevelt his word, and I know he'll keep going until Isaac is caught."

"I hope he does, he killed my brother too, and I want justice for him." Dolores sniffed. "I don't suppose we'll ever know what happened in that Grand Junction hotel room."

"I'm sorry to admit it, but I'm afraid we won't," Tate said. "We couldn't even find anyone who saw Isaac get on the train for Grand Junction that day—as a man or a woman."

"I think that's what worries me the most," Kedra said pushing her beans around on her plate. "He seems to be able to transform himself into anyone. I know him so well; the way he moves—his mannerisms. But I wonder if I could pick him out of a crowd, if he was in disguise, in character."

A waiter came to the table. "Miss Moore, I have a note for you."

Kedra read the note aloud. "Mr. Scrogin is satisfied. You are free to leave Denver whenever you choose."

Everyone cheered.

The night was one of complete frustration for Jack. Three hours before dawn, he turned the train station watch over to Luke and a new crew of deputies. He headed for his hotel, completely exhausted and discouraged, but not defeated.

Isaac Moore's picture and description, in his known male and female forms, had gone out over the national wire service and by tomorrow it would go international.

Jack threw himself down on his bed, without undressing, and closed his eyes. He was asleep in minutes.

52

Saturday, July 4, 1908

Kedra was in the midst of a wonderful dream, when she was suddenly awakened. A hand covered her mouth. The muzzle of a gun pressed against her temple. Her eyes flew open and she stared into Isaac's cold blue eyes.

"Don't make a sound, if you want to live any longer," he hissed. He sat on the edge of her bed and removed his hand from her mouth, but kept the muzzle of the gun pressed against her temple. He tisked out a sigh, "All my hard work, all my careful planning, and you still managed to wiggle off my carefully baited hook." He shoved the gun tighter to her head. "But I won't be denied my revenge."

Kedra pressed her lips together, trying to think of something she could do and not get killed.

Nothing came to mind.

She gripped her covers to keep her hands from shaking. "Why do you hate me so much, Isaac? What have I ever done to you?"

"You stole my father from me. I knew as soon as Eli brought me to the ranch that he would always love you more than me. At first I tried so hard to make him proud, but I could never outshine *you*. Then, when I found out you weren't even his daughter—"

"You know about that? How did you find out?"

"Do you remember that drunk he went on when you turned twenty-one? I poured him into bed that night. He was in a very melancholy mood—talkative too. He spilled his guts to me about you. He was afraid you would get married soon and leave him." Isaac laughed. "He told me everything I needed to know to make him give me what should have been mine—not yours. That's why I blackmailed him. I knew it was the only way I'd get my share out of him, because he was about ready to throw me out and give everything to you. Oh, and don't tell me you didn't guess I was blackmailing him?"

"I knew, but Eli never told me what you were holding over him. I didn't know, until my uncle Zedekiah told me, who my real father was."

"Well, *princess,* I hope you enjoyed your moment of triumph and your brief family reunion." Isaac cocked the gun. "Get up!"

Kedra pushed back the covers and stood.

"Turn around and put your hands behind your back."

Kedra started to turn and quickly swept her arm toward the gun. Isaac grabbed it and wrenched it behind her back, knocking her in the head with butt of his gun. She cried out and dropped to her knees.

"Shut up," Isaac growled hauling her to her feet. "Don't try that again or I'll kill you right here."

"Where are you taking me?"

"You'll see," he said, chuckling.

"At least let me get dressed."

"That won't be necessary," he said tying her hands tightly behind her back. "You aren't going far, besides I think your nightgown is quite pretty."

He pushed her toward the door.

"Can I put on some slippers?"

"No, and keep quiet if you don't want your brains splattered all over the hallway."

Kedra clamped her lips together, trying to keep her teeth from chattering with fright. The night was warm, but the clutch of fear was cold. As they went out into the hall, she shivered beneath the fabric of her thin nightgown.

Isaac laughed softly into her ear, his gun pressed to her back. "Don't fret, princess, you won't feel cold for long."

He pulled her down the hall to the stairs leading up to the roof.

The night was fading and the stars were nearly gone when they stepped out onto the roof.

"Dawn is such a romantic time to die," Isaac said theatrically, dragging her across the roof.

She struggled desperately to free her hands from the ropes, pulling backward, resisting him. But she was no match for the power of his lean muscles. He dragged her to the edge of the roof, next to the hotel's lighted sign, on the cut off corner of the building.

"No, Isaac, please," she gasped as she saw the noose secured to the steel fitting of the lighted sign.

"Yes, *dear sister,* this is going to be your end. What a delightful end too. Just think of poor Marshal Garrison when he finds you in the morning hanging from this sign. Think of your uncle and friends, because that's what I'll be doing. In fact, I intend to stay around for the show." His eyes shot sparks of hate at her. "Your precious marshal is no match for me. Do you know that I checked into this hotel yesterday, hoping to see the sad expressions on the faces of your loved ones when your guilty verdict was announced?" He smiled demonically. "Who would ever think to look for me here? It put me in the perfect position to take my revenge, once I knew you were free."

He ran a finger down her cheek. She tried to pull away from him, but he held on to her with a steel grip, his gun still pressed to her back.

"I almost left when I heard the news, but then, I hate to give up, especially when victory is so *close* at hand. Besides, I know every lawman in the country is looking for me. Waiting a few days will give me a better chance of eluding them."

He jerked the noose over her head and tightened it around her neck. The gun pressed into her back, urged her to the edge of the building. Isaac stopped her when her toes were over the edge.

She locked her knees and gripped the edge of the building with her toes as he pressed her body out over the edge of the building. He kept her from falling by holding the rope around her neck, taut.

The pressure of the rope against her windpipe cut off her breathing. Her vision blurred. She twisted her head and neck, letting the rope cut into her throat, hoping to relieve the pressure on her windpipe, took in a gasp of air and did the only thing she could.

It amazed her how sincere a few simple words could be, when offered up to heaven amidst the most dire despair. She asked nothing for herself, only that those who loved her would find comfort, particularly Zed.

Isaac reeled her in unexpectedly.

She didn't waste her reprieve on words. She used the moments he offered her to breathe.

"We must wait until the sun breaks the horizon."

The glow on the eastern horizon promised a beautiful day. Kedra looked away from the growing light and continued to pray.

Jack jerked upright up in bed, awakened by a voice of thunder, the words reverberating in his head. "Isaac's hatred will only be satisfied when he's killed you, or watched the state do it."

Kedra!

He pulled on his boots, grabbed his coat, checked for his guns, and raced to the stable behind his hotel. With only a bridle over Soldier's nose, he burst out of the stable and rode the big stallion hard until they reached the southwest corner of 18th and Welton Street.

Movement on the roof of the Adams Hotel caught his eye. He brought Soldier to a skidding halt.

His hand shook as he drew his gun.

With the backdrop of the growing dawn, he saw the rope around Kedra's neck, tied to the heavy steel sign of the Adams Hotel. The man standing behind Kedra was her height and Jack only got glimpses of him. He looked to be elderly, white haired and frail, but Jack knew him for who he was—another of Isaac's characters.

Confronting Isaac would only make him push Kedra from the roof. He couldn't shoot Isaac because Kedra was standing directly in front of him. Jack swallowed his fear and tried to look at the situation with the cold calculating eyes of a veteran U.S. Marshal.

"Still," he whispered into Soldier's ear and the stallion became a statue.

The light grew in the east.

Isaac spun Kedra around until she was facing him. His hand grasped the back of her head. His gun hand ran around her waist until his arm encircled her. He pulled her to him and kissed her ruthlessly on the mouth.

Shock and revulsion held Jack motionless for a moment before he shook it off and brought up his gun.

Kedra fought Isaac, jerking back, hard.

Isaac let her go.

She careened backward and plunged over the edge of the building.

53

Jack fired twice in rapid succession. The shots were accompanied by the most fervent prayer his soul had ever uttered.

Isaac staggered backwards as Kedra fell.

Time seemed to stop.

Sweat trickled down Jack's back. His heart felt as though it would burst out of his chest.

The seconds drew out unbearably.

Had he made the shot, or would Kedra jerk to a sudden stop?

The breath *whooshed* out of him as she fell past the fourth floor windows.

Digging his knees into Soldier's sides he barked, "Move."

Soldier bolted across the street. Jack pulled him up next to the large awning covering the front of the hotel's first floor drugstore.

Kedra hit the big awning, hard.

Jack winced as she bounced, came down hard again, and rolled the rest of the way down the awning, right into his waiting arms.

He had her, and for a moment all he could do was hold her next to his heart. His anxious fingers found a pulse in her neck. He drew her face to his, feeling her breath on his cheek.

Her eyes were closed and she lay limp as a ragdoll in his arms. Gently he unwound the rope, which had wrapped itself around her neck as she rolled down the awning, loosened the noose and drew it over her head.

"Walk," he said to Soldier, guiding the stallion with his knees. When they reached the front door of the hotel, Jack said, "Stand."

Soldier stopped and Jack drew his leg over Soldier's head and slid off his back.

The night clerk's eyes bugged out as Jack strode across the lobby with Kedra in his arms. "Get a doctor—now!" Jack barked at the stupefied clerk, and then demanded, "What room is Miss Moore in?"

"Miss-Miss Moore?" The clerk consulted the guest registry. "We don't have—"

"Miss Long-Sight," Jack amended.

"Room 316."

"Send the doctor up as soon as he gets here."

The clerk gaped at Kedra and blinked.

"Move!" Jack roared and ran for the elevator.

Jack laid Kedra down on the bed in her room, took the knife from his boot sheath, rolled her gently to her side and cut the ropes that bound her hands. Like her throat, they were badly rope burned and bleeding. She'd obviously tried to wiggle her hands free of the ropes.

He rolled her onto her back, went to the washstand and poured water from the pitcher into a matching bowl. The water was tepid but would feel cold against her skin. Taking several washcloths from the drawer of the washstand, Jack plunged them into the water and wrung them out. The first one went on Kedra's forehead. Two more were laid against the rope burns on her neck. With the last two, he wrapped her wrists.

She moaned and moved her head.

He sat down on the edge of the bed.

With a startled cry she came to. Her hands flew up, as though to defend herself.

Jack caught them in his big hand, running his other gently down the side of her face. "You're safe. It's all over. The doctor is on his way. Everything is going to be all right."

She stopped struggling and went limp, but the terror in her gold eyes stared up at him. "Isaac tried to—he wanted to—he meant to—" she croaked out.

Jack laid her hands down on the bed. "I know, but he didn't succeed."

"What happened? Where is he?"

Her raspy voice told Jack her windpipe had been bruised and her throat must be sore.

"I'm not sure. I'll go get Zed for you, and then I'll look for Isaac."

"No!" Her arms flew around his neck. "Don't leave me here by myself. Isaac might come back to kill me."

Jack cradled her in his arms, feeling tremor after tremor of fear course through her. He tightened his arms around her. "I won't go anywhere until the doctor gets here."

She rasped, "Tell me what happened? All I remember is—falling." A convulsive shudder rocked her. "I was sure the rope would stop me, break my neck—kill me. Why didn't it?"

"Well, I believe it was because a miracle answered the most fervent prayer I've ever said." Jack grinned at her. "It consisted of just two words."

"What words?"

"Help me. When I looked up and saw what Isaac was going to do. It was still too dark to see anything more than the shadow of the rope attached to the building's sign. Then, just as he kissed you and let you go over the edge, when you shoved away from him, a sunbeam burst around the building. For an instant, as the rope played out, I saw it clearly and fired at it." He gave her a wondering look. "I'm a darn good shot, darlin', but I'm not that good. I believe heaven interceded at that point. But I didn't know it until you kept falling."

"But then, why am I still alive?"

"You can thank that big industrial strength awning over the drug store. I knew it was your only chance."

She searched his face, a frown between her brows. "How did you know to come?"

He told her about the voice of thunder.

"So much for the still small voice."

"There are times I sleep like the dead, and it takes more than a whisper to wake me up."

She dropped her arms from around his neck and he laid her back on the bed.

"Zed told me what you were planning to do if I was convicted."

"My job is to bring criminals to justice, not hang innocent young women."

"Even if it means breaking the law yourself?"

"Defending the innocent would never be breaking the law, even if it was seen that way by some."

"A very diplomatic answer."

A knock sounded on the door. Jack called for the doctor to come in, his hand in his pocket, gripping his gun, in case it wasn't the doctor.

A sleepy, elderly man with a large black bag came into the room. Jack sized him up. He was too short and stout to be Isaac.

"You'll be in good hands now, and don't worry, it will only take a moment to go get Zed," Jack said, squeezing her hand.

She held onto his for a moment. "I haven't thanked you for saving my life. You will come back so I can, won't you?"

"I will—when I can." Jack walked over to the door. "Right now, I'm still a U.S. Marshal with a bad guy to round up, and I don't know how long that will take."

"Soon, I hope," she croaked out as he closed the door behind him.

Jack woke Zed, and briefly told him about Isaac's attack on Kedra. He told Zed he should probably wake Sarah and let her know what had happened too, in case Kedra needed the sympathy of another woman.

Zed was pulling his shirt over his head as Jack opened the door.

"Where are you going?" Zed asked.

"To see if Isaac is still on the roof. He fell backwards when I fired. I'm sure one of my shots hit him, although he wasn't my target."

"Do you want me to come with you?"

"No, Kedra needs you more than I do."

Jack cautiously opened the door to the stairs at the end of the hall. The light in the stairwell was dim. He looked at the steps leading up to the roof and saw several small drops of blood. There was blood on the steps going down too. Jack followed the blood down to the second floor hallway. Here there were smears of blood along the wall. They stopped on the door of room 205.

Letting his boot and his gun lead the way, Jack crashed through the door, and took the room in at a glance.

An elderly man was sprawled on the bed. His hair was white, as were his bushy eyebrows and full beard.

Jack approached the bed, his gun fixed on the elderly man.

"A doctor, I need a doctor," the man whined, pitifully.

"Amazing," Jack muttered, staring down into the ice blue eyes of Isaac Moore.

The disguise was remarkable, but equally so was the fact that both Jack's shots had hit Isaac. One bullet had hit him just under the right collarbone. The other had penetrated just below his ribs on the right side.

With the utmost care, Jack searched and removed two guns from Isaac's body. Then he pulled the wig from his head and the fake beard from his face, leaving only the, now comical looking, eyebrows.

"Get me a doctor," Isaac demanded with aristocratic disdain.

"There is a doctor attending Kedra right now. If you answer my questions, I'll send for him."

"After you get the doctor," Isaac insisted.

Jack shrugged. "I've got time. Do you?"

He'd seen too many fatal gunshot wounds not to know Isaac's time was limited and there was little a doctor to could besides ease his pain.

"All right," Isaac groaned. "What do you want to know?"

"Where are the emeralds?"

Isaac pressed his lips together.

Jack waited, staring coldly down at him.

A shudder of pain loosened his tongue. "False bottom . . . satchel."

Jack dumped the contents of the satchel on the floor, and pried up the false bottom. Inside, he found a sack of unknown jewelry, which he assumed must be Bessie Louder's. He put the sack in his jacket pocket and pulled out the Mi'kmaq leather bag, which Kedra had described to him. He opened the neck of the bag. Half a million dollars in emeralds glimmered up at him. They, too, went into his pocket. Next, he extracted a black velvet box with Mrs. Capshaw's pearls and pocketed them as well. At the bottom of the satchel, he found Kedra's braid. He rearranged his bulging pockets, before sliding the braid in too.

"The doctor . . . call the doctor." Isaac's voice had gone from demanding to pleading.

Jack called the desk and requested they call room 316, and send the doctor down to room 205, as soon as possible.

"While we wait for the doctor, I want to know why you killed everyone in the express car. That wasn't part of Kedra's plan.

"I've said . . . all I'm going to . . . say," Isaac moaned.

Jack reached for the telephone. "I guess I'll just call the desk and cancel my request for a doctor."

"No!" Isaac coughed and licked his dry lips.

Jack filled a glass with water, lifted Isaac's head, and put the glass to his lips. Isaac drank thirstily. When he finished drinking, Jack laid him back on the bed, covered his wounds with towels from the washstand, and stood back.

"Why?"

Isaac moaned, pressing his hands against his wounds. "Because Harry . . . betrayed me. I have only loved three people in my life, my O'Shea Grandparents—and Harry."

"How did Harry betray you?"

"He fell in love with that . . . that filthy Indian. He was supposed to make *her* fall for *him*, string her along—set her up as our scapegoat, for whenever we got wind of—a big score. The day he learned about the emeralds, he told . . . me he would help me steal them and escape the country—to . . . to start a new life, but he didn't want any part of the spoils. He was going to give up his heiress fiancée to marry . . . Kedra and live in some backwater town as a rancher. I didn't know how Kedra felt about him, but I wasn't about to let her win. No one—especially Kedra, was going to take . . . Harry from me. That's when I decided to kill him.

"What happened in that express car?"

"When I came out from under the bed . . . Harry was opening the safe. The old marshal was asleep on the bed, as we'd planned—except he wasn't. He must not have . . . drunk enough coffee. Just as Harry reached into the safe . . . the old man sat up and shouted. I turned and . . . fired. He fell back—I thought he was dead." Isaac gasped out. "Then, quick as a flash I turned back to Harry . . . and shot him." Isaac coughed and groaned out a laugh. "He was so surprised."

The gleam in Isaac's eyes told Jack how much Isaac had enjoyed killing his cousin, exacting his revenge for Harry's betrayal. It sent a shiver through Jack.

"I was reaching in the safe when . . . the old marshal leaped at me . . . and tore off my mask. We . . . scuffled." Isaac swallowed and licked his lips. "I—I managed to turn my gun into his chest . . . and fire."

Isaac's eyes lit with triumph. Jack's grip on his gun tightened. He forced himself to lower his weapon and step back.

"I don't remember the marshal pulling Kedra's pendant from my neck. I had planned to—to plant it in Harry's hand. But I'd been there too long . . . too long." Isaac's head thrashed back and forth. "Too many shots . . . fired. Knew . . . Drew would—would stop the train. Only time to . . . grab things from the safe . . . shoot the prisoner—get out."

The increased stumbling of Isaac's reply told Jack he had little time left and there was still a couple of questions Jack wanted answered.

Quickly, he asked, "Why did you kill Drew Ellis?"

'He—he was . . . getting . . . scared—couldn't risk . . . him making a deal . . . with the cops to . . . to turn . . . me in."

"How did Swindler get some of the emeralds?"

"Open window . . . dropped some . . . when Effie banged on my door they rolled . . . under . . . the bed." Isaac groaned and closed his eyes.

A knock on the door sent Jack to it. He let the doctor in, stood back as the doctor examined Isaac's wounds, and took a bottle from inside his medical bag. The doctor injected Isaac with a heavy dose of morphine, waited for it to take effect and then turned to Jack.

"It's the kindest thing I can do for him. The collar bone wound could have been treated, but the other one—" He shook his head. "I'll stay with him until he passes. It shouldn't be long."

There's no need, Doc. He was a wanted fugitive and I'm the U.S. Marshal who shot him." Jack showed his badge. "I'll stay—"

Isaac let out a long sigh and didn't take another breath.

"Is there anyone who will want to bury him, Marshal?"

"I'll see to that. Could you have him taken to the city morgue?"

The doctor nodded as he drew a sheet over Isaac's body. "What was his name?"

"Isaac Moore."

"Not *the*—"

"Yes. But I'm sure it's not the name he's registered under here. I'd appreciate it, and I'm sure the hotel would too, if we took care of removing him as quietly as possible, under whatever name he was using. It might also be better if the hotel isn't told how he died."

"Yes, that kind of publicity is never welcome. Leave it to me, Marshal. I'll call your office when Mr. Moore is in the morgue."

54

The courthouse was closed when Jack arrived, but not the jail or the marshal's office, although, at the moment, they were only minimally staffed. Most of the police would roll in just before dark, when the Fourth of July celebrations got under way, and the citizens started getting rowdy.

Darrius Jones was the only one in the U.S. Marshal's office when Jack ducked through the door.

"How long have you been here?" Jack asked the deputy.

"Just got in— I'm supposed to relieve Luke at the train station stakeout at nine."

"There won't be any need for that now. Isaac Moore is dead."

"What? How?"

Jack briefed him, displaying the emeralds and Mrs. Capshaw's pearls. "Call Luke and tell him the news. I'll send it out over the wire. After that, I'd appreciate it if you'd take Mrs. Capshaw's pearls back to her. I'd do it myself, but I'm going to be up to my neck in paperwork for the next couple of hours."

"Be my pleasure." Darrius grinned and put on his hat. "This Fourth of July is shaping up to be a humdinger."

"It will be even better as soon as Luke returns Señor Ortiz's emeralds," Jack said, following Darrius out of the office.

The district court's secure telegraph was located at the end of the hall. The clerk immediately perked up when Jack entered. It was obvious he needed something to do to pass the time on this holiday.

Jack briskly dictated four telegraphs to him. "I'm hoping for a response to that last one," he said.

"I'll bring it down to your office, Marshal."

"Thanks."

Jack spent the next hour laboring through his report on the death of Isaac Moore and the recovery of the stolen emeralds. He was interrupted by Marshal Laramore's arrival and forced to retell everything that had happened.

He finished briefing Luke by showing him the sack of unknown jewelry. "Be sure you make Bessie Louder submit a list of her stolen jewelry before you return anything in this sack to her."

"I'll be sure she only gets the jewelry she can describe to me."

Anxious to be done, Jack handed Luke the bag of emeralds. "Why don't you make Señor Ortiz a happy man? Tell him if he finds there are still a few missing, that I'll have Effie search Isaac's room. But warn him that there's no guarantee they'll ever be found. Swindler may have taken some of them out of the house before Kedra caught him."

"At this point, I don't think Señor Ortiz will complain. Just getting the bulk of the emeralds back should be enough to sooth his high strung nerves," Luke said and left with the bag of emeralds.

Jack had just finished his report when the telegraph clerk poked his head into the office.

"I got replies to three of your telegrams," the clerk said.

"Just set them on the desk," Jack said, stuffing his report into an envelope, addressed to the Justice Department.

After the clerk left, Jack set aside the telegram from the Justice Department, and read the one from President Roosevelt.

Well done, Jack!

Will Forbes has been avenged and the honor of the U.S. Marshal's office upheld. I knew you were the right man for this job. Now it is my pleasure, although with regret, to accept your immediate resignation. I have so informed the Department of Justice. Good luck to you, Jack. Let me know where you settle and if you ever find that rarest of females—one who doesn't want to go to Paris!

Teddy Roosevelt

Jack smiled and put the telegram into the pocket of his shirt. He opened the telegram from the Department of Justice. It was a formal acceptance of his resignation.

Happy Birthday, he congratulated himself, tucking the third telegram into his pocket, unopened.

It was nearly noon when he left the courthouse. He saw at a glance that Soldier was in a foul mood.

"Don't look at me like that. You know I had to finish this job. Now we can go back to the hotel. I'll brush you down, give you a double ration of oats, and leave you alone for the rest of the day—all right?"

Soldier snorted and tossed his head.

Jack knew as soon as it dawned on the big stallion that they were headed for the hotel, because he had to keep reining him in. It took forty minutes to groom and feed Soldier. Another thirty ticked by before Jack was bathed, shaved, and dressed in clean clothes. He left his hotel and hopped on a streetcar to the sound of children setting off firecrackers in the street.

Ten minutes later, he knocked on Kedra's door. Sarah answered and Jack looked over her shoulder at Kedra, sleeping peacefully. His disappointment must have been obvious to Sarah.

"I know she wants to talk with you, Jack. She's been somewhat anxious about it, but she needs to sleep too. She is bruised from head to toe by that fall and her throat is very sore. Why don't you check back in a little while?"

"Jack?" Kedra's voice rasped from the bed.

Jack gave Sarah a consulting look.

She stepped aside. "Come and get me when you leave."

Kedra held out her hand to him and asked him to sit on the edge of the bed. He took her hand and searched her face. There was a bruise on her cheek. She was much too pale and there were dark smudges under her beautiful eyes.

"Are you going to be all right?" he asked.

"Right now," she croaked out, "I'm not so sure. Every muscle in my body hurts, and I have bruises in more places than I can count."

"Forgive me, but I couldn't think of any other way to rescue you."

She took his hand, brought to her lips, and kissed it.

He sucked in a startled breath and managed to cover it by clearing his throat. The contact of her lips on his skin nearly unleashed the feelings he wasn't ready to confess—hadn't found the words for yet.

"I'm not criticizing you, Jack," she whispered hoarsely. "Your quick thinking saved my life. Bruises are a small price to pay for that. Her hypnotic eyes turned molten. "Saying it is so inadequate, but I mean it with all my heart—thank you." She brushed away the tear that rolled down her face and said, "Now, tell me about Isaac."

He told her everything, feeling her reactions in the grip of her hand. When he finished, her grip relaxed.

"I've brought you a few things."

"What things?"

From the inside pocket of his jacket he pulled out her pendant.

Her eyes misted over. "Would you put it in the box on the dresser, please? That's where Nahtow's chain and the earrings are. I can't wait to show it to Zed. He can reattach the pendant to the chain."

After the pendant joined the earrings, Jack took her totem from his pocket and clipped it to the end of her braid.

She smiled radiantly. "Now I feel like myself again."

"Well, at least you're beginning to, but I have one more thing I hope will help you feel better."

He pulled the unopened telegram from his pocket and handed it to her.

She took in a sharp breath. "From my grandmother Barlow?"

"I had a friend track her down, and as soon as I knew the outcome of your trial—I contacted her. I hope I haven't upset you by doing that."

"No—not at all." She handed the telegram back to him. "I'm too shaky. Read it to me, please."

"Dearest Kedra,

For so many years I have longed to know what became of my daughter Caroline and her child. The last letter I received was in May, twenty-two years ago. Carrie said she and Seth were taking the Nahtow to Utah to join with those of their religion. She was so excited about the coming birth of her child. I waited and waited for news. It never came. I sent men to search for her, but no trace of her, or the Nahtow, was ever found. Long have I mourned over her. But now I will rejoice.

Come to me Kedra. Your Uncle Zedekiah is also welcome to come. My arms long to hold you, my eyes to look upon you. There are tickets waiting for you at the train station in Denver.

Marshal Garrison told me what a terrible ordeal the trial was for you—and yes I know all about it. He said you need time to rest and heal. I agree. Come to me, Kedra, and together we will find healing for my old wounds and your new ones.

With love,
Grandma"

Kedra was wiping her eyes with the sheet when Jack finished reading.

"Zed agrees you need time away from all the ugliness you've been through. Go meet your grandmother and stay with her for a while."

"Does Zed know about my grandmother's invitation?"

"Not yet, but he told me yesterday that he wanted to take you away somewhere to rest. I'm sure he'll be in favor of going to your grandmother's."

Jack folded the telegram and handed it to her. "Her address is at the bottom.

She held the telegram to her heart and squeezed his hand. "Thank you for finding her and writing to her." Her hypnotic eyes pulled him in with a concerned expression. "Where will you go now that this case is over? Is it on to a new case?"

"No. As of a couple of hours ago, I am no longer a U.S. Marshal. This case was to be my last, and I only took it because Will Forbes was a dear friend of mine."

"So what will you do? Where will you go?"

"I intend to do just exactly what I told you I was doing when I showed up on the High Peak Ranch. I want to buy a ranch. I want to live like ordinary folks. I'm tired of chasing criminals."

Her eyes welled up. "Will I ever see you again?"

Those gold hypnotic eyes, fringed by thick black lashes tore at his heart, but he couldn't tell her what he felt. She'd been through too much. Her life had been torn apart. Everything she thought she knew about herself had largely been a lie. He couldn't complicate her life with another life altering decision or add any more emotional stress.

It didn't feel right.

Still, he couldn't keep himself from brushing her lips with a soft, lingering kiss.

The feel of her fingers moving along his neck made him jump up and stride to the door.

"Jack?!"

He looked back at her as he opened the door. "I'll come for you, darlin'—when it's right," he said and shut the door firmly behind himself.

55

Philadelphia—New Year's Eve, 1908

It was beginning to snow. Kedra felt the wisps of cold air seep in through the lead glass panes of the floor-to-ceiling window at her back. It felt delicious. Her longing to escape the stuffy, overcrowded ballroom, intensified. But she couldn't escape. This ball was in her honor. It was her grandmother's way of telling her how much she loved her and showing all the Philadelphia matrons how proud she was to be the grandmother of an Indian princess.

Kedra spotted her grandmother sitting across the room with her cronies, deep in conversation. Her mother's letter had been her introduction to her grandmother. As her grandmother read it to her it became an instant bond between them.

Kedra smiled. Her grandmother, Martha Barlow, was a force to be reckoned with, and Kedra adored her. She had learned so much about her mother and herself from her grandmother. Her grandmother continually commented on how much like her mother she was, in mannerisms and spirit. It was Kedra's only regret about leaving tomorrow morning.

She and Zed were taking the train west. They both missed the majesty of the mountains and the sparsely populated places the west held. Zed hadn't said where they were going, but it didn't really matter. She just wanted to put on her buckskins and ride through the wilds of the mountains. Zed said that was her Indian blood. He knew because he was feeling the same way.

A barrage of voices brought her back to the cluster of eager young men around her, and their effusive compliments. She dismissed their compliments, but she couldn't dismiss their demands to know who had the next dance. *I wish it was Zed, but he's undoubtedly enthroned in the library with his friends, and my Barlow uncles, discussing everything from mathematics to animal husbandry. I wish that's where I was.*

Zed hadn't spent much time with her in the last month. His invitations to visit classmates from Harvard kept him traveling around New England.

Her grandmother had seen how much she missed Zed. She'd invited Zed's friends to the New Year's Eve ball, effectively keeping Zed in residence in the large manor house owned by Kedra's Uncle Benjamin, where her grandmother now lived.

The demands to know who her next dance partner would be, increased. She reluctantly consulted her dance card, and raised her eyes to her fawning crowd of admirers to announce the winner.

His name died on her lips.

Jack Garrison walked into the ballroom. He was as tall as the Rocky Mountains and just as rugged. Debonair in a black tuxedo, which put every other man in the room to shame, he strode across the room.

She couldn't take her eyes off him, but noticed the wave of women's heads that followed his progress through the room. His eyes never left her as he crossed the dance floor.

"Miss Kedra, the orchestra is about to start. Who is your next dance partner?" a man at her side asked.

Jack's long arm reached over the men around her as though they didn't exist and took her hand. "I am," he said and whirled her onto the dance floor.

Kedra stared up at Jack, unable to find her voice in the midst of the storm of emotions that swirled around her. She hadn't heard from Jack in six months—not one word. Exasperation finally won out. She may not have heard from him, but he hadn't been out of her mind for a single day. That kiss, that stupid kiss, plagued her waking hours and haunted her dreams.

He danced her once around the room in silence, and then said, "You are a nonpareil. There isn't a woman here that is your equal in beauty or spirit."

Her dress was indeed exquisite, a Christmas gift from her grandmother—straight from Paris. It was ivory silk overlaid with gold lace and beaded all over with amber. It was the loveliest dress she'd ever owned.

"Thank you."

Her clipped response widened his eyes.

"You don't seem particularly pleased to see me," he said.

"Should I be? Not one word from you in six months and suddenly, with no warning, you crash my ball and steal me away from my dance partners."

"I'll have you know, I'm here by invitation."

"Who invited you?"

"Your grandmother—Zed asked her to send me an invitation."

"You have been in contact with Zed?"

"I've been helping him write the Nahtow account of the massacre. As one who saw things he didn't, he's needed my help."

She pressed her lips together, hurt that he and Zed had been in contact without her knowing anything about it.

"I can tell I'm in trouble, and we need a private place to talk," Jack said, dancing her through the doorway before she could protest.

He danced her down the hall and into a small salon.

She escaped his arms as he closed the door and searched for the light switch. She whirled around to face him when the light came on; illuminating her grandmother's personal sitting room.

"It's obvious you're very upset with me. I won't deny you have reason. If it will make you feel better, you can scalp me—I've never liked this hair anyway."

His hair was longer than it had been when she'd last seen him, long enough to curl on the ends. She was torn between the desire to pull his curls out and run her fingers through them.

"Why haven't I heard from you in six months?"

"You needed time to heal—think about what you wanted to do with your life. Besides, I didn't have anything to offer you then."

"And you do now?"

He pulled her over to a yellow striped, satin settee and sat, tugging on her hand, until she reluctantly sat down. It was a little settee and forced her to sit right next to him, but she kept her posture rigid.

His arm ran along the back of the settee until it was around her shoulder. His other hand claimed hers. Before she could protest, he said, "In all the remembering I did for Zed, during the time our families traveled together, I remembered something that belongs just to you."

She frowned and stared at the silver studs in his shirt. "What?"

"The night before the massacre, your parents were sitting by themselves, near a small fire, talking. In my four-year-old way, I intruded and sat down next to your mother. She looked at my thumb, which still hurt from my blood brother ritual with Daeden. Your father said he was glad I was now a blood brother to his nephew. He told me my friendship would help Daeden and the other Nahtow children fit into the new life they would find in Utah. Your mother agreed and then jumped as though something had struck her."

Kedra's eyes came up. What was he saying? It sounded familiar.

"She told your father you were awake, took his hand, and put it on her belly. Your father smiled and proclaimed that the baby would be a fine brave, strong and hardy. Your mother asked if I'd like to feel the baby kick. I have to admit I was a little scared. I'd never felt a baby inside a woman before."

The tingling sensation in the top of Kedra's head surged through her body. She knew this memory. Somewhere in the recess of her soul she'd always held this memory, but never believed it was real.

But could her auditory memory really extend back to before she was born?

"Your mother put my hand on her belly and I felt you kick her, hard. I told your father that the baby would be my friend and blood brother, just like Daeden. Your mother laughed and asked what I would do if the baby was a girl."

Kedra couldn't breathe. She knew what he was going to say.

"I promised your mother; if you were a girl, that I'd marry you, take care of you"—Jack's green eyes melted her heart—"*love you.* And I do—my magnificent little savage."

She pushed away from his tightening embrace. "Then why did you wait six months to tell me how you felt?"

"Because I didn't have a home to offer you."

"A home?"

"I do now. I bought Sylas Beck's ranch, down below Glenwood Springs. I hired Buck Gilbert to be my foreman. He and Grace Cohn got married a month ago. They've been coming to church with me, and are getting baptized in a few weeks."

"What? Sarah hasn't told me any of this!"

"Well, I asked her not to. I wanted to surprise you. Anyway, the ranch is the prettiest place you'll ever see. There are meadows and forests and a set of cliffs that fall away into a hot springs pool. I've named the ranch Cliff Springs and I can't wait to take you there." He paused. "The house isn't more than just a cabin, and Sylas was such a hermit that he didn't even have electricity, running water, indoor plumping or a telephone. I couldn't ask you to come and live like that."

"Oh, so you think a house with amenities equals a home, do you?" She glared at him through narrowed eyes. "I thought you were a smart man, Jack Garrison, but you don't know anything! Maybe those red curls have twisted into your brain." She glared at his curls. "That must be it, because you should know better. A house isn't any woman's home. Her home will always be here." She pressed her hand against his chest. "It doesn't matter to me about plumbing or lighting, my home is, and always will be, in your heart—where ever you happen to be."

He gave her that smile that made her tingle all over and tightened his arms around her. "Then it's high time you came home, darlin'."

He brought her home with a warm and welcoming kiss that told her all that was in his heart. She responded with everything he needed to know about her feelings for him.

A cheerful voice interrupted them. "I take it that everything has been worked out satisfactorily?" Kedra's grandmother asked from the doorway. Her bright blue eyes sparkled with approval, while her angelic halo of white hair belied the impish grin on her face.

"Not quite," Jack said.

"Well, hurry up. I want to announce your engagement at midnight and get this party going again. All the men are standing around waiting for you, Kedra, and all the women are pestering me to introduce them to you, Jack." She consulted the clock over the fireplace. "I'll give you five more minutes," she said and shut the door.

"Just how long has my grandmother been aware of your intentions?" Kedra asked accusingly, her gold eyes sparking with annoyance.

"I told her when I initially contacted her. She agreed you needed time to find your feet again *before* I told you how I felt."

"So she's kept your secret all these months too, has she?"

"I did try to tell you my intentions the day I left, but I didn't want to make you feel obligated by gratitude to return my feelings." He took her hand and placed it on his heart. "Everything I feel for you is right here and if you'll be patient with me, I'll find the right way to tell you." He smiled ruefully. "I'm very, very glad that worldly comforts don't mean that much to you. As inept as it was, I wanted to show you how I felt by fixing up the cabin for you. It now has lights, a telephone, running water, and an indoor bathroom—if that doesn't upset you too much. Not only that, but Flyer is getting fat and needs you to ride him, and Swindler is driving me crazy. I kept him in a cage for a month until he took to me. Now he won't let me be, please marry me and rescue me from that varmint."

Kedra couldn't hold back the laugh. "When we met, I'd been trying for weeks to get Swindler to return to the wild. I felt sure he would when I came here. Now you tell me you've domesticated him, and it serves you right if he's driving you nuts."

Jack groaned. "How could I have guessed, with you feeding him late night treats?"

"I was weaning him with less food each night. And I don't intend to let you put this problem on me. You'll have to coax him to leave."

"Does that mean you'll marry me?"

Her brows contracted, she had every right to be upset with Zed, her grandmother, and, especially, Jack. They'd all been communicating behind her back, keeping secrets—being over protective. Jack deserved a piece of her mind.

On an exasperated sigh, she expelled her annoyance, giving in to what her heart wanted. She looked up at Jack's anxious face. They had been betrothed—by his own admission—since before she was born. She touched the crease in his chin, ran her fingers through his thick, bright curls, loving the feel of them, and murmured against his lips, "Yes."

Kedra Nahtow Garrison—January, 1909. On the day of my marriage to Jack Garrison, my Uncle Zedekiah Nahtow, also known as Long-Sight, conferred upon me the custodianship of the book of Nahtow and all the records my ancestors have made over the last thousand years. He says it is my right, by blood and royalty, as the only known, direct descendant of our first parents, Elan and Nahtow.

The responsibility for the records is now mine. I must decide if it is time to bring them forth. I will go to the library of my ancestors this summer, when the snow has left the mountains. The responsibility for the library weighs heavily upon me. I will go in fasting and prayer, seeking the Lord's guidance to know what I should do.

Epilogue

Cliff Springs Ranch—June 1947

"**Grandpa and I were married** in the Manti temple two weeks after we left Philadelphia," Kedra said.

"Why did you choose the Manti temple, Grandma?"

"It was the first temple I ever saw. It looked just like a royal castle. The Powell's took me there after I graduated from high school. I promised myself that someday I would be married there."

Jack took hold of Kedra's hand. "I'm still amazed that a gloriously beautiful Indian princess would marry a saddle tramp like me."

"You aren't a saddle tramp, Grandpa."

"That's what your grandma thought of me when we met."

"Actually, I was very attracted to him and didn't want him to know it," Kedra confided.

"She took my feelings on quite a roller coaster ride, before she finally agreed to marry me."

"How soon after you got married did you go to the library?"

"In July of that year, Grandpa, Uncle Zed, and I went to find it."

"Was it hard to find?"

"No, the necklace and earrings map led us right to it, but it was very treacherous to reach. Time and erosion had taken a toll on the way leading down to the door. Grandpa only let me go down after I agreed to let him hold onto me with a rope," Kedra said.

"What was it like inside?"

Kedra's face lit. "It was as though I finally understood who I was and what a remarkable people I descended from." Her gold eyes held the gold eyes of her granddaughter. "As soon as I walked into the library, I knew what my mission was and what I had to do."

"What—what did you have to do?"

"I had to move the library."

"Why?"

"I didn't know why—at least not then—but as soon as I said it to Zed, he confirmed my feeling, even though he too didn't know why."

"Did you move the library? Where is it? Do you know why you were supposed to move the library, now?"

"It took nearly ten years to move all the records out of the library," Jack said. "We went every summer and worked for a month to do it."

"But where did you put it?"

"The library is now under the house. When we started to build the house, we built a carefully designed vault to hold all the books in the Nahtow library," Kedra said.

"During the time we were moving the books, we came to understand why they needed to be moved. The access to the library is over the edge of a narrow land bridge. The white men call the bridge the Devil's Causeway. It's about twenty-five yards long and three feet wide. It drops off for thousands of feet on each side. Over the years the causeway has become a tourist attraction," Zed explained.

"That made getting the last of the records out of the library difficult," Jack said.

"We didn't want the library to become public knowledge. It is a sacred place to generations of Nahtow, a place where their chiefs guarded the honor of their people. There are many pictographs on the walls of the library, Nahtow's and Elan's swords are there, along with many other ancient artifacts. My heart told me to keep these things hidden from the eyes of the world," Kedra said.

"Will I be allowed to see them?"

"When you are older, we will take you to the Devil's Causeway to see the original library," Kedra promised.

"Have any of my cousins been there?"

"No one from your generation has been there, or been down to see the library under the house either," Jack said.

"Why? Isn't Casey old enough?"

"Yes. But caring for the library isn't your brother's calling," Kedra said solemnly.

"Whose calling is it?"

"That was something that troubled me for a long time," Kedra admitted. "Your Uncle Ryder has all the Nahtow gifts. He has helped, and will continue to help, with translating the records whenever he can. However, the calling of custodian of the Nahtow library isn't his."

"And your aunt Jessie is too far away to help," Zed said.

"I didn't think your mother possessed any of the Nahtow gifts. She has tried to help, but finds the Nahtow language very difficult. That left me with a very big problem, until ten years ago." Kedra smiled.

"What happened ten years ago?"

"You were born. I was there when you came." Kedra blinked back tears. "You had my eyes and my hair. In you I saw the heart of the

Nahtow. When I put you into your mother's arms, and she told me what she and your father had agreed your name should be, I knew she possessed the greatest gift of all my children. I was certain you were the one that had long been prophesied would come forth to complete the great work which all the generations of the Nahtow had labored so tirelessly to accomplish."

"*Me*?"

"Yes, my sweet child—you. Of all my grandchildren, only you, possess all of the Nahtow gifts. Only you can read, write, and speak the Nahtow language. When you first saw me with my pages from the book of Nahtow, your desire was to learn to read it. Your immediate grasp of the language was amazing. I was so grateful and happy that the Lord had sent you to be the next custodian of the Nahtow library."

The girl's mouth dropped open. She looked at her grandparents and great uncle with awe and not a little fright.

Jack chuckled and hugged her. "We don't expect you to take over being the custodian of the library today."

"And not for many years to come," Zed added.

"But if you are willing, I will begin to tutor you and take you into the library so you can become familiar with everything that is there." Kedra fixed her granddaughter with a sober expression. "This is a sacred trust, one you are not to share with anyone else. The existence of the library must not become public knowledge, you must not even tell your cousins—at least not yet."

"Do not let that frighten you. There are others of the Nahtow blood, though not the royal line, which will come forth and desire to help in this work, I have seen it. You will know them when they come for they will possess the gold eyes and long sight of the Nahtow. They will help you, and from among them you will find a companion," Zed said prophetically. Then solemnly, he took the totem from his hair and clipped it in hers. "It is time you wore the totem of your people."

"This all may seem pretty overwhelming right now," Jack said. "But there is plenty of time for you to grow up, have fun, and still do this work—if that is what you chose." He smiled down at her with an infectious grin. "Now, after all you have learned today, how do you feel about yourself?"

The child searched the faces that surrounded her. She ran her hand over the silver clasp and down the white feathers and tiger-eye beads of her Nahtow totem. Standing up straight and tall, she said, "I am Elan Nahtow Gilbert, the Nahtow princess, prophesied to come forth to be the custodian of the Nahtow library, and"—she lifted her chin and smiled at her grandfather—"I am very beautiful."

Author's Notes

For those of you who love history, I have outlined *some* of the important historical facts found in **CODES OF HONOR** and their sources:

—JC

Books:

The Book of Mormon; Mormon Chapter 6, pages 478-480
History of the Church, Vol. 1, pages 183-185. The Mission to the Lamanites

Frontier Historical Society Museum—Information:
(1001 Colorado Avenue, Glenwood Springs, CO 81601, 970-945-4448)

Bowles family: Pictures and history found at the museum

Events held in Glenwood Springs in 1908:
Colorado State Democratic Convention: June 15th and 16th
Colorado Druggist Convention: June 17th, 18th and 19th
Eleventh Annual Strawberry Day: June 20th

Glenwood Springs telephone directory, 1903:
Charles W. Darrow—Attorney At Law
Cohn Groceries & Meat
Dr. G.W. Pell Jr.—Veterinary, 115 9th St. Phone 403
Doctor L.A. Robinson
J.C. Schwartz—Furniture store owner and licensed Embalmer
The Manhattan Restaurant, 714 Cooper Avenue
Mayor Drach
Voorhees Livery Stable

People and Businesses from June 18, 1908 Glenwood Avalanche:
Ada Reese—Star of the Glenwood Opera House (10 cents a show)
BT Napier & Company, 808-810 Grand Avenue
Ed Wallace—Strawberry Day Committee
Glenwood Avalanche Newspaper: H.J. Holmes—Editor
Miss Donna Parlee–Piano Teacher (studied at Alma College, Toronto University)

Internet Research:

Adams Hotel: http: //denverhistorytours.blogspot.com/2008/06/adams-hotel.html

Bosco, Henry: Owned a brewery in the basement of a saloon which later became the Denver Hotel in Glenwood Springs.
http://thehoteldenver.com/History/TheHotelDenversGrowingYears/tabid/108/Default.aspx

Colombian Emeralds - Wikipedia, en.wikipedia.org/wiki/Colombian_Emeralds

Devil's Causeway - Hike to Devil's Causeway in Flat Tops ...
www.rockymountainhikingtrails.com/devils-causeway.htm

Internet Images of the Flat Top Wilderness Area:

E
N + S
W

The Devil's Causeway

The Footstool of God

The Great Altar

Jade, invaluable through time - Viaje a Guatemala
www.viajeaguatemala.com/jade-invaluable-through-time

Pluck and Luck magazine was created in... - Museum of ...
https://www.facebook.com/FinanceMuseum/posts/10151693633678904

Rough Riders - en.wikipedia.org/wiki/Rough_Riders

Sioux Treaty of 1868 www.archives.gov/.../siou...
National Archives and Records Administration.

The last "Treasure Coach": Black Hills Gold Rush - Wikipedia, the free encyclopedia. en.wikipedia.org/wiki/Black_Hills_Gold_Rush

White River National Forest - History & Culture
www.fs.usda.gov/.../whiteriver/...

William Howard Taft, Roosevelt's hand-picked successor to the White House
www.pbs.org/wgbh/americanexperience/features/general.../tr-politics...

www.ingramcontent.com/pod-product-compliance
Lightning Source LLC
Chambersburg PA
CBHW021527250626
47154CB00006BA/2009

* 9 7 8 0 6 9 2 4 3 5 5 4 0 *